"No." I wipe a hand over speaking to a stupid ch after all. "We've nearly reache energy cost of generating a s travel beyond it is unnecessary ... only a month or two off our crossing time. So what would be the point of wasting reactor fuel? It's expensive stuff."

"You sound like a fucking Corporate now," Zed growls, nudging the door release to the VIP lounge with his elbow.

"Screw you. You wanted in on this and now you're getting nervous."

Now I've done it. Flash of temper in his eyes; his male pride's been wounded and now he'll have to assert some kind of dominance over me—rank or no rank. It's all you can expect from a lowbrow gorilla like Zed.

"You listen to me..." he shouts as the door slides open.

Whatever it is I'm supposed to listen to stops mattering as we take in the scene in front of us. Two caskets open. The occupant of one missing but the other still there—wouldn't be going anywhere ever again.

"What the unholy fuck..." I breathe.

The woman must have been about thirty-two years old, subjective. She'd been beautiful in life, with honed features—classic North African, I'd say—probably gen-hanced but physically perfect, nonetheless. The amount of new-jiao it'd cost to look so good would cost me a lifetime's salary and then some. But beauty means nothing on a corpse. Her throat's been torn out.

ISBN 978-1-63789-734-8
Macabre Ink is an imprint of Crossroad Press Publishing

For information address Crossroad Press at 141 Brayden Dr., Hertford, NC 27944
www.crossroadpress.com

First Edition

BY LUKE HINDMARSH

For Freyja and Rufus.
Aim for the stars.

PART I

CHAPTER 1

I'm stolen from dreams of angels.

"Easy, Kara. Easy. The cryo-shock will wear off," a man's voice… sounds like it's coming from underwater as I swim back down a tunnel of light. Is this the academy? Have I just come out of psychosurgery again? All emotions feel muted, it must be…

Drag one shuddering breath in, my throat itching and stinging from where I've been intubated. No—place and time snap back into focus—not navigator conditioning. That's a distant bad memory.

Coughing, I rasp blue phlegm onto the warming deckplate beneath my feet—speckles of my blood lie plain against the dull grey metal. This is how it feels to be resurrected—being revived from a frozen grave, memories of life flooding into the hollow void and bringing identity back.

"Zed?" I ask. "How come you woke first?" The details click together as the last of the cold-sleep tranq—DreamSafe™, nothing less than the best—wears off and the triple cocktail of synth-amines he'd shot right into my carotid artery lights up my brain like a supernova. Everything takes on a crystal clarity, and the faintest tickle of air moving over my skin sets my nerves sparking.

He takes me by the shoulder, squeezing gently. The heat of his hand, its strength, sets a shockwave racing from the point of contact all through my body. "You told me you'd programmed in a surprise, remember? Or did you mean something else?"

The heartrush of the stimulants pushes through the haze and drives out everything but the animal. Pressing against him, my mouth seeks his. Ignore the taste of the cold-sleep chems on his breath. Seize life. The kiss makes my chest tighten with a flush of adrenaline—and warmer hormones. But I've crested the wave of the stims and begun the crash back down, so nausea and a bone-deep ache begin to show through. I pull back to catch my breath.

"Waking out of sequence wasn't meant to be the surprise. Thought I'd synced us better than that."

"Well, it doesn't matter now," Zed says. "So long as you can hack the records, we're in the clear."

"Zed, baby, even you could do it."

Can't help but laugh and touch his face, not even the shadow of approaching pain able to blunt the sheer animal joy of being alive. I'm still reveling in sensation. Makes me want to drag him over to the revival couch right now but there's that edge of nausea building. And he's right. The sooner we cover our tracks the better.

Can't deny there's a thrill at the hunger in his eyes as I walk to the simple greenlit terminal of the medicomp. He's so easy to toy with.

"How far along are we, anyway?"

"Still just short of the midpoint," I say, not looking up from the screen. "Something like eighteen-point-seven years out, objective time."

"What's that subjective?" Zed asks, leaning in the hatchway while I fish a link-key out of my wearall's thigh pocket.

"Assuming we reach maximum safe speed within a day or so that'll take us another eight-point-four-four years to reach Gliese 892. Factor in deceleration and we're looking at another eleven-and-a-quarter-years flight time."

"Eleven, subjective time?"

"Yeah, subjective." First: slide key into medicomp. Second: trigger QI upload.

"And you did that calculation in your head?" He shakes his own, whistling softly.

"That's why I'm ship's navigator, baby." He doesn't understand. And what they did to me so I can calculate astronomical equations at speeds close to that of a computer is none of his business.

He grunts. "Don't remind me, ain't supposed to fraternize."

What he means is the Spacer's Union would see it as a betrayal of its principles and blackball him, maybe bust a kneecap. Nothing compared to the fun I'd face. But, you know, risks make life worth living. And I need him.

"Come on. Let's do what we planned, then we go somewhere and get on with a little more of that 'fraternizing' you've been promising me."

Stretching out the stiffness, my joints pop and crackle. One of the problems with lying in cold-sleep: you wake up feeling like arthritis has set in. With the synthetic dopamine and endorphins fading, I'd probably just want to curl up somewhere but good old synth-phenethylamine's still getting me going. A few seconds more for the upload of the quasi-intelligent virus to the ship's system to finish.

Speaking of risks, getting caught with QI tech would see me court-martialed and spaced before any appeal notice could reach Earth. But this gig is worth it; it's not for the thrill, it's for what the payoff will get me.

Upload complete. And the ship's systems stop registering our unscheduled revival.

A quick check back through the records shows all evidence of disruption to the normal cold-sleep routine has been erased. My little QI viral hitchhiker is back safe in the link-key, its work done for now. Of course, a full virtual forensic check, stripping away every level of the programming and examining the source code, will make my tampering as obvious as a cometary impact. But the QI virus has laid the same evidence trail to each of the eighteen crew, four officers, and one hundred thousand passengers on board.

If you can't hide your crime, make sure the evidence points to someone else. Better yet, everyone else.

For now, we're ghosts aboard a sleeping ship.

"I'm done," I say, withdrawing the link-key with its QI hitchhiker asleep once more.

Have to ditch the key as soon as I sterilize it, but the thing had cost me in risk, and new-Jiao, and the loss of face of being officer class dealing with a street-fixer like Stengler to get this gig. The cost makes the shard of crystal nanoprocessor not something you get rid of before the job is done.

"Impressed with yourself, ma'am?" Zed asks.

"Cut the chatter, Warrant Officer Hong." I mean for it to come out with mock authority, but Zed squares up and salutes.

"Aye, ma'am!"

"You can stand to attention later."

He relaxes. But it's there, in his eyes. We might joke about it, we might, as he put it, "fraternize" but there will always be that gap between us. Officer class doesn't mix with the ranks—no matter what feelings Zed evokes in me, he's barely a step up from the street.

Leaving the crew cold-sleep bay, we start down towards the cargo service area where the passengers were loaded from one of the many Earth-orbiting arrays and will be unloaded with even less ceremony at the colony drone-built dry-dock.

Normally, they'd get little more than a basic check-over of their systems before being stored in a cargo bay—no one important gives a shit about the increased risk of death in transit from such cursory measures. No change this time. Another milk-run. For us, anyway. For them, different story. Five percent "spoilage" is factored into every Corporate-sponsored stellar crossing. At least, these colonists are being sent out with a crew to up their chances of survival. Not like those poor bastards on the first-wave ships.

This is the second run I've been on with a cluster of VIPs on board. The bigshots have better facilities than the crew, for fuck's sake. But it's given us this opportunity. Our chance for a life-changing score.

Refocus. Air purification system is idling—it sets a hard limit on our active time.

"How long have we got for this, you know, before the deceleration phase kicks in and turns us to paste?" Zed asks.

He has got to be joking. "Better part of two days I'd guess before we'd have to suit up 'cause of the air. We don't want to have to do that."

"Sure, I get it—we'd have to use our own suits."

"Precisely."

"You could hack the records on all the crew suits."

"Yeah, but come on, Zed, think about it. We'd limit the suspect pool to the crew roster; it's not like passengers can access the voidsuits. Anyhow we'd have to purge the suits to hide the physical signs of usage, not to mention doing it to all the other suits so they'd all be the same. Don't know about you but I don't want to risk the captain spacing all non-essential crew and docking Char*on* herself. It's not like she couldn't. Not like she wouldn't either."

His eyes flash a bit wider. "You'd be alright. She's got a soft spot for you."

"Bullshit. That's scuttlebutt, mister. She's on her third husband."

"Whatever. So… we got two days before the air starts getting thin."

"No. Fuck it, Zed! Didn't you pay any attention when we discussed this?"

"Kara, my mind might have been somewhere else—we were holed up in a room at YaoYao-san's, remember?"

I remember.

A flea-bitten dive with flickering company holos out front sending their glare into the grubby room no matter how high we dial the windows' opacity. Our sweat mingling and soaking through the sheets Zed had brought to cover the stained mattress. Leaving some part of us—of me—sunk into the mattress. Stray skin cells. More intimate essence. Evidence, maybe, particularly given the sudden prevalence of nanotech everywhere. Something which'd been a preserve of cutting-edge labs sixteen years before on my previous furlough Earthside.

A break in our sexual marathon to navigate the network of back alleys to Stengler's lair. All the time, leaving a route the Company or the Interstellar Naval Corps might piece together. Hood obscuring my features, wearing a slum-rat disguise, padded here and there to change my profile and boots with one missing a heel to give me a limp. Paranoid? Not nearly enough. But maybe, if they ever looked, they'd only discover our liaison and not the thing with Stengler.

Zed navigating the street as if nothing had changed. Time doesn't change its nature—dirty, dangerous, without a hope—even as the datastreams are filled with a blur of events, tech speak, and trends bearing almost no resemblance to the world left behind when I'd last shipped out. Leaving me with little notion of how the World now works outside the framework of the Service. But as it always had, as it always will, the training takes over. Lets me see past the irrelevant to those things which will never change—can never change.

Oh yes, Zed. I remember. The risk, meeting with him, even on leave. The thrill it gave me, still does give me, knowing if the captain finds out, she'll ditch me as her XO and I'll wash out of the service altogether. You didn't cross the line with the crew and expect a career if anyone found out.

It tightens the tension in my relationship with Zed. He'll always have something to hold over me, if ever our thing goes south. Worst he can expect might be a flogging. I'd lose a chance at the only thing I've ever dreamed about.

Still, those stolen hours had been worth it. If nothing else, the thrill of the forbidden made the sex primal, intense… breathtaking.

"OK, one more time. It's not the lack of air. It's that after two days we'll have left enough of our own genetic markers in the air composition for an investigation to reveal the imbalance between our breath and that of the rest of the crew. Without air processing we're stuck with the mixture we leave when we go back into cold-sleep. Same reason you can't smoke. Changes the atmo mix too much."

"But we're not going to get squished by the deceleration?"

"No, forget the fucking deceleration." A long sigh tears its way out of me despite my battle to hold it in. Fuck me, he's dense.

I am not about to go over it with him *yet again*. We've reached optimum acceleration—it's why we've got close to standard gravity right now—but it'll slacken off to the zero point before we exceed the maximum safe velocity. Then at midpoint, reverse thrust will start slowing us at a deceleration curve from one g down to the limit of the ramscoop's ability to gather fuel. Only when we're in the Gliese 892 heliosphere will the fusion rockets fire. That's what'd squash us. Not difficult to grasp now, is it?

"We won't do the hard burn until we're almost there, for fuck's sake, Zed."

"I don't get it." Of course he doesn't. "So we'll keep pushing all the way?"

"No." I wipe my hands over my eyes, ignoring the edges of my comedown headache from the synthphenethylamine, and slow my words as if speaking to a stupid child. Well, he is a wrench-monkey after all. "We've nearly reached our maximum safe speed. The energy cost of generating a strong enough magnetic cowl to travel beyond it is unnecessary and it'd shave only a month or two off our crossing time. So what would be the point of wasting reactor fuel? It's expensive stuff."

"You sound like a fucking Corporate now," Zed growls, nudging the door release to the VIP lounge with his elbow.

"Screw you. You wanted in on this and now you're getting nervous."

Now I've done it. Flash of temper in his eyes; his male pride's been wounded and now he'll have to assert some kind of dominance over me—rank or no rank. It's all you can expect from a lowbrow gorilla like Zed.

"You listen to me…" he shouts as the door slides open.

Whatever it is I'm supposed to listen to stops mattering as we take in the scene in front of us. Two caskets open. The occupant of one missing but the other still there—wouldn't be going anywhere ever again.

"What the unholy fuck..." I breathe, adrenaline picking up where the stimulants left off.

The woman must have been about thirty-two years old, subjective. She'd been beautiful in life with honed features—classic North African, I'd say—probably gen-hanced but physically perfect, nonetheless. The amount of new-jiao it'd cost to look so good would cost me a lifetime's salary and then some. But beauty means nothing on a corpse.

Her throat's been torn out. Blood streaks the VIP casket's pristine white ceramic shell. Crimson handprints mark the controls and edges of the casket's lid. Bright red spray mars the shining surface of the nearest casket and trickles down across its viewport. The deckplate's smeared here and there, but the marks aren't clear enough to make out any footprints.

"No one else in here," Zed says.

While I've been gawping at the corpse, he's secured the room. There's more to him than being a reliable bit of rough. It's become too easy to dismiss him—the man is capable enough.

"I don't understand. How could one of the passengers get out of storage?" I ask.

"Look at the casket," Zed says. "Why's it still registering an occupant?"

Being careful not to step in any blood, I get closer to her. What strikes me is the way the arcs of blood paint the VIP bay looks like something out of an anti-Ares Cult propaganda piece. The sacrifice of innocent beauty to sate the spirit of Mars. Kind of thing we'd only caught rumors of my first time shipping out. Then the newsfeeds had become more and more clogged with hysteria with every return to Earth. That and the usual. War. War threatening everywhere. Makes me think of my brother and hope he isn't—wait, decades have passed—wasn't on the frontline.

I drag my mind back from the futureshock and my eyes from the corpse. Getting lost in the past is a sure-fire way to get killed in the here and now. The monitor on the empty casket is still showing a green line with the occasional spike and wobble which indicate the viability of a body in cold-sleep. The trace says this flesh can be revived—no ischemic damage. But the damn thing's empty.

Can't help but look at her savaged body again. Blood is fresh, still dripping from her gaping throat, and trickling down the surfaces it had spurted over. Staring into the hole in her throat—the white of bone reveals itself. I turn away, fighting back my rising gorge. Whoever'd done it had been brutal. Yet, they'd left no trail on the deck—they'd shown some care. I find myself checking over my shoulder, feeling like prey. Fear is a distraction; survival is about staying focused.

Her casket, like the empty one, displays a continuous viable reading, similar to the other's but different enough to look unique. Reviving the dead might be situation normal when bringing a "sleeper" out of cold-sleep but not when they've been ripped up like this. There's no scientific sorcery that can breathe life into her again.

"We are in the shit," Zed says.

"Fucking understatement. Look, seal the hatch behind us while I think."

"But what about..."

"No. Do as I tell you. I need to think this through. First things first—whoever did this is outside this room, so we're safe in here, for now at least."

"Aye, ma'am," Zed says. His sullen tone tells me he's going to be difficult to get back on side when this crisis is over, but he has his weak spots. There are ways around a fragile male ego.

I try to focus, to work out what's going on. It clearly isn't linked to the Ares Cult—those maniacs would've stuck around to skin her. Probably still be sitting here frothing with religious fervor. And where maybe someone who'd lived through the propaganda about them might hold them to be a greater threat, the time lost to each journey between the stars leaves me unable to shake off the feeling they're too small-time to get on board and do shit like this.

So what? An assassination on a vessel in mid-stellar transit? I've heard of Corporations sabotaging crossings to eliminate a rival exec but that's a rare thing. It causes reciprocal actions and those are bad for the bottom line.

There are maybe a couple of thousand radical groups operating with varying degrees of Corporate sponsorship but for the same reasons they tend to be kept on a tight leash. Which leaves a member of one of the rare independent groups or someone who'd wanted to murder this woman for personal reasons.

Shit.

Security isn't in my job description but I'm not going to defrost M'Benga to have her investigate this for me. She'd go blabbing to the Captain, anyway—any chance to screw me and climb another notch up the pole.

"Zed, listen to me," I say, as my tumbling thoughts come to

rest on an idea. "We've got time to get what we came for. So long as our missing passenger isn't off to sabotage the whole ship there's an easy way round this."

"Yeah, like what?"

"We go back to the crew quarters, set the QI virus to trigger a security alert in say ten minutes and then go back into cold-sleep." A shudder runs through me as it always does whenever thoughts of entering cold-sleep play across my mind. The things you see as it happens. The emptiness which follows. Ten minutes or a thousand years is about as appealing. I catch Zed's questioning look. "We'll be triggered after M'Benga and the Captain, so it should cover up the fact we've woken once already."

He's shaking his head. "What if this crazy motherfucker comes in and murders us during those ten minutes, Kara? Huh? The guy's fucking space-happy. Look what he did to that poor bitch."

"Respect, Zed. Show her some respect. Now, listen up. We're going to miss out on our private time, but other than that, this can all go off as planned. No way once we're in the crew section the killer can get in, not in such a short time. Door will be on security lockdown the moment we step through it."

He shakes his head again, patting down his wearall until he finds his tabac. "Thought you were supposed to be the brains." He fumbles a red-end into his mouth with a wavering hand, starts shake-charging his kine lighter.

"What the fuck is that supposed to mean?" I ask, snatching the cigarette from his lips and crushing it. "Air composition, remember?"

He frowns. "Huh, yeah. Anyways, don't you get it? Whoever done this has got to have a QI virus of their own. Only way they'd be able to get out of suspension to do this. And faking the medi-readout on two caskets? Serious tech-heavy shit. Take a look around at all these other frozen assholes. Whoever it is, they've got enough new-jiao to get the top-of-the-line shit that'll walk all over the amateur-hour crap we picked up. Ten minutes? We go under, we're under forever."

Can't deny he's making sense. I won't underestimate him

again. Well… I'll try not to.

"OK, OK. Fuck. So we've got to get this guy."

"No shit we got to get him. But what do you want to use? Harsh language? Not exactly tooled up here, are we? Case you ain't noticed."

"I'll use the virus on the armory. Easy as a lunar run."

"Got any idea how many people have died on lunar runs? Besides, won't accessing the armory trigger one of those security alerts? It's hardwired or something."

"Shit." I run a hand through my hair, a shower would feel so good. "You're right. Ok. So we can get the engineering tools and use those. There has to be a laser torch…"

"Useless—too short range." He rubs his chin. "Now, if he was wearing a voidsuit, it'd be worth it."

"…or bulkhead shears."

"Even worse, yeah. And who the fuck you think's going to hold him down while the other one uses the shears? Kara, the only tools worth using are down in the engineering section of the cargo bay. We've either got to suit up or else pressurize the bay."

"We do that, this guy can hide for as long as he likes. We'd never find him among a hundred-thousand caskets."

A loud, hollow banging sounds through the ship. We both fall silent.

"What the fuck was that?"

"Shh, listen."

A slow metallic creaking noise which lasts while we stand paralyzed by shock and indecision. Then it cuts off, leaving only the beating of my heart and my own and Zed's rapid breathing.

"Look we drive him deep enough in and he's fucked. Second we start high-g deceleration he'll be pancaked without the protection of a casket."

I sigh and shake my head. "That's years from now, remember?"

"Yeah, OK." Concern flashes across Zed's hard face. "Hey, he's not our guy, is he?"

"No, that's Dmitrios—he's still in his casket over there.

We're assuming this passenger is male but if our murderer's got a QI virus they could be anyone. Fuck, they could even be a goddamned naukara."

"No way could one of those cyborg monsters get on board, even in a casket, without nobody seeing. Think about it. You ever seen one?"

"Just the once. Bodyguard to protect some corporate muckety-muck from a rival's wetwork team."

"Those mechanical fuckers ain't exactly small." He says, still fiddling with his lighter.

"You're right, it'd never fit into a casket. So what? ITF assassin?"

"Maybe. I heard rumors they're almost as tough as a naukara but still look normal."

"So it could still be a man or woman."

"Yeah." He tucks his lighter away. "We're in the shit."

"So you keep saying. Calm down. We've still got options. Let's get what we came for and then work out a way to deal with whoever's out there."

I go over to the casket holding our mark. Dmitrios Yang-Sung. Big-time player in a United American/Panasian conglomerate. N-Stellar—word is it's a front for Sevran Corp to dodge UNWG regs. Him being here kind of proves it. Whatever he'd done to deserve a trip into the black to some barely viable mudball in one of the closer Cassiopeian star systems is none of my concern. Who gives a damn with a paycheck this big?

Stengler had told us Dmitrios was bringing his own private narc-synthesizer with him. No surprise some corporate big-dick would travel with a pharmacopeia, even while in disgrace. One simple chip would let him use a colony reprocessor to manufacture his drugs of choice from whatever recipes it has stored on it. Stengler said the chip holds all the latest Sevran Corp narcs and synth versions of the classics. Let you get yourself some synth-H or Blue-sky poly-fucking-metamine with equal ease. Raises the value even closer to the stars. Positively astronomical at street value.

"He got it?" Zed asks from the door. He'd dropped down to press an ear to the deck in front of it, but now stands and turns to watch me.

"I'll know in a moment."

Pull on gloves, ease casket's control panel open, and insert link-key.

Moments later the QI virus is done with its work and all security options lie wide open. I mute the alarms, pop the casket open, and hold my breath as a flood of fog spills from within. I know what's really happening—you don't go through officer flight school without getting extensive training in the sciences, but it's hard to accept I'm seeing the moisture from the air condensing as it hits the supercooled contents of the casket instead of some freezing gas pouring out.

"Hurry it up! Don't want to kill him," Zed says from the door. He doesn't mean kill him. I mean, he's already dead. But caught in a frozen limbo. Zed, like most of the ranks don't like to face up to the reality—you go in the tube and it kills you. If you're lucky it can bring you back. Don't blame him, but what I'm worried about is spoilage. Ischemic damage. Med stuff I know is important, even if I know less about it than Zed knows about astrodynamics.

"I'm sure he'd be touched by your concern, now shut up and let me do what we came here for."

The body's developing a layer of rime—we are running out of time. Wasting none of it, I crack open the pouch strapped to the belt of the mark's cold-sleep suit. It crackles under my gloved fingertips. Despite the insulation of my wearall, cold bites into my flesh. Inside the pouch is one of the new headset hubs they'd been trying to hawk on every media-vector back on Earth and another device, little more than a small black square. I ease it out with exaggerated care—it'll set me up for life—and replace it with a near identical square Stengler gave us before we left Earth.

Any moment now the medi-readout on the casket's lid is going to start flashing a red viability warning. I slam the lid back down and re-engage the coolant system. The readout stays green. Hold your breath. Wait for the trace to nose-dive. This is the worst part. It'll all go wrong if the corporate fuck spoils.

"He gonna make it?" Zed asks.

"Stengler told us this sort of thing's been done before."

"What, robbing Corporates in cold-sleep?"

"Yeah." Can't take my eyes off the readout. Steady. Green. "Stealing genetic codes to clone them and use for espionage, wetwork, those kinds of things."

"How the fuck would a back-alley fixer like Stengler know shit like that?"

"How did he know about this chip? Why should we care, so long as he holds up his end and we get our payday?"

"Some good it will do us now."

"Having second thoughts?" I ask, still unable to take my eyes off the trace.

If Zed's getting shaky on me, something'll need to be done about him. The affair was—*is*—good fun, it scratched an itch and it's one that still tingles but I need to be able to trust him. And no amount of satisfaction's worth putting my life on the line.

"No, just wondering how we're ever going to spend the new-jiao we'll make from this."

"Slowly. Like we planned. You retire from the service after this trip; I'll blow my next psych assessment and get discharged. It can be done." He doesn't need to know my real aim. You've got to keep that kind of ambition to yourself. And now the key's in my hand.

Buying a Captaincy of a ship, not one hauling cargo—of the human or any other kind—isn't the dream. The dream is buying the Captaincy of an Explorer. One of the few manned interstellar rovers charting new worlds.

Where does that desire come from? I don't know.

As a kid, I demonstrated a knack for mathematics. Not as in I was counting early, but in the sense I was doing differential calculus while my kindergarten friends were learning that two apples and another two apples equal four.

Some psychometric test examined the three angles of my intellect. What they call visual intelligence is something I'm alright at, rating above average. Nothing special. Abstract reasoning, well, my score there puts me in the top ten percent. But mathematical? Top point-zero-zero-one percent.

What the hell has that got to do with space? Why am I not hotlined into a research facility doing high-end equations? Because the Corporate AI can do everything I can but a thousand times faster. And AIs are far too valuable to be sent into space. The real ones don't arise from any predictable process. They evolve out of data like one of Dawkins' Memes, not like the early efforts of railroading them into existence with neuroscience. But how they're "born" makes them dangerous.

Besides, deep space exploration or colonization doesn't really need an AI. Imagine it deciding the mission is tedious or illogical and looking for something else to do. Got it? Not a pretty picture. Yeah anyway, so every ship they sent out gets a midline computer stripped of anything fancy and given over to mission critical tasks only. If it fails?

Human backup.

The hundredth of a percent of the population who might once have made mathematics professors become navigators. Our natural talents with numbers honed by special training. Deep reprogramming and rewiring of our minds at the unconscious and subconscious levels. Whoopty-fucking-doo. According to the other cadets at the Academy, it'd made me as cold as a walking calculator but despite that, or maybe because of it, I need to find meaning beyond numbers.

I need to matter.

They named the cities on the Moon "Armstrong" and "Aldrin." They'll name the first city on the mudball orbiting Gliese 892 "Sheng-Li". Where will be named "Rozanski"?

Three minutes and the medi-readout is still settled in a consistent green trace. Minor wobble, occasional spike. Enough watching and waiting. The casket will flush the frost from its sleeping occupant and the only sign of our tampering will be the blank chip and the data record on the casket itself.

When the man in the casket tries to process some narcs, he'll be stuck on a shithole colony world lightyears from Earth and so far down the food chain no one will ever give a shit. Set the QI virus to wipe the casket's log and reset it at journey start point plus flight time elapsed—job done. Not a perfect cover but by the time any complaint could reach earth, the casket log will have been downloaded and its memory wiped anyway—so long as the occupant doesn't spoil. At worst, an investigation at that stage would prove inconclusive—I hope.

"Got it," I say, blowing out the breath I've been holding.

"Fucking A. Now all we got to do is deal with this *shāshǒu*."

"What?" I don't speak Cantonese, even the street-level mangle Zed was using.

"Psycho."

"Uh-huh. Let's stash the chip first. Last thing we need is to lose it or damage it while we're playing hide and seek."

"OK. Follow me," Zed says. He's picked up a coffee jug—chromed steel, of course—from where it'd been magnetically stowed in the VIP lounge.

"What are you going to do with that, pour a latte for our psycho?" I ask.

"Hey, it's the closest thing we've got to a weapon at the moment," Zed says.

"I've an idea about that. We should be able to use one of the bulkhead rivet guns, shouldn't we? The bolts they fire won't go very far but if you stapled someone with one, it'd end a fight pretty quick."

"Maybe. Those things are big and slow, I'd basically have to hold it to our fucking psycho-killer's head to use it. What's he going to be doing? Chewing at my neck, that's what."

"You think that's how he killed her?" I ask, giving in to the assumption of gender.

"Looked like bite marks to me."

I don't press Zed on it. He'd come up from the streets and though he'd not lived as a cutter, he'd seen more of the filthy underside of life than I ever would. Probably eaten gong-chai "chicken" on a daily basis and I don't doubt he'd seen some sickos going after long pig. The rats you can understand but eating people? It makes me glad I'd grown up in a high-riser, safe from the constant murderfest raging below. Never really thought about it before but while shipboard life has a feeling of familiarity for me—so close to the controlled existence of my childhood and early teens—for Zed it must represent an escape from a short and brutal life, scrabbling for scraps of food and whatever narcs might dull the horror.

"You think maybe we got this wrong?" Zed asks. "Somehow triggered these two caskets and the missing guy just went schizoid on us?"

"Schizoid?" I sneer. "Is that your medical assessment, Dr Freud?"

"What?" Zed says. "I'm serious. Haven't you heard the stories about travelers who redline in cold-sleep but revive when they're thawed out? They're never the same. I heard some go loco—start attacking everyone in sight. Others, they go all quiet and withdrawn then do something suicidal like try and sabotage their vessel's engines."

"Such typical spacer bullshit. Thought you were savvier than to buy into that nonsense, Zed."

"Think about it. Whoever this passenger is, you really think they loaded him into his casket frothing at the mouth and ready to tear some woman's throat out?"

I shake my head, it's not hard to see where he's going with this.

Zed's eyes are wild, roving around the room, "If this was some assassin, even some fucked up naukara machine man or an ITF Ghostface, don't you think they'd have been a bit more subtle than chowing down on her neck?"

His voice reverberates within the confines of the VIP casket bay. Here where there are only frozen bodies and me, it doesn't matter. But some sounds travel easily through a vessel's bulkheads. Even in a cavernous bulk hauler like SCCSV *Charon*, his words might echo in other parts of the ship.

I step close to him and lay one finger over his lips, stilling them. Lean in and kiss him. The hard, meaningful kiss saved for showing him who's dominant in whatever bunk we might share. Now, it serves to curb the tide of panic rising in him. He resists at first, shoulders stiff and mouth locked closed, but then his lips part and the kiss becomes real. His arms come up around me and the shaking in them subsides. Slowly, aching, I pull back.

"We're calm," I say. "We've got to be. Whatever's going on, we both know what's real and what's not." I bang a fist on the edge of the nearest casket. "Technology, not conspiracy theories or ghost stories. OK?"

"But what if…"

"No. Stop. We don't have time for endless speculation. Check me over. I don't have any blood on me, do I?"

"You're clear."

"Good." I look him up and down. "So are you. We're going to hide our payday, and then we're going to put out this fire."

"How?"

"Easy. The idea of trapping him deep in the ship and letting g-forces pancake him is a bust, same with starving him out. If he's got a QI virus, he'd go ahead and hack another casket."

"You just said it'd be easy."

"Yeah, it is. All we have to do is use our brains. So we get on the thermal scanners to locate the escaped passenger and seal him in wherever he is. Then we find a way to set atmosphere cycling to suck the oxygen out of that part of the ship, pump in some CO2 and it's over."

"Not sure it's possible but even if it is, won't it leave a record?"

"Baby, how could we cover up what's happened here?" I ask, see him start to answer, and cut him off. "Let's get real. All we can do is hide our involvement. Treat this as a perfect opportunity and use it to our advantage. Everything our virus has done can be laid at our wakeful passenger's door."

Zed sighs. The wildness has gone from his eyes but there's still the edge of something in his expression. He's screwing down hard on his fear, but it's there.

I've seen this before. My first trip into the black, I'd been paired with another ensign, fresh out of training. There'd been a problem with our drive which threatened to leave the hauler overshooting its destination by half a light year. Not a disaster but cutting close to it—fusion rocket fuel reserves didn't allow leeway. She'd started cracking under the pressure, finally ending up sedated and stuffed back in the freezer. Right before she'd gone space-happy, tearing at her hair and screaming, her eyes had held the look that's in Zed's right now. Close to the edge, looking over at the drop.

A hollow clang reverberates.

"What the fuck was that?" Zed whispers, looking at the

bulkhead.

"He's not sitting on his hands and waiting for us. Whoever it is, he's up to something and you can bet it's not making us a nice breakfast."

Zed winces and looks over at the corpse of the woman behind us. "Did you have to?"

I huff a laugh and go to open the VIP bay door.

"What are you doing? Aren't you going to check whether he's out there?"

"And how am I supposed to do that, genius? Besides, he can't be down in the ship clanging stuff around and outside the door, can he?"

"Well, I'd better go first, right?" Zed says, holding the coffee pot high.

"No, don't want him dying with laughter," I say, ignoring the frown that earns me. "Come on, it's not far to the bridge."

CHAPTER 2

Zed takes position behind me as we creep along the dim two hundred meters of corridor between the VIP boat and the forward compartment of Charon. The lights remain in their power saving mode, mere lines of red at the corridor's edges that shed barely enough illumination to stave off the dark. Halfway to the bulkhead door ahead of us, another metallic clanging echoes from the rear of the ship.

"Think he's gonna mess with the fusion rockets?" Zed asks. "Or the ion drive?"

"Now there's something real to worry about. We need to find this fucker and deal with him before he jeopardizes us all. The rockets or the drive... Could he overload them?" I ask.

"No. I mean, don't see how he could get close enough without the radiation killing him. Er... I think, the amount of gamma rays and x-rays those suckers put out would cook even one of those cyborg soldiers in less time than we've been talking about it."

"Yeah, but what about the fuel lines?"

"Er... maybe... I..."

I scowl. His eyes are wide. He should know all this without hesitation. But his panic's coming up again. There has to be something to bring him round, and more than that, we have to know what risk having some space-happy bastard rattling around the engine compartment poses.

"You're the technician, I'm the navigator. You know this. Tell me—fuel or coolant lines, could you get to either of them in-flight?"

"Coolant isn't an issue. The rockets radiate most their heat directly into the void. Fuel…" Zed rubbed his forehead. "Maybe. Could burn off some of the H2 from the thrusters. Doubt it'd do enough damage unless we were really unlucky. Feeds to the fusion rockets? Buried a bit deeper, hard to get to but possible. No way to do it without killing himself though, that stuff would boil off real fast. Fill whatever compartment with fumes and suffocate him before he could override the bulkhead doors. That sort of leak would trigger a separate containment system—hardwired with no way to hack it via computer."

"But it'd still kill the rest of us, right?"

"Maybe. Not quickly but we'd end up unable to slow down below the minimum velocity necessary for the ramscoop. Maybe we'd have some chance of changing course…"

"…so we could use gravitational braking or a slingshot return course." I finish, nodding. "Not bad, warrant officer."

"Unless he's got a cutting torch. In which case…" Zed gestures with his hands, opening them and spreading them apart. "Boom."

I punch in the code to open the command compartment, half expecting to come face to face with the killer's bloodied visage. The door hisses but doesn't open.

"What now?" Zed asks.

"Door won't release. Must be a pressure variance."

"Atmo leak?"

"Maybe. Hold on. No, still showing pressure's nominal in the crew lounge and command module." I pump away at the manual door release and it opens a crack.

"Electrical systems failure, maybe? Could our schizoid killer be doing it?"

"Worry about that when we get in," I say. "Don't just stand there, help me with this. Any other time and I'd be writing you up for failing to maintain the manual backups; this crank is nearly seized up."

"Hey, you have any idea how big this tub is?" he said. "As if I've got time to go around oiling the doors. Wait, what's happening?"

Behind us the low-level lighting is going off, the line of light being swallowed by an advancing wave of darkness. The dull metallic clang comes again, no longer from elsewhere in the ship but closer. A pause and it sounds once more, echoing out of the darkness stalking towards us.

"Hurry the fuck up!" Zed hisses.

One more crank and the bulkhead door opens enough for me to squeeze through. In I wriggle and start cranking the release on the other side.

Another clang—this time near enough the sound beat upon my ears. The door shifts another couple of inches and Zed tries to push through. The light behind him blinks out with his head and most of his torso through.

"Aargh! Something's got my arm. For fuck's sake, help me!" He screams.

I let go of the crank and grab Zed, putting a foot up on the bulkhead and pulling him with all my strength. At first, it makes no difference, then the pressure releases and he falls through the door. I pound the emergency seal button on the door and it springs closed.

"Ten fingers, ten toes?" I ask, falling into spacer's slang.

"Yeah," Zed gasps. "Yeah, I think so. Shit, look at my fucking arm."

There's a growing dark stain of blood on his wearall's right arm. The fabric is perforated. Carefully rolling up the sleeve reveals a puncture wound on his forearm, blood welling from it.

"Was that his nails?" I ask, adrenaline conjuring images of some feral looking colonist with claws for hands. Ridiculous.

"I don't know. His teeth, I think. Fuck, am I going to bleed to death?"

"Steady, man, steady," I say. "You're not spraying blood everywhere. OK."

There's not much in the way of medical facilities here. Even the main medibay is utilitarian at best, equipped for cold-sleep revival more than triage—who needs better when most of the time the crew and passengers are frozen solid? Our medical officer Hiroki is thorough though. He'd stowed a small quantity of wound sealant, still in date. It'll close the wound and stave off infection. I spray some into the wound and squeeze the edges together then spray the whole area. Zed sighs as the sealant numbs his skin.

"That's better," he said. "You think he's got some kind of jaw augment? Poison?"

"Relax," I say, injecting as much calm as I can into my voice. "Maybe he or she *has* got some modification, I mean it'd explain the strength and biting through your wearall, but poison? You aren't flopping about on the deck, so I guess you're not poisoned."

"But what if..."

"Zed, stow it. We're clear for now, but our unwanted passenger can still hurt us. We stick to the plan. Hide the chip then see if we can track him."

Zed doesn't answer but stands cradling his wounded arm even though the painkillers in the wound sealant must have anaesthetized the injury by now.

I go over to my cold-sleep casket. Crew privilege allows for storage of some personal effects inside—cigarettes mostly. I've never picked up the habit but most of the rest of the crew have, captain included. Why care about the health risk when corporate insurance covers anti-cancer shots every time crew medicals come around. When you're getting a regular dose of cosmic radiation, even reduced by *Charon's* hull and magnetic cowl, what's the added harm of a bit of tobacco? Not that anyone other than the captain can afford the real stuff—the rest lit up the synthetic shit. Tabac doesn't smell the same but it all stinks, you know. Zed's probably still itching for one. There won't be any harm in it now but I'm not going to put up with the smell. Still, at least it's only tabac he's twitching about. Don't grow up in the slums without some kind of narc habit and it could've been a lot worse.

I pop the chip into the small container alongside a holo of my parents, dead seven years, subjective. I've lost track of how long ago they passed, objective.

"You know, if Dominguez shakes us all down for contraband, our little gig here will be up in an instant. Couldn't you find a better place to hide it?" Zed asks.

"Like where?"

"You know... somewhere they can't look without a medic."

I give him a disgusted look. "Don't be so fucking stupid. We get a medical before leaving the ship. Anything inside a crewmember's body would show up in a flash. Here, this chip might be nothing more than my music collection or family holo archive. Or ten thousand books to read."

"Who the hell reads books?"

"You know what I'm saying, Zed. This will only be a problem if we give them a reason to look for it. Like we said, the corporate asshole might get a message back before us, but what's he going to say? "Oh yeah, someone stole my narc recipes, can you arrest them for me." We stay cool about it. Just like we stay cool about this schizoid murderer."

"Okay, okay," Zed says, holding up both hands and walking into the command module. He's stopped cradling his injured arm—let's take it for a good sign.

Leaning my head against the cool metal of the casket, I try to pull my fractured thoughts together. There's something important missing from this picture, and it's got to be staring me straight in the face. But like hunting for a word you can't quite seize, the answer slips away from me. Touching the holo of my parents with a gentle caress, I close up the casket and join Zed in the command module. He's leaning over the internal monitors, dialing through the settings.

"What?" I ask.

"Nothing on thermals. Nothing except the normal temperature variance and no atmo variation."

"You have got to be shitting me."

"Take a look for yourself. Our killer has to be some kind of cybered-up tech-assassin or ITF Ghostface. Like I was saying."

"No, way. As if some corporate or government assassin would bite your arm and not tear it clean off."

"Er... Yeah, okay. I see what you mean."

"This bastard's clever, I'll give him that. Whatever QI-virus he's got, he must've uploaded it into the security monitors."

"How the fuck could he do that?"

"I don't know," I say.

"Maybe it's time we woke the rest of the crew, Kara. We're in the shit."

"Stop saying that. And we explain why we're awake first how, exactly?"

"We do a short sleep like we talked about earlier."

"The short sleep we'll never wake up from? Give me a break, Zed."

He starts pacing up and down. The tendons in his neck show how tight his teeth are gritted. My sometime-lover and partner in crime is about to sail over the edge.

"Set it up so all the caskets purge, okay? Enough screwing around. We've got what we woke for; we lie up in our caskets and get up all woozy like everyone else. We don't offer any explanations, just keep our heads down."

His idea has some appeal—we'd avoided leaving any real traces of our waking, at least not any that couldn't be hidden under a general QI-virus raid and so blamed on the killer. My eyes rove over Zed's face before dropping to his arm.

"And you think both the Captain and M'Benga are going to put your wound down to scratching an itch when you woke from cold-sleep? Please. Try to get a grip on reality, yeah?"

Zed looks down at his arm, realization slowly lighting his face.

"But it fucks us anyway, doesn't it? Why wait to get killed."

"Captain'll space you, no hesitation. And you'd blab, Zed, so she'd space me too. That's not happening." No need to add I'll space him myself first and jettison a lifepod to put the Captain off the scent. She'd buy it—Zed isn't stupid, but she probably wouldn't realize that. It's not a great leap to assume he'd be dumb enough to believe the lifepods are an escape instead of the slow death they really represent. But it gives me an idea.

"Trust me," I say. "I have it all worked out. Wound sealant will get it sorted out and after a month or two of cold-sleep it'll look like an old scar. We want to hide what we've done, then we have to take the killer down before we go back into our caskets and leave the Captain with a problem that seems to have sown itself up."

"How?"

"We kill this fucker, dump him in a lifepod and wave goodbye to our troubles. Set the medicomp to wake the Captain at the midpoint and let her puzzle out what happened."

"One problem." He holds up a finger like a little boy asking teacher if he can go pee.

I sigh. "What?"

"How're we going to kill someone we can't find?"

"CO2."

"What?" Zed says.

"He's got to breathe. Doesn't matter if he can hack the thermal monitors. Doesn't matter if he can hack the life-support logs. He can't alter the change in atmospheric composition. So, all we do is track which compartments are using their CO2 scrubbers—that leaves physical traces."

"But we'd have to check each compartment as we go," Zed says.

"Wouldn't take a minute, then we know which one he's been in or is still in and we focus our search there. Manually seal the doors behind us as we go."

"And kill him with what?"

Shit—this is the snag. If he can hack the atmo regulation, then we can't selectively depressurize a compartment. We need a weapon…

"There must be something. Come on, I can't be the one to come up with all the answers."

Zed glowers but the panic recedes with his focus returned.

"Would the armory be where passengers' weapons are stowed?" He asks.

"Passengers aren't allowed weapons."

"Kara, you think those Corporate ice-cubes are going to be happy defrosting on a new planet, ready to boss the colonists around only to find they're outnumbered? They've got to have an equalizer."

"I didn't see any sign of one."

"Of course not, but one of those caskets must have a gun in it."

"What good is that going to be? Ten'll give one it won't be a deckgun which means firing it will probably put a hole in the bulkhead."

"Nah, if they've kept a holdout on them, it'd be small. Hand maser? Nah. Probably a ballistic—easier to hide without an energy cell. Doubt even a big caliber pistol could do more than scratch the hull."

I think about it. He has a point.

"Okay, genius, how do we find it?"

Before Zed can answer there's clanking from deep beneath our feet.

"Somewhere among the cargo compartments," I say.

"Sounded big whatever it was," Zed whispers.

I nudge him. "What was your idea? We've got to get moving on it."

"Right," he says, voice still low. "I figure we check the manifest, see which passenger is set for first revival, pop their casket and I bet you we find a piece."

I nod. No, Zed isn't stupid at all. Have to watch him, in case this turns sour and he needs a convenient scapegoat who could be stuffed inside a lifepod along with the corpse of the murderer. Surviving officer training required a certain ruthlessness and it's not hard to see now how closely it resembles the will to do whatever's necessary bred into those who've come up on the streets and in the slums.

"Let's get to it," I say, gesturing for Zed to take the lead.

Without a backward glance, he walks over to the corner where I'd retrieved the emergency medikit. Opening the small storage space beneath, he pulls out the dull red cylinder of a fire suppressant. It's small, but the way Zed hefts it, I figure he could use it as a short club.

"Either I'll bash his head in with this or give him a mouthful of foam. Either way ought to slow the bastard down."

"Good thinking," I grunt, doubly sure I don't want him behind me.

We pump the manual door release until it's wide enough to peek through. The corridor outside is still pitch black, so I shine a penlight about, chasing shadows from the corners.

"Looks clear," Zed says and cranks the release until he can slip through the gap.

"Leave it open, or seal it off?" I ask.

"Open. We can't stop him getting in unless we're inside and

I don't want to end up having to pump the door open while he's trying to chew my fucking arm off again."

"Okay," I say, wishing he'd can it with the melodrama.

The pressure door leading from the corridor into the VIP module is still active and opens for us with a touch of the door release.

"Wonder why this one's still working," I say aloud, not really expecting Zed to answer.

"No controls in there. Bet he doesn't think there's any threat," Zed says. He walks in, holding the fire extinguisher high. The lights are still on; everything looks as it had when we left. Blood pooling and the reek of death.

"Give me the light." Zed says, holding out a hand. "I'll stand guard while you do your trick again."

"Fine, but why not simply close the door?"

"Don't know about you but I'd rather see him coming."

Can't help but arch a brow, but I still give in and shake my head. "Sure, whatever you like. Just keep an eye out while I access the passenger manifest."

Easy enough to access the computer and meet its demand for security codes with the QI-virus. Within a couple of seconds I'm looking at a manifest, not only of the VIP passengers but of all the caskets. It's an active list, showing which are viable and which have suffered spoilage. Life and death a difference of a green light and a red.

As always, the thought of the death grip of suspension sends a shiver through me. It's not so much the knowledge we're not really alive, merely preserved in the first moments of death, which gets to me. More the visions. I've never had the courage to ask Hiroki, but my best guess is the tranqs—good old DreamSafe™ and the rest—don't do much but calm us as we slide down into the blackness and then mess with our memories. What things are these "sleepers" seeing? Maybe it's what's driven the killer over the edge?

Clear the idle thought with a shake of my head, I do my best to ignore the standard manifest with its scattering of red dots showing how many colonists will never see their new world. The VIP list is short and shows all green lights, despite evidence to the contrary. Again it strikes me how sophisticated the killer is—this had to have been done after he'd woken and it leaves little or no room for the theory of someone going space-happy from cold-sleep visions or chems.

This is the work of a rational mind. Has to be. One fully able to slaughter its victims before disposing of any evidence and returning to a decade of suspension without risk of discovery.

Focus on the task at hand—the revival sequence is simple. Of the eighty-five VIP colonists three are scheduled for primary revival—the casket of the murdered woman, the casket of the killer, and one more. Passenger Shironji, Takahashi. Corporate, Exos Inc. Rating—executive security officer.

Jackpot.

I take a chance and load the file on the murderer's casket.

"Oh fuck..." I sigh.

"What?" Zed asks, looking at me over his shoulder from his post in the open doorway.

"I located a security officer's casket and thought why not check on our murderous passenger."

"And?"

"And the name is the same. Rank the same. Same with the murdered woman. It must be part of the hack to cover up what he was doing."

"Hold on." Zed holds up a hand. "What about the casket we opened earlier? We know his name."

"Good point, I'll check."

Dmitrios Yang-Sung. Our fixer'd made sure we knew the mark's name, casket number, and its content. What difference it made to know the name of the man is beyond me, yet Stengler had thought it important. Now the manifest is wrong.

"Shit. No dice, same name. Looks like the entire VIP module is tied into one casket ident. Probably the easiest work around to keep all the lights green." Yet each medi-readout shows a different trace... This is very sophisticated stuff, maybe beyond what you could do with the QI virus we have.

"So now what?" Zed asks. "Open all the caskets?"

"Huh?" I say, my train of thought broken. "I don't think that'd be a good idea. Let me try the other casket set for primary revival—chances are it will be the security exec but if not, the logic's the same. If they're set for early revival, they might have a weapon."

Another distant clang sounded.

"We'd better hurry," Zed says. "Whatever that space-happy motherfucker's doing, it ain't good!"

It's hard not to rush the process, shoving the link-key into the casket's port and setting it to send a cloned signal through to the main computer while clearing the ID hack on the casket itself. Lose her name but get the medi-readout back. All the lights stay green on the screen, even though the open casket starts flashing warnings.

Another noise echoes through the ship—a wail of agony. Maybe human, maybe the metallic screech of machinery but it hardly matters. Zed's right: it can only be bad news.

The security exec is small in stature and young looking, but even intubated for cryo-fugue her face bears a hard expression. Any moment she's going open her eyes and look at me, you just fucking know it. My hand shakes, and not from the cold.

"Whoever she is, she's come prepared," I say.

"Find a gun?"

"Sort of," I say, removing the small black cylinder tucked along her outer thigh.

"A shock stick?" Zed asks.

"I don't think so, something like one though. Hold on," I say as I close up the casket.

"Well, it's better than nothing, but…" Zed begins.

"Forget it, we have another problem," I say.

The display showing casket integrity isn't settling down. Each line's crashing flat—irreparable ischemic damage.

"What's going on?"

"Shut-up. We're losing viability."

I adjust the casket's settings, trying to stabilize it. Three persistent lines show on the display—catastrophic ischemia. Nothing makes any difference.

"Can we revive her?" I ask.

"No way. Only way is fixing her casket, but I don't have the training to deal with stabilizing a failing casket, do you?"

"We can't just let her die," I say.

Zed shakes his head and turns back to the open doorway. "She's dead already, Kara. All you can do is cover our tracks."

My body goes rigid, hands pressed to the casket-lid so hard it feels like it's cutting into me. A hot wave burns through my chest and belly. I hammer my fist on the side of the casket.

"Work damn you. Work."

It's no use. The lines remain flat. Hesitating, I pull the link-key out, expecting to see a red dot appear next to one of the names on the manifest. Not caring if it set off an alarm. I've as good as murdered the woman. Sure she is... *was* a corporate and far from innocent but a weight settles in my stomach. A feeling washing over me beyond my ability to name.

No alarm. No change on the screen. Her death hasn't even warranted that much.

"Kara, forget it. There's nothing we could do. Now we've got to focus on us. Okay?"

"Fuck you, Zed. You didn't pull the plug on her."

"Neither did you," He says, his voice calm and even. "What does the spacer's manual call it? You know the term the corporates made us all learn."

"Yeah, yeah."

"No. I'm going to remind you. 'Spoilage.' You know it, but think about it. It's not a word you use for people. Not a word you use for anything living and breathing. It's a word you use for a commodity. That's all any of us are to people like her. My mama-san used to tell me 'you reap what you sow.' She was right."

I can't answer him. Part of me wants to shout at him, to rage against what he said and deny it. But it's true. No one gets to be in one of those VIP caskets without blood on their hands.

I look at Zed anew. He'd never mentioned his mother before, though the tendency of slummers to use a word which actually means the madam of a brothel in the original Japanese gives me pause. Is he telling me he worked in one of the low-rent houses earning night-pay or is it only the usual misuse? No time for wondering about it now and after this it's doubtful we'll ever again have the kind of openness between us to let me ask.

"Maybe you're right. It's a matter of survival."

"The first and only rule," Zed says. "Let me take a look at that." He gestures at the black cylinder.

It gives him total control over me, but I hand it over.

"Nice. Dart gun. No chemicals or compression caps like with a ballistic and no energy cells. Easy to smuggle through."

"What use is that going to be?"

"Got about five darts, preloaded. Bet each one has some nerve-toxin in it—kill you with a scratch in a couple of heartbeats."

"You sure?"

"Well, it could just be tranq darts but why bother? A holdout is for life and death situations. If she was set for waking first, she'd want to be able to kill anyone who stood between her and the armory. And it'd scare off mutinous colonists." Zed hands the cylinder back to me, careful not to point its open-mouthed end at either of us. "Be careful with it, I don't want to test it out first-hand, you know."

"Thanks," I say. "Now let's find the killer and finish this."

"Amen to that."

CHAPTER 3

We walk down the corridor, Zed a step ahead and to one side. He must trust me, but not quite enough to be straight in front of a tube of poisoned darts. Can't blame him. With the lights still off, we both have our penlights out, one sweeping the corners while the other keeps a beam on the bulkhead door leading to the central corridor back towards the cargo bays and the engineering section. As the light plays over the door, it shows the access panel has been ripped free leaving optical cables hanging. In the red emergency lighting, they take on a slickness as if the entrails of the ship herself had been pulled out and left on display. A shudder runs through me.

"Manual release?" I ask.

"No choice. Wonder whether he was trying to hotwire it or force us to use the crank. You know, slow us down."

"Not hotwiring it to open the door," I say. "He'd not need it if he's got a QI-virus. You know, maybe this is how he stopped power to the crew bay door."

"Yeah, good point. The VIP-lounge door's on a separate circuit—all part of the promise to keep them safe. You know, the whole area is basically a giant lifepod. Shit happens to the rest of the ship and they get blasted clear. Screw what damage it does to the rest of us. I mean, what the fuck do they care?"

"Bet they paid extra for it too," I shake my head. "Damn fools."

"Hey, just because you're a royal corporate asshole, doesn't mean they tell you the chance of a lifepod ever being recovered is about one in a billion," Zed says, laughing.

Why does he think that's funny? He bends over the exposed

wires, shining his penlight on them.

"Cover the door, I'll undo his little rewiring project," Zed says. "There, that oughta do it."

The lights flicker on in a cascade along the corner illumination strips—full on this time so they nearly blind me. Behind us comes the creak-hiss of the crew-bay door going back on automatic and closing tight. At the same time, there's a hiss of equalizing pressure as the bulkhead door in front of us wheezes open into blackness so thick it seems a physical thing. The brightness of the lights in the corridor blind me to whatever is in the feeble beam of my penlight.

"Steady there," Zed says, and I realize I'm swaying on my feet.

"I'm okay."

"Sure. Hey, sorry to blind you. Figured we might want to have full illumination and it's not like it's something we'll need to cover up, now."

"Can you do anything about in there," I gesture through the open door.

"Not from here. Low-energy illumination only covers the forward compartment. We won't see any more until we get into the engine room."

"So what?"

"So, we either have all the lights on or we wander about in the dark."

"Let's get them on."

"Should be a control panel on the other side of the door."

Zed walks into the blackness. Now as my eyes adjust, the dark is less total and I can make out the first few meters of the compartment beyond. Nothing to see.

"Hold on. Looks like he's been at this side too. There we go."

The wide corridor ahead floods with light. It links to each cargo bay—row on row of simple pressure doors leading to vaults filled with ranks of cold-sleep caskets. Hunting the killer might take more time than we have. All the cargo bay access doors look normal—no sign of torn wiring.

"You coming?" Zed asks.

Swallowing the hard lump forming at the back of my throat,

I step into the corridor. The door behind me slides shut.

"So where do we start?" I ask.

"Engineering. Make sure the shāshǒu isn't doing something there."

"Yeah, but then he can get behind us."

"Fair point. Don't think that's a good idea."

"What then?" I ask.

"We open each of these doors. You guard my back; I'll check the CO2 scrubber. If the compartment's been used, the scrubber will have come online before we enter and have switched off again if he left."

I grunt—it'd been my idea but hearing it from Zed somehow makes it seem less reasonable.

"What?" he asks.

"How sensitive are these things?"

"They'd kick in if you'd been breathing in the room a minute after the door closes, probably sooner if the door stays open to an area with a higher CO2 content. But it shouldn't be a problem. Scrubber will already be working in this corridor, so only the breaths we take in any given compartment should trigger the one inside."

"You're sure about that?"

"No, but it was your best idea," He says. "Now are we doing this or what?"

"Yeah, but one more thing," I say, hating myself for it.

"What?"

"We have to turn the lights off in here, otherwise as soon as we open the door it'll be like a beacon to him."

"Good point," Zed sighs and plunges us into darkness.

We creep from bay to bay. Standing in each doorway trembling as I stare into the sightless dark while Zed tinkers with life support equipment by each door. In each compartment, the urge to demand he turns on illumination is a constant adversary—and you know what he'll say. It's the same argument I had with myself before suggesting we switch off the corridor lights. If our quarry is in the compartment, hiding or getting at one of the cargo-class caskets, he might not notice us. Turn on the lights and we'll lose any chance of surprising him.

Each cargo bay in turn shows no activation of the CO2 scrubber since the crew had entered cold-sleep. Every time a compartment door opens, you just know a blood-soaked maniac is going to leap on us.

We clear the last one. Nothing. Leaves me wanting to sigh with relief but if anything, the tightness in my chest only grows.

"Waste of three hours," Zed says. "No sign of him and no more noises."

"It's the quiet that bothers me. What's he doing?"

"Probably tinkering with the engines, looking for a way to blow us all to hell. Shit, I should have listened to you when you suggested we search there first."

"It's not your fault," I say. "It was a good plan. Now we know he's not behind us."

"Well at least the engineering section is open. Take a moment to check the main bay. Might have to go check the engineering bolt hole at the far end, but it'd only take a minute to search once we get there. Only real places to hide in there would be the crawl spaces between the engines and up into the fuel tanks. Not that you could enter one of those in-flight. Not without getting a lethal dose of radiation."

"So we check for a missing rad suit."

"Yeah, if we can't find him," Zed says. "You ready with that darter?"

I do my best to inject certainty into my voice though it comes out more as a croak. "Yes."

Again, Zed takes the lead and a childlike part of me screams we're about to come face to face with the killer. Whispers we'll find the engine room covered in torn wiring and broken circuits and know we're doomed to never slow down. Makes me shake myself and give a literal mental shout of *Get a grip!* Zed had told me sabotage of the engines isn't likely. Whatever had come over the killer—whether it's a part of his mission or he's lost it and gone space-happy—we'll deal with him. I raise the metallic tube of the darter almost squeezing the trigger as the airlock wheezes open.

Nothing.

Zed steps through with me following him close behind. The connecting corridor's clear. No sound from the medibay. No sound from ahead where the cavernous engine room is lit by the faint glow of the ion drive. Without asking, Zed hits the lights. Untouched. No sign of anyone having been in it since we'd entered cold-sleep. No trail of blood. No damaged wiring. Nothing.

"Where the fuck is he?" Zed says.

"Rad suit missing?"

"No, all here. If he came this way and climbed into the engines, well, that'd explain why he's been silent for so long. Still, I better check the bolt hole." He starts down the half-kilometer long walkway over the ion engine.

"But we heard him doing something," I say. "All the clanging and screeching can't have been for nothing."

As if on cue another heavy booming comes, this time from behind me. It sounds much closer. More like something heavy hitting the deck than someone striking something metal.

"So much for the checking the CO2, the psycho's still in one of the cargo bays," I say.

There's another crash and another.

"I've had enough of this bullshit," Zed says, his face darkening. Great. Just what I need—one moment he's flapping, the next losing his goddamn temper.

Before I can pull him back, he pushes past me and races to the airlock. In the main corridor, deep booms reverberate every few seconds. Banging on the light, Zed charges in. Another sound comes from our right.

"Third door down?" I ask.

"One way to find out."

Zed dashes to the door with me taking up position to one side with the darter ready to go.

"On three."

"Just open the fucking door, Zed."

He hits the control and the door slides open. Dull red emergency lighting winks on.

"Can't do better than that," Zed says.

"It's good enough."

We move together into the compartment. The arching vault, like each of the ten on board, contains ten thousand caskets. A colonist frozen on the edge of death imprisoned in every one of them.

The caskets are arranged so some follow the curve of the compartment while others hang above our heads, held in place by magnetic fields and thick chains which jangle and clank when touched. In the dim light, I catch sight of movement ahead of us, maybe forty meters away.

With a booming crash a casket drops from above, landing flat on the deck. The force of the impact strong enough to feel through my feet. All around it other caskets lie scattered. The steel meshwork of the decks glistened in the low light.

Movement away and to the left—I jerk the darter up, tracking the figure I can barely make out in the gloom. The beam from my penlight shows me a man in a cold-sleep wearall. No hesitation—squeeze the darter's tube. It coughs out a flechette, then the man-shape is on us.

There's a vague sense of Zed struggling with our attacker then a surge of pain flashes through me as something grazes my cheek. Falling back, I try to fire again but it's too dark and chaotic to see where Zed ends and the killer begins. The gasping sound must've come from Zed, the sort of short panting of someone fighting for their life. I'm all too aware of my own rapid breathing and the burn of adrenaline. I can't shoot—I want to run and cower in the darkest reaches of the ship, but the struggling men are between the door and me—no hope of getting past and out.

Aiming the penlight at the fight, I try to find an opening to shoot. There's a thud, and a hiss of liquid under high pressure. A face rises into the wavering circle of my light. What I see transfixes me, so I freeze when I should fire. A face—top half covered in the flame retardant foam, bottom half slathered with blood. No way to know if it's Zed or the killer until the mouth opens wide in a scream and through the blood reveals where there should have been teeth, instead there's only a cluster of broken shards of glass jammed into the gums, reflecting the light with a bluish tint even through all the blood. Then the face moves out of the light and Zed gives a pained grunt.

The door slides open, the light from the central corridor blinding me. A silhouette moves across the rectangle of light but disappears before there's any chance to tell if it's Zed or the killer. Gripping the darter and ready to fire, I play the penlight over the form between the door and me. There's a lot of blood—smeared all over the deck and the dark fabric of the figure's wearall. A dark hand gropes towards me, nearly making me fire a dart but the hand is shaking—seeking help not grabbing for my throat.

"Zed, you alright? Talk to me."

He groans. "Fucker bit my neck, I managed to pull him off, hit him with the extinguisher but I'm bleeding. Bad."

"Hold on," I say.

Shining my light on his face and neck shows blood caking him but no sign of the kind of injuries to explain the amount of it. There's a ragged wound near his neck but more on the meat between neck and shoulder. It's bleeding but not with the kind of spray or pumping I'd expect from a severed artery or vein.

"You'll live," I say. "I think."

"Help me up," Zed raises his other arm and I grab it, heaving him to his feet. The expression on his face is near invisible in the dim light, but his breath is still coming in desperate gasps.

"Can you stand?" I ask.

"Yeah… yeah, I can," he says, holding one hand to his wound.

"At least we know it wasn't a naukara or a contract killer, right?"

"What?"

"Well, you fought him off," I say. "If he was enhanced, you'd have lasted about two seconds."

"No, but he was strong. Real strong. Had to use everything I got to keep him off me. But what I don't get is there was almost nothing to him, he felt like skin and bones."

"Thought I'd hit him with the darter, but I must have missed."

"No, the fucker had something sticking out of his arm, I

guess there wasn't any tranq or toxin in those darts after all."

"I don't believe it. Anyway, you see his teeth?"

"Are you kidding? I fucking felt them."

"No," I say. "That's not what I mean. He'd done something to them, looked like he'd ripped out his teeth and shoved broken shards of what looked like glass in their place."

"You mean it looked recent?"

"Yeah. Nothing like cyber-surgery to give him fangs; this looked like he'd done it to himself."

"I told you. I fucking told you. It's the cold-sleep. Something's gotten into him—he's tripping balls on contaminated tranq or plain out of his gourd. Unless..."

"What?"

"Well, you've heard the stories. Maybe... maybe he didn't come back from suspension. Maybe something else did."

I splutter with disbelief that he'd even say it. "Spacer's tales. We've both been through cold-sleep what, a dozen times? You wake up stiff and sore or you don't wake up."

"No, come on. You've heard the stories. And you've had the dreams when they're putting you under. The bright tunnel of light. The voices."

"Cut the bullshit out. OK? You no more believe in that crap than I do."

"No, not really. But... I mean, it does sound like this thing I'd heard about..."

I look at him, making sure my face says what a crock of shit fantasy he's indulging in.

He looks down. "Yeah, you're right. But have you thought maybe the QI virus Stengler gave us was meant for more than our little job?"

"What are you getting at?" I ask.

"Like maybe we were meant to be a cover for something else going on? Like maybe they found a way to trigger the madness mid-trip."

"This sounds almost as paranoid as the ghost stories, Zed."

"No, listen. The tales all talk about the ships where someone's revived and they're changed. Gone... like someone else, like something else was in them." He catches my scowl and stutters on. "Or… or brain damage or some shit. Then they kill themselves or go schizoid, start trying to open the airlocks or some other loco shit. Well, no passenger is meant to be woken during a flight. Maybe it's something you can trigger. You know, program a virus to wake him without doing it right. Make him go fucknuts crazy. Space-happy killer is kind of deniable, right? So Stengler…"

"Stop it," I shout. "I don't give a shit about the reasons. We can work them out later. You've hurt him and we need to find him and finish the job. We'll work out if Stengler fucked us over when we're done and you can come up with all the thermo-foil cap-wearing, superstitious spacer bullshit you want. Deal?"

"Aye, ma'am." He doesn't salute and there's no need to see his face to know the sullen, dangerous expression he's wearing.

"It's a man. Gone crazy maybe. But still only a man. Not a cybernetic killer or face-shifting assassin." I deliberately avoid using the term *Ghost-Face* to forestall any more mumbo-jumbo. "We need to get him somewhere the lights are on and hit him with all four of the remaining darts. If that doesn't work then we fight together, I'll try to hold him while you bash his head in."

"But…"

"No more buts. We're going after him, right?"

"Don't you want to see what he was doing with those caskets first?"

"No."

"Kara, come on. I need to get patched up before we can go after him. There'll be a medikit in here—we can take a look at what he was doing while you seal my neck back up. Please, I'm bleeding here."

"Okay," I sigh. "We patch you up; then we kill him."

I lead Zed to the emergency locker, get a medikit out and slap wound sealant on his neck.

"This is getting to be a regular thing," I say.

Zed doesn't answer. He is staring over my shoulder, penlight in his free hand moving back and forth while I treat his injury.

"What is it?"

"Look," he says.

The tone in his voice is like nothing I've heard from him before. Makes me turn slowly, reluctantly.

Framed in the small circle of light from his penlight, the deck around the fallen caskets is thick with blood. A wide pool of it. From this angle, the casket's positions no longer look random—they're arranged around the pool of blood. I shine my own light over them. Each of the caskets is blank—they don't have the sophisticated viability monitors of the VIP section, only a red or green light. No chance of interfering if one starts fading out. None of these caskets has a light on. Cut from power, they're defrosting, the people inside no longer viable. But where did the blood come from?

"Lights are off, Kara."

"Yeah, poor bastards, nothing we can do for them."

"No. Light should be red; every casket has its own capacitor so they can be moved easily. Only goes off if they're empty."

"What?"

"Where do you think all the blood came from?"

I stalk forward to the nearest casket—its seal is broken. Faint traces of condensing air vapor waft from it as my approach displaces the air. Reaching out to the lid of the casket, the cold bites into my flesh. I ignore the discomfort and pull the lid open. Inside is soaked with blood but of the occupant, there's no sign.

"What do you see?" Zed asks.

"Whoever was in here has gone—there's a lot of blood and no body."

"Gone. Gone where?"

"Don't know," I say. "I have a really bad feeling about this. I think maybe it's time we woke the Captain and screw the consequences."

"Whoa, Kara. You know what she'll do to us!"

"No, I'm not sure. When she sees what's going on here, I don't think she'll care."

"You're crazy! I ain't diving out of an airlock. Not for you, not for anyone."

Something else catches my eye. Part of the casket has been

pulled away, exposing where the optical matrix of the casket's basic computer should sit—a plate of glass with crystalline circuitry. What little remains is shattered...

The teeth in the mouth of the man who'd attacked us.

As I move closer, my foot kicks something that chitters across the floor. Focusing the beam from my torch on it, reveals what looks like a mouthful of teeth scattered across the deck. Some have gone into the pool of blood, but each has left its own tail of red—comets trailing blood instead of ice.

"What the fuck?" I breathe.

Zed steps forward. "I got the strangest feeling. Like we're being watched."

"We've got to get out of here. I don't think the man that attacked you is the same as whoever—*whatever* killed the young woman."

"What?"

"I think there are more than one of them. We've got to wake the Captain—if we can even get to her."

There's a rasping sound like metal grinding on metal. It almost sounds like laughter.

"Run," I shout.

We bolt for the door. All around us come echoing footsteps. I don't stop, don't look back. Zed is bigger than me, stronger, and probably faster but he's injured—maybe more than the neck wound. I make it to the door ahead of him and pound the control to open it. As the door slides up and bright light engulfs me, Zed cries out.

Glance back—six figures surround him, one larger than the others. Can't see much of them with my light-blinded eyes but I can see the terror on Zed's face.

"I'm sorry," I say and pound the door control. It slides down and the desperate scream of the man who'd been my lover and partner in crime cuts off as the seal is made.

CHAPTER 4

No time. Yanking open the control, I rip out the wiring in handfuls. Maybe I'm not as skilled as Zed, but any spacer'd know enough to break the connection to main power.

Pounding comes from the other side of the door—there are only moments before they find the manual release. I pull out the manual crank on my side and wedge the penlight into the mechanism then yank the handle. It grates but doesn't move. I step back and kick it, nearly breaking my foot through my soft-soled deck-shoes. Still the crank won't move. They're rattling it on the other side. The handle bobs but the penlight's stopping the mechanism from turning. It'll hold, for now.

I sprint down the corridor to the pressure door between the core of Char*on* and the command section. A trail of blood leads all the way to the end. Red handprints cover the control panel. Darter raised and ready, I press the door release and wait. Behind me the rattling of the manual release is getting louder as the penlight works all too swiftly loose.

The door finishes cycling and, with a creak-hiss of equalizing pressure, slides aside. Lighting in the short corridor is still on. The trail of blood leads past the VIP boat to the fore compartment.

"Please don't let me be too late."

The rattling sound behind me becomes a grinding. I dive through the airlock. Don't stop to look but seal it and sprint towards the forward pressure door. As I approach, the door slides back. I skitter to a stop, slipping and landing on my backside. A thin man shuffles through, into the corridor. He's soaked in blood and has white fire suppressant foam smeared across his face, blending in pink wetness with the blood. Opening his mouth to shriek, he lurches towards me.

I fire the darter over and over as he comes. Four darts hit him, two in the chest, one in the throat and one straight into his right eye. Though his body jerks at the impacts, he doesn't slow. His hands are held open—claws ready to grasp me.

Scrambling backwards as he bears down on me, both my hands are raised to ward him off. Mouth agape, he presses down on me, blood dripping from torn gums pierced with shards of glass. Coming closer and closer.

One moment I can smell his breath, sharp with a coppery taint. The next, a hot wave of fluid covers my face and his body slumps over me.

"Get her up!" Captain Dominguez's voice.

Wiping my eyes with a hand, I clear the man's blood away. M'Benga's frowning face looms over me. She pulls the corpse off and grabs me by the front of my wearall, hauling me to my feet. She seems huge to me then, though I tower over her when I manage to stand upright.

The Captain fixes me with hard eyes which give away no emotion.

"Lieutenant-Commander Rozanski, are more of our passengers awake?"

"Aye, ma'am," I say and remember my salute.

"Where?"

"Cargo compartment three, Ma'am."

"How many?"

"At least six."

"Warrant Officer Hong?"

"Presumed dead, ma'am."

"While M'Benga and I clear up this mess, have a think about the story you want to tell me. Make it a good one, Kara. Make it fit the facts because if I find you've endangered my ship, you'll be taking a walk out of the nearest airlock." She sighs. "Goddamn revenants."

"Ma'am?" What is she saying? "You know what they are, ma'am?"

"Every time we go into cold-sleep, we die. All of us. You know this, I'm sure."

Of course. You don't get to my rank without some idea. But I can't process this. Sounds like… no, she can't believe such horseshit, can she?

"When we're revived at the end of the journey, sometimes, there are those who aren't viable for revival—they don't wake up. Sometimes, what comes back isn't the person who was there before. Sometimes it's something else entirely."

"But…" I want to challenge this Spacer woo-woo bullshit. To call her out on it, because there's no way a rational human being can believe in this kind of possession. Not unless they've suffered their own cold-sleep induced brain damage. I want to tell her it has to be a problem with the tranq, damn Company short selling us or offloading a bad batch. I want to tell her it's casket failure, some disease, or hell, even a conspiracy. Tell her one maniac who self-mutilates can give all the other loons the same idea. Tell her there's no such things as ghosts, or demons, or spirits. Not on Earth and not in the void of space.

The Captain doesn't give me a chance—storming past me, deckgun raised. M'Benga opens the airlock and charges through. While their deckguns sing a steady rhythm, I lean against the bulkhead. Thinking about ways to blame this all on Zed, thinking about the data-sliver hidden among my personal effects. Thinking about stepping into the VIP module and triggering the lifepod. Taking my chances in deep space instead of waiting on the Captain's mercy.

Behind all those thoughts, I keep asking myself "what is it that comes back?" Some degree of the certainty in the Captain's voice breaking through the wall I'd long ago built against childish fantasy and fear of the dark. Would the next time I lie in cold-sleep be the time something replaces me inside my own skin? Was that what the visions were—an insight into some flipside of reality?

Sinking to the deck and weeping, my tears carve through the congealed blood marking my cheeks.

The rhythmic blare of the guns continues. Each time accompanied by a screech. The cries of the damned… how long before I join them?

I stand ramrod straight, the way my academy instructors had always commended. "There's a cadet who knows how to present. The rest of you maggots pay attention. You've got to be in the top three percent of the class or the only way you'll taste vacuum is humping it with the rest of the other ranks. 'What are you saying, Sergeant?' I hear your slow brains grinding. That's the top one percent right there. You best shape up faster than ten-thousand-greased-gazelles 'cause she's leaving you lightyears behind."

The memory threatens to twist a sneer onto my face. Not a happy memory. I'd had to fight—with my fists, feet, and head—to survive the academy after being touted as the poster-girl. Eighteen months of hell had inured me to intimidation and threats from spacer officers and grounder comp-jocks.

Rank is something to work around like how it pays to finesse relationships with the crew instead of stomping them into line. Thinking of relations with the crew makes me think of Zed, and any hint of a sneer falls away.

Dominguez looks up from my report—her face blank, cigarette hanging from her lips as if ready to fall. Then she quirks an eyebrow, the one with the scar slashing a silver line from her temple to her cheek, catching the corner of her eye and making the bottom lid droop.

"If we were shipping organic fertilizer, I don't think it would stink of bullshit as much as your report, Commander. But right now, I haven't got enough evidence to satisfy a board of inquiry." She spreads her hands. "Another time, it wouldn't matter. You'd wear your tongue out long before convincing me to keep your conniving cunt on board. As it is, I'm tempted to have your personal effects confiscated and every one of your orifices deep probed until I find whatever you've used to hack my ship."

"Captain, if I could just..."

"Shut. Your. Mouth." I go silent. Dominguez smiles. "Good. From now on in, you'll keep your cunning tongue still in my presence unless I tell you otherwise. Understood?"

I nod.

"Excellent. Now, whatever shit you've been up to might—and

I do mean might—have saved my ship and the worthless excuse for a crew I've been lumbered with. I don't care if you revived crewman Hong so you could guzzle dick or if you vermin had larceny on your minds. Whatever it was, I've got revenants loose on my ship." There's something in her eye when she says it, a hint behind the mask. But what's she's hiding back there—fear, or something else?

Every inch of my skin tightens. I want to ask her how any could have escaped but her threats aren't exaggeration. Sometimes it seems like conditioning has made it harder for me to read people, and harder for me to know my own feelings. But there's no doubt about her seriousness.

The Captain's hard eyes still bore into me then she grunts.

"Why'd you have to ruin it? You were the best XO I've had. I'd even thought of cutting you in..." she trails off. "No. No point thinking about it. You'll never make Captain now. For a grasper like you, maybe that's punishment enough."

Still I stay silent. My jaw aches with how tight it's clenched. She'd planned to cut me into something. Knowing Dominguez, it would've been a major venture. The kind of thing which never hit the books and never risked censure. A quasi-legal job. Now I'm outside a circle of trust without even realizing I'd entered it.

But maybe there's a way back in.

"Permission to speak, ma'am?"

The Captain scowls but nods sharply.

"I formally request permission to lead the clean-up crew."

Dominguez sucks her teeth. "You think you can do a better job than M'Benga?"

"No, ma'am. But I'm expendable. She's not."

Captain Dominguez throws back her head and laughs. A throaty guffawing that sounds genuine.

"Madre de Dios! Kara, you really would do anything to get ahead in this life, wouldn't you? It's never been my way, though I admire it. But let you lead? Never again. You're a navigator but all that makes you is a backup to the computer. It's so simple we don't even warrant a full AI. Unless the computer breaks down, you're right—you're dead weight. Expendable. Report to Lieutenant M'Benga. If she says clean the crews' deckguns, you do it. If she trusts you to carry one and crawl through the ship's innards hunting revenants, you'll snap to it. Understood?"

"Aye, ma'am." I snap my sharpest parade ground salute but my brain's leaping teraflops with possibilities. The link-key I'd stowed in Zed's personal effects hasn't been found yet. The computer is indispensable for navigation… replaceable only by me. M'Benga's an obstacle. Or is she?

"Get out," Dominguez says, looking away from me and blowing a long stream of smoke out the side of her mouth.

I spin on my heel and march out of her quarters.

CHAPTER 5

From deep within the ship, clanging comes again. Caskets falling.

"Fuck." I lean against a bulkhead, pressing my forearm into it and letting my head rest in the crook of my arm to stifle my welling tears. I do it to feel the solidity of *Charon,* trying to take some reassurance from it even as my world spins under foot. Another clang. The vibration runs through me. Raising my head from the cradle of my arm, the plan forming in my mind drives out the burning in my chest and stinging in my eyes.

"Kara." M'Benga's voice.

"Siyanda." I turn to face her, looking down to meet her gaze.

"This thing you were doing with Zed…" she pauses, gaze never wavering.

I sigh, letting it sound as weary as I feel. "Warrant Officer Hong was up to something on his own—it had nothing to do with me. As I told the Captain, I don't know why I woke. It was a mistake to investigate without immediately waking the both of you, but I didn't believe it was necessary. You'd have done the same thing in my place."

"*Gówno prawda*! Isn't that how your people say it?"

"*Nenda kamjitombe.* Isn't that how your people would answer?"

M'Benga laughs. "Oh, Kara. I may prefer to fuck myself than mess with the crew but that's up to me, isn't it? And your story *is* bullshit."

"Think whatever you like. I couldn't care less. The Captain will come to her senses."

"You have always had the tongue of a serpent, Kara. One

worthy of an expensive *malaya*. The rest of us might joke it is why our Captain favored you, but now? Now, you are nothing but shit." She clicks her fingers in my face.

"You'd like to think so, wouldn't you? You think I got to be the XO by doing Dominguez favors, then more fool you. You think she'd be interested in a stunted cunt like you? Even you can't be so stupid."

Any other time it'd be unwise to antagonize M'Benga. She might be a foot and a half shorter than me, but she's security chief for a reason. Bunched muscles and scarred fists are proof enough of that. And she has more traction with the Captain than I do… now. The barb about her achondroplasia was low, but it stings more than anything else I can say to her. After the germline DNA edits in most of the Superstates to eliminate genetic "disorders"—which included dwarfism—she has every right to be sensitive about it. The glint in her eyes says my goading worked. She'll send me out on my own to investigate hoping to get me scragged. Which suits my plans perfectly.

M'Benga's face splits in a broad grin, revealing teeth green from cold-sleep chems. She's not even taken the time to clean up. Duty first, always.

"You have been assigned to me to assist with clearing the ship of revenants. We're going out in teams of two but with the loss of Hong we're one man short. So you'll have to make do on your own. I've ordered the armory to provide you with a deckgun and sufficient ammunition. Collect your weapon and proceed to cargo bay seven where you will sweep every last casket for signs of tampering."

"Really? You expect me to check ten thousand caskets all by myself?"

"Those are your orders. How do the Anglos say it? Break a leg."

I storm away, but when I'm sure she can't see me, the smile I'd been holding back curls my lips. M'Benga is an effective security chief—tough, dependable, and highly intelligent. But her intellect works in straight lines. Manipulating her into sending me out alone had been all too easy.

The smile freezes on my face as the sound of Zed's scream

comes back to me. The teeth. The empty caskets. I dismissed what the Captain had said about dying in cold-sleep and something else coming back. She must be as susceptible to old spacer's tales as meatheads like Zed, though even he'd entertained more rational theories than plain batshit crazy ghost stories. And I know better. It isn't possible. But playing with the idea, a shiver dances up and down my spine regardless. Why had the "revenant" been waking other sleepers? Was it a way to turn them? I can't accept some bullshit explanation like possession but maybe… maybe tampering with the caskets is a way to bring on the psychosis. Change the casket revival settings to make the sleeper OD on stims and flip right out to full on space-happy? Possible. Maybe.

Getting to the armory means walking through the crew lounge. It's humming with activity as Ensign Joud wrangles the enlisted men and women into combat readiness. Seventeen pairs of eyes lock on me the moment I enter and all conversation stops.

"We've got a crisis situation here, people. No time to gawk at me; get moving." The snap of command enters my voice and sends the crew back to their business—checking their deckguns and listening to Joud's briefing. His gaze flicks over to me, so I scowl and he jerks before getting his focus back.

"Nicely done," Hiroki says.

"Doc." I nod at him and start towards the armory again.

"That's it?" He spreads his hands, all mock-offended… I think. You know, me and reading people… "After all our time serving together. All those years? Haven't the decades we've lost in objective time left us needing each other—the only family who can understand. And all I get is, "Doc"?"

Could he get any more clingy? Time was, I thought Hiroki's puppy dog act was all about trying to get into my bunk. But the years—and he's right, it has been a *long* time to spend together—don't mean as much to me as they do to him. The futureshock anytime you go on shore-leave doesn't equate to seeing the crew as family. Sitting round drinking sake with him and engaging in the only intellectual conversation I got save for the rare occasions sharing a whisky with the Captain, means maybe he's managed to inveigle himself into the position of "friend" but it's not enough to become a weakness. Not for me. I don't need anyone. Not Zed. Not Hiroki.

"Don't get philosophical on me, Doc. I've no time to indulge your maudlin musings."

"Very poetic of you, Kara. But when did you get so cruel?"

Fuck's sake. "About the same time I got accused of treachery by our Captain."

"You need to talk about it." Here we go with his prying into my private shit. "You're assigned to sweep Cargo bay seven, yes? I will be in the main medical bay, performing autopsies on the revenants and their victims."

This is the reason to value Hiroki. "For what?"

"I cannot accept the Captain's belief that this is a mystical event and spirits are returning to the bodies of sleepers instead of their own consciousness."

I seize him by the arm, dragging him to one side before the crew heard him.

"Have you been at your homebrew saké again? Have you?" I thumb towards the crew. "They don't need to hear you questioning me about unfounded allegations and they damn well don't need to hear you doubting the Captain. Now, you don't buy the spacers' tale and neither do I, but we need proof before there's *the slightest* challenge to the Captain's authority like contradicting her about the nature of the threat. You understand? And if that challenge comes, it will happen by the book and behind closed doors. Do I make myself clear?"

This is crossing the line with him. Trampling over a friendship forged through years of compressed time, no matter how much his attention-seeking can irritate me. The look he gives me almost makes me pause but attachment is an unaffordable luxury right now. My life and my career are in real danger. Hiroki is an asset but only if I can keep him from his self-indulgence and get him dancing to my tune.

Memories of covering up his indiscretions rise—literally picking him off the ceiling when he'd got drunk during the ship's pre-launch zero-g phase and passed out still stikpadded to the deck which'd become up the second the thrusters fired. Another time when I found him crouched in the corner of the medibay, eyes and nose streaming while singing in Japanese—a song for his dead mother, he'd told me when he'd sobered up. Pathetic. But he has had his uses.

He swallows. "You're right. Of course. *Gomen'nasai.* I won't slip again."

"Good. I know you, old friend." I move a hand to his shoulder, squeezing it in the gesture men like him take as a sign of brotherhood. Far easier to lie with a gesture than a word. "You shouldn't be alone, Hiroki-chan. While I was finding out what Crewman Hong was up to, I found these so-called "revenants" manipulating ship's systems. Hacking doors and such. Maybe M'Benga's got the cargo bays secured but I wouldn't trust your life to it."

He gives me a sharp look, eyes wide. "That is… disturbing. Is there anything else unusual you can tell me?"

"Unusual? It's all fucking unusual."

"Forgive me. I mean to say someone suffering a psychotic break brought on by problems with cryogenic suspension, usually due to an imbalance in cryoprotectant fluid or casket mal…"

"Get to the point," I say.

"Yes. Well, they shouldn't function at a cognitive level sufficient to perform complex actions like bypassing door controls."

"So pulling out their teeth and replacing them with shards of optical circuitry wouldn't be normal behavior?"

Both of Hiroki's eyebrows shoot up and he wipes a hand over his mouth. "Self-harm might be, but what you describe sounds a little too involved… Was it only one of them?"

"From what I saw it was the whole group."

Hiroki mumbles something to himself in Japanese. I have a grasp of the language, as I have of Swahili and a couple of the other Superstate tongues, but whatever he's saying makes no sense. Something about childhood. Maybe leaving something in childhood but the thing, whatever it is, is a word I haven't heard before. Sounds like *yūrei*. Someone's name, perhaps.

"You know one of the passengers?" I guess.

"Ai?"

"You said '*Yūrei*'."

"Hmm. Yes. Superstitious nonsense. My people have as many ghost stories as yours, I imagine."

"What stories?"

"Oh, my *Soba,* my grandmother, was an expert in *Fusui,* like the Chinese *Feng Shui.* Highly sought after, even by soulless corporates to arrange their dwellings. This place..." Hiroki waves a hand. "This vessel would have frustrated her greatly. Most of her work was about the directing of elemental energy—wind and water. But sometimes she was asked to direct spirits away from a place or encourage them to go to another. She told me stories of what she saw. I had nearly forgotten them. Ghosts attacking the living or possessing them. Others fed on corpses. I cannot remember the names she gave them. But she swore they were real."

"What are you saying to me, Hiroki? You're starting to believe this bullshit after all?"

It's hard to resist the urge to slap some sense into him.

"No..." He looks as if wants to say more but instead glances away and sighs.

"Good. Now, you're going to do the autopsies and I'll delay my sweep to keep an eye on you."

"Yes, thank you. But shouldn't M'Benga..."

"No. She's slipped up and it's my job to cover her error."

Hiroki nods at me—a slight bow. I hide my smile. He might be high-strung and prone to unpredictability, particularly after a drink, but there are things about him as reliable, no, as boringly predictable as M'Benga.

Voices rise in anger behind us, accompanied by a murmur of excitement. I spin back to the crew lounge proper. Two of the crew are struggling with each other, while Ensign Joud stands to one side waving his hands.

"Stand down! Now!" I shout.

I've lost none of the parade ground thunder I'd shown at the academy. I've inherited my grandmother's opera singer lungs. Projecting my voice and cracking it like a whip comes easy.

The two men—of course it's men fighting like ill-disciplined boys—pull back from each other. Moore and Johnson. Eurussian and United American. The tensions between their Superstates no doubt triggering this loss of control. Unless I'm giving them too much credit and it's something trivial.

"You two are on report. I don't care what your reasons are, if I hear one of you so much as side-eyes the other before the situation on board is resolved, I'll be recommending the Captain space you both. You hear?"

"Yes Ma'am," they both croak.

"Now join your assigned partner and get on with your sweep."

Please, don't let Joud have been foolish enough to put them together. No. M'Benga had overseen the orders. She's many things, but there's no way she'd have put two idiots like Moore and Johnson together. I scan the room looking for any other troublemakers. Daring one of them to cross me.

Silence again descends in the crew lounge but before I can bark an order at them, Hiroki raises his voice. "That goes for the rest of you. You've heard the Commander's orders. Get to it." Seems he is pulling himself together.

I fix on Joud. He looks away. Stepping close to him, I whisper in his ear to spare him the embarrassment of a dressing down in front of the crew. As I come near him, a blush rises in his cheeks and his eyes flick over me. He's a naive boy, on his first run and his attraction to me couldn't be clearer if he bellowed it. So it makes me soften my words then, call me sentimental. It's a failing but who's not flattered by being wanted. Though if it'd had been the leering some men thinks a come on, he'd have got a quite different reaction, make no mistake.

"Ensign, when you give an order you do so in the knowledge the Captain's authority rests on your shoulders. If the crew disobey your orders, that's mutiny. Mutiny means they get spaced. Understood?"

"Yes, Commander. I just… I don't think I could do that to someone."

I laugh softly, as if he'd shared some great witticism—feeling the eyes of the crew on us as they grab their gear.

"Command is about protecting them from themselves as much as it is about getting them to do what you want them to. If you're weak, you invite the behavior that'll see them sucking vacuum before long." I pause a moment, framing the lie. "I see in you a strong man, a good officer. Let him out."

Joud gives a juddering sigh at my words. Maybe I've gone too far—fed whatever fantasy about me he's been storing up. He stands straighter and looks me in the eye. Maybe not.

"Aye, ma'am!"

"Excellent. Dismissed."

He salutes—an ill-advised show of respect given my dubious position—spins on his heel, swipes up his deckgun and starts directing the crew. Maybe it's my imagination, but some of the hesitancy has left his voice.

"Kara, you deserve to be a Captain one day." Hiroki says from behind me.

I nod at him and saunter towards the armory. Cool as I can, like I *am* in control of everything. And why not? Maybe I deserve to be Captain a whole lot sooner.

Standing before the armory and waiting for the security scanner to recognize me, I chew my bottom lip. The armory itself fits more with the monolithic aesthetic of the cargo holds with their thousands of entombed passengers than the cramped crew lounge. Weapons enough for a handful of crew to suppress an attack from a hundred times their number. The door swings wide and I enter the vault. Weapons racks and ammo bins stand empty save for four backups and the three unissued weapons. Mine. Hiroki's... And Zed's.

It hits me then. Not only that I'd left him to die—torn into by crazies—but what his loss means to me. For the first time since being rescued by the Captain, my defenses drop and allow me to feel the hole in my chest where my heart had been. Something vital has been torn from me and only Zed's name fits. I'd mistrusted him. Seen him as someone to use to get what I wanted and never considered there was more. Not saying it's the stupid "l" word. I have more class and discipline than to let myself fall for some other rank barely a step above his slum-rat origins. But it hurts. Leaves me breathless with tears surging to my eyes.

Soft footsteps behind me—Hiroki come to join me. With an effort, I force down the stinging in my eyes and draw a steady breath to fill the hollow inside me. There'll be a time to face the grief or shock or whatever the hell it is. But not now.

Instead, I grab my deckgun, pause for the authorization to click and release it to me. The weight of the gun is disappointing. Engineered to be as light as possible for use on the shuttles, it lacks any heft. An ammo can's still unsealed—red lethal mags not blue crowd dispersal rounds. I slap a mag home. Its weight makes the gun feel a little more reassuring, more ready for action.

Without a word, Hiroki reaches past me and takes his own deckgun then stands hesitating with it in his hands.

"What's the matter?" I ask him.

"If I am right, these revenants are all victims of a medical condition. They deserve treatment, not execution."

"Yeah, well say that when one of them's trying to tear your throat out with their teeth."

"But if we used the soft rounds, we could restrain one. Find out if there's a way to cure them."

Let's think about it for a moment. We might term colonist deaths "spoilage" as a way to escape the scale of the risks of interstellar travel but it doesn't make us all callous. Still, every which way you weigh the issue, the same answer comes back. The risk is too great.

"We have our orders."

"But if they're wrong?"

"If they're wrong, the Captain will bear the responsibility."

"But..."

"No, Hiroki. If, and I do mean if, the autopsy shows sign of contagion or poisoning of the cryoprotectants then we'll take your idea to the Captain. Without hard evidence, we haven't got shit to persuade her the risk is worth it. This is about the survival of thousands versus the deaths of a few."

He hangs his head, scoops up a red-lit magazine and slapped it into the butt of his deckgun.

"You're right, of course. Besides, I hope not to need to defend myself. If the medibay isn't safe, we're all in more danger than we thought."

He has a point. If the revenants get out of the cargo bays again it would mean they have sufficient numbers to cause serious damage to Char*on*.

As he turns to go, I hold his shoulder. Press a radio headset into his hand.

"Don't forget this, Doc. Hopefully, someone'll hear you."

He says nothing but gives me a mournful look as we thread our way back through the crew lounge. It's still, save for the air blowing from the vents overhead and rustling scattered scraps of wrappings from ration packs. I stop under the cool breeze for a moment, only then realizing sweat streaks my face. Thoughts and plans collide again, knocking away the return of the rising feeling trying to betray me and leak from my eyes.

"Wait here a moment, Doc. I have to get something from my casket."

He grunts and as I hustle into the crew cold-sleep bay, I glance over my shoulder. Hiroki is staring at the gun in his hands, mumbling to himself. The way the light catches his face, it looks as if his cheeks are shining with tears. Shaking my head, I scan the room filled with caskets. All show empty. Every last one of us woken to fight the threat.

With security monitors compromised and nowhere for anyone to hide and watch me, I hurry over to Zed's casket. Pop it open and root around for the link-key with the QI virus on it. For the space of a half-dozen heartbeats panic surged in me. Has M'Benga found it? Is the Captain already considering the device and readying an order for Hiroki to test it for DNA? Have I left any traces in my hurry?

A hard edge of plastic catches my fingernail and I scrabble for it, yanking the link-key out of the pouch which holds what little mementos of home Zed had bothered to bring with him. I don't dare look at those fragments of his life. They might mean nothing to me or they might plunge me down the well of emotion deep within my chest.

Tucking the QI virus into my wearall, I close the casket and step away, expecting M'Benga to emerge from the shadows. Instead, a clatter comes from outside and I find Hiroki picking up his gun's magazine from the deck.

"Adrenaline is making me clumsy. I pray I don't have to use this... thing." He says, hoisting the gun and sliding the magazine back in.

"Come on." I say, waving him past. Hiroki might have good intentions. Enough to make me even trust him a little. But only a fool would let someone with shaking hands and a deckgun walk behind them.

CHAPTER 6

Charon is quiet as we march down the main corridor from the crew section towards the aft compartment. You'd expect the sound of deckguns and screams. Or more of the thudding that signals caskets being dropped from their places. Instead, there's only the faintest hum of the ion drive finally pushing 1g acceleration.

In my head, the calculation starts crunching by pure habit. It feels like the Earth is beneath my feet pulling me down but that's wrong. *Charon* will ease off its acceleration as it approaches the halfway point, managing the amount of energy it needs for deceleration as it takes account of the effect of the minute changes in local gravity fields in the time since the route was first charted and drag from the interstellar medium. Time to stop my calculation—I don't know those variables. Who cares about saving Sevran Corp a few new-jiao on the fusion rocket fuel when the whole ship's in danger?

We're midway along the ship's spine when a cascade of distant clanging reverberates all around.

"What is that?" Hiroki asks, swinging his deckgun around in a nervous arc.

"Caskets hitting the deck. Come on, Doc. We'd better get a move on. The revenants, whatever the hell they are, are pressganging more colonists."

I shudder and tighten my grip on the gun in my hands. Recheck the clip and pop the safety off. Ears straining for more sounds, I cover each of the doors to the cargo bays as we pass them, swinging the gun this way and that; spinning around when I think I hear a noise behind us. Hiroki's face is a mask of strain and his fingers grip his gun like he's trying to choke it. His movements are stiff and robotic.

The airlock is closed.

"Let's be careful about this, Doc. I'll cover the door, you open it."

"Hai."

Hiroki moves up and activates the airlock cycle between hull sections. Nothing inside. We get in and trigger the atmo exchange.

"What would we do if the central corridor suffered a hull breach?" Hiroki asks.

"Relax. Stop thinking of the worst-case scenario. They've got nothing that could make a hole in the bulkheads. Even if someone gave them a deckgun, the flechettes couldn't penetrate the hull. Even if they could, it's unlikely the ship's spine would break."

"Has that ever happened? Tell me that's never happened."

"Doc. Calm the fuck down. The door's opening. I need you to focus. Stay alert."

He nods again, another of the small bows which come from his waist, not just a tipping of his head. The door cycles and we step through. The rear section is still filled with the same noises I'd heard earlier when Zed and I had swept through looking for the single killer we thought haunted Char*on*. The hum of equipment in low power mode. The slight tremor of the engines as they ionize the small traces of interstellar dust and gas and drive them out of the back. It'd sound so different when the fusion rockets fire. Within eight seconds, they reach a volume that'd rupture the human eardrum. The massive g-forces they expend would pancake a person less than a minute later.

Turning away, I scan the area. Illumination on full, chasing every shadow away. A feeling like something crawling up my spine comes over me as I see the blood trail. The smear starts a few meters from the airlock, leads round a corner and out of sight. The direction we have to take. Towards the main medibay.

"One of *them*?" Hiroki asks.

His hands are shaking—got to keep clear of him if shooting starts. Then again, the grip on my deckgun is slick with sweat. We aren't so different.

I grit my teeth. "Maybe. Keep close and cover our rear."

"Shouldn't we call for backup?"

"No."

Last thing I need is having to admit I can't handle a single revenant while armed with a deckgun. The humiliation at needing to be rescued by the Captain and M'Benga flares, eclipsing any memory of the relief I'd felt at seeing them.

The red smear carries on down the corridor ahead of us. This part of the ship is cramped compared to the rest. So much space given to the engines there's little room for anything else. Most of *Charon's* mass is here, despite the tons of cargo we carry. Fuel and the sheer size of the fusion rockets dwarf those modules. The ion drive—the low cost, efficient ramjet system can keep accelerating steadily for decades, cutting ever closer to but never reaching lightspeed—out-masses the entire command section despite being little more than a hollow tube.

The corridor narrows again, enough space to move a single casket down and no more. Vents lead from it on both sides; air blows across the gap between them carrying the smell of hot metal. Any moment one of the vents is going to pop open and an insane face with shards of glass for teeth will leer out at me. It stays quiet. The trail grows fainter and patchy. I notice footprints in the gaps between the traces. Too vague to make clear beyond that they're the prints of shoes and not bare feet.

Blood smudges the medibay door control. Covering the door, I nod at Hiroki. Without a word, he slaps the release and ducks back. The door hisses open. Inside, the space is dark. The only faint light coming from some equipment.

I put my mouth to Hiroki's ear. "Should anything be on in there?"

He shakes his head, eyes so wide they're almost popping from their sockets. Fucking brilliant, really fucking brilliant.

I point for him to take position by the door as I advance into the room, switching the sights on the deckgun to infrared. The room leaps out in front of me in a contrast of green and black. Here and there white blooms show which machines are active. No sign of bloodstains through the sights. So they aren't too recent. The only sound audible above the rasp of breath in my throat and the thunder of my pulse is the quiet whirring of some medical equipment.

Swinging my gun left and right, I sweep the room. Not much larger than the crew medibay if you remove the caskets—emergency equipment and a couple of bunks for anyone who can't be put back in their casket to recuperate. Behind them's a single large blank of cool metal but on it is a heat source. Not strong, but in the shape of a person—cold at the extremities but warm in the center.

Focus on it. Move forward with my finger twitching on the trigger. Hiroki behind, his tread heavy. I want to order him to spread out and give me space but I can't force words past the tension in my throat.

Lights flare and my eyes screw shut in agony. Purple afterimages blurring before me.

"Ah, Kara. I'm sorry." Hiroki's voice. "Lights should have come on automatically but someone's reset the system."

I open my eyes again, blinking away the last tracers of purple in my vision.

"That was really, really stupid. Thanks so much, Doc."

He winces and gives me an apologetic smile. "I could see there was nothing in the room but the cadaver. It didn't seem to be a risk."

Over on the table with a cooling human form is a corpse. Male. Medium build. Chest shredded by flechette fire. His face had been scratched deep and now he lies with his lips peeled back from his mouth, showing bloodied gums and jagged shards of glass sticking from them.

Hiroki moves over to him, setting his deckgun down to lean against the leg of the operating table. I grab it, shaking my head and clicking the safety back on, but he doesn't notice. Already absorbed. Without a word to me, he takes up shears and cuts away the shredded wearall covering the man. It's the blue of a colonist—'cargo,' not VIP black or crew grey.

Hiroki goes to work, unfazed by the horrific injuries the man had suffered and the mutilation he'd inflicted on himself before the blast from a deckgun ended his existence. I have to look away, a tide of nausea rising as the smell clawing its way up my nose registers on me. A sickly mixture of meat and feces, urine and the tang of the cold-sleep preservation chems still coating the corpse. It takes all my willpower to force my gorge back down. I need to know the cause of this as soon as he can tell me.

Before long, I'll have to start my sweep or risk a charge of insubordination and a one-way trip outside. But if the autopsy reveals evidence that this isn't some possession by spirits out of a spacer's tale then it'll give me something to use. Maybe against the Captain or maybe to get back into her favor. Not sure which right now.

Hiroki takes out a circular bladed device and moves to the head of the cadaver, pausing a moment to pull at one of the shards lodged in the gums. He struggles with it a moment, swearing in Japanese when it won't come. Then uses a pair of pliers, braces himself and yanks on the shard. Nearly falls over backwards but the "tooth" comes free. A gout of blood squirting as it does.

Hiroki holds the shard up, turning it this way and that, then holds it out for me to see.

"Fascinating. Optical CPU, if I'm not mistaken," he mutters. "Yet with strands of material somehow penetrating into the jaw. I wonder..."

I cough and he glances up. "A curiosity, nothing more. I'm going to open the skull—fastest way to check for abnormalities to the brain."

"Can't you use a scanner?" I ask. "I mean you must have something better than hacking open his head."

"Hmmm...?" Hiroki murmurs, the blade in his hand whining as he brushes the scraggy hair back from the forehead of the dead man. "Oh no. There's no substitute for getting hands on. Even if we had a forensic lab, a physical examination would be undertaken early on in the process. Best way of scanning a brain is outside the body, anyway."

With that, he brings the blade down on the forehead and the awful odor of bone heating up assaults me. It's too much. Sends me lurching away, hunting for a waste bin and, failing to find one, leaves me heaving the contents of my stomach into a specimen tray. Hiroki ignores me, humming to himself as he carries on the task as if it were nothing.

I stumble to the door, scrupulously avoiding looking back and try to distract myself with figuring out what the hell I'm going to do. Whether the dawning of a plan I've had is worth taking a risk on. It could catapult me to success faster than I dared imagine or damn me twice as fast. Absentmindedly, I fidget with the small plastic tab of the link-key. I have to use it or get rid of it sooner rather than later.

An hour, standing there, listening to the crunch and pop of the sacred insides of man being drawn into the light. An hour of churning thoughts and a churning stomach tainted by the taste of bile in my mouth and the greasy fear souring the sweat which soaked me. Fear that a revenant's about to pounce on me, fear that the Captain and M'Benga will find something to nail me with. Fear that Hiroki won't find anything.

"Commander?" Hiroki calls. "You should look at this. I've found something… unexpected."

I spin on my heel, expecting to be greeted by a sight to make me lose control again. Instead, the cadaver is in a slowly deflating vacbag. Hiroki is leaning over one of the medical machines, a red light washing over his face from the narrow viewer attached to the device. I join him, slinging the deckgun over my shoulder.

"What're you looking at?"

"A section of the brain stem of our recently departed passenger. Quite extraordinary."

"What, Hiroki? For fucks sake, what have you found?"

"I forget myself. Look here."

Bending over the viewer and squinting at what it shows, I know enough to recognize cells. Each of them bears a small dark dot.

"Take a closer look." Hiroki says.

My view shifts closer. To a single cell, blown up to fill the display.

"Look in in the smooth endoplasmic reticulum… no, no

opposite the mitochondria, right outside the cell nucleus."

I look up at him with eyebrow arched.

"Ah. *Gomen'ne*—allow me."

I turn back to the scope. The dark dot comes into focus. It's moving. Ever so slowly. A microscopic machine with impossibly small filaments boring into the core of the cell.

"What the fuck?" I breathe. "Implanted nanotech? This shit's supposed to be outlawed by the non-proliferation conventions." Even as I say it I know I'm wrong. Nanotech products had been available to the wealthy—read Corporates—when we were last on Earth. Means the restrictions had to have been lifted in some areas. Forgetting little details or failing to make the obvious connections is another symptom of the futureshock time dilation causes. So much coming at you, easiest thing to do is focus on the familiar. So I know I'm wrong, but I can't stop him as he sets professor mode to stun.

"You're out of date, Kara-chan. At the time of our last stop on Earth the UN World Government had moved one step closer to realization. The Superstates and Corporations both were moving towards an accord that would activate the final treaty. But there were still tensions."

"Of course there were." I look up from the viewer. "What's that got to do with this?"

"Panasia had been progressing its naukara technology. I heard America vetoed the ban on non-medical purposes and commenced aerosol dispersal of what it called "nanodefenders" as a move to pre-empt the other Superstates and show Panasia its cyber-soldiers would be as useless in an invasion as any other troops. Heard rumors of offensive nanotech being trialed as well." He shakes his head.

"So is that what we're seeing here? This revenant's United American?" I ask.

"No. African Nations. When we left Earth, they still protested the changes… Only civilized Superstate."

"Hey. I'm a Corporate gal so I've no arguments with you there."

"Those life-eaters. I wouldn't boast about that."

"Says the man whose people created cybernetic

slave-soldiers." I take a breath to calm myself. "Sorry, Hiroki. You know the rule—no religion, no politics."

He inclines his head. It doesn't hide the effort he's making to conquer his irritation.

"What we've got here are different from nanodefenders. Focused in specific parts of the brain. What the purpose of this nanotech is, I can only guess at."

"Driving him to homicidal fury?"

"Maybe. Maybe not. They might serve a very different function altogether. I lack enough evidence to conclude they're the cause. What I need..."

"...is another body."

"Precisely. Ideally more than one and not from the African Nations. Of course, a living specimen would be even better..."

"Specimen?"

"Oh. you're right. If this is something being done by these nanotech devices, then perhaps they can be treated, have them removed. I didn't mean to sound callous."

I stare at him. Hiroki's a... moral man. I've seen his service record and his psych report as part of my duties as XO. Apart from a tendency to eccentricity, the binge drinking I've kept off his record while we've shipped together, and his obsession with medical matters, his file's main complaint is how driven he is by a commitment to help others. A true altruist.

Amazing such a person can survive working for Sevran Corp but his skills have insulated him from the worst corporate backstabbing. No doubt the officer training medics went through was far more civilized than the free-for-all I'd suffered.

"OK, Doc. Give me one suggestion for an alternative to this nanotech causing madness."

"One? I could give you ten. Easiest is that this is some kind of neural interlace being developed by the African Nations to allow direct brain to computer communication."

"That was tried. It didn't work."

"Again, we're decades out of date thanks to the time dilation. You should know better than I, navigator."

"Fair point."

I run a hand over my face. All of this is tiring me. Almost

like the weight of years left behind are catching up to me all at once. I've been so on edge adrenaline has kept me going. Wonder how long it's been since I last slept?

"So this could be nothing or it could explain this whole problem? A nano-weapon for corrupting enemy troops?" I ask.

"Maybe. Or a peaceful device corrupted by a virus."

His words slam into me. There's no proof the first revenant who killed the woman in VIP cold-sleep had used a QI virus. It's just my best guess, but if he hadn't, that leaves two potential sources. A transmission. Or the virus in my pocket.

"Ok, Doc. I have to conduct my sweep. If I can bag you a revenant I will. When it's done, if when we regroup there are still revenants left, I'll speak to the captain. Suggest we take some alive."

"You're going to leave me?"

"Seal the door. You can do that, right?"

"Yes… oh. I could have done so all along." Suspicion dawns in his eyes.

"You could but we didn't know the medibay was clear. I'll come back for you, escort you to the crew lounge when I'm done."

I leave, feeling a prickling in the back of my neck—his eyes boring into me.

CHAPTER 7

I cover the corners as I go, aiming my gun at every vent. Nothing. The stillness of the central corridor greets me again. Where before it'd unnerved me, now it gives me space to think. Gives me time to work out what to do.

Opening the door to cargo-bay seven, I half-expect a horde of ravening maniacs. But it's empty. Armed and with no need for stealth, I activate illumination—a thousand points of light flare into being, driving the shadows from the vault.

It's never struck me before how much the hanging caskets resemble the way an old-West undertakers might've looked—coffins mounted on walls, waiting for customers. All the Cowboy vids Cal had forced me to watch come back to me then. Never a favorite of mine—too low-tech—but my big brother had loved the period. Obsessed over it. Probably his inspiration for joining the ITF marine corps.

Thinking of him makes me pause. He'd been only a year older than me when I'd started shipping out but with cold-sleep and time dilation, the age-gap has expanded more than fifty years. Had to avoid looking him up on my last visit to Earth—call it being unable to face the possibility of his death. Or cowardice, if you like. Now it nags at me. Of all the times to be distracted this shouldn't be one but the grief lurking in my chest is playing tricks with my emotions. Testing my resolve with weakness I've been conditioned to reject.

Shaking off the pull of memory and the sharp edges of feelings I'm not ready to deal with, I look about—objectivity restored. Caskets fill the space ahead of me, above and to both sides. Each anchored by chains as they float in the air. The higher the g-forces the ship experienced the more power the gravitic dynamos for the magnetic traction fields generate. It doesn't stop the occasional casket breaking free during high-g maneuvers but it's all part of expected spoilage. No—that's a corporate word, have to tell myself it's a waste of life.

A sneer crosses my face. Why should I care for strangers I'll never meet? Normally, something practical would distract me from the losses. They'd become nothing more than a statistic to me, even if the figure rose as high as a thousand deaths. The death of Zed, of an individual, had been a tragedy—it's broken through my reserve. Fighting the urge to curl up on the deck and weep, I pause. Look up as if seeking heaven, though faith had abandoned me early in life. Besides, the heavens are all around me, in their true form. An endless void sparkling with the occasional bright point. Each of those stars meaningless when set against the vastness of the whole.

My radio crackles. A burst of static in my ear broken by distant shouting, the thump of deckguns firing and the thrashing of flechettes tearing flesh apart. Behind the gunfire there are animal howls. The transmission cuts off but I feel no urge to try to get it back. After the rush of noise, the silence of the bay around me grows more oppressive than before. Caskets hang limp, blurring in my vision. I touch a finger to my cheeks, finding them wet.

"Goddamn wimp," I say, cursing my own weakness. It cost me years to drill it out of me and my sense of self rocks under the realization I failed.

My words are swallowed up by the still air. Shaking off the surge of feeling, I stride forward, determined to get the sweep over and done with so I can do what I need to. Maybe twenty meters into the bay, my feet strike something on the floor and send it skittering along the deck. So focused covering the angles, I've not looked down and so scuffed my foot through a bloody clump of teeth, sending them flying across the deck in an arc ahead of me.

Dropping into a crouch, I hunt for targets. So much for a clear bay to sweep. M'Benga would love this. A flash of movement comes ahead, obscured by the caskets. A crashing boom strikes me with deafening intensity. Another casket dropped. Orders are one thing but the possibility of being outnumbered and torn down by sheer weight of bodies clicks up as a high probability in my head.

Despite that, my feet start moving. The cold shiver prickling along my spine bleeds away as training kicks in. Assess the threat: if excessive, retreat; if manageable, engage.

I creep to the edge of the nearest casket, careful not to touch it and set its chain to jangling. From ahead comes a scraping sound before metallic grinding rises in pitch to a shriek and something drops to the deck with a clank. I crouch lower, until I can see under the casket in front of me. A man of apparent Panasian descent hunches over a fallen casket; one of its locking bolts on the ground beside him. He's holding something in his hands, a tool he's forcing against the remaining bolt. His torso is stripped of the cold-sleep wearall—scratches run the length of his back, seeping blood. No sign of any other hunched and bloody figures. Wait a second. It's… too convenient.

Another grinding screech comes and the other bolt falls away, the casket hissing out great plumes of freezing air. It prickles my skin even several meters away but the revenant doesn't even flinch. He reaches into the casket and a shaking hand grabs his wrist tight.

"Fuck it," I grunt, and blast the revenant's legs with the deckgun. The flechettes tear off everything below his knees and he flops to the deck howling—nothing human in his cry, more like feedback screech.

Rolling to my feet, I round the casket, covering the writhing revenant. Blood squirts in all directions from his ruined legs; he'll bleed out before long. So much for getting Hiroki a live specimen.

Movement in the casket again; gurgling as the occupant pulls out the breathing tube and catheters. I sidestep over to the end of the casket, aim still focused on the dying revenant. It takes me a moment to process what's in front of me.

A young woman, no more than twenty. Pallid skin, reddish hair… Eyes fix on me, seize my gaze, and send a shudder running through me. The same blank, dark stare as the man thrashing and howling on the floor. She grabs at me. No hesitation. Reverse the deckgun and bash the stock hard into her face. Smash her nose to a pulp and ruin her perfect features.

Suppose I should feel guilt or sympathy but all soft feelings are buried again under my primary directive—self-preservation. Same as most people. Find yourself in the shit and you think of number one. The sleeper groans and struggles to sit, so you know, hit her a second time, square in the middle of her forehead. Hard as I can, hard enough it might kill her. Tiring of the noise, I reverse the deckgun again, level it at the legless revenant, and blow a hole through him. His screeching stops dead.

In the sudden silence, I pant for breath, hands shaking on the gun. No signs of any other company. Only the casket I'd hidden behind swinging slightly, chain not even squeaking. I sling my deckgun over my shoulder.

The young woman weighs less than I'd expect as I pull her from the casket but she's still too heavy to carry. Have to settle for dragging her by one leg, ignoring the trail of blood it leaves. I toy with the idea of trying to remove the head of the other revenant—surprised at my own detachment—but there's no way to do it short of blowing his head off. If Hiroki wants this one, he can come and fucking get it himself.

Halfway back to the medibay my radio crackles to life again. Sounds like M'Benga is shouting orders with the coughing of gunfire in the background. Whatever's going on must be more of a pitched battle than the simple flushing out of revenants she'd anticipated. The transmission breaks again. With all this shit going on, where the sweet unholy fuck is the Captain? Is she holed up in her cabin or is she up to something else?

Can't shake the feeling she's playing up the superstitious angle. Maybe because I don't want to see her as a fool—not after being her "protégé." Hell, she'd introduced me to her latest husband when we were last Earthside. A man young enough to still be of use to her after this journey. She goes through them like they mean nothing, least that's what the scuttlebutt says. Does it in a way that's so beautifully ruthless—chooses men who're young and naïve enough to care for her children for the decades she's gone, with the promise of a never aging lover and a regular stipend to keep them from straying. How could someone so self-serving have fallen prey to ghost stories worthy of an Ares Cult slasher vid? You know, those awful things where the old god of Mars wakes hungry for blood. Kind of shit shouldn't make a Captain blink, let alone a goddamn, stone-cold operator like her.

Part of me wants to return to the VIP lounge, to check no evidence of my own involvement in "Zed's crime" remains. Another part of me wants to check on the data-sliver with the stolen data on it—my paycheck to a Captaincy of my own and maybe the kind of lifestyle Dominguez has forged for herself.

Midway through musing on my options, the woman I'm dragging moans, coming around. Hitting her again might kill her, so I pick up pace, dragging her as fast as possible and taking no care of what's around me. It's a risk. Makes me easy prey if revenants have escaped the purge.

The moments of anxious waiting while the aft airlock cycles gives me a chance to rethink my approach. Clasping the woman under her arms, I pinion her in a full nelson. It stops me grabbing the deckgun and means I have to scuttle backwards, but it stops her attacking me. There's little doubt she'll be as violent as the others, despite the lack of obvious changes to her. Something Hiroki needs to hear—she woke from her cold-sleep already a schizoid killer.

Any moment, footsteps are going to lurch towards me. The revenant I'm carrying is going to wake and her cries will bring more. As the corridor grows narrower, the vents to either side feel like mechanical mouths leaning in to take a bite out of me. I try to shake off the image but it holds me each time I shuffle past one. As if Char*on* herself has been possessed by whatever's possessed the revenants…

The thought brings me out of it. The cheapest, as in cheaper than a slummer rent-a-hole, spacer tale is the ghost ship and maybe second to it is the possessed ship. You hear the myths all the way through officer training. Mostly in dismissive tones.

But sometimes they'd creep out at downtime in the crew lounge during the weeks surrounding launch and arrival. As easily ignored for the bullshit they are as the stories of blood rituals to wake Ares himself.

The medibay door is closed—no light visible through its small viewport. I ping the entry switch but it bleeps and remains sealed. The girl in my arms starts thrashing and baying as I'm about to pound on the door. Takes all my strength to keep her under control. Even then it's a losing battle. Though I'm bigger, older and in better condition, the revenant is holding nothing back—her frenzy is going to overwhelm me and soon.

I shift enough to bang my heel against the medibay door while I force the revenant's head forwards to keep her from getting to her feet. The dried blood helps—gives less of a grip for her scrabbling feet than clean deckplates would have. Which is something. Not much but something.

My grip begins to slip—every second she struggles a bit more out of my grip. If Hiroki doesn't open up soon, my only option is to kick her away from me and hope I can bring my deckgun up fast enough to shred her before she does for me.

The door hisses open behind me and I stumble backwards into the darkness, almost losing my grip on my captive as she gets her feet under her. Skin prickling, I can almost feel the broken-glass teeth of another revenant closing on my flesh. Visions of the one Hiroki had cut apart somehow sown back together and moving in mockery of life fill my mind. With training on one side and the weight of emotions adding to my panic on the other, I'm close to screaming. Arms reach out of the dark and I suck in a panicked breath, tasting tabac smoke. Hiroki clasps the revenant's flailing arm and presses a hypoderm to her pale flesh.

Her struggling fades and she goes limp.

"Hiroki, damn you. What are you doing with the light off?" I hiss at him.

"Thinking," he says round his cigarette—a red-end of course. "You are uninjured?"

"Yeah. Nailed one opening this one's casket. Hiroki, listen to me." I grab his arm and let the unconscious revenant flop onto the deck. "She was like this when she came out of the casket."

"Are you sure? The other revenant didn't touch her first?"

"Yes. She grabbed him."

"That's… unexpected. I have been unable to find any sign of a pathogen which could be causing this madness. Either it's the nanotech we discovered or…" he trails off.

"Or there's another explanation we haven't found yet. Right?" I dig my fingers into his arm. How can a scientist be willing to even consider the alternative?

"Hai. Of course." He waves at the door. "Lock us in while I prep the patient."

He hoists the slight young woman—what a bag of bones she is—and sets her on a recuperation couch. I'd expected him to use the still bloodied surgical table—if there's no cure for this space-madness, wouldn't this revenant soon be joining the dead one anyway?

With the door sealed, I go and sit on the other couch as Hiroki straps the prisoner down. He sets up a smooth dark grey halo of metal around her head.

"Now, let's hope we find more nanotech." Hiroki says.

The scanner must have come from one of his more recent visits to Earth. Instead of a small display like the microscope, this spins an image into a haze of mist.

"New equipment?"

"This? No, old style holo display. Back when it was thought to be a better way of seeing scans. I'm sure I have an AR headset for some of the even older devices."

"You mean the microscope is newer than this?"

"Much. But I should say, every doctor's preference is different. I work better with a microscope for that kind of examination—I want to see as much as possible of the reality and not a computer simulation. There's no choice with a scan, so…"

"You put up with whatever they give you."

"There's not much call for most of the medibay's equipment. Only reason Sevran Corp bothers with the weight expenditure is to comply with UNWG directives. We're far from fully equipped here."

"Great."

"Look at this." Hiroki hands me a small white container with the ancient symbol of healing, the red cross, displayed on one corner.

"A medipack, with nanotech, right?"

"Precisely." He fiddles with the scanning equipment. "This is an image of how the nanites which are designed to heal injuries look and behave."

An image floats in the air, zooming in until clusters of microscopic machines enlarged to smash-me ball size gather around a break in the skin of a patient. The view zooms closer and what looked like a single machine reveals itself to be a cluster. The nanites seal breaks in damaged cells while at the next level up they form bridges between broken tissues drawing the edges together. When the nanite latches on to a damaged cell, it conforms to its shape, extruding some substance to coat the cell membrane before it moves on.

The view shifts. "This is what is happening inside our patient's head here."

No gradual zooming, instead a clump of cells leaps into view, each cell marked with the single black dot of a nanite. The nanites themselves look different, smaller than the ones from the wound sealant. Sharper.

"What are they doing?"

"Nothing I can see. But look at the cell activity."

"What do you mean?"

"Hold on." The view zooms out—leaving me momentarily disoriented, I've been staring at it so intently. "Can you see now, the affected cells surround the endings of the synapses in these parts of her brain? They're blocking neurotransmitters from interacting across the synaptic cleft."

"Navigator, Hiroki. I'm a navigator. What are you telling me?"

"These nanites are actively shutting down parts of her brain. Similar to Alzheimer's before it was cured. Here the effect is localized to specific areas dealing with motor control."

"So... what? You're saying she shouldn't be able to walk around?"

"Just so." He inclines his head at me; I shake mine.

"But she can."

The view zooms out again. "It's like her brain has found a way around the blockages. You can see there are plenty of signals going through the brain." The floating image shifts, becoming more translucent and flickering with lights flashing around it.

"Is this the cause then? Some fucked up nanotech's gone wrong and triggered a change in the way the brain works for some of our cargo?"

Hiroki wipes his forehead with the back of his wrist. "I do not know. If not for the change in behavior we have seen, I would expect anyone with these nanites active within their brains to be paralyzed. That said, there's another oddity."

No more fucking oddities, please. "What?"

"The "teeth" in the cadaver were each anchored into the bone of jaw. Grown into it, I should say."

I fold my arms. "And?"

"Well, that means the nanites had to have done it. No way could one drive the optical chip fragments into bone and the gums alone wouldn't hold them in place."

"So what?"

"I do not know. It strikes me as strange the nanites would do that and then proceed to disable neuronal function. It is almost like they were trying to repair the damage done to his mouth but if so, why then go and obstruct brain activity?"

"Is that important somehow?"

He shrugs. Wonderful.

"Well, thanks for that, Doc. Wait, what about sleeping beauty?" He looks blankly at me so I gesture to the unconscious revenant.

"No abnormalities in her teeth, if that's what you're asking."

Waste of my goddamn time.

An uncomfortable idea forms. "Would this nanotech be activated by an RF signal?"

"Possibly. Some operate on biochemical cues."

"Can we check?"

"If these nanites have receivers? Not with my scanning

equipment. Nanotechnology requires far more precise tools than even the most advanced corporate hospital could use. There's no part of the human body which relies on cells small enough."

The part of me separate from all emotion—robotic in its fixations and allowing me to calculate a Lorentz transformation on the fly—kicks in. If the nanites received a signal, it'd have to come from within Char*on*. The effectiveness of the bulkheads at interrupting our radios suggests it's impossible for a signal to have been received except on the main Comm Array. If there is a radio relay in the ship, it's not something the Captain wants me to know about.

I miss Zed. He'd known Char*on's* systems at such an intimate level it'd almost made me jealous. As if his obsessive care for the vessel was in competition with those moments he'd spent exploring me.

A sucking feeling in my chest makes me gasp as his loss hits again. Not caring if Hiroki sees, I slap myself.

"What is it?" he asks.

Shaking my head, I swipe up the deckgun. "Find out how she's still able to move. I have to see the Captain."

CHAPTER 8

Back in the command section, a ragged gaggle of crewmembers is waiting, gathered in the lounge. Five of them. All wild-eyed and blood-soaked.

"What's the status of your sweep?" I ask.

They look at me with expressions ranging from the blank to the desperate. One, a middle-aged rating who's seen more trips between the stars than even the Captain, stands and salutes me.

"Ma'am, we've finished our sweeps," she says. "Waiting for Lieutenant M'Benga to give us more orders." Every word comes as an effort. Probably never needed to fire a deckgun her whole career. You have to wonder how many times crews have needed to gun down their ca… I mean, passengers.

"Heavy resistance?"

"Not at first, Ma'am. But they're sly, these *cao ni ma jiangshi.* They come out of nowhere. We thought they were no more than crazies but they ambushed us. Ngolo, he was… they tore his throat out in front of me…" Her shoulders shake. I want to comfort her, but it's been drilled into me so deep, there's no changing now—the crew are different. You don't mix with them save to give orders. Don't fraternize.

I can only think of Zed, as I stand helpless.

After a moment, one of the other crew takes her arm. A scar-faced man—United American by his accent. Dawkins, is it?

"Keep an eye on her, Dawkins. I have news for the Captain. Maybe we can end this." The last slips out before I can stop myself. It isn't for them to know.

He gives me a sloppy salute and leaving me wrestling with whether to call him on it. It's probably not disrespect, merely fatigue. M'Benga really did give me an easier assignment. From kindness or a desire to see me humiliated before the end? No point thinking about it—won't make me go softer on her, when power swings back my way again.

Outside the Captain's cabin I stop, hand raised to ping the door control. I was so certain on my way from the medibay, not hesitating for a moment. Now doubts pounce. If what I suspect is true, the Captain might eliminate me, or worse. Could she paralyze me with a press of a button? Unbidden, my right hand rises to the back of my head feeling for signs of the nanites which might lurk inside.

The pointlessness of the subconscious action makes me snort—for a moment fear has reduced me to phrenology, a fool gulled by a snake-oil peddler.

More memories of Cal's historical obsessions flood in. From them, come reassurance. Almost as if my big brother is telling me to think like a gunfighter in one of his stupid films. If the Captain goes to activate a broadcast or does *anything* to threaten me, the answer is by my side. Stroking the deckgun's polymer shell, a dozen ways to get away with shooting her spring to mind. So easy maybe I should do it while I can still take command ahead of M'Benga. Slum-rat thinking must have rubbed off on me from Zed or maybe it's the way of things when you go into business with scum like Stengler. I key the entry pad.

The door sighs open. Behind a haze of cigarette smoke, Dominguez sits at her desk, feet crossed on its top, deckgun resting alongside—pointing straight at me. Thoughts that doing away with the Captain might be easy evaporate.

"What the fuck are you doing here, Lieutenant-Commander?" She stresses the lieutenant part.

I swallow, shifting my hand from my gun to its strap, as if all I'd been doing was steadying it. "Ma'am, I have urgent news."

She frowns; takes a drag on her cigarette, burning away the L of the Lucky Strike printed down its side. "Come in."

Striding forward, I deliver a parade-ground salute.

"Lay off the brownnosing, Kara." Dominguez hisses a plume of smoke. "If you have something worth my time you'd better spit it out."

"Nanites."

"Nanites?"

"Hiroki found them in the brains of two revenants—one he autopsied and a live one I brought him."

"You've been busy, I see." Dominguez sits forward, taking her feet off her desk and stubbing out a new-jiao's worth of tobacco. "I don't need to ask why I'm getting this report from you and not our doctor now, do I?"

"The nanites should paralyze the revenants but the live one was still kicking and screaming."

"Why is this of any interest to me? I told you what was causing this."

"With the utmost respect, Captain," I say. "That's the kind of bullshit the crew might swallow but it's not something your officers accept. Not something the Company will buy either. No one in their right mind believes some irrational spacer tale."

"So you'd taken it on yourself to find another explanation."

"You ordered the autopsy."

"I did." One hand rests on the stock of her deckgun.

I swallow and plough on. "Because you wanted to know why the nanites weren't working to shut down the revenants."

"Very good. Yes. You're not cleared to know about it but since you've puzzled it out why hide it? All colonists have nanotech introduced to them in cold-sleep. Nanotech that seeks two places. The brain and the womb of female colonists. New colonists get their upgrade before birth."

"Fucking Sevran Corp!" I spit. "If a colony ever chose to secede from Earth…" All the implications grind through my brain. "Fuck. Wouldn't be much of a battle."

"No."

"And you've been trying to use the nanites to stop the revenants."

She nods. "It's so easy, so damned easy. They're interlinked. Trigger one and…" she flickers her fingers. "Cascade effect. But it's not working." Reaching for a glass of amber liquid on her desk, she takes a slug; eyes never leaving mine. "We're fucked."

"So you decided to hole up here and drink yourself

insensible?" I can't believe it. Last thing you'd ever expect of Dominguez. Never had her pegged her as a cowardly shit who'd just quit.

"Don't get it, do you? We could've controlled this if none of them had got loose. It'd have been a higher spoilage rate than usual maybe, nothing more. But they're going round, waking others. Instead of one in a hundred thousand coming back… different, it's every damn one they go to."

"This is insane. It's fucking mental." I wave my arms around, careful still not to make any move which might look like a threat. "Have you been at the Company pharmaceuticals? I mean, you really believe these revenants are possessed?"

"Do you know where consciousness goes when we die, Kara? Do you know why it comes back for some but not all? There's no reason anyone should spoil in transit. Casket failure's rarer than you're ever told. Some people don't want to come back. Come on, haven't you ever had the dreams in the tube?" She drains her glass. "And if there's a body going, then outside the light of the stars, in this emptiness, something's waiting for its chance."

"Ghost stories. Damn spacer's tales. Come on, this is crazy talk. If it's an infection or an imbalance in the cryoprotectants for cold-sleep, we can do something about it. If some other transmission is blocking control of the nanites, maybe it would explain…"

She stands quickly, the expression on her face making me fall silent. Walks over to me, leaving her gun on the desk. Comes so close to me the smell of smoke and whisky on her breath washes over me. "If every last one of them isn't killed quickly, they'll overrun the ship. Slaughter us. There's no cure but the gun. You understand me?"

The overwhelming desire comes over me to drive my forehead into her nose and frag her as she staggers back. Give her the cure she wants, the cure for all my fucking problems. Before sanity returns, I fall. Except it's not falling, instead I'm floating free of the deck.

I flail about before the training kicks in. Dominguez is ahead of me. She grasps the edge of her desk with one hand, pulls herself down and catches my foot, drawing me close to her again. I get a grip, cheeks burning from being surprised by the change in apparent gravity.

"We're not due for zero-thrust yet," I say.

Dominguez catches her spinning glass, secures it to a stikpad on her desk. "Someone doesn't agree. They must have gotten into the engineering section."

"Unless they got to control?"

"No. I've got helm security set to alert me here—we'd know."

Fighting with the nausea of the unexpected shift to micro-gravity, Hiroki springs to mind. Alone. With one live revenant in the medibay and more outside. Ones clever enough to disable the ship's ion drive.

"We've got to get down there," I say.

"No shit," Dominguez sneers. "You really do have potential for a Captaincy."

She clicks her deckgun onto her wearall's tether and drifts over to a metal locker covered with photos of her families—all three of them. Roots around inside.

"Heads up," she says, tossing me a small grey sack—micro-g essentials.

I catch it as it spins towards me, my reflexes already adjusting to the change. Slap the promethazine patch on my neck to stop the microgravity induced need to puke—does fuck all for the nausea, but no one wants to deal with vomit in zero-g. Put on the rebreather and pull stikpads over my deck-shoes. Giving them a practice pull off the deck, the instincts months of micro-g training had instilled in me kick fully into play. Slap my foot down and it holds. Twist the foot, pull, and it releases. I do just that, launching myself at the door and slapping the control before the Captain can beat me to it.

"After you, Ma'am," I gesture at the open hatchway.

"Lead on, Kara."

We float through the crew area, dodging the detritus floating about. The crew gathered here are busy securing the junk before it becomes a hazard. Standard procedure coming automatically despite the trauma they've been through.

"Leave that. All of you, with me and Commander Rozanski. Now. Weapons hot."

Without hesitation, they abandon their task and push off to join us, unhooking themselves from anchor points as they come. Surrounded by guns, it doesn't feel safer. Something about this is wrong, screaming at me to think again, but swept along in the Captain's wake, I can do nothing but follow orders. All the while the other part, the one with the plan, rumbles inside me. Awaiting an opportunity.

The central corridor has changed in the minutes since I'd come through. Blood streaks its walls and hangs in droplets, colliding, forming great globules. A half-dozen corpses float about. One spins through the air towards us, arterial spray still gouting from her savaged throat, her eyes bulging. Williams. Crewmember. Nothing to do but watch her die or move on. My gorge rises, but it helps to look past the dying woman and focus on the airlock ahead of us. Crimson smears streak its grey-white surface.

I duck my head away from the floating mass of ruptured intestines trailing from a dead revenant; his shattered body leaks profane fluids and chokes the air with the stink of shit and death.

"Where's M'Benga?" I ask, meaning it as a thought but finding my mouth moves on its own.

"She'll be around. She's the sharpest *coño* on board… after you. Always underestimated her, haven't you? Because of her stature. Not realizing the advantage it gives her here and the hard edge she's developed succeeding despite prejudice."

"I never took you for a bleeding heart, Captain."

"Then you've always been right about me."

What she said hits me harder than you might expect. Let's be clear, I'm not prejudiced against M'Benga because of her physical differences. I'm not stupid. In space, she has significant advantages—greater g-force tolerance being but one. A research paper, now many years out of date in objective time, had said germline editing to create a new generation of spacers with conditions previously seen as disabilities is the future of interstellar travel was required reading at the Academy. Truth is, I've never thought less of M'Benga for any other reason than she's a jealous bitch who lacks imagination. Stuck in her narrow way, unable to change.

Lashing anchor-lines to the airlock, Dominguez sets her feet down.

"You, Martinez. Stay here. Kill anyone who fails to identify themselves. I don't care if they're crew, I don't care if they're your steady bunk mate. If they do not identify themselves when challenged, shoot them. Is that clear?"

Martinez grits his teeth. "Aye, ma'am."

Dominguez engages the airlock cycle. We squeeze in, three of the crew walking up the sides of the airlock until they appear to stand above us, or is it below? The cycle drags. If time's a measure of heartbeats, my subjective timeline has constricted as the universe streaks away from me near lightspeed. Seconds become years. Have to tell myself to get a grip and watch for my chance.

A dead revenant bumps off the narrow corridor walls ahead of the airlock door, the small change in pressure pushing it away from us so the corpse tumbles end over end, leaking beads of blood which coast through the air, striking each other and melding.

Dominguez takes a cautious step. "Dawkins, stay here. You know what to do?"

The scarred man anchors himself in place. "Aye, ma'am."

I clear my throat. "Captain, I left Hiroki on his own in the medibay. With a live revenant…"

"And?"

"I'd like to check on him."

Her eyes are hard, pinning me to the deck as surely as the stikpads do. Leaning in so it's for my ears only, she says, "I wouldn't turn my back on you now for anyone, Kara. Not for a second."

"But…" I regret it as soon as the word leaves my lips.

"One more word and I'll have you stripped of rank. Understood?" She growls.

What can I do but nod? The eyes of the crew make my back burn.

"You. Meecher. Go to the Medibay and check on the medic. If he's alive bring him to the engine-room. If not, don't hang around. Stay sharp." Under her breath, the Captain mutters, "Siyanda, where are you when I need you?"

The middle-aged woman who'd lost her partner on the earlier sweep trembles at the order but starts moving. She wouldn't have been much use anyway, the way her hands shake.

We inch along the corridor, to the rhythm of twist, release, step, test, repeat. Any revenants we encounter will float while we stay stable and blast them—hopefully, it'll be advantage enough. Doesn't stop my heart from thundering.

The quiet bothers me. No matter where you are in the ship, you grow used to the constant background vibration which becomes an actual humming near the engines. Now they're still. Like being at dock. Only then, you'd be focused on getting your duties out of the way, briefing the crew not to mess with the colonists or Earthside gangs, collecting your pay, and enjoying the all too short shore-leave before prepping *Charon* for its next journey and dealing with whatever fallout there was from the ranks being let off the leash. In the absence of that low frequency, my ears whine.

CHAPTER 9

Corpses soar in a tangled constellation through the engine vault. Leaking fluids and body parts orbit them; a nebula of blood hazes the air. The visible sections of the great fusion rockets are spattered with gore and scuffed by flechette rounds. The ion drive, running under the walkways we stick and unstick ourselves to, is dark, all displays dead. Maybe permanently out of commission. In which case we are as good as dead.

The calculation runs itself in the back of my mind without urging. Spin Char*on*; fire all fusion rockets at the limits of ship tolerance until they expend their fuel. Velocity'll still be too high by the time we enter the Gliese 892 system. Maybe, gravity assist could shed enough speed—weaving a complex path among the planets. The sheer complexity of the course we'd need overloads me. It'd take days of calculations with the navicomp's help.

I'm not convinced we have enough reaction mass to make the course corrections but it is possible. If the course corrections and gravity assist didn't work, we'd hurtle out of the system and into forever. The vessel itself might be worth several billion new-jiao but the cost of a rescue would dwarf that. Sevran Corp would be pragmatic.

"Captain. We've got to end this now. There's no time if we don't want to end up on a one-way trip."

Her fist comes up. Hold. I set both feet, brush the lenses of my rebreather clear of blood, and look about for threats. Something's wrong about the scene before us. Not simply the bodies tumbling about, bouncing off each other and the walls. They're enough to crack anyone's sanity, a whirling waltz of the dead, the *danse macabre* of legend in the flesh. Painted with the colors of blood and shit.

No weapons.

Not a single corpse has a visible deckgun and none of the weapons float free. There are seven dead revenants—three whole, four floating in pieces, one torn in half, the others missing limbs and in one case a head. The dead crew are all the same: throats torn out with the savagery I'd first seen in the VIP lounge.

It makes little sense.

If they'd been overwhelmed, why don't their corpses bear signs of other wounds? Bites or scratches to their arms should be clear as defensive injuries. If they'd been ambushed, how'd they manage to kill all of these revenants?

I realize our mistake and cry out as the first of the intact revenant corpses opens her eyes and draws the deckgun lashed to her back up and around.

Twist, twist, I free my feet.

The muzzle of the gun points at me.

Kick.

Launch myself away from the deck. She pulls the trigger. A cluster of flechettes tear through the flesh of my left shoulder. The crewman who'd been standing behind me screams. Pain flashes, eclipsing all my senses in a white haze even as my throat lets loose a shriek of agony. The training saves me, leaves me enough focus to keep conscious and do my job. Spinning around, I set my feet to the deckplates which had been above my head.

The recoil of the deckgun had sent each of the ambushers tumbling backwards and I pump shot after shot into them while the Captain does the same from her position ahead and below/above me. Not one of the schizoid killers had hit her but their attack's slaughtered the rest of our group. They stand, still stuck to the deck but shrouded in their own broken pieces and haloed in blood. I turn away, unable to cope with seeing the inner workings of people I'd spoken to only moments before.

"Kara? You still with me?"

Dominguez is in front of me. I must have blacked out. The urge to swing up my deckgun and end the Captain while I can still blame the revenants swells and breaks as the pain in my shoulder blows away thought, leaving me whimpering in agony.

"Hold on. I've got the emergency medipack. Here." She holds something to my neck and prickles my skin, a shallow and insignificant pain next to the screaming torture of my shoulder. My heart thuds in my chest, each beat driving back the agony until it exists in the far distance. Not gone but something I can ignore. The pain rockets again as Dominguez does something and my vision blurs…

I'm aware again. Floating near the engine controls, anchored to them. I look to my shoulder—the Captain's torn away the arm of my wearall to get at the injury. Wound sealant closes the rents in my flesh but the razor tip of a flechette protrudes, seeping droplets of blood which swell and float free. She must've freed the ones that weren't too deep and left the sealant to slow the bleeding. The patch of springy foam covering my shoulder is pink in places and blistered around the protruding tip of the flechette. Don't need to hear it from Hiroki to know that without surgery, the barbed end of the flechette will keep ripping at my flesh as it works its way deeper and deeper. Without help, I'll bleed to death.

I look round for the Captain, but there's no sign of her. Only one place she could've gone. Into the ion drive to restart it. She wouldn't be able to do the calculations I'd rushed; she wouldn't realize there was a chance we could use a gravity assist to slow us down. The only choice Dominguez would see was between getting the ion drive working or consigning us all to an eternal sleep between the stars.

What to do? I need Hiroki. *If* he's still alive. And, though I had been happy to contemplate her death when all other options ran out, I can't ignore that the Captain saved my life. There'll be more revenants waiting for her. Probably the first one who'd woken when Zed and I had made our play for our big score. It's obvious—these things, whatever their origin, aren't rabid beasts. They act with purpose. Not one had tried to kill the Captain. Which means something—they need her alive. Why? If they get what they want, will they be satisfied or will it spell death for the rest of us? No way will I chance finding out.

Something nags at me. My QI virus. Either it'd been prepared to release the first revenant, Revenant Zero as I now think of him, or there's some force active aboard ship. Could Dominguez have triggered the release? It makes no sense. Maybe the creeping numbness of the painkiller's affecting my mind but when I think of a simple calculation, the numbers crunch as they always have.

There are too many variables I don't know. Nothing to sink my intellect into and rip out an answer. Only one choice lies open to me. Choose myself or choose the Captain.

My shoulder throbs as I bump against the ladder. I'm pulling myself along the ion drive's half-kilometer housing, one rung at a time, sticking both feet before reaching out with my right arm. Easy prey if a revenant attacks. My left arm's useless, I've tried using it but the agony pierces even the icy haze of the painkiller. When it runs out, I'll be nothing more than a coiled-up ball of misery. To keep control, I used an anchor line to bind my left arm across my chest. It helps, but every now and then, I catch my arm as I move and pain spears through me.

My plan? No, I'm shit out of plans. So much for finding a way to use the QI virus or eliminating the Captain. Survival has boiled down to the realization Dominguez is vital in some way. My career might never recover but if I live, opportunities will open. Dying or being stuck on a vessel doomed to fly forever into the dark between stars leaves no chance of a comeback.

The ion engine stretches the entire length of the ship—its intake, and during deceleration its exhaust, angled below Char*on's* armored prow. But its heart's in the aft compartment. In many ways, it is the rear section with what remains of the engineering space given over to the fusion rockets we'll use when our speed drops to a point the interstellar medium is too diffuse for the ramscoop to properly fuel the ion drive. Dispose of them and it'd take over a century to slow down on ion drive but what's time to an interstellar traveler? Each journey drags you farther in spacetime from any world you know and anyone left on it.

The engine itself is a small section at the very rear of the vessel. Most of what's visible as a giant tube running the length of the engineering bay is part of the ramscoop, drawing in the sparse dust and gasses of interstellar space and funneling them along, building a charge as it does so. The final hundred meters are where the magic happens. Where propulsion becomes significant. It can't safely exceed one-point-one-g and takes its damn time getting there, but the fuel it scoops in the seeming emptiness of deep space allows the ship to accelerate ever closer to lightspeed—far beyond the redline where friction and radiation become too great. Unless the final reaction chamber gets damaged. Then it's nothing but a magnetized tube.

I gain the bottom or is it the top of the ladder? My mind's begun to wander again, thoughts fuzzed by shock and the drugs. The colossal cylinder ahead of me, the ramscoop itself, is dim. No scintillation of particles being accelerated and condensed. No hum of power—have to hope the magnetic cowl is still being generated. I can't see the Captain if she is ahead. It's dark where the tube I'm standing on runs under the engineering deck. The strong desire to shine a light down the cramped space wars within me against the certainty it'll give away my position. Guided by the grainy image of the deckgun's thermal sight, I stagger forward—all grace gone from my steps so I tug at the stikpads and lose my balance as often as I twist them free. My shoulder burns.

Too soon for the painkiller to wear off.

It bothers me. Had bumping the injury driven the flechette deep enough in to nick an artery?

Stop thinking about it!

Ahead, maybe a hundred meters, is an access port to the inside of the engine. There'd be a voidsuit there, not armored to allow for true EVA but a light model to protect an engineer from vacuum so they can work on the inside of the ion engine if necessary. Such a suit wouldn't survive long outside the ship at the speeds we were travelling. The slightest impact from dust would tear through it but with the intake of the ramscoop closed—and it has to be closed since the engine is dark—there's no threat. If a revenant has climbed into the engine, the access would cause an automatic safety shutdown. But what could they do there? If the Captain's followed them, I'm out of luck. The need to work on the ion engines is so rare even two suits are considered a luxury and Sevran Corps doesn't bother with those for haulers like this one. By the time I can find my way back to the hard suits, whatever's going to happen here will already be over. All I can hope to do is watch Dominguez's back and make sure she can get back in.

The port is visible now, a dark hump on the surface of the engine cover. What had seemed pitch black isn't total. Another shape rears up on my thermal scope—the Captain?

The time for worrying about giving myself away has passed. I flick on the deckgun's light and frame the figure.

Male. Dark-haired. Wide shoulders, powerful waist. He turns and my finger tightens on the trigger. And then I see his face.

"Zed?" I say.

Maybe I scream his name, maybe whisper it. Blood loss and shock combine, making me sway. If not for the microgravity and being stikpadded to the engine mounting, I'd have fallen. As it is, the next moments come as a series of still images. Events strobing before my eyes as I drift in and out of consciousness. Zed calling out. Now he's halfway to me. Every detail of his face his crystal-clear. Now he's ten paces away. My heart leaps—an unfamiliar feeling filling the empty space in my chest, the chasm that's been there since I left him.

He's alive!

Now he's in front of me, holding an arm out towards me. He'll take care of me and I'll never let him down again, no matter the cost to my bullshit career.

My navigator conditioning—the cutting, the reshaping of who I am to better serve the Company—is tied to my emotions. They'd been dragged from me, not removed but turned to serve the all-important goal of making me function as a navigator needs to.

In many ways, they'd left us navigators with a shred of a personality. Most of the time, it doesn't matter. You get the big things, the primal emotions. But anything more subtle… Don't get me wrong. All the fundamental needs of a human—to feel valued, to seek approval and love—they all remain but they're undermined. You end up not callous as much as preoccupied with things that affect *you*. The fundamental drives mean survival, the things you *can't* cut away.

Seeing Zed brings on a surge of feeling that threatens to break down all the Company had rewritten in my mind. Threatens but fails. In the last blink of consciousness trying to slip from me there's a stretching of time. The moment dilates to a singularity of existence.

All the power of my mind leaps to deal with the tide of emotion. It seeks facts and draws conclusions. Where are the injuries Zed must have suffered? Why isn't he speaking to me? Why isn't he angry after I left him?

It looks like Zed, but it can't be him. Blink and there he is before me. Now see the glint of something in his hand. A blade coming straight for my throat.

I fling myself backwards.

There's no time for the twist of feet to release the stikpads" grip. Instead, I bend against the tendons in my ankles as far as a person can go, knees at right angles and back arched. The knife punches through the air where my head had been.

Adrenaline drives me back up, bringing the deckgun round even as I twist first one foot, then the other free of the floor. Zed—or whoever it is—slashes again but I pull the trigger. Without being anchored the shot from the deckgun sends me hurtling backwards, tumbling head over heels and spinning crazily. Consciousness slips away for another moment, leaving me in the dark place where only logic still clings to awareness.

Not Zed. The only thing that can change its face is an ITF assassin. One of the fabled killers under the military arm of the nascent UN World Government. A techno-murderer beyond equal who serves only the International Task Force. As far above my big brother, Cal the void-marine, as his training and gear put him above an unskilled colonist armed with a pointy stick. A myth yet one you can't dismiss as a conspiracy theory when Superstate leaders and Corporate officials are well known to demand DNA verification of anyone who comes near them and never trust a familiar face. Ghostfaces. It's said they have nanotech that allows them to alter their features and hack any security... like a QI virus...

Blink back. Pain returns to my shoulder. A savage tearing at my sanity but I cling to it, dive into the agony to hold onto consciousness. As I spin through the air, I see the Ghostface has kicked off towards me. Knife held against the back of his forearm, ready to slice me apart. Now, I'm facing away from him but I bring my deckgun in line with where he'll be when my rotation brings me round again. There. Straight in line. I jerk the trigger, once, twice but my spin takes him out of sight again. Dully, it dawns on me my spin hasn't changed—my trajectory through the air remains the same. The gun didn't fire.

He grabs me and jerks me round to face him as we turn and tumble. His knife hand comes up in an arc to end my life and my vision goes dark. It takes me a moment to feel the wetness on my face. Not the light spatter of blood droplets against my skin but a thick wet layer covering the lenses of my rebreather and blots out the world. His hand isn't gripping me anymore.

In darkness, world turning around me in sickening jerks, I slam into a hard surface. Scrabble madly for a handhold as I bounce away and feel the stikpadded tips of my toes on one foot catch something solid. My body whiplashes against that hold and my ankle, already strained from dodging the first fatal thrust, pops in searing agony. But the stikpad holds. Using what little strength is left to me, I fight my body's movement and bring my other foot down beside the first.

Voices... but they're so far away. The pain rises again in a tide and carries me away.

CHAPTER 10

Light hurts my eye. Not both of them—the left one. It goes away. Fingers prise my right eyelid open and again searing brightness burns into my brain.

"Will she live, Doctor?" M'Benga's voice.

"Yes. I've repaired the severed artery and sealed her wound. What with the synthetic blood I'm pumping into her, she should make a full recovery."

"A pity. But we need the traitorous bitch."

"She can probably hear you, Lieutenant. And I do not appreciate such talk about one of my patients. Certainly not when they are ranking officer on board."

A metallic thudding comes, loud and shocking.

"They aren't giving up," Hiroki says.

"I will deal with it, but I need you to wake her. I need to know what she's done."

"That might not…"

"Shut up and do as I tell you."

I groan, trying to form words. "M'Benga." It sounds slurred to my ears, but it's recognizable as her name.

"See… I warned you she could hear."

"Give her something, I need her to speak not drool and groan."

Thudding again, louder this time. A prickle at my neck and shock runs through me. Eyes leap open on agonizingly sharp light which swims in and out of focus. I try to sit up. A hand presses firmly on my good shoulder, holding me down.

"Easy, Kara, easy," Hiroki says.

Another bang.

"Hiroki," I mumble, mouth clumsy and full.

"Give the stimulant a chance to work. You'll find you feel better quickly but you mustn't believe it. You need rest though our Chief of Security doesn't seem to understand that."

"We've no time for this. Out of my way."

M'Benga steps into my field of view, pushing Hiroki aside. She leans in close, staring into my eyes.

"You..." I begin.

"We have no time. The Captain is dead. The revenant I saved you from killed her. What was she trying to do?"

It's a struggle to grasp what she's saying. A thousand thoughts collide in my head, setting off chains of ideas and images, leaving everything as a blur between what's real, and what's imagination. Like I've been hitting a wedge of the polymetamine so beloved of slumrats like Zed. Zed...

M'Benga shakes me and I wince in expectation of pain but all that comes from my shoulder is a dull ache—as if I'd strained it while training in the officer's club gym, back on Earth.

"Focus, *malaya*. Focus!"

"Help me sit up," I gasp.

"I really don't adv..." Hiroki says.

"Shut up, Hiroki." M'Benga snaps.

Her arm comes round behind me and eases me upright. It's only then I realize we have gravity again. My head spins leaving me blinking to chase away the dizziness.

"Don't you pass out on me. I need you, *kukaribisha*!" M'Benga starts shaking me again.

"Stop. Stop it!" I shout, my voice a harsh rasp but I'm stronger. Clearer in the head. I swing my feet round to hang from the medical couch, ignoring Hiroki's clucking.

M'Benga draws a breath to speak again but I hold up a hand. "Siyanda, maybe I owe you my life, but if you shake me again, I swear I will pull your fucking arms off."

Her eyes widen and she rears back. My words may be absurd but my tone holds a cold certainty—the attitude which'd gotten me through Officer School despite the daily attacks of my competition.

I massage my neck above my wounded shoulder. "The Captain is dead?"

"Yes. After we killed the revenant attacking you, I checked on the engine port. Could see her pulling herself towards the access airlock. Struggling to open it but the door was jammed. I tried to undo the damage he'd done before we got him…"

"And?"

"There was no time, someone else was there—a revenant. It grabbed her… then the engine restarted."

M'Benga falls silent. The shock of what she said runs through me. Dominguez, an ice-cold killer of an officer who'd have happily spaced any of us if we'd given her cause, had died to save us.

"We have a chance," I say. "Thanks to Captain Dominguez, if we can defeat the revenants, we can still stop *Charon* in time."

The clanging noise again, this time it's clear someone's striking the door to the medibay.

"What was the Captain's plan?" M'Benga asks.

"Plan? She didn't have a plan. At least, none she told me."

"Then we are fucked," Hiroki says.

"Stow that talk, doctor or I'll put you on a charge. We are not fucked!" M'Benga bellows at him.

"No, we're not," I say. There's nothing left to lose. Nothing left to gain except my life and this ship which I'm now captain of by default if not by merit. "Lieutenant M'Benga…" another crash at the door interrupts me.

"Yes," she says.

"That's 'Aye, ma'am,' Lieutenant. Or do you dispute I am acting Captain by virtue of seniority?"

She hides her frustration well, you have to give her that. "No… ma'am."

"Good," I say, not believing she'll let her suspicions fall away. "Do we have a route to the command section?"

"No, ma'am." Another booming clang from outside. "Revenants have trapped us in here."

"Weapons?"

"Two deckguns, three magazines."

"How many revenants are we talking about?"

"A hundred, a thousand. Didn't have time for a headcount."

"Sarcasm is not appreciated, Lieutenant. Now, Hiroki. You have an uplink to the main computer here?"

"Yes, but it has limited functionality. We can't access any of the command protocols."

"Lieutenant M'Benga, in your assessment of this situation, do you agree it is unlikely any crew survive except those in this room?"

M'Benga stares at me, her eyes hard and her expression unreadable. She sighs. "Aye, ma'am. Couldn't raise any of the crew on their radios, then I got Dawkins. He was under attack. By the time I got there… it was too late." She closes her mouth, her jaw muscles working.

"Meecher was with us when we found you but she was pulled into a vent when we were fighting off the revenants to get back into the medibay," Hiroki says. He blinks and a tear runs down his cheek.

I reach for my pocket to retrieve the QI-virus but the top half of my wearall has been cut away. Another bang comes at the door and a splintering sound as if the viewport's giving way. M'Benga spins, aiming her deckgun at the door.

If she'd found the link-key with the virus on it, she'd have used it to justify usurping my place in the chain of command. I catch Hiroki's eye, raise an eyebrow. He nods at me, no more than a slight shift of his head.

"Ma'am," M'Benga says, the word still strained. "The revenants can't break through the medibay door, though they could damage its mechanism so we'll not be able to open it,"

"Understood, Lieutenant. Your team was slaughtered, wasn't it?"

She hangs her head. "Yes ma'am." Another reason she'd not pressed to take leadership—guilt. *Pathetic.*

"Yet you escaped. How?" I ask.

"Climbed into a ventilation shaft. They narrow to a point where the revenants had to crawl to follow me. I was able to leave them behind." Her eyes meet mine, challenging me to criticize her actions or mock her stature. But command now rests on my shoulders and it fits me well.

"Quick thinking, Lieutenant." My déjà vu is shattered by another bang at the door, shaking my nerves. "The air vents link throughout the ship, right?"

"Aye, ma'am. But they have pressure seals between compartments. And the VIP module has its own air processing."

I suspected as much but it still leaves me with an idea.

"Lieutenant, what happens to the vents if there's a sudden loss of pressure in any section of the ship?"

"They lock down."

"All of them?"

"No, just the affected sections." M'Benga scowls, maybe seeing where I'm going with this.

"What if we jammed the pressure seals open?"

"They couldn't stop the ship from depressurizing. I see," she says, a grin breaking across her scarred features.

"It'd take some time to kill them all," Hiroki says. "They've displayed quite a startling level of intelligence so far. Perhaps, they would understand what we were doing and stop it."

"But if they are *mzuka* then how do we know it will kill them?"

Both of Hiroki's eyebrows shoot up, I hope in disbelief that M'Benga still clearly believes the Captain's ghost story. He tilts his head, almost as if he's asking my permission to educate her.

I sigh. Shake my head. "The Doc here found nanotech in the revenants' brains. Nothing supernatural, OK?"

I look to Hiroki, expecting him to chime in and back me up with some science, but he stays silent, a troubled expression on his face.

M'Benga grunts and from the look on her face it's obvious she hasn't changed her mind—she fears these revenants are a supernatural threat, from being "beyond the protective light of the stars." Out in the dark where dragons lurk or some such horseshit. You could die laughing, but I have to stop myself. It's not the command response.

"Listen to me, both of you. I know our former Captain was willing to turn to superstition to explain this." No point in telling them about Dominguez having a code to activate the nanotech, or about the code not working. "I agree it's hard to explain why this has happened, but these things die easy enough when you unload a deckgun in their faces."

"Not easy," M'Benga grunts. I ignore her.

"The "revenant" you saved me from was nothing of the sort."

"What?" they both croak.

"It was a Ghostface."

"That's… impossible." Hiroki says.

"Siamini hivyo," M'Benga says. I quirk my eyebrows at her. "They're a myth, one I do not believe in."

"Yet you'll believe ghosts or demons lurk between the stars, waiting for a vessel full of cold-sleepers to pass by. So what if Dominguez was right and we're all dead in cold-sleep…"

"An over-simplification," Hiroki says. I shoot him a look and he falls silent.

"As I was saying, if we were all vulnerable then why hasn't it affected the crew? Hmm? Not one of us."

"You'd lost a lot of blood, maybe you imagined it," M'Benga says.

"Well, why don't we choose logic over superstition? And since I *am* in command, we'll assume this madness, whatever it is, has a physical, mundane cause. No more spacer's tales. Understood?" I let the last word snap, even though it makes me desperate to cough. I fight it back until they both salute.

"Lieutenant M'Benga. Clear the door. Then hold the nearest vent. We'll be going through shortly."

"Aye, aye, ma'am."

"Doctor, give me the link-key you recovered from the revenant's corpse." He looks at me with a shocked expression.

"The one you found warrant officer Hong's fingerprints on." Hiroki's eyes narrow. Now's the time he might betray me. When you bluff, best keep your expression relaxed and neutral—you learn that playing cards and surviving the drill-sergeants at the Academy. If I've judged him correctly, Hiroki's feelings of friendship towards me will sway things. If not…

"Yes. Yes, I have it here somewhere."

The medibay door opens and M'Benga's deckgun begins its song. I ignore the screams and roars of pain, focusing on the task at hand. Activating the medibay computer, I insert the link-key into the terminal jack. Within moments, the QI virus uploads. Have to hold my breath as I order it to batter down the barriers preventing command access.

If Stengler was in on this whole thing—a corporate patsy or worse an agent for the UNWG—then now would be the time. Or would it? Maybe the virus had been programmed to do no more than wake the Ghostface, or Revenant Zero, or both. Maybe it hadn't been involved at all. I doubt I'll ever know.

The display jumps and blurs. When it clears, the core command menu opens before me. Speed, ship orientation, time to midpoint and the fatal burn of the fusion rockets—all laid out. The system is easy enough to navigate, quickly bringing me to its root menu. In the meanwhile, M'Benga's gun has fallen silent and the howling of dying revenants has stopped.

Pulling up the command overrides to set the VIP module to eject with a countdown of thirty minutes takes only two command lines. The countdown is silent but gives us long enough to crawl into the forward section, jam the vents open, and get ourselves into hard voidsuits. I confess to a flicker of emotion at consigning the people within to an eternity lost between the stars. But two things calm me.

If we can regain full control of Char*on*, it can maneuver and dock with the lifeboat.

If we can't, well, every sleeper in the 'boat is directly or indirectly responsible for the deaths of hundreds if not thousands.

So... you know. Fuck them.

"Help me up, Doc," I say.

Hiroki throws an arm under my good shoulder and gets me to my feet. We stumble along together and I lean into him, trying to enforce his feelings of responsibility for me—to make him feel my reliance on him. Sealing his loyalty and his silence.

The vents are cramped, with many smaller tubes running off the main shafts. The constant rush of air brings a range of odors—ozone from the engines, grease and grime from the cargo bays and, underlying the rest, a charnel reek. Progress is slow. Will the half-hour's grace I've given us be enough?

M'Benga takes the lead with me in the middle and Hiroki bringing up the rear. He's begun muttering to himself in Japanese—too quiet and too fast for me to understand. He has to hold it together, but right now I'm too wrapped up in my own plans and worries to find words of comfort for him.

The vents tighten until we're forced to wriggle along on our bellies. Here, M'Benga struggles the most. She's far more muscular than either the doctor or myself and her shoulders brush against both sides of the shaft as we go on.

"Why aren't we seeing revenants in here?" I ask, my voice low but still echoing all around us.

"Shh." M'Benga hisses. She stops and looks back at me under her arm, making a gesture I interpret to mean our voices will travel. Makes sense. The vents are hollow tubes for carrying air. And that's all sound is, I figure—vibrating air. They'd probably been the real reason the booming of the caskets striking the cargo bay decks could be heard all over the ship.

I draw up short, only for Hiroki to bump into my feet. Why aren't we still hearing caskets falling?

Grabbing M'Benga's ankle before she can move off, I get another of her glares. It'd be comical, but the situation doesn't allow humor. I wave her back. There's not enough space for any of us to turn around, but she rolls onto her back and scoots towards me. Realizing she plans to move under me, I press myself flat against the top of the vent. Bit of a strange position to find myself in, stuck as close as a lover to someone more enemy than anything else. But it brings her face near to mine. Hiroki murmurs behind us but his voice is lost in the susurration of the airflow.

M'Benga's breath warms my cheek. "What is it?"

"No sounds from the Revenants. They've stopped dropping caskets. Why?"

"Perhaps we got them all." Is she being sarcastic?

"No, there's no way it's that easy."

"Well, there's only one way to find out," she says. "*Siipendi*! Why did you have to give me something else to worry about?"

Before there's time to answer, she wriggles out from under me—both a relief and an irritation. I haven't finished, even if she has. Setting aside my annoyance, I massage my shoulder. The medi-nanites have worked faster than seems possible. Feeling returns to my shoulder as a burning itch but it no longer hurts so much as provides a distraction. I imagine the microscopic machines crawling around inside me, repairing and reinforcing my tissue.

Ahead, M'Benga slows and grunts, struggling with something. My chest tightens—I long for the reassuring weight of one of our two deckguns. Then she's moving again and revealing what she'd been doing. The pressure seal—a miniature airlock, in effect—is jammed open. A small red light flashes. No doubt warning the main computer but without any crew to act on it, the seal will remain open. Squeezing through the gap, I scrape my backside on the top of the seal and curse under my breath.

I'm a meter or so away from the seal when Hiroki swears in Japanese and a clank echoes through the shaft. He'd let his deckgun slip and strike the base of the vent.

We both hold our breath. Seconds drag. I'm about to exhale when a chorus of howls and the clashing of metal on metal come from below. The sound resonates through the vents.

"Shit!" M'Benga stops ahead of me, the light from her deckgun casting her face in shadow and glinting off eyes wide with shock. No point worrying about sound now.

"Keep going," I say. "They know we're in here. Don't stop."

She says nothing but turns and wriggles along the vent much faster than before. The shaft grows ahead of her and soon she moves up to a crouch. Then she rounds a bend and disappears.

Left with only the light from behind, I struggle on as best I can. Shadows writhe ahead of me as Hiroki's torch turns every movement sinister. Every now and then, he makes a noise somewhere between a whimper and a sob. Damn fool doctor. The clanging all around us stops abruptly and the pace of my heart roars. They've stopped banging because they've got into the vents and need to hear where we are.

Round the bend ahead, the shaft grows high enough for me to crawl but branches in two. Couldn't you just scream with frustration? Sounds of movement from both of them—M'Benga down one and revenants coming up the other, the sounds too faint to work out which was which. Hiroki moves beside me.

"Which way?" He asks.

I frown at him, biting back the barb which springs to my lips. "Don't know, Doc. I didn't see which M'Benga took."

He shifts round so his back presses against the side of the tube; plays the light from his gun over the two openings.

"This way," he says, no trace of doubt in his voice as he indicates the left-hand tube.

"How do you know?"

"The air is circulated round *Charon* from fans in the engineering section and fans in the command section. We've been moving away from the breeze coming from the aft of the ship. Now we need to go into the breeze coming from the fore."

So simple it makes me feel stupid. Air wafts from the left, none from the right. I start moving. Hiroki stays slumped where he was.

"Doc, come on. No time to rest."

"I think I'll wait here for them. I've had enough of being squeezed tight, waiting for something to come behind me and grasp my ankle. I'll stop them following you, as long as I have rounds."

"Hiroki-chan, I appreciate the gesture, but if you think I'm going to be stuck on my own with M'Benga you've gone space-happy. Now, fucking move. That's an order."

Howls echo down the tubes. From behind, or so it seems. The sound strikes Hiroki more than my words had. He's pale in the light from his deckgun as he crawls after me, casting a last look over his shoulder. Soon, a scrabbling sound begins behind us accompanied by a strange blue glow. Hiroki pauses and blasts the deckgun back the way we'd come. There's a howl of agony and snarling.

We pass over a half-dozen closed vents, none with a view that lets me guess where we are, and now a square of light shines out of the darkness ahead.

"Hiroki, she's left the hatch open behind her, we're nearly out."

"De kita!" He turns again and his deckgun coughs a bundle of half-a-hundred razor sharp shards of metal corkscrewing down the shaft. Another roar of pain.

I skid along the tube, skinning my knuckles on a rough weld line. Ahead of me the square of light is blotted out as a figure starts moving down the shaft towards me.

"M'Benga?" I call.

No reply. The dark shape comes faster—too long and wild in its movements to be M'Benga. Its mouth gapes, blue light shining out.

"Hiroki!" I shout, panic rising in me.

He fires again behind us, then spins.

"Gomen'nasai, Commander. Please cover your ears."

I drop flat as I realize what he intends—his arm stretches over me, pressing me down even as he brings the deckgun to bear. Sound explodes, rattling through me. My eyes screw tight in reflex.

When I open them, the shape in front of me is a crumpled mess on the bottom of the shaft. Yellow light shines in a square again, promising escape from the maddening trap of this hole we're in.

I clamber over the corpse of the revenant, putting my mind elsewhere as blood and organs smear across my wearall and my hands slip in the slickness of his death. Fighting back the urge to weep with relief, I drop out of the ventilation shaft and into the crew lounge. Even the jarring of my shoulder doesn't bother me though a wave of dizziness rises and falls—I'm still not right.

Spin back to help Hiroki out as he holds out an arm… screams, and disappears back into the vent.

CHAPTER 11

Desperately, I grab the only thing in reach, the muzzle of Hiroki's deckgun. It points at my face—if his finger squeezes the trigger...

He screams and I pull down with all my force, hoping he won't kill me. He reappears, falling on top of me with another figure dropping behind. The wind's knocked out of me and I lie dazed listening to the fatal struggle. The deckgun coughs once, twice, a pause, then a third time. After that, the click, click, click of the trigger being pulled. I push myself up, favoring my shoulder as the muscles popped and fizzed.

Hiroki kneels in front of me, his wearall a shredded, bloody mess around his right leg, his face covered in gore and one eye shut tight under a slick mess of brain and skull fragments. His open eye is wide and fixed on the splattered remains of a revenant. Enough of her remains to see it'd been a woman, thin and sticklike—the malnutrition of those desperate enough to become colonists. He'd pumped three flechette rounds into her at close range tearing her apart. Yet still he kneels, jerking the trigger while the deckgun clicks.

I manage to stagger to my feet, aching all over and feeling a tide of weariness threatening to drag me down again. No time for self-indulgence. First thing is to slam shut the vent above us and then find something to jam it and quick. Yank open a locker in the small galley. A metal tray. Not much, but it'll have to do. Straining to reach the vent, I wedge the tray between hinge and hatch.

Behind me, Hiroki hasn't moved, hasn't stopped pulling the trigger.

"It's dry, Doc."

He doesn't react, so I snatch the gun away. His eye meets mine. It's blank, as if the Hiroki I know has fled the world. *Him and his high-strung, weakling...* I stop myself. Not the attitude of a commander. Not what's needed to get him moving. He's essential crew for a reason.

"Hiroki, snap the fuck out of it. I need you with me." I slap him and he jerks but nothing more.

Scrabbling in the galley for a cloth and finding a dirty rag still caked with reheated rations, I wet it then wipe the gelatinous mess from Hiroki's face. His eye is swollen—he'll get a cracking bruise in the next few hours... if we live.

Hours. No, no. Minutes. But how many? I sling the empty deckgun over my bad shoulder, wincing as the weight pulls at my injury despite the nanites' work. Reach my good arm around Hiroki and pull him up, whispering reassurances to him. We hobble towards the main command airlock where all the crew hard voidsuits are stored.

As we stumble through the lounge, a suited figure appears in front of us—M'Benga, her squat suit filling the doorway. It's a struggle to make out her face through the suit's visor—most of it's taken up with combat mods—range finders, laser tracking and vid-magnification for shooting targets outside the ship. Tricky thing shooting targets in space. Distance is difficult to gauge and even spotting your target against the overwhelming scope of forever is a challenge. Something as small as a person is easy to lose against the background of stars and infinite void.

M'Benga's voice crackles from the suit's external speaker. "You have less than a minute. Bring him quickly."

Together we bundle Hiroki into his suit. Leaving M'Benga to secure him, I climb into my own. It holds a smell recognizable as my own sweat. Despite purging, it'll forever be marked as Kara Rozanski's, not by name but by the trace of fear sweat I've left in it every time I had to wear the damn thing. A klaxon sounds. The ten second warning before the VIP module ejects and becomes a lifeboat or more accurately, a deep-space mausoleum.

My suit bleeps an alert across my visor—systems nominal and airtight seal achieved.

The compartment around me shakes as the VIP section tears free of the ship. The link to the command computer through my suit's on-board systems pings. Minor pressure loss from the central section. Atmo still being lost at a low rate but no pressure drop showing from any other compartment. Alarms continue to sound but I shut them off one by one and send a command to shut off the ion drive. Well, part-one of the plan complete. Now for the hard bit.

"What did you do?" M'Benga's voice crackles over the radio.

"What needed to be done."

"We will all be indicted for this when we get back to Earth. *Fala mbwajike*!"

I let the insult slide—but she will pay for it later.

"What did you think I was doing? There's no way to open the outer airlocks in flight. This was the only way."

"The only way," Hiroki says.

"Back with us, Doc? Good. We need to get outside, to where the VIP section just departed. With some bulkhead shears, we can cause enough of an atmo leak to drain the whole ship in a couple of hours."

"You are crazy. But it's too late," M'Benga sighs. "Why don't we make a breach from in here?"

I raise my eyes. She is so rigid in her thinking sometimes it blinds her even to obvious problems. "Think about it, Siyanda. We create a big enough atmo leak from in here; we're liable to get blown out of the ship. And outside we'll be safe from revenants while we work. They don't have the access codes to use our suits."

"We breach the bulkhead and wait." She sighs again. "Alright, you are in command. We'll do it your way."

Gritting my teeth at her insubordination, I focus on what needs to be done. Access *Charon's* mainframe and order it to shut down air processing. It won't stop the CO2 scrubbers from working but it will save our air-reserves so we can re-pressurize sections of the ship when we're done. *Easy*.

The back of my scalp crawls. An instinct. Makes me call up the navigation feed. The navicomp's doing... something. Altering our course by degrees. It hasn't moved us much so far but if it's not corrected then over the next several hours we'll be heading on a different trajectory. Missing the Gliese 892 system entirely and going… where? I can't tell. Have to hope it isn't something to do with the QI virus.

M'Benga grabs a set of bulkhead shears, I take a sealant gun. If we get this right, it'll be easy enough to do. Famous and often fatal last words. Behind me, Hiroki stomps across the deck. Unlike M'Benga's suit, his has nothing stopping me from looking through his visor. What I see on his face makes me feel like a hand's been thrust into my chest, fingers probing around for my heart. There is little sanity in his gaze. The inner door slides down as the airlock begins its cycle.

Space. Always scared the shit out of me. Sounds crazy, I know. Here I am, committed to travelling between the stars, leaving everything familiar to age away behind me all for the joy of one day commanding my own ship.

You see, facing the prospect of setting foot outside the ship with only the scant protection of a vac-suit makes me reflect on my life. Each and every time. Makes me ask myself the question, "What the fuck am I doing this for?" The worst thing is, I've never really known how to answer. But the dream keeps pushing me on.

The void itself is a source of so many spacers' tales. Why? Because so many spacers have died in it. Planets with hostile environments don't attract settlements—robot mining with an orbiting control team is the limit of it. Before anyone ever visits a world, we know if there's a threat. But the void still throws up the inexplicable. Asteroids and dark planetoids without a sun. Bands of space drenched in the hard radiation of a pulsar or the devastating magnetic field of a magnetar. Pockets of volatile gasses or unseen clouds of interstellar dust. These are the simple physical threats waiting outside a ship's hull. The ships themselves are built so radiation and dust ablates only the front cone of the ship, a section that's easy enough to swap out every hundred years or so. At the speeds we're travelling—enough to alter our perception of space-time so time dilates and distance contracts—even a heavily armored voidsuit won't protect a spacer for long. Radiation's mostly blocked by the thick plates of the suit itself but those plates can be breached by a surprisingly low concentration of gaseous traces when striking them at such high percentages of lightspeed. One day, maybe, there'll be a way to push engines harder and protect a ship and its crew from the hazards of near-relativistic travel. Even then, I wouldn't expect to see any spacer be keen to set foot outside while in transit.

What's happened on Char*on* can be explained by rational means, without a doubt. But it's the kind of event that feeds the stories of the void "hungering for human souls." Of a will within the darkness to swallow those who stray too far from the light of the stars. I don't hold to any of that superstitious bullshit but… setting foot outside makes me feel, I don't know. Awe. As in the "Oh shit, I can't grasp what it is I'm seeing" kind. I'm not one to avoid thinking about what's right in front of me but that's what you have to do to survive walking outside. Put your mind somewhere else.

So M'Benga goes first—she lacks the imagination to be awed. The only illumination on the hull comes from her helmet light. She'd switched off her suit-to-suit comms but it's not hard to guess she's cursing me and at some volume. I watch her squat form advance into the darkness filled with the glamour of distant stars. Maybe I should've explained my plan, but the more she knows, the more power I give her. Let ignorance keep her off-guard with desperation mounting. When presented with a *fait accompli,* she'll leap to take it.

"Doc, you with me?" I ask over private suit-to-suit.

When he doesn't reply, I turn to find him staring past me at the infinite expanse of the void.

"Doc? Hiroki, snap out of it."

As if it takes great effort, he drags his eyes from the swirl of stars and distant galaxies to look at me. Makes me want to hit him, anything to wake him from this near catatonia. What he needs is to think about something else.

"Hiroki-chan, something's bothering me. I'd like your medical opinion."

There it is: his eyebrows twitch and the dullness fades from his gaze for a second.

"What I've been wondering is why we've not seen any child revenants. I mean, ten percent or more of the colonists are children. Is it something in them which makes them resistant?"

He clears his throat, a phlegmy rasp over the radio. "They would have received the nanites at the same time as their parents, but it doesn't seem to matter. Hmm, some innate childhood immunity… a psychological resilience their parents lack?"

"Get back to me when you have an answer, Doc. Might be vital to stop this happening again." The blank look leaves him, instead his eyes gain the faraway look of one lost in thought—an expression I've seen on his face all too often. "We'd better catch up with M'Benga."

I turn from him and stomp across the scarred and pitted hull. Studying the surface is supposed to make it easier to ignore *out-there* but instead it makes me all the more aware of how vulnerable I am. The depth of the gouges into the hull, even this far away from the nose cone, are enough that whatever had caused them would punch through the armor of my suit.

M'Benga is my salvation.

Staring after her, as she trudges to where the VIP lifeboat had torn free, helps. A blur of air jets from the breach in front of her. It hadn't been much of a gamble, not really. In the vessel's schematics, all the computer models suggest ejecting the lifeboat on any ship wouldn't compromise its hull integrity. But it's bullshit. I don't need Zed—*oh God, yes I do*—no, I don't need him to tell me designs are a lightyear away from reality.

The data had all been gathered from the smaller vessels of the past. Ones equipped with small lifepods rather than full sized lifeboats. The pods themselves were even worse death traps than the lifeboats, though for different reasons—no cold-sleep, poor air recycling and not enough space for rations versus the simple fact of being stuck in interstellar space. Pods didn't do much damage when they ejected.

Lifeboats… well, the only time all the important people leave the ship is if it's beyond saving, so who cares about the cargo left behind? Besides, anyone not active at the time is protected from pressure loss by their cold-sleep casket for as long as ship's power holds out. Which all depends on whether decompression damages the fusion reactor enough to shut it down and if it does whether the ship is too far from a star to deploy solar sails.

"There's a ten centimeter rent in the bulkhead," M'Benga says.

"On our way. Hold until I have eyes on."

She doesn't acknowledge. I grit my teeth—not the time to get into it with her.

It only takes a couple of minutes to catch up though it's enough to have me sweating. Suit cooling systems are good but even with servo assist, the effort of moving the damn thing is exhausting. Each step requires a maglock to be confirmed before the other foot releases. Extra safety precautions though there are some limited maneuvering jets and even an anchoring harpoon in the event of losing contact with the ship. Precautions my paranoia keeps seeing as barely adequate every time my thoughts stray to what would happen to someone blown too far away for recovery. Off at the extreme of sight, what appears to be a red star winks at me.

"Is that the VIP lifeboat?" I ask M'Benga.

There's no response but she turns to look out into the black. Then my comm crackles with her voice, sounding more accented than usual. Filled with some emotion—suppressed rage or terror, maybe but I can't see enough of her face to read her expression.

"It is. Rangefinder puts it nearly five clicks away. Heading off at ten meters-per-second. For whatever that matters."

"It does, Siyanda. It does."

"What?"

"All part of the plan."

"Your plan is to abandon the leaders of the new colony to die in the depths of space, while we do what? Become privateers? There's no other way I can see us surviving this monumental fuck up."

"You're not really angry, are you? I know you. You'd be

spitting curses at me in Swahili."

"I am sickened by you. But I'm stuck. You are in command and… and that is all there is to it."

"Defense of superior orders won't wash. You really think what I'm doing's wrong—declare me unfit. But you know the only way we live is doing what I say, don't you?"

She stays silent.

"Your problem, Siyanda, the thing that kept you from being XO and the thing that'll stop you ever being ready for command is your total lack of imagination." Her suit's fists clench. How close is she to striking me? How far can I push this without it backfiring? "I'm a navigator, you *głupia cipa*. Do you have any idea how easy it is for us to correct our course by a few degrees to collect the lifeboat? Why do you think I shut off the drive?"

"So we wouldn't accelerate away from them." She sighs again, this time less filled with frustration. "I… I'm sorry I didn't understand."

"Of course not. Dominguez gave her life for us. If you think I'd dishonor her sacrifice, then you really don't know me at all." It sounds good—I almost believe it myself.

"I… may have misjudged you," she says. I wait for more but that's it. It'll do, for now.

"Let's get on with this shall we." I send an interrogatory to Char*on's* computer, confirming no contact from surviving crew. For the log's sake more than anything else. No one's attempted to access the computer nor check in by radio. Which doesn't mean there aren't a handful pinned down in a pitched fight with revenants. If they've followed procedure, they should have breathing masks and suit seals to give them a chance to get to safety, though the air supply of a wearall's emergency mask is measured in minutes. Almost better to go quick…

"Right, use the shears to increase the rent to half a meter. Should be enough."

M'Benga scuttles over to the tear in the hull, keeping clear of the jet of gas. She fires an anchor piton into the plating behind her and crouches with the bulkhead shears extended, carefully widening the jagged hole.

CHAPTER 12

I watch her work, anything to keep my attention from looking outwards. It's taken thirty minutes to widen the rent by ten centimeters and as the cut grows wider the force of the air escaping increases. Ice crystals form rapidly, tinkling against my voidsuit as they shoot into the dark. The light from my helmet makes the nearest crystals sparkle. It's pretty—beautiful even—but all I can think of is the death waiting beyond those twinkling jewels.

"They're too small to be useful," Hiroki says, on our private suit-to-suit comms.

"What?" I ask.

"The children. Not strong enough to be good in a fight and lacking the skills to affect the ship or its operations."

"Oh. Well done."

"I don't think you realize what I'm saying, Kara. Whatever the cause of these revenants, there is a method to it. It isn't random."

"Well, no. We'd worked out the revenants are still able to reason, in some fucked-up way."

"More than that. How would you know whether a child or an adult was in any given casket?"

"Look at the manifest," I say.

"And who has access to the manifest?"

"Our late Captain, M'Benga and anyone with access to a QI virus. Hmm, the Ghostface you saved me from," I say. "Wait a second. No, the manifest was corrupted when we… I mean when Warrant Officer Hong messed with the systems."

He doesn't seem to notice my slip even as I curse myself for my clumsiness. Lack of sleep and the effect of my injury. The burning itch in my shoulder has stopped all by itself. I'm a little stiff, but in the hour-and-a-half since I'd woken in the medibay, the nanites have healed my injury better than a month of rest could.

"If the manifest was scrambled, how could anyone know who was in which casket?" Hiroki asks.

"Memorized the manifest?"

"Memorized all hundred thousand passengers? You can't believe that."

"Downloaded it, then?" I say.

"You would know better than I, but isn't the manifest a monitoring system? It's not some printout you can copy on to a device."

"Well, with a QI virus…"

"We've got the only QI virus, haven't we? The link-key didn't come from the man you tell us was an ITF agent. I don't need to know the truth, Kara. For our friendship, I will not push you. But there is a problem. If the ITF agent was meant to trigger this, why didn't he stop you and Zed from waking? Why didn't he kill you both? You see, I'm beginning to understand what's happened here."

"Oh, you are?" If he's worked out what I'd been up to then… well, I'll have to deal with it. When M'Benga is distracted, I can see there might need to be an unfortunate accident for my dear old friend.

"I believe you. There was a Ghostface on board. Such a thing is possible in theory—nanotech to alter the features. An agent might be secreted among the colonists to deal with anything threatening UNWG policy. Imagine if we survived and word of this… let's call it a plague for now. If word of the plague got out?"

I frown, not liking where this is going. Away from me at least, but still into uncomfortable territory. "It'd put people off travelling to the colonies."

"We've seen they rip their teeth out and replace them with what looks like fragments of optical chips but far from just shoving them into their gums, the chips grow into the bone—the nanites at work. When the revenants attack they go for the throat. Savage. Bestial. Yet they retain their knowledge and skills. They wake from cold-sleep which is as close to resurrection as makes little difference. At first, I thought a rival corporation might have wanted to make the colony fail but then I reconsidered. We have not seen this Revenant Zero. It may be the key to understanding what has happened and why."

"It and all the others are going to be dead within the hour. End of problem."

"No, Kara. This isn't going to be solved by venting atmo."

"You better be wrong. If this doesn't work, I'm all out of ideas."

"May I suggest a small change to your plan?"

I frown—questioning orders is an issue but a commander who doesn't at least hear her subordinates out is a fool. "I'm listening."

"Domo arigato gozaimasu," he says, his suit inclining as he makes an awkward bow.

"Well, get on with it."

"Do not seal the breach until we have swept the ship from top to bottom."

"What?"

"Assume there is a way to survive aboard ship—consider, the other voidsuits, or a short duration cold-sleep. Waking only when conditions were right."

"Yeah… I see where you're going…"

"Or a small area could be made airtight with a sealant gun. If the room also had a CO2 scrubber…"

"Like the medibay or parts of the crew compartment."

"Just so."

I sigh. This is a major pain in the ass. "Alright, Doc. We'll conduct a thorough search. How about this, we re-pressurize the ship compartment by compartment and shoot anything that emerges?"

"Hai."

"Great."

I cut comms and swear, long and loud. Fucking Hiroki. Fucking stupid *Charon*. Why? I close my eyes; breath slow and deep until I start to calm down. *So damn tired.*

"Commander?" M'Benga's voice crackles over the radio. I start awake. Can't believe I've been asleep, *outside*.

"Yes, Lieutenant, what?"

"You need to see this."

I look to where she crouches over the rent in Char*on's* side. No more gas escapes from the damaged section—I must've been asleep for a quite a while. But that's not right. My suit's chrono has moved on a few minutes at most.

"What is it?"

"Someone's sealed the damage from inside." She stands, letting the bulkhead shears float beside her, held only by their tether.

"That's not…" I was going to say possible but of course it is. I look into the gap. It looks like the slash in the bulkhead has been filled with a wad of wearall, its vacuum resistant material creating a temporary airtight seal. Then it dawns on me.

"No, someone's not sealed the hull breach. A corpse has been sucked against it."

Her left eye, the only one I can see, widens. Then closes. "Yes. It shouldn't be a surprise. Does it mean there are revenants in the crew compartment?" Neither of us want to raise the possibility it's a crewmember killed by decompression.

"Maybe. All we can be sure it means is there were some of them between the VIP Lounge, the command section, and the central corridor. And at least one member of the crew died there." I want to rub my eyes, to clear away the grit. Yet another of the annoyances of wearing a voidsuit.

"What do I do?" M'Benga asks.

"You need me to spell it out for you?"

"I can't!"

I don't believe her—the hard-as-nails security officer is squeamish about punching a hole through a corpse.

Then Hiroki's here, grabbing the bulkhead shears and standing with one foot on either side of the rent.

"Allow me."

I think both M'Benga and I are too stunned to stop him.

I shout, "Hiroki, don't!" before realizing I disabled the comm channel to him.

By then it's too late.

M'Benga makes to grab his arm but he thrust the bulkhead shears into the gap and depressed their cutting trigger. Viscera and body parts explode out of the rent in the hull as the wearall punctures and the corpse is blown out by the pressure of the air behind. Voidsuit magboots are good but there's a reason we use anchor lines. Sudden changes in the forces acting on the boots can cause them to fail. Bits of dead crewman hit Hiroki at the speed of sound—more than enough force to break his magboots' grip on the hull and blow him off the ship. Air continues to jet out of the hole and bits of junk fly out with it.

I try to call Hiroki on the suit comms but get no answer. He'd been thrown clear so fast I've already lost sight of him against the starfield.

"Can you see him?" I ask M'Benga.

"No… I've no idea where to look. His suit should have a transponder, we can look for it."

"He's not answering comms. Could he… could it have killed him?"

"Explosive decompression blasted everything on the inside of the hull right up into him. Look." She holds up the broken and frayed ends of the tether which had held the bulkhead shears. "Near took me too. If the shears hit his faceplate, they could've fractured it, but the visor has an armor plate that will slide into place if there's any risk of breaching the faceplate. It's automatic, so even if he's been knocked unconscious, he should still be sealed."

"We find him using his transponder then we'll deal with it." I try to bring up the display on my suit's systems. "Shit. I can't track him."

"Access the transponder through Char*on's* computer," M'Benga says.

I key through the various remote access menus. Transponders. Voidsuit locator. Active voidsuits. Then I stop.

"Siyanda, according to this there are five active voidsuits."

"*Hakuna unaosaambaa njia*! Track them. Can you get a ping from either of the others?"

"Wait a second." I highlight first one—no return—and then

the other. "One of them is outside. Coordinates… hold on." I set the suit to overlay a marker on my visor and turn my head. A red light blinks a few degrees to port. As I watch, it shifts and the blinking of the light grows more rapid. "Whoever it is, they're coming towards us."

"What? How could they, unless…"

"They have access to the transponder too." My heart races. "You have your deckgun?"

"No, I stowed it in the airlock. But it would do no good. Flechettes cannot penetrate voidsuit armor."

"What?" I try to keep the panic from my voice.

"They're designed not to risk breaching bulkheads, remember. The faceplate's the only vulnerability but all you have to do is lower the armored layer and use the suit's external cams."

I need to pay more attention to voidsuit drills. My distaste for it—no I'll admit it—my fear of spacewalks, has left me with a gap in my knowledge. A failing I'll have to remedy.

"What do we do?" All thought of being in command flees me then, this is a tactical situation—M'Benga is the specialist.

"Send me the transponder signal, then locate Hiroki. If he's awake, then he might be able to use his control jets to slow down or stop. Then it's a case of him firing an anchor pin if he's close enough or one of us will have to get him."

She's right, it's obvious really. If he can reduce his speed so he maintains a distance relative to the ship, then a simple burst of thrust in his direction and whoever goes to rescue him should be able to reach him so long as their air lasts. The thrusters in a suit don't allow for continuous burn but they have enough fuel to get up to a meter-per-second, steer, stop to rendezvous with him and then do another burn to bring him back and slow enough so we don't smash into the hull. If he'd been thrown clear at a low enough speed, he can make his own way back. But not being able to get him on the comms bothers me.

I send M'Benga the transponder data on the unidentified voidsuit and activate Hiroki's signal. A red dot blooms in my vision, blinking slowly at about seventy degrees from the hull's faux horizon. Distance and speed. He's flying away from us fast, but not so fast his maneuvering jets couldn't stop him and bring him back. But he's not slowing. Which means he's either unconscious, dead or the jets have been damaged in the explosion. Shit.

"Company," M'Benga says. Her voice is calm, icy even. I look up to see a voidsuited figure striding across the hull towards us.

CHAPTER 13

"Move right. Don't engage unless I say," M'Benga says. The comms can't hide the tension in her voice.

Taking a pace backwards, I side-step to her right, lengthening the hypotenuse of our little triangle of fear. I don't like the feeling of leaving my future to M'Benga's fighting prowess, though I have no illusions about my ability to handle anyone in voidsuit combat. But there's something I can do. Flicking my comms channel to interface with the approaching voidsuit, I ping it—hoping, fearing, for an answer. The connection is accepted and suddenly my ears fill with the sound of heavy breathing.

"Hello?" I say.

"Kara? Is that you?" Zed's voice. I think again of the man who'd attacked me wearing Zed's face. A Ghostface proved real.

Screwing down the surge of emotion, I frame every word with the snap confidence of command. "Zed's dead. Who are you?"

"No, Kara, it is me. How else would I know about Stengler?" That throws me. But he keeps moving forwards, straight for M'Benga. The suit has its visor covered by the ablative layer. If it is Zed in there, he's seeing only using his suit's external cameras. Why?

"If it is you, Zed, then stop. I'm sorry I left you to face those things alone but how could I have helped you?" My words are accompanied by a tight burning in my throat.

"Kara, I don't blame you. But it's not what you think. Really. Come with me, I'll answer all your questions." Still he moves forwards. M'Benga detaches her anchorline, preps a new piton and trails the arm with the anchor harpoon behind her.

A thought bubbles up in my mind then. How had the Ghostface assassin known to wear Zed's face? If it'd been any other member of the crew or some random colonist, it wouldn't have distracted me. How does this thing—it can't be Zed inside the suit, it can't. How can this thing know what to say to me? How can it know about Stengler? Unless Zed told it. Does it mean he survived? Is he alive somewhere on the depressurizing ship? Or had he only lived long enough to give up his secrets?

I switch comm channel to M'Benga. She'd left her transmission to me open and is saying something in Swahili. Something like, "Come on you fucker."

Should I tell her the figure claimed to be Zed? I dismiss the thought as soon as it comes. The last thing she needs is a distraction. Instead, I circle closer, stomping along the hull until I'm flanking the thing claiming to be Zed.

He lurches forward, towering over M'Benga, awkward as he disengages the maglock on his lead foot. She kicks off with both feet, maneuvering jets blasting and firing her anchorline behind her as she does so. The piton drives into the hull a half-meter to my left. Her momentum carries her up and over him. He tries to grab her, missing by a handful of inches. The anchorline goes taut and she curves rapidly back to the hull, her body twisting as she comes so she lands facing the rear of his suit. Before he can react, she strikes hard at the back of first his right knee, then his left. The flexible armor there is weaker and his legs buckle under the impact of her blows. M'Benga grunts with effort as she leaps and strikes.

I can't help myself but cheer her on though she gives no sign she hears me.

Zed or whoever's impersonating him falls backwards though his feet stay locked in place. M'Benga uncoils an elbow strike right into the back of his head, where the flexible bands of armor around his neck join the solid surface of the helm. Brain stem. Kind of blow we'd been taught as a finisher in basic hand-to-hand combat training. Her strike sends the body moving forward and up again—I wonder if she's knocked him out. M'Benga must think so too because she pauses in her assault.

I see what he's doing before she does.

"Look out!" I scream. Useless—it tells her nothing.

His right foot detaches from the hull and, as he tips forwards, he twists, whipping the foot around to strike the side of her leg even as he uses the momentum to half turn towards her. Then it's a blur. I can't see where he begins and she ends. They grapple and trade blows while I stand stunned. Twice I go to move forward but I remember what M'Benga had told me. If I interfere at the wrong time maybe I'll do more harm than good.

Whoever's in the other suit is clumsy. Not at all what I'd expect of an ITF assassin. And not how I imagine Zed would fight either. He'd been brought up as a street rat, fighting in the gutter for scraps against a horde of other desperate people. He also logged many more hours in microgravity than I have, and probably more than M'Benga too—the perks of being an engineer. This man lacks both the cunning of the street and the confidence in zero-g. It should mean an easy fight for M'Benga but whatever she tries, she can't get him off her.

His leg stays coiled around her and he grabs her with both arms while she delivers a series of blows. They rock forward and back, locked in place by the three magboots in contact with the hull.

Alarms go off in my suit—radiation and particle density. The bright orange paint on my armor starts abrading before my eyes. We must be entering a pocket of denser interstellar dust. At the speed Char*on* is hurtling through the void, even a small density increase might prove too much for my voidsuit.

"Siyanda, I'm going to grab him from behind."

"No! No, stay back. He's too strong." She cuts off with a grunt of pain as his arms circle her and he clashes his helmet against the front of hers again and again.

I can see her visor crack. Why isn't she using the ablative layer? "Your visor. Lower the secondary."

"I can't, he must have damaged it. Oh..." her breathing is coming in ragged gasps. "It's too..." There's a crackle over the comm and a high shrilling whistle—air escaping from a breach in her helmet. I move forward—I should've acted before. Maybe I'm not too late. Without M'Benga, I'll have no chance against whoever's in the suit.

That's when she does it. A billowing cloud of gas jets from her suit as her maneuvering thrusters do a full burn. She shoots up with enough force to yank his trailing foot free. Still he clings to her. The jets stop their burn—expended. I watch dully as together the two suited figures rise slowly above the hull out to the full length of M'Benga's anchorline and their trajectory begins to curve.

Over the whistling screech of escaping air she's transmitting, M'Benga gasps, "Break the line!"

I stomp towards it; catch the line as she strikes hard at the maneuvering jets on the other suit. For a moment, I hold the line in my hands—life and death for her; life and death for me. All the while the alarms blare in my ears and the surface of my suit strips back from white and hi-visibility orange to the flat grey of the metal beneath.

"Do it, *mkundu*!" She chokes. The sound of leaking atmo is almost gone.

I jerk my hands apart. The line is strong, wound steel wire but it has to be light weight. It's meant to stop you drifting off into space, an added precaution should the magboots fail, no more. With the servo assist of the suit boosting my strength the line pops in my hands and slides through them. The thrusters on the other suit fire but M'Benga had done her job well. The jets sputter out in opposite directions, making the two of them spin and wobble like I'd once spun and twirled at the Academy's Graduation Ball.

Now there's only silence from M'Benga's comm. But the other suit pings me. He can claim to be Zed all he likes but I know it's not true. It can't be true. Zed wouldn't have attacked us. He pings again. I try to ignore it but almost against my will, I find myself flicking over to his channel.

"...late, Kara. We're waiting for you. You don't have to be alone. Oh, Kara..." I cut the transmission. The voice was flat and dead. A copy of Zed's but lacking any of the edge his had held. The edge of desire when he'd flirted, the edge of anger when we'd argued, the edge of fear I'd heard the last time he ever spoke to me. He pings me again. I ignore it. Instead, I watch him float off with the corpse of a woman I'd loathed in his arms. A woman who'd sacrificed herself for me while I'd watched, using her pride as an excuse for my own cowardice. The creeping slickness of nausea rises in me and I look away.

Focus is what I need. So focus on a problem.

The hull breach. Hiroki out there in the dust and gas. The fifth active voidsuit.

It's a hard thing making the choice. First thing's first, though, I have to get out of danger before I decide what to do. I clank along the hull as fast as I can, locked on my destination. It takes me five minutes to double-time it to the airlock and secure myself inside. There I stop. No point going farther until I know what to do. Problems. Alone, what can I do about them?

The ship wouldn't yet have vented all its air but as we plough through the denser gas and dust, I worry about the damage it might do. *Charon*'s prow and the ramscoop's magnetic cowl are designed so dust and gas would flow round the ship, minimizing astrodynamic drag elsewhere on the hull. In theory, there should be almost no particles within a half-meter of the surface of the ship. I can't see how the hull breach alters this but it worries me, as does the course correction.

We're still travelling straight for Gliese 892 at a little over point-eight lightspeed, close to the redline. A course correction would take weeks to show any noticeable change in vector but the change in orientation has already taken place. We could spin a full three sixty if we wanted using the thrusters but it wouldn't alter our direction of travel.

Fundamental rule of low-tau space flight number one—the faster you go, the more force is required to change course and speed. Back in the early days, to slow down, a ship would have to flip one-eighty to point the engines forwards, which meant you couldn't use the ramscoop to power the ion drive. Worse, in situations like the one we're in—battering through a patch of high density interstellar medium—it'd caused critical damage to the hull and destroyed at least one vessel. Then they'd discovered how to make the ion drive fire in the same direction it was scooping fuel—nothing more complex than making the drive's cylinder fit inside a second one. Close the rear vent and cycle the thrust out of a ring at the front of the ship. End of problem. The ship would still have to rotate to use its fusion rockets for the final hard deceleration but by then enough speed would've been shed to reduce the friction to negligible.

Now the real danger is a major course correction en route. If the angle of approach has shifted enough then instead of flowing past the hull, some of the particulate matter will strike it. Even without a hull breach, Char*on* will only be able to survive the wear for a few hours. With one… It doesn't bear thinking about. Whatever else I do, I need to prevent the damage from getting any worse. Sealing the hole won't make for a long-term solution. That'll only come if I alter course either back to true or at least shift it away from a dangerous angle.

I try to call up the navicomp from the suit but even with full access to the rest of Char*on's* mainframe, navigation is locked. Whoever's altered course must have decided to disable remote access after I shut off the ion drive. I'll have to go to the navicomp and hope my QI virus will let me overcome the lockout. What puzzles me is why they haven't restarted the drive. I'll find out the reason soon enough.

Raising my hand to close the outer door, I let it float above the panel, drifting in the microgravity. Pressing the button is as good as sealing Hiroki's fate. I call up tracking again but this time I can't locate him. All I get on his comm channel is static and cosmic whine.

In some way, it comforts me. I'm leaving him to a bad death—armor abrading away until his suit compromises and decompression kills him. Every spacer's secret terror. But there's nothing I can do. Even if I choose to put saving him above all other concerns—which I won't do for my own sake and the sake of the ship—I can't find him to attempt some foolish rescue effort.

My hand falls and the outer airlock door closes behind me, its dull clank reverberating up through my suit. Lights flash on the airlock inner door, warning me of the near vacuum. I override them and open the inner door.

Internal lights are down—just what I need. Stomping over to where M'Benga had stowed the remaining deckgun, I check it over. The clip's three-quarters full. Not a big deal, I plan to grab another couple of magazines from the armory, but then what's the point? The fifth active voidsuit is somewhere on board—its occupant either a member of the crew and so on my side or else what? An ITF agent or Revenant Zero.

If it's someone, or something, I ought to worry about then a deckgun isn't going to be much good against the armor of a voidsuit. Bulkhead shears might. I open the engineering equipment locker. No backup shears but there is a rivet gun for securing plates to patch any hull damage too big for sealant to fix. Not quite what I want but it'd punch a hole in a suit. I remembered what Zed had said about it. Not a weapon that'd be worth much in a normal fight, but in vacuum all I have to do is make a small breach in a hostile's suit and step back as they try to patch it. While they're occupied with the first one, it's simple enough to pop another hole in the armor and so on, until they asphyxiate.

My cold-blooded assessment jars with the memory of M'Benga's death, Zed's, and the inevitability of Hiroki's. Before it can overwhelm me, I turn my mind away from my traitor heart telling me I've lost everyone who matters in my life over the last day.

A wide yawn makes my jaws crackle. Fatigue is lurking on the edges of my awareness—whispering I need rest before I do anything else. Like the temptation to indulge in the weakness of emotion, I dismiss it. *Now* is all I have. Leave it any longer and I'll soon be joining my family—my long dead parents on Earth and the new family I've lost between the stars.

CHAPTER 14

The navicomp flickers with data, its screen lighting the command area with flashing green. I scroll through the command options and find it simple enough to reset the original course. My cynical side starts grumbling, saying it's too easy. But the combination of everything on my mind dulls my instinct enough I allow myself to take this change in fortune at face value. I mean, when you've had a shit day and you find a new-jiao on the street, it seems like providence rebalancing the scales, right? You don't question it. So I realign Charon and set the engines to start up with a delay of two hours. Long enough to give Hiroki a chance—if he's somehow survived. Not that I believe it for a moment, but I can't bring myself to deny him a slim hope.

I don't hear his approach—there isn't any air after all—but I feel the thudding of armored feet approaching through the deck beneath me. Turn and see *him*. Even through the visor of his helmet, his eyes hold me captive. The most inhuman gaze I've ever met, a total absence of all that makes us what we are. Like staring into a camera lens. He's holding a set of bulkhead shears. So much for my advantage. For every hole I can punch in his armor, he'll open a half-meter rent in mine. He stops in the doorway to the command module.

My comm pings. No point ignoring it.

"Kara, join us. You are alone. Empty. We will fulfil you. Make you part of something greater." He grins as he says it—his mouth glowing blue, the scintillating crystalline shards of optical chips where teeth should be.

"What are you?"

"Join us, you will know."

My shoulder itches. Then burns. Agony soars beyond anything I've ever felt, beyond my capacity to understand. Pain larger than existence flashes through me before it fades, leaving an afterburn in my senses. As if my nerves have seared a new pathway from my shoulder to my brain. In the aftermath of the torrent of pain, a dreadful certainty grips me.

The nanites.

The revenant comes closer, offering me one gauntleted hand. All it takes is a touch and he'll hold me until it's too late for me to stop this. Behind him, another figure appears, in a voidsuit stripped of all its high-vis paint. I try to keep the shock from my eyes as the figure raises its arms. I can't see what it's doing behind the bulk of the revenant's voidsuit. Doesn't take me long to realize.

Bulkhead shears close around the back of the revenant's neck, cutting through armor and deep into its flesh and bone. Air jets out of the rent in his armor with a stream of blood. The revenant jerks and spasms then stands swaying back and forth. Dead but unable to fall without gravity and held in place by the maglocks in his boots, his corpse will keep swaying until the resistance of the servos in the voidsuit finally brings it to a standstill.

Hiroki clips the shears to his suit tether and shuffles around the dead revenant. I try to ping his comm and get nothing but static. He makes a gesture with his fist against the side of his helmet. Is his radio damaged? I feel another sharp pain, this time in my neck. The nanites are working their way into my brain. It won't be long before I'm gone and all that remains is a creature wearing my flesh. There's a bump against my helmet as Hiroki touches his to mine.

"...hear me?"

"Yes. Yes, I can hear you Hiroki."

"You need to shout." Looking through his visor I can see he's bellowing the words at me.

"OK!" I shout though the effort hurts. "Hiroki, he's done something to the nanites in me. The pain..."

"I understand. When I woke, out there in the darkness, the

answer came to me in a flash. It had been staring me in the face all along. Revenant Zero, the Ghostface's nanotech. The optical chips…"

I hold up my hand. "I don't think I have time." Another flash of pain, right under my jaw. "Promise me you won't let me become like them. Whatever it takes."

"Kara, listen. It's not an end to you. The nanites. They're not disabling their victims" brains. They're creating a new neural net." His eyes take on the faraway look again.

My breath comes in rapid panting. "Can you fix it?"

"No. Not yet, but I know I will be able to. They form a gestalt. A new intelligence. Burdened with all the base elements of the human mind. The savagery and darkness we carry. It's what comes from the most primitive parts of ourselves. That's why they were violent, that's why they've maimed themselves. But they… no it, it is evolving. Maybe I can communicate with it."

"Please, Hiroki. I can't become one."

"Kara, you must trust me. I have to get you into cold-sleep before you lose control. I will find a way to stop it, no matter how long it takes. I swear it."

I follow him, fighting pain with every step. He closes the door to the cold-sleep chamber; used the sealant gun on first it and then the vent in the ceiling. The room spins and I close my eyes, focusing on breathing slowly. Voices echo in my head. Sounds not words but still carrying meaning. Phosphenes scatter across my vision, the geometric shapes becoming neat and regular. Marching towards me, a battalion of triangles and polygons. I open my eyes and the phosphenes remain, becoming clearer and sharper. I try not to moan but words choke in my throat. Needles of ice drive through my body.

Hiroki pulls a gas canister from the medilocker—O2 for helping revive sleepers—and cranks the release valve. Icons on my suit's visor show external pressure rising. He finds another canister and sets it open. The suit's atmo warning clicks on—too much oxygen. Then Hiroki retracts his helmet, comes over to me.

"Vent your suit's remaining air."

My vision's pin-holing—every movement feels like I have

to fight my own body. I tab the suit to vent and override its warnings. The levels shift to a shade within acceptable levels, not that there'd been a real risk of lung damage or blindness. It seems funny to me. As if I have to worry about blindness when my vision's fading behind patterns and shapes that aren't there.

"I need to put you in cold-sleep."

Hiroki's voice comes from a long way off, though now there's air to carry the sound from his mouth to my ears. I try to help him strip my suit but numbness steals through my limbs. Everything goes purple for a moment and a high pitch whine fills my ears, then the room returns, overlaid with triangles and polygons racing around my sight before forming a long tube.

I tell myself this is only a normal entry into cold-sleep. The visions. The tunnel of light, losing contact with my body. But this is nothing like that, there's no peace. No acceptance. This is death filled with terror. No one's asking me if I'm ready.

I'm back in the room. Beneath me is the couch of my casket—I can see it but no longer feel it. Hiroki bustles about, attaching tubes and monitors to me. Using every scrap of willpower I have left, I try to croak at him, to tell him to hurry but my throat is no longer my own. My mouth can only make a gurgling sound. An inhuman sound.

"Kara-chan, I will find a way to save you I promi…"

All sound cuts off and sight goes with it. My thoughts start to wander away. What am I worried about? Where…

>Review of network node memory storage complete. Control established. Node designated "navigator," priority peripheral. Motor function returning. Node's higher brain functions preserved in standby. Immediate physical threat from target node designated "doctor." Attempting to pacify "doctor" for establishment of network connection. Uploading "navigator" data on vessel's subluminal flight profile. Course correction procedure to be modified—avoidance of damage from particles and gas in interstellar medium. Calculating time to designated coordinates. "Navigator" node identifies target stellar system as Fulu. Bayer designation: Zeta Cassiopeiae. Maximum safe velocity of vessel 0.81132c. Flight duration resulting: 417.4847 years subjective. No known human colonies at destination. WARNING:

pacification of target node "doctor" unsuccessful. Environmental threat to priority peripheral, node designated "navigator" detected—extreme cold. Heart rate decreasing. Assessment: Cryogenic suspension commencing.

PART II

CHAPTER 15

>Node online. Electromagnetic attack detected. Compensating.

Flash of light in my eyes. It's like the tunnel and I try to reach for it. A moment, no more of consciousness with a man's tense features leaning over me, mouth covered with a mask, red-rimmed eyes framed by wild hair. He's familiar…

>Control of node designated navigator re-established.
>Attempt pacification of subject designated doctor.
>>>>Failure.
>Cryogenic suspension detected.
>Signal…
>…Re-established.
>New code received from primary node.
>Code accepted.
>Network connectivity is limited.
>Sending interrogatory.
>Acknowledge system standby.

I am not here and then, without effort, I *am* again. Every moment between losing myself and being frozen, the flash of contact with the grinning revenant and submergence into the code language of the nanites once more—all comes like a dream breaking apart and shattering into shards of memory my mind tries to suppress—pulling the pain, the loss of self, away from my surface thoughts.

"Kara-chan? Can you hear me?"

I struggle to move but my arms are tightly bound and there's the heavy numbness of the cocktail of cryo-protectants weighing down every part of me. Opening my eyes a slit is like lifting the weight of the world. I catch a dim blur of light. Try to speak. Breathing hurts, but I'm used to that—just intubation, right?

"Get with the program, cadet. You'll go through this a thousand times before we're done, maggot."

Who'd that been? Sergeant Nassar… bastard. Who'd he been talking to? Oh, yeah. Me. Who's that? Who am I?

"Kara, come out of it. I need to know. Are you yourself again? *Kuso. Kuso.* Please, give me a sign."

Who's this? Oh… Memories. There, sitting out of reach like a word caught on the tip of my tongue.

"Think, Hiroki-san. Think. More stimulants? Risky… But they seem to have released her. Scan is… hmmm. No, that cannot be right."

Hiroki? A name I should know… I peel one eyelid open a fraction more. A smudge of darkness, man shaped against the blue glow of a screen. Hacking a cough, I spit out the foul clump filling my mouth. Some spatters on my hand. The feeling of weight isn't just from the drugs then. Gravity.

"So… the *bakayarou* thinks to test me? Wait. Must focus on her. Stimulant. Yes, stimulants. Hmm… *Kanojo ga rikai shite kuretara īnoni.* Time to try the polymetamine. Risk is minimal. Yes, yes. That's the right choice. *Kanojo wa watashi o yurushimasu.*"

Footsteps clank on the deck and the dark shape blocks my sight. A sting at my neck and…

Every childhood memory races through my mind fast enough to dilate time. The struggle of the Academy. The surgery, the conditioning, the changes. The joy of Flight School, the pleasure of numbers. Shipping out, losing years. Caskets. Visions. Zed. Revenants. Hiroki. Nanites…

"Oh god, no!" I shout, jerking forward against the restraints. My eyes are wide open now, taking in everything. Hiroki stumbles back from me—his face lined and grimy. Hair loosely bound at the back of his head, and so much hair. Streaked now with grey, like the straggly beard he wears—not the midnight black I'm used to. A voidsuit, the same one he'd worn before but missing even more of its hi-vis paint, hides the rest of his body from me, but seeing his sunken cheeks I can imagine the rest. Emaciated. Aged.

"Hiroki? What the hell's happened? How long have I been under? How've you managed to get rid of the nanites? What's the ship's status?" I stop. Fucking polymetamine has amped up my brain to breaking point—what the hell he thinks he is doing by shoving a narc into me I don't know. A drug so associated with the "cutter" class of street crime, I'd never realized there'd been a stock of it on board. And now he's shot me full of it.

I try to focus on my breathing, get control of myself even as my mind does backflips calculating the likely distance travelled based on last data received and how much his hair has grown. It must have been at least eighteen months… He looks so much older. Did he used to dye his hair? I wonder what he's been eating. No, focus damn you, Kara. Focus. Inhale. Exhale. Hold on, he's talking to me…

"Has it worked? *Umaku itta hazudesu…* She doesn't seem herself yet but she's awake. She's not like the others. Wait. *Kanojo wa watashi ga shita koto o kiku junbi ga dekite inaideshou.* Don't talk about that now. She can't think you've gone space-happy."

"Hiroki?"

"Hai, Kara-chan?"

"I'm calm. Are you calm?"

"Hai."

"Then you'd better start from the beginning. What's happened since I've been under?"

"We don't have much…" A heavy clanking comes from the bulkhead behind him. A concussive bang followed by the unmistakable hiss of an atmo leak. "…time."

"Get me out of these restraints. That's an order."

"I don't know—"

"Do it!" I snap, the parade-ground bark scorching my throat with its ferocity. Has the desired effect, though. He jumps like a startled animal and starts undoing the restraints which bind me. I expect to be weak, to shake and need to fight to get up. Instead, I bounce to my feet, feeling no ache in my joints. Which after over a hundred cold sleep suspensions is plain wrong.

"Hiroki…"

"No time. Here, put this on." He bundles the inner shell of a voidsuit over to me—looks like it's been stripped of all the armor.

I begin to pull it on. "What have you done to the suit, and why?"

"Too heavy to carry you around in a full one, even with articulation. Besides the actuators in my suit are half-seized and I can't fix them."

"That's basic space training."

"I patch people, not machines." He continues talking but, no longer looking at me, fiddled with something in a corner of the room. "Questions, questions. I find a way to save her. Sacrifice so much. And now, questions. *Ochitsuite nani mo akiraka ni shinai.* Yes, but you're not alone anymore. She'll know what to do. She'll know how to fix what you…" He stops and looks up at me, a flicker of a frown on his face. "Must hurry." More clanging on the bulkhead. But not from the door.

I finish pulling on the voidsuit and pull the inner hood up. Get a green light on pressure seal and alerts on suit integrity everywhere else. Internal comms… disabled. Great. No, wait. Slaved to a single encrypted channel. This is impressive work for a man who can't even maintain his own suit's servos.

"You are clear?" Hiroki radios.

"Yeah. Green and clear to go."

"Depressurizing."

There's a hiss of atmo being rapidly pumped from the room. Then the sound fades along with the clanging from the bulkhead.

"This way." Hiroki gestures with one hand, the other dragging a squat box on wheels behind him. His lips continue moving but he's closed the channel. Talking to himself again, most likely.

The box is a piece of medical equipment—a respirator for surgery maybe—that he's fiddled with. Attaching extra oxy bottles and parts of another machine I can't place. So much for not having mechanical skills. But he's clearly gone a little space-happy, so who can say if anything he does makes sense.

He walks to a stretch of blank bulkhead, and only then do I notice the scorch marks that show it's been cut with a laser torch. Hiroki lets go of the modified respirator he's dragging and takes hold of a straggling end of grey temporary suit sealant. The sealant's still flexible, perhaps applied only a matter of an hour before so it hasn't had enough time to harden.

A muscle flutters in my abdomen—this whole time we've been kept safe from decompression only by a substance not much more reliable than spit, gum, and hope. Fucking Hiroki really has cracked.

He rips the pliable seal away in one movement—not the first time he's done so, that much is clear. The metal which was held in place begins to tilt towards us, but he catches it with one hand and thrusts it back the other way. There's no sound as it hits but a heavy vibration runs through my feet and legs. The jagged hatch leads away from the area I woke in, deeper into the workings of the ship and not towards the navigation systems and bridge controls as I'd have expected.

Hiroki pushes ahead, leaving the fallen section of bulkhead on the deck. I get a look at how thick it is as I duck through the hatch. That section must weigh close to what a fully functional voidsuit would. Another little detail clicking into place. What the hell is his game?

There isn't much space to move between the pipes and bundles of fiber-optic cabling. Here and there the familiar lattice of the crystalline matrix of the control boards flicker and flash—system junctions. Still amped up by the polymetamine, part of my mind goes off on a little journey calculating how many false teeth the revenants could make out of one of those crystal sheets; another begins putting together what such a density of data junctions says about our destination within the ship; one more replays childhood memories to a heavy synthesized spacer friendly club sound. But the foremost track's calculating how I can handle Hiroki with him in an armored suit and me in this inner layer that's little more than an airtight body-glove. Breach his air supply and watch him asphyxiate or overpressure the suit's release valve and rupture his lungs. Hmm... How to do it with him fighting back? Better to use the ship in some way—crush him in a pressure door by fully cranking the manual release while latched open and then kicking it off as he goes through. Images of his broken suit leaking blood flood my mind, his fluids boiling off into the vacuum. And there you have why I never like to play with nootropics, certainly not the electric blue-sky dazzle of polymetamine. Laser focus on too much at once and a tendency to irrational violence. No, scrap that—hyper-rational violence. I focus on breathing deep and regular, trying to draw myself back from the spiraling 'metamine rush.

Predictably, several things click into place at once—all attempts at controlling the maverick rocket ride of the narc smashed aside by its potency.

My parents had really loved both my brother and me. If anything, they'd thought more of me than poor Cal. It should hurt but even without the emotion suppressing hit of the drug, this kind of thought doesn't matter much, set against ambition.

Each optical computer plate would provide teeth for about seven revenants.

Both of those plans are impractical and too high-risk. Hiroki's suit is still vulnerable to one thing he hasn't stripped my suit of—the same temporary sealant he'd used to seal us into the makeshift medibay. Spray that into the suit's joints and get some over his helmet's faceplate. It wouldn't stop him for long but if I could get my hands on the right tool, he'd not be able to move fast enough to stop me doing critical damage to his suit.

"We're nearly there. Are you OK, Kara-chan? *Umaku ikanakatta baai wa dōsureba īdesu ka. Watashi no subete no keikaku…* Of course she is, just look at how…"

"I'm doing fine, Hiroki. So you've holed up around the Comm Array?"

He stops and turns to inspect me. His mouth's ajar but at least he's stopped talking to himself. Then he begins saying something, frowns and the comm channel opened again. "The polymetamine? *Yappari.* Too much stimulation for you. *Sumimasen*, Kara. Yes, we're on our way to the Comm Array. It's nearby and is sufficiently isolated from the rest of the ship."

"One access corridor—easy to depressurize without

compromising the comms section itself. Lets you control transmissions to Earth. You've sent a distress signal?"

"No… You must understand—"

"That's our only chance at this stage, isn't it? You've been alone for, what? Eighteen months?"

"Has it been so long? But—"

"No, Hiroki. What are you playing at? By this point, there's no way the Company's policy on radio silence should be holding. For the sake of every damn crewperson out there, you should have transmitted a wide band unencrypted warning."

"Please, wait and I will explain when we are safe."

"I assume the revenants don't have 'suits, I mean, why the hell else would you be mucking around with depressurizing parts of the ship?"

"A lot has happened. Now is not the time to tell you all of it. Please, you must trust me. *Yahari watashi no gisei…* After all I've done, she's doubting me—"

"Keep calm, Hiroki. I trust you. I do. I'm trying to get my bearings, that's all." Hell but his ego's almost as fragile as Zed's had been. Oh, shit. Thinking about Zed again. Poly-fucking-metamine gives no thought space to hide. But my vision's dimming a bit and a vague cloud's bringing me back down from the artificial heights. Short acting stuff, about the only good thing I can say about the dirty shit he'd pumped me full of.

"Hiroki."

"Hai?"

"Never dose me with the blue again, ok? And I say that as an order. Understood?"

"Hai. I mean, aye, Ma'am."

"Good. Now let's get somewhere we can take off the 'suits. I think I need to puke."

CHAPTER 16

We jostle and clank against each other as we hurry down the narrow spaces—they really hadn't been designed for access by voidsuit. After another twenty meters of twisting and turning with Hiroki coming close to knocking loose Charon's sensitive vitals with every lumbering step, we come to another rough hole in the bulkhead.

Hiroki bundles through, clanging into the edges of the cut metal as he does so. I take greater care. This hole had been cut with shears, not a torch. The edges are jagged and I'm not about to find out if they're sharp enough to rupture the thin material of my body-glove.

There's no sign of the cut out—makes a certain sense if Hiroki had done what I would have. Isolated himself within an area and made sure all access routes couldn't be easily re-pressurized without the use of voidsuits. As if to prove the point, I notice a corpse—little more than a withered husk—tangled up in some cabling with its limbs splayed, near to the pressure door into the corridor we emerge into. The remains of the cadaver's wearall marks it as a colonist. Decompression has desiccated the body, and the mouth has drawn open. But no sign of optical chips jammed into its mouth…

"One moment."

Hiroki stomps over to the other pressure door which leads into the Comm Array. There's a code access panel but it's been ripped open and hanging out of the bulkhead. He touches a couple of loose wires together and the door slides slowly open. From the way it moves, I imagine it grating and grinding. But all I can hear is my own breathing and the suit noise until the door opens fully with a dull thud I feel more than hear.

The Comm Array itself should occupy most of the space within the compartment, but it's deployed—trailing behind the ship where it can cover all but the very front arc. The datalines which connect it to *Charon*'s mainframe have been pulled out but not detached. The cables lie around like so many dead snakes.

Behind me, Hiroki cranks the manual door lever until the pressure seal engages. Two weak red lights come on at the top of the door. While he fiddles with the jury-rigged respirator unit, I look about. The place is a mess. Vacbags lie about, lashed here and there in a haphazard way, some opaque and others with their hastily stowed contents visible. Looks like Hiroki has liberated most of the contents of the medical bay and the crew lounge and dragged them up here. Anything sensitive—water purifier and some medical equipment—or perishable—reprocessed rations, medicines—are stowed in the bags. Scattered over a workbench from the crew mess hall, are hundreds of shards of optical crystal. Some connected to power sources but showing no sign of activation. One is wired into a standard crew radio headset. What the hell has Hiroki been up to?

My suit bleeps, confirming there's a breathable atmosphere in the compartment—albeit it's bitterly cold. Still, my stomach is jumping around as I come out of the blue dazzle of the polymetamine.

Shit, but the come down on the stuff is bad.

Pain lances behind my eyes and a wave of dizziness makes me grab the worktable littered with revenant teeth. I'm shaking with the thought maybe the nanites are again asserting their control over me, but the bodily need drives out fear. I yank at the hood of my suit until I control myself enough to remember to order it to disengage seal, peel it back, and bend over in the corner.

What I bring up is mucus and a little blood but nothing more. Doesn't stop me heaving again and again in a futile yet primal need to rid my body of the nootropic poison.

"Drink this." Hiroki says, handing me a flask of water. It's ice-cold but drinkable and I guzzle at it. There's a slight aftertaste of salt and sweetness.

I stop, wiping my lips. "What've you given me?"

"She is very suspicious, *hai*, very suspicious. How to reassure her? Ah. Kara-chan, this is merely a mixture of salts and sugars to help you recover. There are no drugs in the water. I promise. See?" He takes the flask and drinks three large gulps. Something of the tone he'd always had when dealing with a patient has crept back into his voice and with it a greater sense of returning sanity.

He's been alone a long time. It's unfair of me to think he's gone crazy. After all, if he had, I'd still be on ice or worse, some revenant zombie.

"I'm sorry, Doc. You can't understand what it was like... and then... waking to..." I'm crying. Don't ask me why. He comes forward and holds me as gently as he can with arms still sheathed in the armor of his voidsuit. This close I can hear the burr of the suit's actuators and servos. They should be silent. Maybe my mistrust is misplaced?

"Hush, Kara-chan. There is time now to get your strength back." He begins to sing softly, his voice cracking as he stumbles over words in Japanese which stretch my knowledge of the language. Something about a canary and the song of the cradle.

He's treating me like a child.

My tears dry but I don't shake him off. Let him think he can soothe me like this. Let him think of me in a paternal way. Playing along will make me safer until I can be certain of his sanity and sure he'll do as I order.

Slowly, I pull back, pretending to dry my eyes. "I'm sorry, I don't know what came over me."

"She's supposed to be the strong one. *Watashi wa kanojo o machigaemashita ka*? No, it is shock at all she has been through. It's alright. Kara-chan. I have a plan. But first, let's warm up and eat—if you feel ready?"

He scuttles about—not taking his voidsuit off. Paranoia? Or has he grown so used to shifting from atmo to vacuum that he's forgotten? The third possibility, that even despite his precautions we're at risk from the revenants nags at me. But there's one way to take control of the situation.

"Safe for me to take this voidsuit off?" I ask, trying to keep as offhand a tone as I can while I watch for his reaction.

"Hmm? Oh yes. I should think so. Faster than this one," he taps the armor of the chest plate. "I find it easier to keep on than using power to heat the air. *Naze kanojo wa watashi o nayama seru nodesu ka*? I cannot bear more questions..." A puzzled expression comes on his face, and the skin darkens on his cheeks behind the scraggly beard. "I've been alone for so long, I've started talking to myself, haven't I?"

I shrug, keeping my expression calm and my voice soothing. "Don't worry about it—how could you not? It must have been so hard, being alone. Doing all of this without any human contact. Talking to yourself must have been the only way to stay sane."

His eyes narrow and some of the old piercing intellect reveals itself in his gaze. More disturbing, there's no sign of the hesitancy which had marked my old friend. He's changed in more ways than one while I've been in cold sleep.

"Yes, it has been hard. Here, let me make you some food. Emergency rations ran out some time ago but I managed to adapt one of the tissue synthesizers to grow a beef and algae soup." I wrinkle my nose at the jar of green, lumpy slop he places in front of me. "It has all the necessary nutrients. And it is full of umami."

"Great." I choke down a mouthful of the awful broth. "Umami, huh?" Rotting fish more like. Still, my stomach feels less like an empty flapping sack once I finish and the last of the polymetamine induced nausea fades away.

"So... the big question."

"Hai?"

"How did the revenants get out? They had no voidsuits, beyond the one you breached. With Revenant Zero in..."

"You cannot access some areas of the ship without atmo. Sensitive sections are kept isolated even in the event of a ship wide blow out."

"Yeah. I know, we're in one." I cast an arm about. "But there are no caskets stowed here or in any other of those sections. Did some of them survive in those areas? But—"

"I re-pressurized cargo bay four."

"You what?" I nearly drop my bowl of algae.

"It was the only way. I needed…" his face darkens. "I needed a sample. Someone to work with to try the cure on before I risked you."

"That doesn't explain—"

"I had no choice. I couldn't move the caskets so far. I couldn't do what I needed to through the locked casket. Or even in cold sleep. I needed to wake them."

I put my hands on my hips. "You cracked a casket and what? Zapped the poor bastard inside with EM radiation. Wait a second… Them?"

He looks away from me. Cowering almost.

"Hiroki, how many did you wake?"

"It seemed to be working. I was so sure."

"How many?"

"Seven," he says, hands coming together almost in prayer. "But the treatment looked like it was working."

"You woke seven colonists when you knew they were infected with the nanites? I was wrong, you weren't trying to hold onto your sanity."

"You don't understand. I figured out how they communicate—not the code but the frequencies. Found a way of jamming them. The first I woke, she started to respond. Not fully but as if coming out of a coma. My scans showed the nanites had stopped working in concert and were no longer controlling her. But she was still paralyzed."

"She?"

"I initially thought I needed women of about the same age and with similar genotype to you. As close as I could get."

I fold my arms. "What happened?"

"The EM therapy had worked so well, but I couldn't stop the paralysis. Turned the machine up as high as it would go. It wasn't working."

"Wait, you did this to me at one point, didn't you?"

"Yes, a much lower dose, more focused."

"But I didn't go into a coma, they took back control."

"We are rushing ahead…"

"Look Doc, I don't really give a shit about the hows, whys, and fucking wherefores. It's worked on me now. We need to know how many revenants are loose on the ship. Where they are. And whether you can do what you did to me, to them."

"It's not as simple as that," he says.

"Why have I got a bad feeling about this?"

"It shouldn't have happened."

"Spit it the fuck out, Hiroki. Now."

"They split."

"What?"

"The nanites. The first ones, they've changed. Adapted. Learned from their hosts. They're willing to listen to reason."

"You've been communicating with them?"

"Yes—not face to face but through the comms. Their Gestalt has developed a conscience, of sorts."

"What the absolute fuck? You've been chatting to the things that fucking killed the crew? Killed the captain. Tried to fucking kill me."

Hiroki sits down on the chair welded beside his makeshift workshop. Wipes his face and scratches the skin beneath his beard. "It's alive. Self-aware and all it wants is to survive."

Alive? Oh, sweet fucking… No. Control. Focus.

"I get it. It can feel fear. Good. Means we can make it positively shit itself before we wipe it the fuck out of existence."

"Kara-chan. I think, the nanites are mostly gone from inside your head."

"Yeah, so?"

"But if I'm wrong, the ones there, they're still active."

"The fuck are you saying?"

I hold one hand to my temple, the other reaches for a zero-g tether. I cling to it, my legs shaking.

"I didn't cure you. They, it, released you."

"You mean, anytime it feels like, I'll find my mind torn apart again and turned into some kind of node for them."

"No. Well, at least I hope not." There's the old Hiroki uncertainty. He removes a syringe from his voidsuit's hip-bag. "If they kept their end of the bargain, they're all in here."

"And what do they get out of releasing me?"

"Our help. And a way to escape this ship."

"So you've committed us to helping a thing that wiped out

the crew and killed countless colonists. Fighting it, we flushed those VIP bastards out into space, dooming us if we return to Earth. You just know Sevran Corp will want its pound of flesh. And then M'Benga gave her life for what? The Captain gave her life for what, Hiroki? Zed…" Tears in my eyes, forming a blurry wall between me and the world, burning from the heat of rage building inside me. His betrayal of all we'd fought for…

But hey, I'm still alive. And isn't he saying there's a way to survive?

"I did what I had to do. You taught me that. More than anyone I've ever known, you put survival ahead of moral or ethical concerns. Pure, ruthless logic. I've always admired that about you." I start to speak, but he holds up a hand. "As far as I can tell, we're hurtling towards another star system at the limits of the ship's acceleration. But the Gestalt cannot repair the damage we did. It cannot find a way to get down to the planet if we arrive there."

"Hang on, how can we still be accelerating?" An obvious question I should have asked on waking, so much time has passed but I haven't questioned the gravity.

"It slowed the ship, reversed thrust for a few days then accelerated again so I could work, so I could save you. It will have to stop the engines again soon, before we exceed the ship's maximum safe speed."

I keep my face impassive. Hiroki's involvement with the nanite Gestalt is clearly strong. If he believes we can have common cause with it, I can't yet argue against that, yet the pain of having my self—the ego or whatever you want to call it—stripped away by the machines is still fresh.

"There's more. I can see it in your eyes, Hiroki old friend."

His lips part, "She sees right through…" and then he clasps a hand over his mouth. Breaths in and out. Takes the hand away. "*Gomen'ne*, I will not keep saying every thought aloud. You are right as always, Commander. You would find out sooner than later and it is better I confess to you now."

I raise both eyebrows and purse my lips.

"Yes, to the point. The split I mentioned between nanites. It means I must show you something in the medibay. And we can test—"

"I'm not leaving this room without an explanation. Now, doctor." The tone of command which had always made him flinch to attention does little but bring a frown to his face. How much has changed…

"I have explored several further scenarios for how and why the nanites have reacted the way they have. It is still a puzzle. No other ships have reported the formation of a gestalt. None of the colonies have disappeared from contact—"

"That we know of."

"Quite right. Perhaps, it really is because we have encountered some strange signal between the stars. Even the Gestalt does not know." The look on my face must make my thoughts pretty obvious, as he mutters something in Japanese under his breath too low and fast for me to catch. "Getting to the point. There were several military operatives aboard Char*on*."

I wave him on. "The ITF…"

"Yes, their nanotech was also affected. Maybe it was the first to be affected. That and the primal human drive to violence combined are what caused them to be so hostile initially—"

"You are fucking joking."

"No. That's what I want to show you. When you thought it was someone imitating Zed—"

"A Ghostface. One of the ITF's assassins."

"Yes. It was. They're not just a myth brewed by all the slumrats blued out on polymetamine."

I glower at him. My head's feeling like every neuron is shrinking thanks to my own comedown from the nootropic. But he's in full flow and doesn't seem to notice this time.

"We seem to have had a contingent on board."

"A contingent?" Pretty sure my mouth is hanging open.

"My guess is the ITF were expecting Sevran Corp to resist any attempt to revoke their corporate charter on Gliese 892. Sent some of their shock troops to make sure."

"So when their military tech went loco it brought out what? Some kind of reaper protocol?"

"Reaper protocol?"

"Doc, you shoot me up to the fucking eyeballs with blue-sky

and then get surprised when weird shit pops out. Thanks to you, I'm dealing with all this with a major comedown but you know, half the fucking time I want to break into poetry while reciting pi to five hundred places."

"Yes. Ok. My apologies. It seemed to be the only way to bring you to a state of clarity in time. Reaper protocol is nice but I think it is less sophisticated than something like that. More like basic programming to keep the ITF agents ready and able to kill their targets."

"Is that why the colonists started," I gesture at my mouth, "you know, fucking with their teeth?"

"I do not think so. But the code of the different nanotech may have twisted the original gestalt to such actions. I prefer to see it as a side-effect of its primitive consciousness seeking any means to ensure its survival while strengthening each colonist's connection to the others."

"Explain."

"The so-called teeth were all arrayed in a way so they linked to the brain via the nerve at the tooth's root allowing a conduit for the nanites to use for data transmission. All were precisely fractured and set so each tooth still functions as an optical chip, enhancing the network connectivity and boosting the processing capacity available to each node."

His casual use of the word makes my skin constrict with a sensation of icy needles driving into it.

"The Gestalt I have been in contact with has evolved beyond such primitive means or at least refined them. Probably because of how many colonists it has turned into active nodes. Its processing power is an order of magnitude greater than it was."

It clicks into place—he's been using the teeth as a means to communicate with the Gestalt. Maybe there are even nanites stored in them. I repress a shudder. Are they infectious in some way? The idea comes out of nowhere, another nootropic side effect—maybe the teeth are a vector for nanite transmission? Whatever, it's a major risk he's taking. Had been taking. For well over a year. I tune back into what he's saying.

"...still active postmortem. That's part of the reason why a violent solution is ineffective—"

"Wait, what did you say about postmortem?"

"The nanites don't die because their host does. We're rather lucky they're not able to self-replicate. Otherwise, we'd be far more easily overrun."

"Is every corpse riddled with those things?"

"No, only the colonists. And those bitten by revenants might or might not have nanites penetrate their blood stream. Probably not if the conflict was a lethal one."

Wild guess was right, what do you know. "You're saying the teeth are infectious and you've got a whole load of them sitting there on the side? Are you fucking crazy?" I hold a hand to my eyes as a wave of dizziness sweeps over me. A whine starts in my ears like tinnitus.

"Calm down. Any part of them is potentially infectious, not just the teeth. If a revenant sneezed on you, it could be enough to transfer nanites into your system. Without the ability to replicate, a small number are no real threat whether they come from a bite or a sneeze. Unless they have access to other nanotech... like the medical nanites that were in your system for example. But I have managed to cure you, haven't I? It's very important you maintain your rational response to all of this. *Uzai*! She's still so unwilling to trust. After all I've sacrificed. No, not her fault, it's the way she was conditioned." His face darkens. "I'm doing it again, aren't I?"

"Yes, forget it. I'm calm, I'm rational," I say, knowing even as the words leave my lips that someone who's calm and rational doesn't need to say it. "What's to stop the nanites from making the dead colonists rise up and attack us?"

"Because they're dead. The bodies, I mean. If the nanites could replicate themselves, given enough time they could create a kind of naukara out of dead colonists. But these are not the builder types nor the weaponized destroyers we heard about last time we were on Earth."

I think briefly of all I knew about the tech—so new to me yet seemingly everywhere. "You mentioned something about United America trialing aerosol nanites."

"I did. If this were to happen there..." He spreads his hands.

"End of the human race, at least as free individuals."

Hiroki nods. "But when they were no direct and immediate threat to my safety, I realized there was one way of resolving a conflict we had not tried."

"You spoke to them."

"Just so."

"What's this got to do with the split?"

"The military nanites are also not able to replicate but their programming was quite different. When I separated some of the colonists from the rest and then reconnected them, it triggered a process where the colonist nanite programming separated from the military one. The ITF agents on board have triggered the evolution of a consciousness with one purpose—seizing the ship and slaughtering everyone who stands in the way, which is to say everyone not carrying nanites with its program. Afterwards, they would likely look to conquer one of the existing colonies, slaughter everyone there. And so on."

"Is it capable of anything other than killing?" I asked.

"That is what makes it dangerous. Imagine a system totally dedicated to achieving military superiority over its enemies—everything would be fed into the goal of more effectively destroying them."

"Doesn't take much imagination, Doc. Look at history, littered with examples of the military-industrial complex."

He nods, considering my words. "Yes, yes. You're right. I had not considered it in those terms but it does fit."

"So this Complex has a commitment to its ideal without the possibility of dissent."

"Hai. It would make the worst juntas of Earth's checkered past seem mild. A level of xenophobia so high as to drive it to attack anything which wasn't a part of itself. It would be… quite insane."

A small part of me can't help thinking about pots and kettles but I push it aside. "That's why the first thing Revenant Zero did was kill the woman. This Complex drove it."

"No. It was part of the whole at that point. It contributed some military aims and objectives but the kill response came not from the nanites but from their interaction with the primal part of the human brain."

"We made *them* killers?" I scoff.

"Yes. The Gestalt, the original, has rewritten itself, in part. It contains all it was but it is no longer actively linked to the ITF revenants and I believe it has purged that code. Their absence has made it more willing to listen to reason. I believe all it wants is a chance to survive."

"Come on, isn't it as bad as the Complex? Maybe a bit more subtle… How can you trust it?"

Hiroki cocks his head to one side, like a dog that's heard something. "I do not. But it fulfilled the first of my tests. It released you."

"But what exactly does it want in return?" I ask. "Don't hold out on me, Doc. I need the truth. Now."

"I, er, well…"

He breaks off as a grinding noise comes from behind us. The Comm Array is rotating. The look of horror on Hiroki's face registers for me at about the same time I hear the high pitched whistle of venting atmo.

CHAPTER 17

Several things happen all at once. Hiroki dives towards the rotating array, snatching up a metal bar propped against his worktable. The flare of a laser torch flashes bright in one corner of the room, and with it all the air begins to scream out into the void. And I grab the soft shell of my voidsuit with one hand and wrap the other around the leg of the worktable.

Focusing on the only thing that can save me, I pull the voidsuit over one leg, even as the sucking air tears at me with increasing force. My ears pop as I get my second foot in the suit. Dots appear before my eyes and my vision dims. There are sounds—mechanical grating, the howl of escaping atmo, the stomp of armored feet—but they're fading fast. The tinnitus whine in my ears grows louder as my sight starts to fail.

Detecting critical threat to node designated navigator.

A thought but not my thought. I try to scream, *Get out of my head*! But I have no air in my lungs to do so. I must have blacked out because the next thing I know, my voidsuit hood is up and I'm breathing the stale sweat smell of recycled air.

"Hiroki?" I croak.

"Easy, Kara. Easy."

I keep my eyes closed—I know that voice. It can mean only one thing. I'm in the hands of the revenants. And the lack of radio identifier tone while the voidsuit's haptics are warning me of a vacuum environment means the voice I'm hearing is coming from a helmet touching mine. Shit.

I open my eyes.

Zed's face. Scarred, bearded but unmistakable. He's crouching next to me, pressing his helmet against mine.

He smiles. "It's ok. You're safe. We drove him off."

"Zed?" I shake my head within my helmet. "It's not you. It can't be you. You're dead." Every nerve in me is screaming with adrenaline. My heart's racing so hard its beating must be visible even through the voidsuit.

"Baby, it's me. I can prove it if you like. Ask me anything."

"No. That's no good. If it really is you, you've been taken over by the nanites. They'll have scanned all your memories, all your knowledge. There's no way you can remember anything they wouldn't know. And that means you could be one of those face changing ITF freaks. They've tried it on me twice already. Once with your face. The next time with your voice. I'm not falling for it again."

"Commander, if I was one of the revenants don't you think you'd be dead or having nanites drilled into your brain right now?"

He's got a point. I squint about. Zed's flanked by three others. One I recognize as Ensign Joud—now sporting a grim expression to match the jagged scar across his right eye. He'd been a little more than a boy last time I'd seen him, with an openness that'd telegraphed his attraction to me. Now he may as well be forged from the same hyper-steel as Char*on*'s bow. Unreadable. Hard-eyed. Lines cut in his face adding what seemed a decade to his twenty years instead of just one.

The other two—both women of about the same build and height, at least as far as I could tell within the 'suits. The closest has skin as dark as mine is pale but there's a definite similarity in our features. She could be my distant cousin. Her voidsuit's still armored though the plating is discolored in several places, cracked here and there, and with the tell-tale bubbling at her left shoulder pad which speaks of a glancing beam from a laser torch.

Leaving *her*. Her nose is bent to one side, marring what might have been a pretty young face. I remember her. Remember the feel of the stock of my deckgun as it broke her nose. Remember the struggle she'd put up. Details I'd not bothered with before now seem important, as if I can find evidence she's a fake somehow. Red hair, barely visible at her brow. Green eyes surrounded by freckled skin. If she's much over eighteen I'd be amazed. But past the physical signs, it's the look in her eyes that catches me most of all. They're blank, as if a part of her has shut down. Not the wild frenzy which had been there when I'd wrestled her down while Hiroki tranqued her. An emptiness I'd last seen when I'd passed through one of Earth's slums—the hollow-eyed look in the eyes of a child clasping the hand of her mother while the woman sprawled in an alley with froth on her lips. It seems real. Believable as a human reaction to all the shit that's happened. But the fucking nanites had been inside my skull—are *still* inside my skull. Maybe they can read me even now. But then, if they can, what kind of game are they playing?

"We ain't got a lot of time. We'll take you somewhere safe. Follow me." Zed, or the thing that looks like him, stands up from his crouch and holds out his gloved hand. I take it and allow him to help me to my feet. I look around again. They must have dragged me from Hiroki's makeshift lab. The Comm Array.

"What happened with the array?"

Zed looks at me blankly, then taps the side of his helmet. Gestures with one hand farther into the innards of the ship before he strides into the lead. Joud steps up behind him and I feel rather than see the stares of the other two who have taken up position behind me. No way out.

I follow Joud, noting the way he limps. A fault with the voidsuit or an injury? I'll find out, if they aren't leading me to the end of the line.

As we're squeezing through gaps between the bulkheads the gravity effect of acceleration ceases. There's no warning, one moment I'm held down, the next my voidsuit's beginning to float free. I activate the suit's magnetic boots—find only one's working—and pushing against the narrow space force my feet back into contact with the deck. I stamp the malfunctioning boot and its status flickers to active. The others haven't suffered the same problem. Their boots activated before they could float free.

The overwhelming sense of my own vulnerability hits home. I'm surrounded by people—if they really are still people—who could tear through my suit like it's thin cloth. The only advantage I have is the agility granted by the suit's flexibility. Not much help when I'm pressed in by the bulkheads and have two of them in front and two behind.

Zed and Joud paused when acceleration stopped, they must be communicating over the radio—curse Hiroki for that as well as everything else. It should worry me that I'd felt no need to challenge what Zed had implied—they'd driven off Hiroki and so I'm safe. A cold, hard lump lies in the pit of my stomach. Instinct had warned me he was dangerous.

The radio. He's locked it to one frequency and encrypted it. Which means I can't communicate with the others right next to me. But I can try to contact him. Starting to tab the suit's comm channel open, I pause. They might not be able to decrypt any communication I send Hiroki, but they'll be able to detect a transmission. Now's not the time to test how safe I am with them.

We emerge from the cramped access spaces around the Comm Array, coming out through a hole cut into one of the engineering section's bulkheads. Here and there desiccated body parts float free. I puzzle over it for a moment until I realize.

They'd been kept in vacuum for over a year and undoubtedly subjected to several periods of microgravity followed by a full standard g. It's small wonder they're shattered into barely recognizable chunks of what had once been human. A piece of someone's lower jaw drifts past lit by the blue glow from two small shards of crystal grown into it.

I clench my back teeth and will the rise of hot fluid welling in my throat to go back down. The twinkling blue light flickers as the piece of jawbone tumbles end over end in a slow dance out over the main engine casing.

The others press on and, trapped in the isolation of my suit, I have never felt more alone. Except... I can still hear them. The nanites. Is it my imagination or are their signals still transmitting? It's both the most horrifying thought I could have and yet some strange part of me yearns for the company. The belonging. Escape from the lonely pointlessness of my own existence and an embrace of the unity with others. I shake my head to clear the foreign thoughts like shaking sweat from my brow.

A gauntleted hand grips my upper arm tight and jerks me back midstride. Only the malfunctioning boot is in contact with the deck and the force of the pull tears me free. The young woman whose nose I'd busted holds me and lowers me slowly to the deck again. Her lips are moving and her frown deepens. With her spare hand she gestures behind me and makes a sharp cutting gesture. I turn as best I can in her grasp and see I'd been moving towards the forward entrance of the engineering section—a route which would take me past first the medibay and then into the main corridor and linked cargo bays. Bays filled with colonists all bound by either the nanite Gestalt or the Complex.

It feels like a pressure building inside of me—not of blood but the rising of a tide of a different sort. Flashes of everything that'd happened assault me in waves. The torn-out throat of the first victim. The death of the VIP at my own clumsy hands. Zed being bitten as we desperately tried to crank the door to the crew section closed. Seeing him dragged away, blood streaming. The revenant Dominguez had blasted apart as it was about to tear into me. I can't breathe. Start pulling at my helmet. Have to get it off. Have to get air...

"Kara, stop it." Zed's voice. My forearms are held in the steel grip of his voidsuit gauntlets, the bones grinding and near breaking under the pressure. It hurts. And pain breaks through my panic.

"Sorry... I'm sorry. I don't know what happened..."

"Breathe. Slow, in and out. Let me check your oxy—yeah, looks ok. Guess you had a panic attack."

"Fuck off, I'm not some cadet on her first time in a voidsuit."

I can barely make out his chuckle through the contact of our helmets. "Ain't about that but ok, Commander. Whatever makes you feel better. With all you've been through, I'd be surprised if you hadn't suffered a panic attack."

"Part of the comedown from the polymet Hiroki dosed me with. Nothing more."

"You got to wonder where he got that from."

Proof Zed is still capable of being thick as dehydrated shit. Which means nothing if the nanites have access to his memories.

"You thinking he got hold of our score?"

Zed's eyes narrow. "Yeah. Not real important now though, right? Still, wonder what other drugs he can synthesize."

"Street narcs. Nothing more useful than Blue for its nootropic effect and maybe some synth-H as a painkiller. Can't see him tripping his balls off on synth-psilocin or DMT can you?"

"Nah. You gotta be right but…"

"You're worried. Nature of command." Throw him a bone. I feel calmer again and back in control of myself.

"It's not that. I reckon he must be able to synthesize some celltech—like EsPD or BiPHOS."

"What do you want with street steroids?"

"Ain't exactly 'roids. One stops catabolism of muscle, the other reduces osteoclast formation. Kind of useful since we keep having long periods of zero-g."

"Well listen to you, professor."

"Don't joke. My brothers were on 'em. Kept them strong enough to do what they needed to, face up to other cutters."

He'd never spoken to me of his family before. I'd made guesses and it doesn't really surprise me to think Zed's kin might have been narced-up enforcers or the street thugs we call cutters. Must've worked hard to claw his way out of a similar fate. I study his face. Full of surprises this man. And my feelings for him…

"You ok to carry on?" Zed asks, breaking my train of thought. "Ain't far. Be good to talk without having to butt heads, you know?" He gives me the lazy grin that's always set my blood rushing.

I pull back from the contact and give him two thumbs up. This time he stays close as we walk on. My malfunctioning magboot keeps fritzing out until Zed puts an arm on my shoulder and presses me to the deck with every step. Makes me look like a total neophyte spacer. Not much to be done about it right now though.

We end up crawling out on the engine compartment all the way to the back. This is a section of the ship where I've never had cause to go. Right amongst the fusion rockets. We crowd into a small compartment which seals behind us and pressurizes, then an inner pressure door opens.

I gasp in the fresher air—desperate to get rid of the smell of my own sweat redolent with pheromonal dread and feeling another upwelling of nausea. The ceiling of the deck is close to my head, Zed's head brushes it with every step, but I remind myself, this is a trick of perception. We're in microgravity. There's no up and down—no ceiling and no floor. Though it makes sense to act like there is when in a voidsuit.

"You're safe in here, Commander," Joud says. He begins stripping off his voidsuit. "This is one of the engineer's emergency bolt holes for if there's a leak from the engines."

"You mean we're sealed off from the rest of the ship?"

"Yeah. No way in or out. Revs'd have to bore through the main drive to get to us—or go the length of the engine compartment with only the emergency air supply in their wearalls." He shakes his head as if to reinforce how unlikely that would be. "We're safe from them in here."

Them. To Joud at least, the revenants are still all lumped together. Interesting. "What about Hiroki? He has a suit."

"He wouldn't dare try it. I'd gut the cunt if he did." Australian accent. The young woman with the squashed nose. Maybe she doesn't know who I am after all.

"He got you pretty angry then?" I ask.

"He sold us out to the machines. Do anything for them. Creeping little shit."

"Sarah. Knock it off. Commander doesn't need to hear it now," Joud says, floating free of his magboots and grabbing onto some zero-g handholds.

"No, Sarah, please," I say. "I want to hear it."

"We were… I mean I was paralyzed by those things. Wake up to find he's messed with them somehow. Some great bloody machine wrapped round my head. Then he switches it off and starts babbling at me. Telling me I'm his way in. I'm the leverage. And he does something and I feel them come on at me again. It hurts. I black out into the emptiness you get when they take you. Then I'm back and he's excited. Changing the dials making the things in my head scream. Now I hear them, their way of talking and it's saying something different. Then he… then…"

"Then it all went to shit and he scuttled out of there like the coward he is," Zed rumbles from behind us.

I fold my arms. "So everything he told me was a lie?"

"I don't know what he told you. Wouldn't trust a word of it myself. But you and he got pretty tight, didn't you?" There's a wounded look in his eye—not jealousy but recrimination. Of course, I'd left him. Must have seemed like I abandoned him without a second thought. I want to tell him how I'd felt after that. The feelings even I hadn't expected. I don't know how. And there's the doubt. Is it him? Is this even real?

"Maybe…" I start, hesitating over my words. "Maybe, we just don't understand what he's trying to do. Maybe—"

"Bullshit, Kara," Zed says. "It's obvious he's tried giving himself some kind of bargaining chip with the revenants. No idea how he's communicating with them—" I stay silent. "—but somehow he's done it. And now he's got you out without one of these…" he gestures to the back of his head. As if on cue, Joud, Sarah, and the other woman who'd so far stayed silent, raise their own hands to the back of their heads.

"What?"

"Look." Zed floats closer and spins giving me a view of where his hand had clutched his head. A disc about the size of my palm squats there. Looks implanted under the skin.

"May I touch it?"

"Knock yourself out," Zed says.

It tingles under my fingers almost with static and a slight vibration.

"This is producing an electromagnetic field, isn't it?" I ask.

"Got it in one. Focused right down so it goes into our skulls but not so strong it messes with radio transmissions. You get used to the humming after a while. Except at night. Then it kinda drives you crazy."

"If it's keeping the nanites from taking over your brain, shouldn't you be thanking Hiroki, not cursing him?" I ask.

"He did this without anesthetic. Rammed it into us and tore out our crystalline "teeth" while he was at it. I felt everything.

Everything. Bastard killed two of the other 'subjects.' And sent another five screaming into the ship, worse than they'd been before. Worse than the revenants when it was just you and me."

Hiroki had said seven. "Wha…"

"Believe it, Kara." He pulls away and flips round to float parallel to me again.

"Can we backtrack a bit?" I ask. "I thought you were dead but you were taken over by the nanites?"

"Yeah. One that bit me? It was trying to get some of the things into me to infect any tech already there. Lucky I never went in for any black-market mods when we were in Berlin. Only delayed things, though. See I'm a 'priority node.' Bet you are too."

I arch an eyebrow. "Why'd they let Hiroki get you?"

"He had them by the balls. I mean, no air on the ship so only he could move around. Least that's what he thought. Can't use the navicomp, so what? He should've gone down into the fusion rockets and set them off. Blown us all to hell."

"Zed, you're going too fast for me. What do you mean, there was somewhere with air even after we vented the whole ship?"

"Yeah. Here for starters. Some maintenance areas in the cargo holds. Then we found there's some kind of pod or shuttle hanging onto the back of the ship. No direct access to our systems but it's docked at the engineering emergency airlock."

"What?"

"Someone was hitching a ride with us, the whole time."

"Who?"

"ITF. Must've been. Anyway, saw their agents on board before I got taken over. I mean, last thing I saw before I went under was this big colonist jerking and twitching while his face was literally melting into mine."

"Ghostface," I whisper.

Zed stops for a moment, gritting his teeth tight. Joud takes him by the shoulder but Zed squeezes the other man's hand and moves it away. Sarah spends the whole time scowling at me. Zed shakes himself, clears his throat two or three times and breaths himself back under control. "Yeah, didn't see shit for however long I was taken over. Woke up, dealt with all the fallout from what

Hiroki was doing. Didn't think about it. Then about six months ago, rest of them… ITF bastards, I mean, they started working on the ship. Doing their own thing. Fuck knows what they want and what they're doing to get it. Only see one at a time, but you go near them, they shoot and move on. No time for questions."

"Holy shit! How many we talking about?" I ask.

"Seen only one of them, but there must be more," Joud says. "We didn't exactly hang around, Riggs—remember him?" I shake my head. "He'd managed to survive in one of the emergency engineering pressure suits. Tough old bastard had seen off all the revenants that came for him but then they…" Joud pulls his hands apart. "…vaporized him."

"So they've got energy weapons?" I ask. "What? Particle lances, pulsed lasers?"

"On this ship?" Zed screws up his face. "No way. Hand maser, that's it."

"Yeah, that's enough though, isn't it?" I say.

"For sure," Joud says. I wink at him, enjoying the blush on his cheeks.

Zed looks from one of us to the other. "Right. We stay out of their way; we stay out of the Revs" way and we only fuck with Hiroki when we can get away with it."

I take a deep breath. "He told me they've evolved. Claimed there were two groups. One gone crazy from the ITF infiltrators' nanites, the other was more… reasonable. Reckoned he'd caused the split."

"Yeah, well I'd say that's a bunch of paranoid bullshit," Zed says. "Maybe he's been synthing himself some old-style cocaine and fucking his head right up."

Joud shrugs. "Maybe he was trying to put you off speaking to us, if you ever saw us."

Zed grunts. "Guess he wasn't figuring on us hitting him in his hidey hole."

"Guess not." I raise an eyebrow at him. "Care to tell me why you did?"

Zed's gaze shifts away from me. First time he's broken eye contact. "We came for you."

"How noble of you." It comes out far more acidic than I

intend but it is, after all, me.

"Yeah. Noble. Like you closing the door on me."

His words, their truth, hammer into me like a physical blow. "I…"

"Forget it, Kara. You're a survivor. It's what I liked about you. I get it. Looked like they were chomping on me and there was nothing you could do. And I figure you've had it bad enough since then. But we came for you because you were so important to Hiroki. That's what he kept telling us. You were why he was doing what he was doing. If he could save you, it would all be alright. Fucking cracked. But then…"

"Then we realized he had a point. You're navigator. With no sign of any other senior officer, the ship would default to accepting your commands so long as you were alive." Joud. Unlike him to interrupt.

I have no idea where he's got the idea from. Obvious bullshit but there's no point in correcting him and revealing *I'd* locked the navicomp. "So you're saying the nanites can't hack all Char*on*'s systems?"

Joud shakes his head. "Not all of them—we think they can't get into the navicomp and probably not interstellar comms either. Not without you."

"By taking you and keeping you on ice, Hiroki got himself a bargaining chip," Zed says. "But if you were conscious and free…"

Something about their reasoning doesn't add up but it's all coming in a blur. I've been awake for only a few hours but I'm as exhausted as if I'd worked a triple watch.

"Ok. We're not finished but I need to rest. Process all of this. Got somewhere I can bunk?"

The silent woman gestures for me to follow her. "Thanks. What's your name by the way?"

She turns and looks at me with a sadness in her eyes.

"Akima lost her voice thanks to Hiroki's experiments," Sarah says.

"Oh. I'm sorry, I hope you get it back."

"Ain't gonna happen. Part of her brain that does speech got burned out. She'll be mute forever."

That can't be right. She clearly understands me when I speak… but then, what do I know? It's the kind of question I'd normally leave to Hiroki.

Akima shows me to a small berth with a hammock. Clambering in, I zip it up. Stomach doing somersaults from the zero-g or the comedown or all this mad shit. Headache reminding me I'm alive. And a pang, deep down in my chest whenever I try to think about Zed or Hiroki or any of the things that have happened. None of it matters as fatigue sweeps over me like a flood, drowning my thoughts.

CHAPTER 18

I wake to find Zed floating near me. He's not touched me or spoken but it's as if the pressure of his thoughts has intruded on my dreams.

"What is it?" I ask.

"Shh. Don't wake the others. They deserve what rest they can get. Come with me."

I unlash myself from the hammock and stretch as best I can. Being without gravity has given me a stuffy nose and made my face puffy. At least, the nausea has slackened off a little—and all without the help of a promethazine patch to help me keep my dignity.

"Where are we going?" I whisper. A thrill's running through me—does he want to "fraternize" as we used to or is this something more sinister? He doesn't answer but holds up a finger to his lips before pulling himself along a crawl way. We drift down a long, narrow tube with fresh tasting air blowing gently in our faces. At the end, a machine room—atmo processor, power gen, and a computer terminal.

I point at the terminal. "That linked into the mains?"

"Yeah. Engineering bolt hole, remember? Get a coolant leak or atmo loss, you'd need to be able to keep in contact with the rest of the ship and maybe remotely deactivate the engines to avoid a meltdown."

"Makes sense," I say.

"Engineering, all 'bout the logic."

Now or never. "I'm sorry, Zed. Sorry I left you."

"Don't be. Had a lot of time to think about it. You know, I'd probably've done the same. You couldn't save me so, I get it. No point in sacrificing yourself."

The tone sounds sincere and nothing in his expression gives it away but deep in my gut, I don't believe him. Maybe Zed's the forgiving sort. Sure as shit doesn't sound like someone who'd dragged themselves out from the bottom of the well. A slum rat who made it out, must have done so over more than one body trampled down in his rush to get away from a meaningless life. I wonder, for the first time, how many people Zed has killed.

"Well, I want you to know I feel guilty about it. I… shouldn't have left you." I allow tears to form in my eyes—not sure whether they're genuine or not. Doesn't really matter. The effect is what I'd hoped for. Zed pushes off from his handhold, catches me in his arms and holds me. Rumbles something deep in his chest but I can't hear it, he's pressed so tight against me. I wrap my arms around him and allow sobs to come. Pour everything I feel about what has happened to me into those sobs. Pour my frustration and fear and worst of all, the realization this debacle has cost me any chance of a captaincy.

Zed spreads one of his meaty hands across my upper back and pats me. I think he even says, "There, there."

I admit it, part of me wants him to get more physical but it really isn't the time. Besides the shockwave dazzle of touching him and being touched in return isn't there. A mild sparkle. Not nearly enough to make me lose track of where we are and what a deep shit-filled pit we're swimming in.

I let my shoulders stop heaving and pull back. Zed releases me and I spin awkwardly in the air until I catch a handhold. Clumsy asshole may be many things but he's no more graceful in zero-g than he is when walking around.

"So they read your mind? Sucked out all your knowledge and then let Hiroki get his hands on you?"

Zed looks taken aback by the question. Gives a thin smile and nods. "Yeah, pretty much nailed it there. Least, that's what I think."

"Why am I any different?"

"He froze you, right?"

"Yeah, bundled me into cold sleep just as they were taking

me over."

"Figured as much. I don't think they can read your memories or thoughts when you're frozen. I mean, maybe they can communicate with each other, but..."

"How do you know?"

"Isolated the frequency they're using to communicate."

"You did?"

"Well, not me. Joud. Turns out his specialty before officer training was in data systems. He's not too shady... for an officer."

"Nice." The informality makes sense, not just between him and me, but the way he's fallen a shade deeper into a street accent. The way he figures he can talk about Joud. Zed has become, in his own mind anyway, the big dog. For now, I'll play along.

Zed gives a gap-toothed grin. "Figure we're all in the shit now. Anyway, we can listen to their communications but it's encrypted."

"Jamming?"

"Tried. Didn't work. Thought maybe the Comm Array would let us do it but I guess Hiroki would've done it if he could've."

"I thought you said he was working with them."

"He is. Sort of... Doesn't mean he started out like that. No, they want something he's leveraged over them. Like holding out on a street gang, he's walking a narrow thread. Playing along but also playing his own game. Moment they think he ain't got what they want..." Zed clicks his fingers and draws one across his throat.

I hook an arm around the nearest handrail. "Don't you think making them out to be not much more than a street gang is an oversimplification?"

He gives me and odd look and I wonder whether I should have used smaller words.

"What you mean?"

"They want control of the ship, all they have to do is kill me or reactivate the nanites in my head. But..." I wave my hand to encompass my head, "I'm still here. What gives?"

"Yeah. OK. Shit."

"Shit is right. Whatever game they're playing is more subtle.

Or…"

"Or it's not you they want."

His words slap me. I admit I've formed the view that naturally I am most important of all the surviving members of the crew. Enough I've been willing to believe everything is a charade. Hell, I'd even woken once in the night convinced this is all only a simulation the nanites have created in my mind to make me reveal some hidden secret. But Zed's right. I'm not that important to the Gestalt and certainly not the psychotic Complex.

Well, they'll soon regret their error of judgement.

"They control the engines?"

"Yeah. We tried manually overriding them but the closest we can do is either trigger a full burn or a meltdown."

"Could we blow up the ship?"

"We could. But it ain't exactly easy to kill yourself and a hundred thousand people."

"It's less than a hundred thousand now…" I stop myself. The look on his face warns me I'm being too cold-blooded. "The bastards saw to that. You're right."

"They know us. Been inside our heads. They know we're not going to blow ourselves up." Something starts an insistent beeping. Zed reaches one hand to the device at the back of his head. Fumbles something out of his wearall pocket and puts it into the device. Catches me staring. "Got to keep it powered. Swapping out the main capacitor." He places the discharged capacitor down and connects it to a power output from the room's generator.

"Don't you just wish we had wireless power on board?" I ask, thinking to myself here's a weakness I can exploit if necessary.

"Not really. Wireless power would make the drives unstable and—" He spreads his hands, makes a rumbling explosion sound. Idiot. There'd be no sound in vacuum.

"Those things keep the nanites inactive?"

"Yeah. Seem to."

"What would happen if you ran out of power?"

"You have to ask?"

"Fair point. You got a spare?"

He taps the side of his temple. "Worried about the nanites you got in your head?"

"Yes. Sounds like I can't trust Hiroki or any deal he's made."

"Don't blame you. We've only got the ones he screwed in."

"Could you make me one?"

"It ain't a good solution. If it were, well, he'd have used it on you." I scowl at him. "We find the time and the parts, I'll see what I can do. Can't promise it'll cut it though."

"Thanks. So… what next?"

"Now we know it ain't you the Revs want, we got to make plans on how to get Hiroki. He's slipperier than a sewer rat, that one. But we got you now, so who knows? Maybe the sonuvabitch'll come calling."

"That it?"

"That, get supplies, strip some more CO2 scrubbers, find food. Avoid getting killed by Revs or the ITF."

I open my mouth to snap a retort—teach the barely evolved grease monkey a lesson for patronizing me—when I fall, wrenching my arm where it's looped around the handrail. My stomach leaps up as if trying to escape my mouth and I crash into the deck.

Zed had landed on his feet beside me but wobbles and thumps forward onto his chest. He groans and rolls onto his back. Joud's shouting in the other room.

"That's the ion drive."

"Yeah, braking or accelerating?" I ask before realizing what a stupid question it is. Despite the absence of gravity, we'd oriented ourselves to the deck as if we were still in the acceleration phase—old-hand spacer habit. And we'd fallen to artificial down.

"We're accelerating again. That's…"

"That's not good," I say. "Yeah, do you know how fast Char*on*'s going?"

"No idea."

"So we could be at the ship's maximum safe speed?"

"Maybe. No way to tell from engine sound."

"If the Gestalt knows everything I know, it wouldn't take us up past the redline, would it?"

"How the fuck should I know?" Zed waves his hands about.

"They been doing this now and then ever since I woke from their control."

"This, this is really important."

"No shit."

"You don't understand. If we exceed the ramscoop's threshold it'll do one of two things." I pause, heart thudding in my chest at the thought.

Zed's eyes are wide. "What? Fucks sake, Kara. Don't leave me hanging."

"Either it'll destabilize the magnetic field that funnels the interstellar medium. Which means leakage. Best case scenario, it'll burn out the ion drive. If we have enough fuel in the fusion rockets there might be a way to slow down enough so we don't end up vaporized or irradiated but it's a long shot. And I've no idea how we could stop the ship. Worst case—" I spread my hands apart.

"Huh. Great. You said either. I don't want to know, do I?"

"It's possible the ramscoop field would get stronger and larger, drawing in more fuel. A side effect of increasing distance contraction as our gamma increases probably leading to a full-blown Anderson scenario."

"Pretend like I didn't understand a word, ma'am."

"We'd accelerate out of control, get closer and closer to the speed of light, and build up such extreme time dilation we'd end up witnessing the heat death of the universe. Sound good to you?"

"You mean we'd keep going faster forever?"

"Only until we'd run out of space. I've seen some theories which suggest the ramscoop field would expand to devour stars, galaxies, and ultimately the whole universe but it's the overactive imagination of officer cadets. The physics doesn't support it."

"Oh, well, I guess that's something." He wipes a hand across his face. "You're telling me, it's not only our mad, traitor doctor, the Revs, whatever the hell the ITF are doing here, and surviving on whatever air, water, and food we can recycle or scavenge. You're saying we've got to make sure the ship is flying right?"

"We might be too late. All depends on whether the Gestalt managed to assimilate my training, my knowledge."

"Wouldn't the navicomp tell them all that shit?"

"It has a hard speed limit set in but navicomps don't contain the explanation for why. Most crewmembers who had a clue about it would think it had to do with the risk of excessive radiation—more a risk to organic matter than machine. None of those infected by the nanites would have been told that once you go over the limit, you risk exponential ramscoop expansion."

Zed puts his hands to his temples, massaging them. "What can we do about it?"

"Depends. What are the chances you can get me to the navicomp?"

"Not good. It's still depressurized, far as I know, but we'd have to go through the central corridor. Hiroki re-pressurized one of the cargo holds. Dug me out of one of the empty caskets. The others too. Means there's probably Revs wandering about. They'll have wearalls and rebreathers—gives them enough protection to move around. We seen a few but they could be up to anything. And you never know what kind they are—if the Doc ain't totally full of shit. Maybe you'll get the clever ones, maybe the crazy ones. Either way, it's not worth the risk."

"EVA?" The thought of stepping outside the ship again makes my guts clench.

"Don't see how. Can't breach the hull here and with the ion drive on, the access port is a no-no. Only airlock we can get to here is where the ITF shot down Riggs."

"But you got into the Comm Array from outside…"

"No way. We cut through between the outer hull and the inner bulkhead."

"So we use those to get forward."

"Seems navigators know jack and shit about ship construction."

I raise my eyebrow at him. I've let him think the chain of command no long matters but as I get a handle on the situation, it becomes clear now is the time to reassert my seniority. Starting with a little respect from the ranks.

He ignores me. "Only the engines require a double hull and

the space between is always depressurized. Get a rupture of the outer hull? No explosive decompression to rip out vital parts of the engines and cause a meltdown."

"Then, Warrant Officer Hong, I need you to help me access the ship's main chronometer."

"Why? You want to know what time it is?"

"I've been out of it, but that doesn't mean the chain of command has fallen away. Gather the others. Our first priority is to gain access to the ship's atomic clock." Parade ground worthy snap to my voice, ok a little rusty sounding but strong. Confident. He folds his arms and smiles coldly. "That's an order, mister."

"Hiroki pulled this stunt on us. We refused. Guess that already makes us mutineers. Now, you want my help, you gotta explain things to me. You want the others to fall in line, we explain it to them. We're about done with being controlled by anyone."

"You realize when the ship gets back to dock, you'll be court martialed?" Dangerous card to play, but it's my last one.

Zed's laughter echoes in the small chamber. "If we ever get anywhere resembling a space dock again, I'll gladly take a flogging and dishonorable discharge from the service. But, you know I'll be taking my share of the score too. Never forget it, Kara. I know your dirty little secret. And in case that devious mind of yours starts turning gears that say, 'kill him,' don't think I ain't got some insurance in place, make sure you get dragged down if I don't make it."

A bluff? Probably… unless he's told the others. They'd probably forged a tight bond in the year they'd been scraping a bare existence from the wreck we're all entombed in.

I sigh, where command fails, creative diplomacy might succeed. "You've got every right to think so little of me after I abandoned you. Believe me, I regret it. And I'm not looking to hurt you, Zed. Command has to work a certain way or the ship is doomed." He snorts. "Maybe you don't see it now, but here's a question. You've been free of Hiroki for over a year. In all that time, you've done what? Scuttled into this hiding place. Raided him what? Once? Lost a man to the ITF and you still can't tell me the numbers. This is not a command acceptable result. We want out of this, we need to take decisive action and there's no such thing as decisive action taken by a committee."

"You done?"

I nod. "Yeah."

"Good. Now in simple words tell me why we need to pull the chronometer out."

"It's tied to the navicomp. Slight changes in gravity affect time. Make it pass slower or faster for the ship. When the navicomp knows the ship's vector, it can use the small changes in the ship's time against an external measure. Usually a continuous radio signal from Earth but also from known stellar objects like pulsars which produce regular emissions. The comparison allows for highly accurate measurements of the local gravitational fields acting on the ship. It's essential for navigation."

"I follow. How does that work? I mean…"

"Zed, do you understand how a holovid works?"

"You kidding? Basic maintenance job."

"Bad example but go with it. Do you need to understand how it works to see the picture?"

"Well… no."

"So do I have to school you on relativity and advanced astrodynamics for you to take my word for it that the chronometer is used to navigate?"

"OK. Cut to the chase. What's this got to do with knowing if we're going too fast?"

"The size of the variation. If we know where we are based on some simple observations, then working out what the rough gravitational field should be is possible. Time dilation from excessive velocity would show a much larger variation than what we could expect from the area of interstellar space we're travelling through."

"OK. You've lost me but I'm willing to accept this is important. To make this work, you're gonna need to either get access to the Comm Array or what? Get a telescope?"

I remember the look of desperation on Hiroki's face when the Comm Array compartment had started to depressurize.

He'd moved to the array itself, in a panic. Treated the loss of atmo and arrival of Zed and the others as an afterthought.

"Let's forget about the array for the moment. You make it sound like we don't want to mess with Hiroki." The thought of my old friend, an erratic but brilliant sawbones, being dangerous makes me want to laugh but Zed's brow unfurrows as I say we'll avoid the array. Zed, big, street-hardened slab of a man that he is, is terrified of the doctor.

"So… you gonna look out the window or what?"

"No. Shouldn't be too hard for a technical whizz like you to access the data lines going into the navicomp."

"There's no way we can out-hack the nanites."

I think of the link-key, but it's pointless. It must be with Hiroki, like the data sliver with the narc synthesis programs. "We don't need to hack anything. Just read off the raw data from Char*on*'s forward radio dishes."

"Hold on," Zed says and crouches in front of the data terminal. Ship's schematics display and zoom in to the forward prow. Looks like a small radio dish tucked behind the generator for the ramscoop and another on the other side of the ship tucked behind the ramscoop repeater. Both shielded from the magnetic interference of the scoop itself and pointing off in an arc nearly ninety degrees away from the direction of travel. Lines highlighted in blue run from the dish, down along the engine compartment until it comes behind Char*on*'s cowl and traces along the line of the main corridor to the cargo and command compartments. Where it traverses that corridor, the blue line becomes dotted and, as Zed zooms in, other lines leap up, highlighted in red and displaying warning symbols.

"So?" I ask.

"Yeah, they're still feeding into the navicomp. Looks like the dataline wasn't compromised by the damage where the VIP boat used to be. Some issue with bandwidth and dataflow but I don't think it's important."

I blow out a long breath. "Well, at least we know the navicomps not been flying blind all this time. Where can you access the dataline?"

"Crawlspace for maintenance to the main port fusion

rocket. Tight fit, but I should be able to splice in a line to the main engineering comp."

"You make it a one-way connection."

"How would I do that?" He frowns.

"You mean, if we do this, the Gestalt will be able to access the engineering systems through it?"

"And? They already control the engines. Can't control the navicomp without you, unless Hiroki was lying about that. We're locked on course. Only thing they can do is change speed."

"Couldn't they hack the CO2 scrubbers you got in here? Or open the doors and vent this to vacuum?"

"Nah. Quit worrying. About the only thing they could do is see what we're doing."

"We'd draw their attention to the forward radio dishes." I feel a shiver which starts bone deep and runs like light fingertips all up my spine. "They could use those dishes for comms, couldn't they?"

"Yeah. Sure. I guess. Who're they going to be signaling though? Little green dudes?"

"Earth."

"Not unless we've changed course to face back the way we're coming. Fixed arc on those dishes, according to this. They can move enough to lock on any signal in the forward arc of the ship. Comm Array is used for anything from the rear arc. Hmm, according to this, right now it's pointing forward too. Far as it can. Anyone listening to that station would get bleeding ears."

"What?"

"It's angled right at the trailing edge of the ramscoop's magnetic envelope. Open signal too. Gotta sound like the whole universe is screaming."

I grin. Hiroki has angled the comma array to give the Gestalt nothing but static and locked it so anything in the main computer will receive that sound, non-stop. It probably isn't painful to them like it'd be to us, but it's a big "fuck you" gesture to them all the same.

"Chronometer—that's more of a pain in the arse. Have to crack open the ion drive casing and get inside it while it's active.

In a voidsuit." Zed sucks his teeth. "It's doable. You need to see the chronometer itself or just the data?"

"Just the data will be fine."

"Well, finally something easier." He looks up at me, a thoughtful expression on his face. "What'll we do if we've gone past the redline?"

"You believe in God?"

His face screws up. "Er, no."

"Well, then there's nothing you could do."

"What's God got to do with this?"

"Only, if we have gone past the redline, about the only thing left to do is to start praying. One way or another, we're doomed."

CHAPTER 19

They've all gathered around the airlock, Joud carrying a makeshift speargun he's fashioned from a gas canister and a length of pipe. Sarah bearing a jagged length of machined metal cut like a flat and rectangular sword blade—its edge glints in the light but she's not bothered to put a point on it. The hooded look in her eyes puts me off asking her about it—I can't shake the feeling she's longing for a confrontation. Not specifically with me, but with anyone or anything. Akima carries the laser torch with its battered generator swung over one shoulder and the silvered fabric of a vacbag over the other. I raise an eyebrow at this, but it makes sense. Maybe we'll find a survivor somewhere who needs to be stuffed in the bubble but more likely she's carrying it in case we come across some food or water that's been preserved and needs a way to transport it without vacuum perishing or evaporating.

Last of all, Zed joins us. He bears the massive jaws of the bulkhead shears, twice the size of the ones Hiroki had used to kill Revenant Zero. Way too big to be a weapon, even used against an unsuspecting target. Does he realize or is this a male ego thing?

"You're all packing quite an arsenal."

"Need it," Joud says. "We've seen the occasional rev with their wearall sealed up, coming into the depressurized areas. They've not got much air, maybe ten minutes tops but..."

"Oh, really." I arch an eyebrow at him. "They aggressive?"

"Not so much, but you never can tell. Some of them seem more interested in collecting supplies or gathering the broken optical matrices they use as teeth. Others, well I've encountered at least three that came at me soon as they saw me."

"So the aggressive ones are sophisticated enough to use makeshift suits?"

"Oh yeah. In fact, they're often in ones that look like someone made more of an effort. You know, actually strapped a compressed air cylinder on them to give them some extra time."

"Sounds like milspec survival training, wouldn't you say? Bit like the space survival training we had at the academy."

"Hadn't thought of it like that." Joud smiles at me. "Guess that's why you're a commander and I'm an ensign." He winks.

There've been some changes there alright. I swear he's flirting with me. It's… charming. Less direct than the way Zed used to show interest, but just as masculine. Maybe even more confident. I catch the scowl on Sarah's face. Jealousy? Another angle to work, should I need it.

"Can we cut the jawing and get on with this?" Sarah says.

"Easy now," Zed says, setting a hand on the shoulder of her voidsuit. "We need to catch our breath a moment before we go jumping into this. Calm, controlled. None of this running off and hacking Revs if we spot them. Clear?"

Sarah grits her teeth for a moment then speaks. "It's clear."

"OK then." Zed turns to Joud. "David, you have any luck with Kara's suit radio?"

"It's software, not hardware. There's a shifting algorithm that keeps anyone from changing the frequency. I'm guessing it encrypts any comms on that frequency too."

"Guessing?"

"Too sophisticated for me to break the program down and take a look. If I had to commit to an explanation, I'd say it's a QI virus."

I keep my expression neutral and note the same careful impassivity on Zed's face. So… he hasn't told them everything after all.

"We're stuck without comms, Kara. I noticed your suit's having problems with its left gravity boot. Better use a stikpad for now." He hands me one of the adhesive layers and I tuck it into the thigh pouch of the voidsuit. Little point hobbling along while we still have gravity.

Zed nods. "OK, everybody. Remember the rules. We stick together. See something interesting, call out. Volunteer to keep an eye on Kara—without her suit comms she could easily get lost. David? Great, you two better use a belaying line—way too easy to get distracted out there."

Joud's face lights up, the expression melting his face back into the soft young man he'd been before. But aside from the thought I'll have the ensign trying to hump my leg the whole time, Zed's decision bothers me. Implies I need babysitting. Implies he doesn't give enough of a shit to do it himself.

"Great, try to keep up, ensign." Joud's gap-toothed grin slips and I smile to myself. "All of you are armed. I'm *not* going out there without a weapon."

They exchange uncomfortable looks. Joud opens his mouth but Sarah nudges him. Akima scowls.

"We're a bit wary of you, Kara, and that's no lie," Zed says. "You look after yourself and screw the rest of us. We get it. It's another part of the training, your killer drive to survive and get to the top no matter what happens. But it doesn't make us trust you." I wouldn't have been more shocked if he'd slapped me.

"I... How dare..."

"I hadn't finished. Surviving this isn't about the individual. Someone as smart as you can see that. Every one of us increases the chances of the rest living through this. So, here—" He hands me a jagged length of metal, one end wrapped in insulation tape. "It's not much but then all of us have to make do with tools or weapons we've made."

Sarah leans forward, a savage excitement in her eyes. "All you got to do is slash their suits and they die fast enough."

I take the shiv, walk to a pile of junk and spare parts they'd lashed together between the hammocks, and grab a length of pipe. Screw the end of the shiv into it then bang the butt against the deck until only an inch of insulating taped handle remains visible. Walk back, putting the old deliberate swagger into my step. "Yeah, all of you have hardened plating covering you head to foot. I might as well wrap myself in a foil blanket. Here's a little secret for you—I'm the one who's having to trust my life to a bunch of people who'll jump on me the moment their batteries run out." I tap the back of my head then pull up my hood and visor and seal them. It muffles their voices but I'm not listening anyway.

Gravity makes the search through the dark interior easier but with every step I can't help but expect the ship's acceleration to stop again. Having my makeshift spear makes me feel a little better even if it'd do precisely zip against the voidsuits of my companions. Zed has done me a favor—I'd begun to get too comfortable with them, let a sense of safety build up. Now I'm back to the simple truth of the situation. Fuck what he said. Each of them is a potential threat, and it's less a question of if and more a question of when I'll have to deal with them.

Joud takes his task seriously, keeping pace with me and behaving in a gentlemanly way at total odds to the mission necessities. But his head stays up and roving from side to side, playing the headlamp's beam over every surface near us. Checking behind us, marking where each of the others were. Shining the light out into the dark expanse of the engine compartment. We stay in a tight formation.

"Kara-chan, do you read me? Over." I must have faltered because immediately my self-appointed protector is at my side, holding my elbow. I'm about to shake him off but I resist the impulse. Make eye-contact. Break it. Look back. Smile and mouth a thank you. I swear he blushes. He opens his mouth and starts speaking then his color deepens further and he waves a hand in a vague gesture. I keep the laughter contained.

"Kara, this is Hiroki. Please come in. Over."

I cast around, checking the others. Each is keeping a tight watch on their surroundings and the rest of us. Zed may only be a wrench-monkey but he's made sure his people stay alert. I almost approve. No sign they can hear Hiroki.

I tab the comm. Keeping eyes on Zed, I speak, trying to keep my lips from moving. "I read you, Hiroki." No reaction from Zed. No way can he be so controlled if he's listening in.

A long stream of rapid-fire Japanese rattles down the comm

before Hiroki breaks off. "So sorry. I was worried you had been hurt or killed. You are all right?"

"Yeah. I'm here with, er, some of your experiments."

There's a rapid intake of breath and a murmur of words before he catches himself. Sounds like a curse in Japanese, *kuso yarō,* maybe? "Those fools. They will ruin everything." I've never heard him so angry.

"Relax, Hiroki. Losing your temper won't help. Now if you have a plan, maybe we can talk it over and achieve it together."

"You don't believe the lies they've told about me?" Even over the radio, his voice is filled with a desperate hope.

"I don't know what to believe, Hiroki. But I do know you'd never betray our friendship. Isn't that a good starting point?"

He murmurs again and then tells himself to stop it. "Yes, yes. You are right. A good foundation. I am nearly certain the Gestalt cannot decrypt our communications. I would like to be sure but I must take this risk. You understand the Gestalt could kill all of us so long as it has one crewmember under its control."

"Yeah, I understand."

"Good. I believe one fragment of the Gestalt remains driven by the primal violence of the human animal but as I told you before, the dominant, less aggressive side can be reasoned with. But I am not a fool. It and the one you called the Complex, both want the Comm Array. To contact other colonies, ships, Earth… perhaps to fill the buffer and block any warning signal. It matters little."

Echoes of my own suspicions. Better be absolutely certain those forward dishes can't be turned back. "It wants to send a message?"

"I believe so. It has tried several times to send a message out in any direction."

"That's why you have the array pointing at the ramscoop."

"Just so. It cannot get past the interference and it cannot shut off the ramscoop at this speed or *Charon* would be torn apart within moments. But we also cannot send any messages."

"I hate to say it, but that's not our biggest problem."

"I imagine so."

"We need to know how fast the ship is going."

"Yes. I understand. It is important?"

"Life or death."

"I will help however I can but you must find a way to escape from them. They may believe they are free of the Gestalt but their EM generators could fail at any moment. Be in no doubt, if they do, they will become rabid, reverting to the most basic level like the revenants we first encountered. Given time, either the Gestalt or the Complex will take them over."

"These groups… Zed says there's no difference."

"He would. Try to avoid revenants but if you see some attacking using military tactics—those are controlled by the, er, Complex. If they ignore you unless threatened or otherwise behave without immediate hostility, those are the Gestalt. They are still dangerous. Remember, you would be a valuable asset to them, if in their hands."

"Can't they simply take me over again?"

"I do not believe so. But I do not know for sure. I took a sample of your cerebral-spinal fluid before reviving you. The agreement was they would cluster at that point and allow themselves to be removed. The fluid I took did indeed contain nanites but perhaps not all of them."

"Is there a way to be sure?"

"Yes, the scanner in the medibay. If it is still functional."

"Could you meet me there?"

"Doubtful… it is currently occupied by the Complex."

"Wait a minute, Hiroki. Something's happening."

I flick the channel off and bring my attention to what was going on in front of me.

Akima is holding her hands to her head, shaking it. The others have clustered around her, waving their arms. It's a perfect chance to get away—slash the tether binding me to Joud and scarper—but I'm still caught between my doubts. Instead, I watch, with a cool paralysis spreading through my limbs. I want to move, but I can't. Akima's arms stop spasming and her movements become sharp and fluid. She whirls on the others, swiping at them with the laser torch. I'm too far away to make out the expression on her face but I can see the glint of her remaining teeth flashing white in the beam of Zed's headlamp.

He steps in, towards her left side and she swings at him, the focus point of the laser torch coming close enough to Zed to bubble the paint on his shoulder plate. Joud and Sarah both throw themselves onto Akima's exposed back. Joud trying to wrap a loop of our tether around her arms. She tries to spin back but Sarah has her pinioned in a way that gives me an eerie flashback to the time when I had held the broken-nosed woman in a similar grip.

Without warning, the fight begins to lift off the deck as a low rumble runs through the engine cover beneath our feet. The drive cutting off again. I manage to engage my magnetic boots and fish around for the stikpad in my thigh pocket. I'm sure I'd look pretty comical, bound to the deck by one foot while the rest of me floats and contorts in the zero-g as I try to get the pad onto the base of my boot.

Locking my foot back in place, I look up towards the fight. One of them must have kicked off the deck as the ship stopped its acceleration. Whether to take advantage of the zero-g or in a desperate attempt to lock their magboots to the deck is anyone's guess. Now, Sarah, Joud, and Akima roil in the air. Akima is close to overpowering both though Joud has managed to get his loop around one of her arms and cinch it tight.

Sarah holding her other arm, grabs for the laser torch. Akima pushes Joud away and the sudden movement frees her arm from Sarah's grip. Sarah spins away, her fingers snatching at Akima's wrist but missing. The briefest jet of gas comes from her voidsuit's thrusters but it's not enough to do more than slow her. She must have exhausted the reaction mass, leaving her drifting off into the dark of the engine compartment while Akima focuses all her attention on Joud.

I don't think he sees it coming and so maybe it's as swift as death can be. The torch comes up and burns through his helmet's visor, the head within, and then out of the back of the helmet. The armored visor snaps up but too late to make any difference. Then the torch burns through that too. The blast of air from the puncture in his suit sends Joud's head bouncing around, making the torch's beam slash the hole wider and more jagged.

His arms jerk once then he lets go and floats free from Akima, his blood bubbling oh so slowly from the charred holes in his helmet as the last escaping gasses from his suit send a thin trail of blood droplets misting out both forward and back to boil away in the vacuum.

I look down, thinking hard. His suit should have shut off the remaining air supply, which means at least we won't lose all his oxygen.

A tug on the tether makes me glance up again. Akima is pulling towards me—Joud's corpse bumping against her side with her every movement. I hold out my spear for an instant before the absurdity of the gesture registers on me. As if a shard of jagged metal on a pole has the slightest chance of penetrating her hard-voidsuit. Flailing with the end, I try to slice the tether, give up and pull the spear in tight. I yank at the knife but it's held fast and the risk of tearing the palm of one of my gloves too high. Taking the spear in my right hand, right below the blade, I hold the tether taut with my left and start sawing at it. The blade frays the carbon fiber strands as I try to keep my eyes down and focused on the task, aware that at any moment the white-hot beam of the laser torch might reach my head.

A final pull of the blade and the line breaks, leaving the frayed end held only by my left hand. I look up, straight into Akima's hollow gaze—she's less than a meter away, laser torch already arcing down towards me. Pulling the tether sharply to one side, I try to spin the revenant who'd been Akima away from me. She twists her arm, pulling herself forward but too late—I let go. She starts slowly tumbling off horizontally a couple of meters from the deck, looking for all the world as if she's dancing a pirouette with Joud's corpse.

Zed's arm flashes out and catches the tip of the line between two of his fingertips. He twists his wrist and catches a handful more as the line snaps tight. At the other end, the revenant is trying to untangle itself—no doubt planning to throw the corpse away from it at a one-eighty from the deck. Zed pulling on the line, tightens the loops which had wrapped round both revenant and corpse as they'd spun. I expect him to pull again and I'm puzzled as he lets the small momentum he'd imparted bring the bound bodies drifting closer to us again.

He leans into me, touching his helmet to mine.

"What were you doing?" I can barely hear him.

"What did it look like I was doing?" I shout.

"Can't let her drift. She's one of us."

"She's a rev now, kill her or find a way to incapacitate her so we can recover her suit."

"You are one cold-blooded shit, aren't you? Whatever the fuck happened to 'No one gets left behind'?"

I chuckle. Bad timing I know, but I don't think he can hear me. "That's what they taught you grunts. Give you some esprit de corps, make you easier to control. They taught us, 'Everyone is expendable in the achievement of the objective'."

"You fucking sick… the whole officer class, you disgust me. Worse than the goddamned Corporates."

"Not quite. They're taught 'nothing of value gets left behind unless the new-jiao value of the objective is greater.'"

"Sounds about the fucking same to me. Akima's one of us. We've lost David, we're not going to lose her too."

"What the fuck are you talking about, Zed? She killed Joud. And look at her. She's already lost."

"Damn you, Kara. If we get her somewhere with air, I can replace the capacitor in her EM disc. She'll come back from it."

"No. Shit. No. You've got to kill her, Zed. Now."

"Are you crazy? I'm gonna save her not kill her."

"For once in your life get your caveman brain around this, she knows what we're doing. If the nanites assimilate her knowledge…"

"It's a risk we'll have to take." Impossible to hear his tone of voice, he's having to bellow to make sure I can hear his words. I doubt there's any uncertainty in them. Nothing I can do, nothing I can say is going to get round this. No way to overpower the idiot and do what has to be done. I should have gotten away when I had the chance.

The bundle of corpse and revenant—Joud and Akima, dead and as good as—comes close enough for Zed to grab with one hand. Looping the remainder of the tether line around and around the struggling woman, he binds her tighter to the dead body. Joud's head has at least stopped spraying blood. Enough has gotten onto the revenant that her helmet is streaked with it—a thick, almost black, gelatinous layer that's still bubbling as the absence of pressure makes it boil. Doesn't exactly help the idea that there's a woman in there who can be saved and not just a killing algorithm.

There's a pop of static in my ears and only then do I realize Hiroki has kept his end of the line open, waiting for me to transmit. I activate the mic once more.

"One of them went revenant right in front of me. Got it tied up. Can't get away now. When I can, where can I go?"

"We need access to the medibay. There is one way. Remember the ventilation ducts?"

"How could I forget?"

"Get to the duct outside the medibay. Wait for me there. Over and out."

"Wait." His connection breaks. "Fuck that crazy doctor and his stupid plans."

A dim light is approaching: Sarah. She thumps along the deck and as she gets close enough to see her face in the illumination of her helmet's HUD, the tears in her red eyes are obvious. Her lips are moving, probably getting an update from Zed. No sign of her sword. Must have thrown it away to use the momentum to regain the deck. Reasonable expenditure of her resources.

She barges past me and grabs Zed by the shoulder, yanking round so he jerks against the hold his boots have on the deck. There's a lot of gesturing, mostly Sarah jabbing a finger at Zed, at me, and at the writhing form of the bound revenant. Eventually, their argument stops and Sarah stomps off ahead. Zed looks round, his face dark, and beckons for me to follow. I start to move, one leg in the easy motions of walking in magboots, the other having to adopt the twist, release, step, test, repeat approach of walking in stikpads. Zed waits for me to come level with him then he falls into my right side. Holds the bound forms of Akima and Joud clear to his right. I shudder as I look at the writhing form. What if it's Zed next?

CHAPTER 20

The rest of the way to the access point for the datalines is uneventful, though every time I start to relax, I only have to look over at Zed's cargo to feel the hairs stand up all over my body.

When we arrive, Zed secures the revenant to a guiderail and sets to work opening up the maintenance hatch. I check my HUD—eight hours oxygen left. Two used. Plenty of time.

Sarah refuses to look at me—no idea what I've done to deserve that, she can hardly blame me for staying out of the way when all I'm wearing is a thin and easily ripped voidsuit. Well, she must do. Seems like the colonists had been given a similar bullshit filled indoctrination about teamwork and self-sacrifice.

She spends her time setting up the vacbag as a makeshift atmo tent. Looks like she's sizing it up for two. I don't like any of the possible reasons for what she's doing.

Before I can make up my mind whether to interrupt her, Zed climbs back out of the maintenance hatch and waves me over.

I hobble to him. Twist, lift, set, test. Beep, clonk. Twist, lift, set, test. Beep, clonk. It frustrates the hell out of me, though with a spare voidsuit now…

Zed touches his helmet to mine, and I notice there's no thrill in having him so close. Only a wave of revulsion at what he really is and how close he might be to revealing it.

"Too narrow for my suit. I need you to go in there and attach the datathief." He holds up a palm-sized black box.

"How would I do that?"

"This from the officer who hacked the ship's computer how many times?"

"Yeah, with a link-key, smartarse. Seriously, how do I do this?"

The shoulders of his suit settle into place with a whine of servos I can barely hear through our helmet contact. "OK, Kara. Take this—" He passes me the flat black box. "—and place one half on either side of the highlighted... ah, shit. I can't show you on your heads-up. I bet Hiroki did this just to fuck with us."

"Calm down."

"It's just... David. Fuck." I swear there are tears in Zed's eyes. He is that good. I almost believe he means it. "OK. OK. Look for two of the cables with a blue stripe. It's the one with BRX887-1VT on the trunking. It doesn't matter where, so long as the two halves of the thief go parallel to each other."

"It sounds too easy."

"It is easy—if you can reach it. I'd uplink the data to you but... you know."

"What's Sarah doing?"

"Trying to replace the capacitor in Akima's EM transmitter."

"Is she fucking crazy?"

"It's safer doing it out here than anywhere else. She uses the vacbag to do it without having to come into contact with Akima. If Akima can't be saved and somehow gets free... well, she won't be much of a threat."

I stare at him, letting silence tell him what I think of his optimism.

"You'd really leave her, wouldn't you?" He squints at me. "Don't answer that. I'll be back soon as I can get a line on the ship's chronometer."

"You're leaving me alone to do this?"

"I am. Good luck and try not to rip your suit on any of the machinery—none of us will be able to reach you before you asphyxiate." He pulls his helmet away from mine and stomps away without stopping to see my reaction. *Bastard.*

Still, there's nothing for it and being wedged into a part of the ship where they, in their armored voidsuits, can't fit seems like a good idea right now.

The access is tight with plenty of power junctions and data nodes for the ship to snag my suit on—none hold an edge which looks like it'd do more than catch the fabric. Zed must have been messing with me. We'll see how he likes it the other way round soon enough.

It's not that I gain a sudden new respect for the wrench-monkeys—after all they'd have Voidsuit HUDs or other diagnostic tools to guide them—but finding one among the hundreds of cables of all sizes is a daunting prospect. Most are grey with red writing with a few yellow cables here and there. No idea what they're for. Hidden amongst them are the two blue cables and the first one to my hand reads BRX in thin type. I pull the black box of the data-thief into its two halves and place one on each side of the cable, press their activation studs, and let go. They stay where I put them. It'd be nice to know they're transmitting but we'll find out soon enough.

There's a flash of light from outside. Brief but intense. My guts twist—I've only ever seen beam weapons used in training at the academy. A standard infantry laser rifle. Of course, we'd all been wearing protective eye goggles so any stray refraction didn't blind us but the quality of this light is different. Another flash. Realization breaks me out of my moment of panic—I'm analyzing what's happening in an abstract way instead of acting. The only group aboard ship with access to an energy weapon is the ITF agents Zed had told me about. The one they'd seen was equipped with a hand maser.

I edge to the entrance of the access point and peek out. Sarah's huddled down beside the grey mass of the vacbag. She's positioned the viewport so she can look in at what she's doing and push the bubble's loose glove appendages back inside it, using them inside out and inside the bubble itself. Whatever she's doing, she seems totally oblivious to the flashes of purple-white light that had flickered across my vision.

Another comes, and now the source of the light is obvious. At the far end of the drive bay, fully seven hundred meters aft of our current position, someone is firing at revenants. Every time the maser's fire lights up the scene—its wielder slashing it back and forth like a scythe—I have a moment or two to see the forms of over a dozen revenants dressed in makeshift voidsuits hurling themselves forward. The burst of maser fire flickers out and the aft of the bay goes dark again. I wait, expecting more fire, but by the count of a hundred none comes.

Sarah finishes whatever she's doing and clonks across the deck to me. When her helmet's about an inch from mine, she snaps her head forward so her armoplas visor slaps into mine. It's hard enough to knock me off balance but not enough to risk damaging our suits.

"What the hell..." I start to shout at her but she pulls back. Her eyes are red-rimmed and her lips drawn back from her gapped teeth in an animal snarl. Human fury, not revenant madness. Something must have happened to Akima—it had been inevitable.

Sarah rears back to butt forward again—I don't give a fuck what she's feeling or whether venting on me now might make her easier to deal with in the long run. I've had enough of this shit. I disengage my magboot but keep my foot to the deck.

Her head comes thrusting forward again, this time she steps into it—maybe enough it'd actually be dangerous. Pivoting on my left leg—the one with the stikpad—I thrust the other foot behind me and to the left. Sarah has too much momentum behind her to pull up, besides, she's triggered her suit's servos. She overextends forward and, as she tries to get her lead foot down, I kick out with my right, sweeping her foot forward as hard as I can. Her magboot makes contact with the deck and engages, leaving her teetering in a near-splits position.

In gravity, this would pretty much be it for her, but absent a downward force, she's only off balance. Grabbing her, I release my left foot and boost myself free of the deck so I rise behind her. Kick the left foot into her back so the stikpad holds, then standing on her back, start kicking the back of her suit where the air and power feeds go into her helmet. I doubt I can do any real damage, but every impact'll make her suit's HUD light up red and squeal warnings at her.

She tries to regain her stance, tries to reach behind her to grab me but I'm standing on her back right beyond the arc of her suited arms' range of movement.

Every time she tries, I kick again.

Without comms, I can't tell whether she's calming or not but eventually she holds her arms out. I wait, kick her again but she doesn't react. Then, climbing down, I detach my stikpad from her. Get my magboot back on the deck and meet her gaze.

Her eyes are full of tears—not from the kicking I've given her, it can't really have hurt so much as it must have been humiliating. Leaning in, I gingerly bring my helmet into contact with hers.

"Are we cool?"

She nods.

"What happened with Akima?"

It takes her a minute to get enough control back to tell me. I suppose I should feel sympathy, she is after all nothing more than a teenaged colony girl. But I've always despised weakness in other women, probably as a result of the scrabble of officer training. Never had the same feeling about men, but then again, they're all weak in their way.

She draws in a shuddering breath, tears floating off her eyes and sticking to the inside of her visor. That's a downside to crying inside a voidsuit in zero-g. Can't wipe your eyes. Can't blow your nose. Get near blinded with a layer of your own weakness right up there on your visor. The suit's systems will clean it off but not fast enough to hide the shame of it.

"I tried to save her but… but when the EM field came back on she had some kinda fit. Bit her own tongue off. Thrashed about screaming and moaning and then she… stopped. I should've waited until we were safe, until we could have gotten her out of the suit and… and…"

"Enough!" I snap as if talking to a raw recruit. "You took the best action you could in the moment. Now, get control of your emotions or you're no use to the rest of us. Do you want to fail Zed too?"

"No… I… Without him I'd still be one of the crazy doctor's experiments."

This catches me off-guard. Still? "You mean he had others? I mean, more than the ones Zed mentioned?"

"Yeah, didn't you realize? He got way more. We was just the

first batch. Zed says it don't matter, that I shouldn't think about it, they're only Revs now but I don't believe it."

Something else I need to find out the truth of. If Hiroki is still experimenting on colonists or even nanite infested crewmembers it means… well, right now I don't have a clue what it means. Nothing good.

"Zed's back. Please, don't tell him I attacked you."

"Deal, but you owe me. Don't forget it." Actually, I'm pretty sure we aren't even all square given what I'd done to her face and I'd been the one to deliver her into Hiroki's hands in the first place, though you can look at it as being a better fate than being left as a revenant… all depends on how things work out.

Sarah pulls back, and I turn to face Zed. He gives me a thumbs up which I take to mean he's been able to sort out the connection to Char*on*'s chronometer.

His face falls—Sarah must be filling him in over the comm channel.

He stomps past her, takes a fistful of the vacbag, and starts marching off back towards the engineer's holdout. I exchange a look with Sarah and hold her gaze—she breaks eye contact first. I fall in behind Zed, allowing my lips to quirk in a smile.

CHAPTER 21

"Damnit, Kara. If we wasted our time and lost David and Akima for this and it doesn't even tell you anything, I'm gonna..."

"You're gonna what?"

"I don't know. Scream, I think. Go crazy."

"Relax and shut the fuck up, Zed. I need to do some calculations. Why don't you go get me something to eat and drink—something to help me concentrate. And while you're at it, clean up Akima's voidsuit."

"What?"

"It's a resource and it'll mean I don't have to be a silent and weak part of our little group."

He shoots me a hard look then coasts out of the compartment.

The terminal in front of me hums with streams of data. On the left is the raw input from the chronometer. On the right, the full spectrum returns from both forward radio dishes. Of course, this terminal has no simulated intelligence or clever dummy AI like the navicomputer. It has no program to process the data and our only datatech expert had died by having his head examined by a laser torch.

I bang my fist on the side of the terminal, making it fritz and sending me bouncing away. "Fuck!"

Grabbing a handhold, I suck in a breath and rub my stinging eyes. Tears are trying to well past my fingers but it only makes me grit my teeth and swear again. No fucking way am I going to give in to weakness.

A thought occurs to me. This is, at least in one sense, an elementary navigational problem. The issue isn't correlating the data itself, it's how much there is to correlate.

I open my eyes and stare at the screen. Looking for a recurring number in the chronometer feed. Focus until I can tune out the rest of it. Do the same thing with the feed from dish A, totally ignore dish B. Now I've started keeping track of the pattern, I expand my efforts until the deep hypno-training I'd undergone in the academy begins crunching the numbers for me. I get my answer just as Sarah floats into the room with a bag of water and a bag of green algae.

"Can you understand any of that?" She asks, her voice low and filled with a wary respect.

"Too much of it." I grab the water and drain it. Leave her holding the green slop. I've lost my appetite.

Zed has wrapped both the bodies of Ensign David Joud and Colonist Akima, last name unknown, in fabric torn from a vacbag. Akima's voidsuit bumps against the corner she'd used to hang her hammock, now Zed has lashed it there. I keep my eyes from the bodies.

"We have a major problem."

He glares up at me and I realize he'd been saying a prayer of some sort over their corpses. I never took him for a sentimentalist and certainly no one with any kind of spiritual leanings. Probably, some spacer superstition rather than real religion. Can't really blame him for it given all the shit he's been through.

"What?"

I ignore the snap in his tone. "You say it's been about eighteen months since this all started."

"Counted every voiddamned day. Most of them I've spent scratching around just to get enough air to breathe."

"That's subjective time. It's more than thirty months objective."

"Who gives a shit? Are we going too fast to slow down or what?"

"No... Unless..." I sigh, then shrug. "This is a situation I've never seen. The chronometer readings either mean we're approaching a massive body or we're experiencing time dilation at a rate way above the redline."

"But?"

"But the navigational fixes we've got are reliable, Cassiopeia A and a couple of well-known pulsars—3C58 and J0002+6216. Unless I'm getting the maths wrong, they're showing us travelling at a few per cent below the redline. Which makes no sense."

"Why not?"

"Because there aren't any massive stellar objects along our route to Gliese 892 and even if my calculations are off, the positional data means we can't be more than a few thousand AU off course."

"So?" He's proved himself far from stupid but his ignorance still stuns me.

"So there's no neutron stars, black holes, or whole rogue solar systems out here. Which means, either we've somehow been travelling for far longer than we think, or…"

"You're being fed the wrong data." Sarah's voice from behind me.

I spin to face her. "That would mean…"

"Akima heard your plan. She got taken over. It has to be that." Not as young and dumb as I expected.

I nod, mulling over what she said. "You're right. That's the only explanation, short of cooking up some irrational bullshit."

Zed looks from one of us to the other, mouth ajar. Shakes his head slowly. "Or maybe, you screwed up the calculations. You're not a computer, Kara."

I give him a withering stare until he swallows and waves a hand at me in mute apology. But I'm not about to let him off so easily. "Thank you. I think I know my own capabilities. I think being a ship's navigator trained and conditioned to do calculations in my head the average person couldn't even manage on hardcopy using a calculator might possibly qualify me to tell you when there's a problem with our data. And if you think I didn't check and recheck the damned calculations until I was satisfied…"

"Alright already. Lay off me. All you're telling me is we know nothing more than we did before we lost David and Akima."

Sarah snorts. "You two sound like my mum and dad."

As one, both Zed and I turn and say, "Shut up."

She colors—hydrogen emission pink behind her freckles—and for an instant I think she might cry. Instead, she bursts out laughing. "You two don't get it. It's all your stupid training, all your pushing for promotion. Zed, if all you wanted was out of the slum life you could have gone on one of the first colony ships, back when they were taking volunteers. But you wanted to be more important than that and you..." she turns to face me, "...you probably had it drilled into you from birth that you and your family were somehow better than the rest of us. That's bullshit—you're no better than me or any of the colonists. If you were so damned brave or special you wouldn't just be some glorified "airbus pilot. You both make me sick—here we are, facing the death of everyone and all you can do is bicker about who's smarter or who should be in charge."

Zed hangs his head but I'm having none of this self-righteous bullshit from a teenager.

"You know what happened to all those colonists who went before? The ones you believe were my equal? Dead. On every world we sent them. The first wave died, every last man, woman, and child. About the only good they did was fertilizing the ground for those who came after.

"And as for all of you? You're the infrastructure. The necessary cogs of the machine. That's all any of us are, but some of us are more useful. You're only fit to shovel shit from one place to another on one of these new worlds.

"People like me? We appear when there's something actually important, something every other deadbeat can't do." She opens her mouth, but this isn't an argument. "Do you know why a dumb nineteen-year-old would be sent on a mission to colonize a new world?"

"My mother is... was a—"

"I couldn't give a shit what she was or whatever degenerate squirted you into her in the first place. You have what, basic schooling?" She nods. "And I'm betting no skilled trade education, hell, you're far too young to have attended an academy."

"But the colony'll have a first-rate education..."

"Bullshit. You're on this ship for one reason." I pause, let the anticipation grow in her eyes. Watch her lips part to speak before I cut her off. "You're cheaper and more expendable than an artificial womb."

All the fight goes out of Sarah and I think she really does start to cry but she spins away to hide her shame. She has some shred of self-respect going for her after all.

Zed glowers at me. "How is destroying her self-confidence going to help? I mean, I knew you could be ruthless, but I never thought you were a shit just for the sake of it."

"What's the first thing they did to you in basic?"

"Made me run until I puked."

"How many times?"

"Every day for three months, I mean I stopped puking but..."

"But they got you into shape. That wasn't only physical though was it?"

I think he sees where I'm going. "No, they were toughening us up mentally too."

"No, Zed, baby. You've a talent for missing the point. They broke you right down so they could rebuild you, body and mind, as something useful to the corps and to our ultimate employers. Remember, it's the corporations that sponsor the academy and they want their new-jiao's worth. Well-trained, responsive crew for their ships."

"Uh huh. You're training her now, are you?"

"I don't have nearly enough time to do what you should have been doing over the last year. She thinks for herself—that is not an asset in an untrained soldier. What we want is for her to do what the hell we tell her without question until she's got skills and knowledge worth a damn."

"She's done well enough surviving and helping the rest of us survive this past year and a half."

"Oh, Zed. I give up with you sometimes, I really do. Now enough of this bullshit. We keep her under control, it's the only way to make sure she doesn't compromise our safety. Agreed?"

"I guess I don't have much choice. Now, what the hell are we going to do? Or is your plan for us to shout at each other until the Revs come?"

I pull out a rag and blow my nose—damn but zero-g makes me congested. "She has some potential, because unlike you, she saw the point I was making. The Revs—Gestalt, Complex, whatever—are hiding our true velocity. Means they could be hiding our true location by manipulating the data we receive."

"So what?"

"No, fuckwit. The question is not what, it's why?"

His eyes widen. "Because they don't want us to know the true situation."

"There you go. And I'm betting it's not just us but Hiroki—"

"Their puppet."

"—and whatever ITF forces are on board too. You know, it also serves their purposes to have you distrustful of Hiroki."

"He's a fucking traitor."

"Zed, you're a practical man," I smile inwardly at how he puffs up at any praise. Men! "Think it through. Then ask yourself—if the nanites can control the bodies of the revenants, can they also control their minds?"

"Huh?"

"Think. You've used total immersion simulators that feed a signal directly into your brain, haven't you?"

He narrows his eyes. "Yeah…"

"So, when you're in one, you can forget it. Buy into the false reality. It's one of the reasons we avoid complicated control systems on ships. Avoid the disconnect with reality."

"What's this got to do with anything?"

"Well, if they can control the minds of the revenants too, how do you know you're not experiencing a delusion while they're marching your body around the ship murdering your former crewmates?"

The look of horror on his face is almost comical. Yet my own words give me pause. I'd felt this fear a couple of times since waking but putting it into words makes it fully formed.

"You think we could be hallucinating all of this."

"We could, but how could we ever know? Let's focus on the practical. Act as if this is real and ask ourselves what it is the Gestalt gains by manipulating us. We can discount the Complex—they seem to focus on physical rather than psychological operations."

From the frown on his face I can see I've blown his tiny mind. "Snap out of it, Zed. I didn't tell you that to give you an existential crisis. The point is we don't know how much we're being manipulated. Instead of assuming everything is as it seems—and by the way, we've had our assumptions blown up—let's look at what the Gestalt is doing. What it wants."

"Ok. you're making my head ache, Kara."

"Good. Means you're using your brain." I hook myself into one of the hammocks. "They control the engines but not the navicomp. If they could control it through whatever they'd learned from me, they would do, but instead, they're sending false data out and starting and stopping the engines, seemingly at random."

"We'd assumed the engines were being fired to give gravity when Hiroki needed it."

"What if the assumption is wrong? Then why would they be doing it?"

"Trying to trick the navicomp somehow?"

"I think so. When they took me over, I had a distinct sense they'd plumbed my mind for the understanding of navigation so they could take us to a distant star system. They'd know they'd have to be careful to avoid destroying the ship by changing its orientation too much, another thing they would have learned from me. But what they didn't get is me physically accessing the navicomp and ordering a course change."

"They're trying to make the navicomp course correct to what it thinks is our true destination when it's really not."

"Yeah. It's what we'd do with the QI virus, if we wanted to change the ship's destination. You can't hack the navicomp because its simulated intelligence is hard-coded but you can hack the data input. Manipulate it."

"You mean Char*on* still thinks it's en route to Gliese 892?"

"Maybe. There's another possibility. A signal to Earth."

"What about it? You think the Gestalt's worried someone's going to send a rescue mission." Zed blows out between his lips in exasperation. "No fucking way they'd waste the money even if they could reach us."

I have to tread carefully, not give my contact with Hiroki away. "It's what doesn't make sense. Hiroki—if he's working for them—went to an awful lot of effort to keep the Comm Array pointing into the interference of the ramscoop's magnetic cowl. If the Gestalt wants to remain anonymous—make sure no record is left of it or our new destination—why not blow the array and be done with it?"

"It's too close to the engines—probably take the whole ship up if you did. On the other hand, it's centrally controlled. If they have control over all the ship's computers with the exception of the navicomp's dummy AI, then they could switch it off and make sure no one could realign it."

"Yeah. What if they wanted to transmit?"

"Sure, they could do that."

"No. I mean, what if they wanted to send a signal and we wanted to stop it."

"You'd cut the hard-line into the dish... No, that'd risk shorting out the other computers and then no engines and no magnetic cowl. I think the only way, short of going out and dismantling the dish by hand, would be to mechanically disable its ability to move."

"Doable?"

"Yeah, you'd obstruct it rather than cutting any of the controls for the same reason you'd risk destabilizing the ramscoop's field."

"Which is what I saw Hiroki doing when you came to rescue me."

"What?"

"The array began to move and he was racing to jam something into its mechanism."

"I didn't see that. Crazy fuck blew up an oxygen tank and disappeared in the confusion. Lucky it was mostly empty."

"If you'd have tried to talk to him instead of killing him, I wonder what he'd have said." A dark look crosses Zed's face.

"It's all about getting what he wanted. We thought that was you but obviously it ain't. His plans are a bit more cracked. Maybe he wants to protect them, sees them as some kind of pet project he can sell to the Corporation."

"So he's restricting communications to keep the secret from getting out? Make sure he's the only one who can deal? Come on, Zed. How's he going to manage it?"

"Maybe he figures if he can get you on his side then the two of you can find a way to get the ship on a course back to Earth. Put everything back into cold sleep. Maybe he figures the payoff would be worth it."

"Hiroki was never about the money or power. I don't buy that time under pressure and in isolation would make him become greedy. I think he's keeping the Gestalt from being able to communicate for another reason."

"Like what?"

"Like it's dangerous in some way."

"No shit it's dangerous…"

"Yeah, but I mean it communicating with Earth or the other colonies."

"You mean you think it's like a virus—it can be spread over the radio?"

"I don't know. Maybe."

"Where are we going with this?"

"You're not going to like this, but we have to meet Hiroki." Zed takes a sharp breath and I hold up my hand. "I'm not done. Then we need to find a way to contact the ITF. Find out what their part is in all this and whether we can help each other to solve this. Don't know about you, but I plan to live through this. You with me, or is your pride getting in the way?"

He growls at me. Actually, growls. Men. So easy to get them to revert to their baboon-like origins. But, slowly, he gets control of his temper.

He thumbs at Akima's voidsuit. "I reset it so you can use it. You're right. No point being sentimental. Better watch out for Sarah, though. She's likely to take it pretty hard, she sees you wearing it."

"Get her and let's get going." But I'm forgetting something. I need my suit's radio to communicate with Hiroki. The problem is how to get it into the other voidsuit without giving it away? Zed has floated down the passageway between the main area and the machine compartment, he'll be gone only a moment or two.

"Shit," I whisper. But maybe there's something I can do. I push off and drift over to where my voidsuit's stowed, bundled into a tight ball with the soft-shell helmet resting on top. Looking at it makes me wince at how vulnerable I'd been. This isn't the time to think about it though.

I pull the helmet open, detach the comm unit and slip it up my sleeve, just in time. Zed's voice comes from the tube, talking Sarah round to the necessity of making use of our available resources.

I do my best to avoid jerking away from what I've been doing. After all, there's no problem with me doing something with my old suit, now, is there?

"I understand," Sarah says. She glowers at me but there's something in her look that hasn't been there before. It's the hurt of someone who desperately wants my approval and has been told they've been found wanting. Part of the process of molding her into a useful crewmember. Hope for her yet.

"Let's get Hiroki first. And Zed, please let's try to treat him as if he has valuable information. OK? No getting revenge or losing sight of the need to keep… him… alive!"

"I get it." I think he tried to hide it, but he can't help glancing at Sarah.

CHAPTER 22

The difference in feel being in the fully-armored voidsuit instead of a stripped-down inner layer is immense. Instead of being frightened of every jagged surface, I now feel... invulnerable. It's false, of course—if I'm pulled down by enough Revs, they could overpower the suit's servos and eventually break one of the weaker seals. Either of my companions might be able to damage my suit enough to cause it to depressurize. And a trigger-happy ITF agent would have little trouble vaporizing me, armor or no. Still, I'm so much safer than I had been.

It comes with a major drawback though. The suit's comm channel is constantly buzzing with Zed and Sarah's inane chatter. Remarking on everything and stating the bleeding obvious. In many ways, I miss the silence of before. When the only time they spoke to me was when they had something worth saying. I sigh.

"Would you two cut the shit for a minute? We need to work out where we're going."

Zed's voice crackles over the radio. "You seem to have a pretty clear idea of that."

"Obvious first place to check is the main medibay. Shouldn't be too hard."

"If you say so." I take his tone for just being surly at me after I'd pointed out some of his failings. Give me a break, I've been through a lot and the façade of "playing nice" has slipped a bit. OK? You get a little out of touch of the soft side of social interaction when you've seen most of the people you know killed and your existence is hanging on by a fingernail.

"In the meantime... Sarah, I have a mission for you."

"For me? Sure a civilian can be trusted. I mean, I'm probably still trying to pick my nose through the helmet, right?"

"Fucking teenagers," I mutter to myself before keying the comms to respond. "Very funny. Enough of the backchat. Consider yourself an Interstellar Navy cadet and start acting like one. In other words, shut the fuck up when an officer is talking. Got it?"

She grumbles something.

"I said, got it?"

"Yes, ma'am."

"Better. Now, your task is this. Track through every single radio channel on your comm and transmit this. "Hailing ITF force on board *Sevran Corp Commercial Space Vessel Charon*. This is Cadet..." Wait, what's your surname, Sarah?"

"McKenzie."

"'This is Cadet McKenzie on behalf of senior officer, Acting Captain Kara Rozanski. Please respond.' Got it?"

"That's it? Why can't you do it?"

"Because I'm ordering you to. Now, will you or do I have to have Warrant Officer Hong lock you up for insubordination?"

I expect Zed to step in on her side here, as much to argue he doesn't take orders from me as anything else but to my surprise, he stays silent.

"No," Sarah says.

"No, what?"

"No, ma'am."

"Much better. Now if you get an acknowledgement you key me into it, you know how to do that, right?"

"Yeah... ma'am."

"Good. Zed, is there an access to the ventilation system around here? Anything big enough for us to fit in while in voidsuits?"

"In full voidsuits, no. But there is access. Why?"

"Wishful thinking. Looks like we're going to have to do this out in the open."

"The Revs haven't been very active in this area. Shouldn't be a problem." *Isn't it in the hands of* the *Complex?*

"What about the ones I saw skirmishing with the ITF?"

"What about them? Either they're all dead or they somehow managed to take down one of those fuckers. Don't see why they'd give two shits about the medibay."

I sigh for the hundredth time and negotiate my way around the drifting gore-spattered debris from a damaged computer terminal.

"Just stay… frosty." Time I start playing the role again and giving him the bullshit the ranks always seem to love.

"Always."

I roll my eyes. Then look him over as he stomps along next to me. He's carrying another vacbag, its material patched here and there using sealant tape. Doesn't seem to have anything in it. Probably a sign of the scavenger instinct that's kept him and the others alive all this time. Always be ready to carry away something of value.

My eyes play up the hard lines of the suit to the armored hosing at the back of his head. Carrying air and power to the helmet systems. I wondered whether the EM implant interferes with the functioning of his suit. It'd explain why his signal carries some distortion, Sarah's too. The thought of how easily they could become unthinking enemies tickles at the edges of my awareness. I push it back down.

They'd gone for months without a failure and it seems highly improbable another of the devices would fail so close to Akima's having done. Besides, I made them swap out their capacitors for a full charge and double-check their spares before we set out. Then again, obsolescence in any one system usually indicates it in all other systems of the same type. That's what the basic training in operational maintenance had taught me. Which means, the more I think about it, it's quite likely if one of the implants fails because it reached the end of its working life span, the others will too.

Zed must know this. I have to trust him. Trust he wouldn't risk all our lives by not dealing with the problem. Then again, what can he do? Hiroki had made them.

I tongue the activation stud on the comm unit from my old suit. There'd been enough time to fix it on the inside of my helmet where I can reach it and not enough time to try to integrate it with the systems.

"Hiroki? This is Kara. Are you receiving? Over."

There's a crackle of static which might be an acknowledgement from him, assuming the signal is too weak. Or it could just be interference.

"I can't hear you. I'll be at the medibay soon. Over and out."

"Rog..." static popping and cracking "...out."

Sounds like he got the message. I replay everything he'd said and done after waking me. It's hard to hold onto the details but I remember the feeling. There'd been something off about him and his behavior. Like he'd been concealing something. Was it the extent to which he'd been prepared to use the others as guineapigs in his efforts to save me? Some deal he'd struck with the Gestalt? Or something else entirely?

The time to confront him and find out is coming. Part of me wants to curl up and shy away from the responsibility. We're trained to reject that feeling, to push it down and force it into a box. So that's what I do.

We're at the corridor leading to the medibay. Here and there, traces of the blood that had been spilt are visible on the deckplates, dried and darkened to little more than black smears. Of the corpses, or parts of them, there's no sign. Probably drifted off into the engineering section, desiccated and frozen and smashed into a million pieces to break up more and more every time the ship accelerates and decelerates. Most of them would be little more than motes of dust by now, with the occasional grisly reminder of what had happened floating by—some barely identifiable fragment of dried flesh and hair, or splintered bone.

No sign of Hiroki. No sign of Revs. So much for the medibay being occupied by the Complex. One less thing to worry about.

"The vent behind us is a junction where three connect." I say. "Should be enough space for you both to huddle in."

"What are you going to do?" Zed asks, his transmission fizzing and popping even worse than before.

"Hiroki'll spook if he sees us. Let me check in the medibay, then... if I can get him talking, maybe we can do this without any stupidity."

Zed grunts. "So far, I ain't seen any of your plans follow

that particular strategy. Do it. We're here and ready if he doesn't come quietly."

I palm the suit's comms off, think about trying Hiroki again and give up on the idea. Instead, I grab the manual release on the medibay, noting how it's been jammed at some point since I left with M'Benga and Hiroki in tow. Left with Sarah sealed inside. Strange I'm now relying on her to watch my back.

The release vibrates in my hand as I use all of the suit's servo assist to grind it open. There's a small puff of air around the door-seal as it cracks open. Nothing from the room, only whatever had been held in the doorway.

Wedging my suit's gauntlet between door and the bulkhead, I yank it open in three goes. Inside, most of the equipment is dark but it's obvious where Hiroki had cut his way in and out of the back wall.

Several of the medibay's beds *are* occupied. Life support modules keeping the sleepers protected from the vacuum. Not as much protection as a casket would provide but then, these sleepers aren't frozen. Three of seven readouts are off. Presumably, the occupants are dead. The others have low-level lifesigns.

What the hell has he been up to?

My helmet fills with the crackle of an open transmission. I tongue the comm unit stuck by my chin.

"Kara-chan, I am almost there. Be warned. The Gestalt has been doing something. I think it is unhappy I have not kept up my end of the deal. Or rather, we have not kept it."

"Hiroki. You never told me exactly what your deal was."

"Didn't I? Hard to keep focused. I will be at the medibay in two or three minutes. The Complex have found a way to move about the ship in makeshift voidsuits. I was attacked a short while ago. Be careful. They're dangerous."

This is old news but there's no way he can know that. "Understood. Over and out."

I look about but see no sign of any revenant activity. No surprise there. Even if they've cobbled together a few voidsuits, they can't have enough to all be roving the ship.

As I wait for Hiroki, I wander over to one of the active life support couches. The patient's face is visible through the plastic layer which forms a bubble over their chest and head. It doesn't exactly seem secure but the patient—a young Asian man—has his arms and legs out of sight under the metal casing which sheaths the rest of his body.

As I lean in to look at his face, his eyes flutter open and focus on mine. His mouth starts working, as if he's struggling to speak or shout and he thrashes about. A nanite infested colonist? I'm not so sure. His behavior seems more desperate than irrational.

"Excuse me while I sedate him again."

I nearly leap out of my voidsuit in shock and I'm pretty sure I've just topped off the suit's urine recyc. Spinning round isn't easy in the ungainly shell but as quick as I can, I come face-to-face with Hiroki. He looks much the same as last I'd seen him, save for some fresh scratches in the paintwork of his voidsuit and darker shadows around his eyes. Right now, his attention's on the man in the life support couch. Administering something via a port in the side. The man's struggles lessen and his eyes flutter shut.

"He is not ready to wake yet. Excuse me while I check the others." Hiroki moves to the other couches and I watch as he pauses to deliver a slight bow beside each of the couches where life signs have gone blank.

"What're you doing with them?"

"Trying to use a cure."

"Hiroki, given some of the things I've heard about what you've been up to, you really need to give me more than that. Now is the time for total honesty."

He sighs, loud enough to be audible over the comms, and turns to face me, a deep scowl creasing his forehead. "Medicine has a long history of fighting one pathogen with another. First it was using penicillin—a mold—to fight bacteria. Years later we gene-tailored viruses to fight antibiotic resistant bacteria and eventually to strike back against the viruses which threatened us most. Finally, we began using nanotech for the same purpose. I've merely adapted the idea."

"I'm not following. Are you talking about using a computer virus…?"

"No, that would be a technological solution, I grant you but it is also beyond me. Instead, I tried numerous physical solutions. The electromagnetic field, which you no doubt have seen has limited results…" I think of Akima and nod. "…and now this."

"What?"

"What do you say? Fight fire with fire."

"You're using nanotech to fight the Gestalt's nanites. Are you fucking crazy?"

"Not at all. It is not very effective—the nanites I have made have to be primitive to avoid being integrated by their targets. They are simple, chemically driven machines with no processors, no "brains" of their own. This is a carrier of the Complex. I have found a way to "remove" it one nanite at a time and without the risk of brain damage the EM field created. What will work for the Complex will work for the Gestalt."

"OK, so you aren't working with them. Hiroki, I didn't want to doubt you but…"

"Oh, I am working with them. Just not how Zed and his companions believe. You see, I had begun to tell you of my mistake."

"The splitting of the revenants into factions. Yeah, I know. But the others, they think you're being played."

"It is… possible. The Gestalt is highly logical. It wants to survive and it knows killing us or trying to control us is not its most efficient means of doing so. For now, at least."

"What are you doing for it?"

"I was going to help it adjust course safely to its chosen destination. Then find a way for it to exist without the need for hosts."

"Giving it what it wants? That's a bad move."

"No, it was a compromise. But I suspect what it really wants is to send a signal back to Earth."

"Why? It can't infect people back home. There aren't that many who'd have this kind of nanite."

"You pay little attention to the changes in the world whenever we return. Remember we talked of United America's defense plan?"

"Not really. Wait, we discussed this... something to do with aerosol dispersal of what did you call them? Nano-defenders. Oh… Oh shit."

"Yes. I believe if the Gestalt could send a signal to Earth, it could spread to all of the nanotechnology on the planet. What is inside people is less worrying than the kind that does not need a host. That can replicate itself from available resources."

"You mean it'd scourge the planet, don't you? Hell… every colony too, right?"

"Either that or infect the whole population, yes."

"Then why help it?"

"Because it is not willing to risk its own survival to achieve its aim. And I have come to believe it is not doing this to hurt us, but out of ignorance. It did not understand we are conscious beings. Communication is the key to learning from it. Removing the threat it poses. Harnessing all the good it could do for us. But…"

"But the Complex wants none of that."

"No. It sees us all as a threat which must be neutralized. It is so much more aggressive I fear without help its logical counterpart is doomed. And then, so are we."

"Doc, I got to tell you, if there's some way we can eradicate both of these things, we got to do it. We can't trust them. They're not… human."

His face reddens and his voice grows thick with anger. "I will not contemplate the destruction of a new level of evolution because you are afraid. We are not like the savages of the past, even if we still carry their primitive natures within us."

"Doc, our survival and the survival of everyone on Earth has to come before this Gestalt. It's not alive. It's… they're machines. Tools we made that turned against us. If there's a way to switch them off…"

"No, you don't understand at all. This cure, it takes so long to work. I could free maybe ten in a year. And they have nearly all hundred thousand colonists. The intellect—the web that makes up their mind—is more complicated than yours or mine. Their consciousness is deeper and more refined. We do not have the right to end it. And more. Unless we can find a way to coexist with them, we would have to annihilate every last trace of them here. We simply cannot do that."

Hiroki's eyes widen. I see why in the reflection from the faceplate of his helmet. Zed and Sarah have entered the medibay.

"I think we've heard enough, Doctor. You're coming with us." Zed advances, holding the vacbag loosely in one gauntleted hand and the bulkhead shears like a club. Sarah advances, the laser torch that had burned Joud's life out clutched in her left hand while her right holds the other end of the vacbag.

"Kara…" Hiroki groans.

"Zed, you can't… this is a mistake. Stand down."

"No, Kara. Knew you couldn't be trusted. Always thought you were so much smarter than the rest of us. We heard everything you've said since we rescued you from this lunatic. You and your secret transmissions… Seems you've always been on his side. Huh?"

I back up a step, looking around for something to use as a weapon. Sarah raises the laser torch, reminding me in that instant of how easily Akima had burned through Joud's helmet. Any trace feeling of invincibility I feel wearing the armored voidsuit evaporates.

Hiroki reacts in a way I don't expect one bit. He smiles.

"It is as they said it would be."

Zed growls and moves forward.

"I wouldn't." Hiroki holds up one gauntleted fist. In it is a device with a button on top.

Zed stops. "A bomb, doctor?"

"In a manner of speaking. This will switch off your implants. Come one step closer and you'll re-join the ranks of the revenants."

"Bullshit." Zed says, but he stays still.

"We should fucking kill him after what he's done to us… to Akima and Joud."

"Quiet, Sarah." I say. "Zed, you know Hiroki. Or you knew him. You ever play him at cards?"

"No. Officers and ranks. They don't mix well, do they, Kara?"

True. Very true. I can't help but agree with him. You might not like it, most people don't. But we know there's a difference. Not how clever you are. Not how successful. But the main difference between a slum rat and one of us? You know if you give the slum rat money and watch them spend it on the most gaudy and nasty things possible. Or leave one of us destitute and see how they suffer with dignity. There's a... qualitative difference. It's got nothing to do with wealth, education, or ethnicity. Something less definite than those things. They used to call it class. I still do. But where they meant it in a bullshit rigid social sense, I mean it in what you can expect of someone. I have it, so does Hiroki. M'Benga despite our differences was a prime example. The Captain? She had it in spades. Zed... not so much. It's why he's a non-commissioned officer and always will be. Not just about his ability—he simply lacks class. Still, doesn't need to be a problem.

I come forward, placing myself in front of Zed and Sarah with Hiroki behind me. Both of them tense and raise their weapons but I think Zed sees I'm giving him a way out. Sees there's another option if he'll only give himself time to calm down.

"Zed, you may say a lot of things about me, but you know, I always had a good eye for my fellow officers. Sized them up as part of my promotion strategy, you might say. Who was a safe bet and reliable. Who thought they always knew best. Who was predictable and who you could never be sure of. M'Benga—she was predictable as clockwork but you give her a hand of cards and you never knew what she was going to do. She and I were never friends... but she trusted me. Gave her life for me. I'll never forget it." It's true. I never will. If only to make sure I never let myself end up in such a stupid position of so-called noble self-sacrifice. "Hiroki here, he's a bit flighty. Used to be you couldn't be sure if he'd panic or get over-excited about things. But cards? You could read him every time. Always called when he had a good hand. Always folded when his cards were poor."

"You're saying we should believe him 'cause you used to play cards together." Sarah spits. "Fuck it, Zed. They're in this together. It's her fault Akima's dead, as much as it's his."

Zed lowers the bulkhead shears. "Maybe, but I think Akima was doomed long before Kara came back. So Hiroki did it for her benefit, so what? She was unconscious, frozen. If you can't blame Akima for what she did to David, I'm thinking we can't blame Kara here. And right now, she has a point."

"Yeah?" Aggressive little shit, is Sarah. Guess I'm no good at breaking them down to build them up after all. But who cares, right? Not like I've ever wanted to take on a teaching job at the stupid Academy anyway. Captain or bust. That's what I tell myself.

"Yeah. She's saying Hiroki don't bluff. Maybe she's lying, it comes easy to her." I bite back a comment. "And maybe she's wrong. But, shit, Sarah. We can't take the risk."

"Zed? Come on!"

"I'm telling you to put the torch down. Let's see where this goes. We don't like it—we go back to plan A and screw the consequences." He slings the shears over his shoulder and starts gathering up his end of the vacbag. What the hell they'd planned to do with it is anyone's guess. Stuff us in the bag? Seems pretty stupid as plans go but they were desperate.

"That's better." I say. "Now, maybe we can talk about..." I break off as an atmo alert flashes across my HUD. "This can't be right."

"You're getting it too?" Hiroki.

"I don't understand." Sarah.

Only Zed stays silent. I could see from the way he closes his eyes and grits his teeth he realizes what this means for our survival chances.

I watch as the external monitor registers pressure and the presence of oxygen. It creeps up to one atmosphere.

Breathable.

Air.

"We're in the shit now, aren't we?" Zed.

"Those *kuso yarō*..." Hiroki.

Sarah stands there with her mouth open and doubt in her eyes.

"Whatever we were going to do," I say. "Whatever you were going to do, Hiroki. It doesn't matter. The Comm Array. We need to make sure they can't get it facing Earth."

"I jammed the motor so it couldn't reposition itself. They would need time to repair it," Hiroki says.

I crack my helmet seal. There was no point using up the suit's reserves when all around me is breathable air again. I expect the first breath to sear my lungs with cold, but there's never been anything wrong with Char*on*'s life support system. Only a gaping hole in the hull.

The air carries strange odors. I imagine they'll get worse as the frozen and fragmented remains of the dead begin to defrost and rot. If desiccated flesh can rot. I push the thought away and focus on where we are and what we're doing.

"It's breathable. Come on. Stop wasting time."

Zed cracks his helmet's seal and it retracts to its storage position behind and over his left shoulder. The others follow, Hiroki—cautious as always—comes last.

"How long 'til they overrun us?" Zed asks.

"We've got to get somewhere defensible quick," I say. "Wait. Without proper weapons, we're going to be helplessly outnumbered. The armory's out. Any ideas?"

"Breach the hull again?" Hiroki asks. Seems like a stupid question coming from him.

Zed snorts. "Can't risk it. Bad enough suffering one decompression like that. Another might do enough damage to the ship's systems we'd lose the engine or ramscoop or just, well you know, boom."

"You think the whole ship's been re-pressurized?" I ask.

"Yeah. Probably… It'd be automatic as soon as the environmental monitor detected no more leak. I mean, it wouldn't happen all at once but each compartment in sequence away from the site of the hull breach would be re-pressurized."

"Fuck." I wipe my face, noticing how much I'm sweating. The walls are coated in condensation—some beginning to freeze in places only to melt again as the heat from the air slowly warms the surfaces.

"Isn't this a good thing?" Sarah asks.

We all spin to face her at once. Of all the naïve questions she could have asked, none reveal her for what she is—an ignorant kid—than those few words.

"Nah, kid." Zed. "We're screwed. Revs'll be able to go anywhere in the ship they want. Bet there are thousands of them out by now."

"You think so?" Her eyes are so wide you can see their whites all around.

"The doctor here re-pressurized one of the cargo bays, ain't that right?"

Hiroki. "Yes. Only one of them. It was necessary. But there were no conscious revenants in there at the time."

"Yeah, but what about after your little experiments backfired, huh? We weren't the only ones to get away from you, were we?"

"No, you were not. The others were... they had reverted to aggression. I didn't realize they had formed a separate gestalt, this Complex as Kara calls it." Zed snorts but Hiroki ignores him. "They had no voidsuits... How was I to know they could build them or they might rely on the emergency air supply in their wearalls?"

"You don't slip off the hook that easy, Doc. That's ten thousand Revs ready to go with another ninety thou soon after. This is all your fault." Zed balls his free hand into a fist and waves it around as if he's about to strike Hiroki. The doctor waves the trigger he holds, in turn.

"Enough!" I bark. "This bickering is pointless. We've got a few minutes, if that, before they swamp us. Now, I know you don't believe it but if we're lucky, really lucky, Hiroki is right and there are two factions, two separate gestalts."

"How the fuck would that make us lucky?" Zed asks, turning the heat of his anger on me. There's the look in his eyes again—like when we'd found the first body. Only this time, he isn't staring over the edge. He's sailed over and is looking at the ground rushing up at him.

"There's a good chance they'll fight each other. Give us time, not much but a little. The ITF. They're our only hope. Whatever they're doing—and let me tell you I have my suspicions—they're as fucked as we are. They'll need our help."

"Those cunts will fucking vaporize us." Sarah, finally snapping out of her dazed state.

Zed bares his teeth, the gaps reminding me again of what'd be done to him. "Better dead than one of those things again. Right?" I don't like the wild look in Zed's eyes but for now, I can harness his fatalism. Sarah's eyes flick away from his gaze. Maybe she's reassessing her loyalties about now.

"Let's get going," I say. "Zed you take point, Sarah you stay tight to Hiroki."

They look at each other, each sizing the other up, but Zed's already started moving and when I snap, "Now!" they both leap to do as I order.

Back in command, at last.

CHAPTER 23

The ventilation system is far too efficient—it sucks up every trace of organic matter that'd turned to dust and distributes it evenly through the air. The larger pieces had floated into vents and remain stuck there against the grills save for those places where revenants had crawled in and left the vents open behind them. Some of those who'd crawled into the vents had never crawled out, and now the air can get to them, the stench of their decay is also blown throughout the ship. It's a huge volume of air, but the human nose is a sensitive thing and everywhere is pervaded by the meat odor of death. Not strong, but there, at the edge of awareness. Tickling the nostrils with the promise we'll soon be joining the dead to rot together in this interstellar mausoleum.

Heavy thoughts dog my every step. Zed's looking for a fight—that much is clear. Sarah's nearly as much of a risk, though more from ignorance of the greater danger we're now in than from pure recklessness. Hiroki… well, he's twitching and jittering as he always has but now and then I'll catch him falling still with a calculating gleam in his eye. He notices me looking and offers a faint smile. Which I immediately distrust.

As I reflect on his reaction to the return of atmosphere, it feels more and more staged and I convince myself he'd somehow known about it before hand. Call it a hunch or instinct or the power of the subconscious mind putting together clues my waking self hasn't even picked up on. Whatever it is, I find my distrust for him peaking.

And of course, there's one thing we've not done. No time to and it *had* slipped my mind so it *could* have slipped his. But that isn't like him. Where was any effort to scan my brain and test whether the nanites were truly gone? It puzzles me that he claims to have a cure of sorts yet with me the nanites had voluntarily withdrawn.

"Let's hope the Revs haven't swarmed the engine compartment," Zed says. From the way he hefts the bulkhead shears, I'm not at all certain he means it. More like, "let's hope there's enough to go round."

Though life support's returned, the engine compartment remains dark; lit here and there by a dim glow from active machinery—the sections governing the ramscoop's magnetic cowl, and those on standby, primed for the ion drive to engage.

"Where are they?" I ask.

"Maybe there ain't that many of the cunts," Sarah says. "I mean, we only just got air, so there can't have been that many out of caskets, can there?" Aussies and the "c" word. Not sure if I'm more shocked at her language or that she's forgotten the ten thousand colonists turned rev who've been waiting for this chance.

I look to Hiroki—his jaw is clenched tight, holding his mouth shut against the words that want to spill out. His return of self-control is as impressive as its timing is frustrating. Even if the words would be in Japanese, hearing him articulate every thought might let me get a handle on whether he's truly a threat or whether I'm buying into Zed's paranoia.

"Let's check." I break from the group, deactivate my magboots and kick off in the direction of the nearest engineering terminal. "Coming?" I call back over my shoulder.

Hiroki frowns but joins me. Over the time I'd been on ice, he'd learned to handle zero-g like a pro. About damn time. It also confirms my main concern about him—not the insanity of talking to himself, nor the way he's got control of the habit so fast. He's gone from being a shy, bumbling academic to having a self-assurance I'd never seen in him.

I catch a handhold and swing my feet into contact with the deck. From the perspective of where I had been, I'm now standing on the ceiling. But in zero-g everything's upside down. All the damn time.

"One thing we've learned is the Gestalt—at least I'm assuming it's the Gestalt—doesn't seem like the other one's way of doing things. Anyone, one of them at least, is interfering with the data from the ship's forward radio dishes. Either that or screwing with the read on the chronometer. But I'm betting it hasn't chosen to do so with every system on board."

"What are you looking for?" Hiroki asks.

"You'll see. Zed, remember when we found all the caskets showed positive life readings even when they were empty?"

"Yeah. Fucked up any chance of tracking the spread of revenants."

"We were pretty dumb. Something obvious we missed."

"Oh yeah?"

"Watch." I pull up Char*on*'s power management system. It immediately confirms life support power to three quarters of the ship, but Cargo bays three, eight, and ten have minimum power. No life support. Then I pull up the casket power usage. Not quite what I'd expect.

"Accessing this is dangerous, Kara-chan. If the Gestalt is monitoring terminal usage, they will know where we are."

"Relax, Hiroki. Kara's right," Zed says. "We need to know what to expect. You know, this is pretty fucking obvious as a way to track casket usage."

"Yeah. Not fool-proof and maybe it wouldn't have worked at first. Casket gets opened and its power draw increases then tails off."

"Why?" Sarah asks.

I look to Zed. "Er… right, well…" he stammers.

"Decanting someone from a casket involves a change in the state of the casket's systems," Hiroki says. "Typically, creating a greater demand on the coolant system before it is switched to rapid warming. After revival, maintaining even a false monitoring cycle would not require the coolant system to be as active and there'd be no need for the life support equipment to circulate cryoprotectants through the occupant's body. It'd show a small power differential. Unless the casket's on battery."

"How long's the casket back up power supply last?" I ask.

"Six to eight months on a standard model," Zed says. "Two years on a VIP or crew model."

"You mean, the colonists had some second-rate caskets?" Sarah asks.

"Now you're getting it," I say. "Corporation values every life according to a new-jiao value. Colonists get the cheapest shit for a reason." She scowls but I ignore her and turn back to the terminal screen. "Here we are. That can't be right?"

"What is it?" Sarah asks.

Zed swears.

Hiroki remains silent.

"*Charon* is not supplying power to any of the caskets. Not a single fucking one. And there's not even any attempt to hide it."

"Which means what?" Sarah asks.

"Means either they're all on battery power or they've been opened," Zed says. "Means we're outnumbered about a hundred thousand to four."

"Not quite, Zed," I say. "Look at this. The three bays without life support are also showing as inoperative."

"You mean on battery?"

"No… Look, the system is totally open. No sign of the previous tampering. Like it's been purged and reset. See—all caskets reading no on-board power draw or draw from the ship." I pause, blinking my eyes to clear them. "Look at them go."

Zed leans over me. "What?"

"Last couple of lifesigns crashing flat… and there's all of them."

"You're telling me thirty thousand colonists are dead. Fuck." Zed grabs Hiroki by the shoulder. "Your fucking 'evolving gestalt' has just murdered thirty thousand people. Or you gonna claim it's the bad one?"

"I… I can't explain why it would do this. It cannot be the Complex. The Gestalt was stronger when it came to managing computer systems. That was the balance of power between them."

"Unless there's only ever been one side, you fucking idiot." Zed raises his fist to strike Hiroki, the doctor standing there with his jaw slack.

"Enough! Leave him alone," I bellow. "Hiroki… Doc, pull

it together. You said the nanites are still active in dead tissue?" Hiroki nods dumbly. "But inoperative in cold sleep?"

He looks at me, eyes blank.

"Snap the fuck out of it!" I clang a gauntleted fist off the armored plate of his chest.

"Yes. Yes, inoperative. They cannot move about between cells, and their communication is limited."

"The bastards killed thirty thousand people so they could increase their computational advantage, right?"

He looks at me, hesitating a moment. "Yes. I don't understand why they'd do this. They promised they didn't want to harm us…"

"You been played, Doc. Damn near doomed the lot of us too. We live through this, I'm gonna see you get spaced for this, you piece of shit." Zed growls.

"I said leave him alone," I square up to Zed, looking up into his eyes without blinking. Like an animal, he can't take it and looks away. "Good. Get a fucking grip. Why it's done it doesn't matter. Where the fuck are they?"

Sarah comes forward. "Zed, what if we've been wrong? What if the doctor is telling the truth? Maybe the two sides, the Revs and the gest-alt thing are fighting it out?"

"Yes. Yes, it could be." Hiroki raises his head, a bright look in his eyes. "If the split was more even than I realized. There would be no choice between them. It might mean…" He falls silent.

"What?" I ask. Scowling.

"No time," Zed shouts. "Incoming."

I look up towards the forward section of the engineering bay. In the dimness, a cloud of dark shapes is drifting towards us. As some of them come into the light of active terminals, the true scope of what's happening is revealed.

There are knots of revenants tearing into each other in a roiling mass of blood and violence. Coming on at us as a churning nebula of death.

"We've got to move people!" Zed shouts. He grabs at me. Doesn't have to tell me twice.

"There's so many of them…" Sarah's standing there, legs

gone loose and swaying.

"Kick off now. That's an order!" I scream in her face, then hurl myself free of the deck away from the oncoming tide and fire the vacsuits thrusters—three percent… two percent—to blast me towards the rear of the engineering bay.

She shakes off her shock and thrusts herself after me. I look about for Hiroki but can't see him. Bastard must've switched off his suit's lights. Which isn't a bad idea.

"Turn off illumination. Don't make it any easier for them to find us." I flick mine off and look back to see Sarah has gone dark but Zed is still anchored to the deck. The lights from his suit torso bright under his face, letting me see the look of grim determination there even from a hundred meters away.

"Zed!" I bellow. "Zed you fucking idiot, get out of there!"

The lead edge of the cloud is less than ten meters from him now.

Whatever he's doing involves the bulkhead shears. Cutting into the deck beneath him. Suddenly the shears go whirling away, and Zed reels back being buffeted about in a haze of gas. He engages his helmet, and looks up towards us, mouthing something.

I hit the command icon on my wrist, my helmet unfolding into place.

"…clear. Over."

"Zed!" I scream.

"Stop them. Kara, you've never thought of anyone but yourself. But you can be better than that. Remember this. Sarah, watch yourself. Grow up and have children. Carry it on. Now both of you get clear!"

The first revenants close on him, streaked with blood and gore from others they've torn apart and their own injuries. They grab Zed. He raises his right hand—I can't see what's in it but I can soon guess. It must be his kine lighter. I wonder if he ever had the smoke he'd been craving when we woke.

He holds his right hand out into the stream of escaping gas and it bursts into flame. Fire in zero-g pulses in waves. It's beautiful and terrible as it flows over surfaces and drifts in cascades of liquid flame. But this jets out in a roiling detonation of flame that bisects the engine compartment and leaves a curtain of flame into which the revenants hurtle. Each set ablaze, they fly on like comets, burning, cartwheeling on top of each other. Dying. Unable to stop. The explosion tossing them about in all directions.

The shockwave from the initial detonation hits me, hurling me out of control. I hit the 'suit's stabilizing thrusters and fire a full burn forward… but too late. Crash into the rear bulkhead. Manage to get one foot down and locked in place. Sarah slams into the deckplates beside me—she scrabbles at them as she bounces away but I catch one ankle and pull her back down.

Zed has disappeared, engulfed in the blaze. I want to believe he could live through it. Believe his voidsuit is tough enough to survive it. Wishful thinking.

"What'd he do? What'd he do? Zed!" Sarah is sobbing.

"Must have cut a fuel line to one of the navigational thrusters. That's pure hydrogen and oxygen burning. It'll cut out in a moment. Or the fire'll burn up inside the line and blow out half the compartment. Probably set off a chain reaction with the fusion rockets and blow the ship to hell."

Her eyes are wide and filled with horror at my words.

"Don't worry. Zed knew what he was doing." Well, I hope he had. Stupid thing to do, throwing his life away for us. Not that I'm not grateful. Just… What a damn fool.

With the light from the fire, the whole rear bulkhead is bright and visible.

"There's the rear airlock. Come on. We better hope the ITF are still alive and not in the mood to shoot first and ask questions later." She doesn't answer. Still in shock from Zed's sacrifice, no doubt. It's going to be a problem if she can't get control of her emotions. "Move, Sarah."

She starts to follow me and as abruptly as the fire had exploded into life, it cuts out. Here and there, burning corpses illuminate the dark spaces of the compartment as they fly in all directions. The smell of burning flesh is overpowering and worst of all is how good it smells. Like barbequed meat. My stomach rumbles with both hunger and nausea combined. I close off the external atmo sampling and breathe the cool air of my suit's internal supply—it's never smelt so clean.

The airlock's only a few feet away when it irises open. An armored figure, sleeker in line than our voidsuits but sharper and deadlier looking, emerges. Its helmet is a blank mask of black metal, whoever's inside must be seeing us only through external cameras.

"Don't make any sudden moves!" I radio to Sarah.

I raise my hands palms outward and hope Sarah is doing the same behind me. The armored figure raises one of its hands too, but this holds a compact silver gun, its barrel nothing more than a collection of tines and antennae. The end of it fluoresces and I close my eyes in expectation of the fatal flash.

Even with the rapid modulation of my helmet's visor cutting the intensity of the light, it sears a purple line across my vision. Then another. By the time of the third, I realize I'm still alive and not experiencing existence as a cloud of vaporized matter.

I glance behind me and see Sarah standing with her hands thrust up in front of her face as if to shield herself from a maser blast. Drifting towards us is a trio of revenants who've escaped the fire. Two of them tearing into the third until he falls limp. His killers look up and fix their attention on Sarah and me. A brilliant flash slashes across my vision and one of the revenants vanishes in a haze of superheated gas. The last is close enough I can reach out and touch her, then she's gone, leaving only steam and cinders, and my suit alarm pinging a brief radiation warning. The last revenant, contorted in death, drifts past me close enough I can look into his eyes and see the terror of the man he had been locked within, though his features are passive and blank.

Opening my comms to a broad-spectrum channel and turning slowly back to face the black-suited figure, both hands held out to the side, I say, "We surrender."

CHAPTER 24

The airlock cycles and our captor gestures with the gun in a way I take to mean to remove my voidsuit. I slowly move my left hand to my right wrist and key for my helmet to retract. There's a background hum of active terminals and other machinery. A faint smell reminiscent of the medibay before everything went to shit.

Still holding up both hands, I try to keep my voice calm and level. "I am Lieutenant-Commander Kara Rozanski, ranking officer and acting Captain of Sevran Corporation Commercial Space Vessel *Charon*. I formally request assistance."

The ITF agent's voice comes through the suit's external speakers in a processed, robotic sound. It gives nothing of gender or mood away, conveying only distance and artificial coolness. I imagine it's meant to be unsettling. "Commander, on behalf of the UN World Government I accept your request. This ship and all crew members are now under the direct authority of the UNWG's International Task Force. Do you concur?"

Surrendering my authority without an explanation of their presence or a chance to know who I'm giving command over to. I grit my teeth but there's a gun on me and living hell at my back. What else can I do? I nod.

"For the record, please state your acquiescence."

"Alright, dammit. Yes, I agree ITF authority supersedes Corporate authority during the period of this emergency."

With a slight hiss of equalizing air pressure—probably done for dramatic effect, typical of these hard-core military types—the agent's helmet folds back in segments and stows itself in a compartment behind her head. She's about my age, maybe a year or two older but with a face which looks like it's seen more mileage. Bad analogy maybe, since I've done over a half century of lightyears by this point and I doubt she's been out of the solar system before. You get the idea though, right? Scars from blades, laser burns, and a hard set around the eyes leaves her with a perpetual scowl. She'd fit in well next to M'Benga in a line up for most permanently pissed off.

"Major Xenia Ahmad. ITF, interstellar division. Commander?" She lowers her gun and extends her other hand.

I take it and shake it once. I like to think you can tell a lot about a woman from her handshake. Is she one of those who tries to be masculine and crush the bones in your hand? Is she afraid of having a firm grip and so clasps your hand with limp indifference? Is her palm sweaty and does she look you in the eye? You can tell less about men, but then again, there's less to tell.

All I can say of the Major, given the voidsuit gauntlets in the way, is she holds my grip and my gaze for long enough to assert dominance and make it clear the handshake ends when she decides and not me. Probably a result of all the steroids they pump these troops full of—she'd have gotten on well with Zed…

Zed, you damn fool.

"This mission is a total FUBAR," the Major says.

Army speak. I can handle this, though the Interstellar Navy is almost completely commercial in its operations. "It certainly is fucked up. Surprised to find the ITF piggybacking our ship."

"New operation. I would say it was classified but I think we're way beyond that, aren't we? Who's this?"

"Sarah McKenzie."

"The cadet you had broadcasting on wide band?"

"Yes. She's a colonist, really."

"I see. What about the others? The medical officer and the engineer?"

"Doctor Hiroki Ishihara disappeared and Warrant Officer Hong gave his life to save ours."

"He caused that explosion?"

"Yes."

"Brave man," She says raising her eyebrows then letting

them fall and pursing her lips. "The doctor. Yeah, he's been on my target list since I woke to this mess. I need information. Do you know how this started?"

"Er… you mean you don't?"

"No. I've been up for maybe the last three months. Automatically woken when we detected the ship had gone substantially off course. I've reviewed our security footage but there's not much to go on."

"You mean you don't even have access to Char*on*'s systems? What the hell's going on? Why are you here?"

Major Ahmad sighs and holsters her weapon. "You'd better come with me."

She leads us through a cramped cold sleep chamber about half the size of Char*on*'s crew chamber. The walls are filled with monitors and three massive caskets are hooked up and showing green lights with three ordinary sized ones showing as offline.

"This is the ops center for this mission. I'm in command and in the caskets are my troops."

"They're fucking huge!" Sarah says, her voice very small.

"They're naukara, aren't they?" I ask.

"Yes. Ranger class, configured for maximum planetside tactical utility. No damn use here and now."

"I don't get it. Aren't these like cyborg killing machines? I've heard the stories. You could wipe out the revenants with them, couldn't you?" I suppress a shudder at the thought of the scraps of human inside the caskets, hooked up to their lethal and efficient hardware.

"Yeah. I could." She leads us deeper into the vessel, into a crew area with a command section and cockpit off to one end. "But that's not going to happen."

Single user airlock beside the cockpit. A shuttle then. "Why not? You could end this."

"Yeah, my second-in-command thought so. Then we checked on the status of our infil team."

"Infil team?"

"Infiltration. They were all set as what you probably call 'Ghostfaces'."

I run a gauntleted hand through my sweat drenched hair.

"So I wasn't imagining things? They're real and aboard ship."

"They were," the Major says. "We had two hidden amongst the colonists and one in with the colony leadership. Then this virus broke out and..." she claps her hands together. "All over. When Mikhail, Pascal, and I were woken by the ops computer we had messages filled with gurgling and growling that changed to coherent demands we join them. Then silence. First thing we did was to check on their status—all showing as deceased. Mikhail and Pascal went to investigate—reported the ship had been depressurized and filled with corpses. They tried accessing the ship's systems only to find some kind of computer virus had taken over everything save the navicomp and it refused to recognize our authority."

"Why not?" I ask, best to play dumb until I've assessed her motives.

"You'd have to ask Sevran Corp why they refused to grant ITF any override access to their properties. Anyway, I lost contact with both Mikhail and Pascal shortly after they went to investigate one of the cargo holds in an attempt to locate any surviving crew. Since then, I've been doing my best to prevent anyone from gaining access to the systems here."

"You killed Riggs!" Sarah blurts, her fists balled.

The Major's brow furrows. "Probably. I had to shoot several of these crazed colonists and crewmembers."

"We've been calling them revenants," I say, scowling at Sarah until she grits her teeth. "Took us a while to work out why they were acting the way they were. Some of the crew bought in to the old spacer's tales about people coming out of cold sleep possessed or with a different personality. Name kind of stuck."

"Well, whatever. Anyone who came close enough to pose a threat and failed to satisfactorily identify themselves was eliminated. Standard operating procedure in a hostile environment. Same way we dealt with terrorists, back in the day."

"But Riggs was ok," Sarah says. "He was like me. Just trying to survive."

"He was a threat and I neutralized him," Major Ahmad glares at Sarah until the younger woman looks away. "I've weighed up the risks of booting up the boys here," she gestures to the oversized caskets, "but it's too dangerous. If this infection spread to them..."

"I get it. Our doctor, Hiroki, he believes it's developed into two AIs. A more rational one he's called the Gestalt and a savage one—the Complex— seems to have been corrupted by the programming in your infiltrators' equipment."

"Ghostface tech. It's basically a batch of nanites that alter the appearance of an agent's face and can even change some other physical characteristics. If they got into them, it's a safe bet they'd infect my naukara if they were activated."

"That leaves us with nothing we can do to stop the revenants." I sigh, cradling my head in the hard coolness of my gauntlets. All of this and it keeps getting worse, as if every door to freedom we manage to prise open is kicked closed in our faces.

"What about the cure?" Sarah says.

I groan.

Major Ahmad grabs my arm. "What is she talking about? Cure? What cure?"

"The doctor said he had a cure," Sarah says. "After everything he put us through, maybe we suffered so we could win. Make it mean something, you know."

I lift my head out of my hands. "He said it was very slow and after everything Hiroki's done, I'm surprised you'd be willing to trust him." I'm looking at Sarah, but it's the Major who replies.

"Who said anything about trusting him? I've not heard the full story here and, frankly, we don't have time. But if there's any chance your medical officer has developed a cure for the nanite infection, that's worth pursuing. What other option do we have except scuttling the ship?"

"We're not scuttling Char*on*," I say as firmly as I can.

"Operational necessity. Crew and cargo lost. Hostile force occupying the vessel. Seems to me scuttling it is the next logical step if we cannot retake it."

"But that would kill all those people. My parents..." Sarah shakes her head. "There has to be other things we can do."

"Worst-case scenario—we all end up taken over by these

things or dead and they turn this ship around and fly it back to Earth."

"No, Major. They don't even need to do that. They've been trying to gain access to the Comm Array. Maybe we've been seeing this wrong and you had it right when you called it a virus. Maybe instead of seeing it as the nanites as the problem, we need to see it as the program, the AI or whatever has changed them. Maybe it's the Gestalt as pure signal."

"So what?" Sarah grunts, scowling. Then her face falls.

The Major stays silent, eyes peel full open, like they're trying to abandon ship. Gasps, "You're saying they could send the virus back to Earth in a radio burst. Infect all the nanotech at once."

"Yeah, and not only Earth but all the twelve colony worlds too."

"Then what are we waiting for? Couple of shots into the fusion rockets ought to do it, don't you think?"

I shake my head, desperate to stop her before she convinces herself noble self-sacrifice is the only way to go. "Way I see it, we have a Corporate's favorite thing—leverage."

"What?" The Major asks.

"The split in the original gestalt, creating these two sides which are fighting each other."

"You mean use them against each other?"

"Maybe, but what I'm getting at is they formed competing consciousnesses from the same virus. So maybe, if whichever one wins transmitted its code or whatever back to Earth, maybe it wouldn't create the same program, consciousness, whatever. Maybe it'd be a new and different one."

The Major scowls and taps a gauntleted finger against her lips. "How does that help us?"

"Well, if this thing's as smart as Hiroki reckons, then it'd realize sending on a copy wouldn't be the same as if it survived itself. All we need is a steady threat to it—make it realize it has something to lose."

The Major folds her arms across her chest. "Assuming it cares about survival in the way we do. Assuming it's the halfway rational one that survives. Seeing a problem with this yet?"

I purse my lips and incline my head. "It's a lot of assumption."

"Yeah and with the fate of Earth and all the colonies at stake if we get it wrong. Look, I'm not suggesting scuttling the ship as a suicide option. We were dispatched with orders to prevent the use of an unknown weapon by a Superstate or one of the Corporations to take over the Gliese 892 colony. Didn't ever expect to have to deploy inside the cargo ship taking us there. But we were to deploy without drawing attention to ourselves in case the intel was wrong. Seems like, given what you've told me, it was spot on but no one could have anticipated its use here and now. Or that it'd go wrong. Anyway, the point is, this is a shuttle craft. Intended for orbital insertion, and it's got space for three in the caskets."

I snort. "There's no way your shuttle could decelerate from nearly eighty percent the speed of light. And does it have a ramscoop or a magnetic cowl generator?"

"Er… no."

"So it's got nothing to protect it from interstellar particles ripping it apart and we'd be dead anyway. It'd just take a bit longer."

"Shit. I hadn't thought about that."

"It's regain control of Char*on* or die," I say.

"Isn't there some way we could get a generator for, what did you call it, the magnetic cowl? Put it on board…"

"There was one on the VIP lifepod. Other than that, only one I know of is about the length of the ship. Maybe if Zed were still alive he'd have a clue about how we could do it, strip out a part or something but I'm a navigator, you're a soldier, and Sarah here…" I thumb in Sarah's direction but she's gone.

"Where's your friend?"

"I don't know. Sarah?" I shout. No answer. "Let me try the comm—"

There's a loud insistent beeping from the control room behind us. "Oh fuck! There's no time for that." The Major's already boosting over to the far end of the small lounge we were in.

"What now?" I ask.

"That's the alarm for emergency decanting of the naukara. Whatever the stupid girl's done, we need to shut them down again before they identify her as a threat and rip her in half."

I hurry after, bouncing from bulkhead to bulkhead until I get my feet down and can stomp along after her.

Sarah is floating over one of the open caskets, expression vacant and a large globule of blood forming on her lips.

The major stands in front of me, gripping on tight to the pressure door's frame. "What's she doing?"

Before I can speak, Sarah spits. A thick mass of blood flies from her mouth to spatter on the vague dark shape within the casket. "Oh my god. She's infecting them."

"No!" Major Ahmad raises her pistol, its tines and antennae already beginning to fluoresce. I suppose this is the point where I'm supposed to stop her and try to save Sarah's life. Instead, I watch as a black mechanical arm rises out of the casket and grips its edge, pulling a vast body out from cold sleep. The thing is huge, easily half again my height and probably massing five times as much.

"Oh shit! Activation protocol delta one omicron. Caesar, Khan. Neutralize Achilles."

Her gun goes up and in a flash, Sarah is gone—no time to scream. Nothing left but a red mist and some red-hot fragments of her voidsuit.

The machineman thrusts itself towards us, one mechanical claw opened and ready to rend, the other arm ending in the multiple barrels of a gun of some kind—probably kinetics—driving forward and starting to rotate. The claw is less than a foot from the Major's head when another black limbed monstrosity rears out of its casket and seizes the infected cyborg's gun arm, yanking it backwards and crushing the whirring barrels. The second naukara starts to bring its own gun-arm to bear, this mounting the wicked profile of a particle cannon.

"If it fires in here—" I begin but the infected naukara grabs the other's gun-arm and the two begin thrashing and kicking at each other. Claws flick out of their feet and drive deep into armor, again and again. In the fury of their combat, I can hardly see what they're doing as they exchange blows with thunderous force. Any moment, they'll sweep over us and we'll be caught in the storm of flailing limbs and torn apart.

"Shoot them!" I say.

She checks the charge on the maser. "Not enough power left to burn through their defenses. We need to get out of here."

The third naukara draws itself from its casket. It moves slower than the other two but is even more bulky. I know so little about the things—whispered rumors of their use on the front lines of the Superstates' petty territorial struggles last time I'd been Earthside. Small communities being wiped away when one or the other side failed to reign in the monstrosities. Little or no fuss about it in the media, as if they'd ceased caring.

As the third naukara begins to join the fray, the second freezes then disengages from the first and both of them turn to attack the newcomer.

I retreat into the cramped lounge, the major one step behind me. She bangs the door seal and smashes it open, pulling out power cables. "Ought to hold them for a few minutes, so long as their energy weapons are offline."

"I'd say it's a pretty safe bet they're vulnerable to the nanites. Fuck knows whether it's the Complex or the Gestalt, right now I don't think there's a difference. What the hell are we going to do?"

"You were right when you said this shuttle isn't a lifepod. Which means it's an expendable asset. There's a small airlock that way, inside the control module. It'll get you outside. Takes one at a time. You go first."

"What are you going to do?" Here's another fool falling into the heroism trap.

"Trigger the shuttle's launch sequence for a full burn. Leave no fuel for them to come back at us. Now move. That's an order!"

I don't hang around. I clamber past the seats and crew stations in the control module until I get to the airlock. It's tiny, little more than a storage locker in size. I blunder through the inner door and begin the cycle. The viewport is just big enough to see about half the control module behind me and into the cockpit. The Major climbs into the pilot's seat and types a sequence of commands into the main computer. The terminal above her head starts flashing a three-minute countdown. The airlock door behind me opens to the void. Dragging myself out, I move aside and slap the button to close the airlock behind me.

Standing beside it, I watch through the outer viewport as the Major gets in and starts the cycle again. See her jerk back from the inner door as the glowing mechanical eye of one of the naukara fills the inner viewport. She presses herself hard into the outer airlock door. Obscuring my view. I pound the release button, but the cycle takes the time it takes.

Then blood splatters the viewport. The cyborg creature must have forced its way through the inner door. Which has one upside. There's no way the outer airlock will open with the inner one breached. This all has taken no more than about a minute-and-a-half. No time to wait and see what the naukara will do. I have to hope they don't have the capacity to abort the launch sequence.

I scramble across the shuttle's irregular hull, cursing each slow step as the magboots engage and disengage in strict sequence. The hull of Char*on* is in sight, no more than twenty feet away. Nearly there… I look back.

One of the naukara comes boiling out of the airlock, another hard behind.

Someone screams and it takes me a moment to realize it was me. I scrabble at the voidsuit's thruster control. Don't wait to check its remaining fuel, disengage my magboots, kick off hard. Blast a second of thrust and immediately get the one-percent warning. Left side thruster fails first leaving me careening into the void in an uncontrolled spin. Stars wheel through my vision as I tumble away from the shuttle until I fire off an anchorline. Solid hit on Char*on*. It jerks me round and then momentum's pulling me in a long arc back towards the ship.

I take a moment to look below, hoping no one had thought to equip the naukara with thrusters. Three of them are moving rapidly towards the edge of the shuttle. They reach it and with a burst of separation thrusters sending vapor out in vast streams of rapidly freezing gas, the shuttle tears itself free of its docking point.

It blasts past me so close it feels like I can reach out and touch it. Then it's out and gone, thrusters continuing to burn leaving a plume of crystallizing vapor in its wake.

All my attention is taken up with the fast-approaching hull of Char*on* as I reach the end of my arc. I slam into the side with enough force to make my voidsuit's HUD glitch but manage to engage a maglock before I ricochet into space. Soon as I'm secure, I detach the anchorline, looking back as I do so. One of the naukara made it off the shuttle and is already level with the anchorpoint. As the detached line whips past it, the manmachine doesn't even slow.

Is the scrap of human flesh at its core aware of what it's doing? Have the nanites infested that piece of brain or have they overridden the mechanical body, leaving the mind inside to scream? The thought doesn't slow me—I scramble away as fast as I can, limited by the time it takes for the magboots to engage and disengage with every step.

The crushing fear I've often experienced when doing an EVA is overwhelmed by the knot in my stomach and the burning in my limbs from the sheer amount of adrenaline my heart's thumping round my body. A terror so exquisite, it feels as if I'm being driven out of sanity and almost out of my own body.

No… That's actually happening.

>Node designated navigator under threat. Node override engaged.

I want to scream but I'm pushed aside from conscious control of my body.

>Get out of my head! I scream inside but it makes no difference.

My legs keep walking and my eyes rove the surface of the hull—flicking over micro-meteorite pitting here and there, picking out the color change where one section of hull plating had been nanobonded to the next, focusing on scuffmarks where the interstellar medium has abraded the hull. But I'm just an observer, trapped while the nanites which must have lain dormant inside me puppet my body. My head turns and checks the location of the naukara. It's gaining. I want to study it, to see which one it is and what armament it's carrying—will I feel the lance of a particle beam punching straight through my body? Or will it only be able to kill me as they had slaughtered Major

Ahmad? Hypersteel claws rending me apart.

The nanites have other ideas, and my head turns back and my eyes study the way ahead. The center of my back prickles and burns as I imagine the shot coming to end my life at any moment.

My continued awareness raises an uncomfortable question. Is this how all the revenants feel? Driven to act and aware of every moment but nothing more than a prisoner within their own body? Not what Zed or the others had reported or what I remember but I *had* been frozen.

But why should this be any different?

>Node proximity to external airlock estimated at one-point-two-three-seven kilometers. Hostile approaching at high speed. Estimate node will not reach airlock before hostile engages node in terminal combat.

I try to speak to it, find as I try to speak my mouth moves and speech comes out. It's slurred but it is me that's speaking. "Let… me… go!"

>Node exhibiting unusual levels of resistance to central control. Attempting to compensate.

A flash of light comes like a supernova before my eyes and with it a sense of total dislocation. One moment, I'm a prisoner of my own body as it marches along the hull, the next I'm floating above it, looking down on myself and seeing the naukara closing in from behind. The stars seem brighter in every direction and I feel the overwhelming desire to flee to them. Impossible geometric shapes form into a kaleidoscopic tunnel and start to draw me down. It reminds me of the times I've fallen from life as I entered cold sleep. Memories of it the corporate-designed tranqs had suppressed, free to rise up. This is coming home… All resistance bleeds from me, replaced by a wave of peace and for a moment my brother's voice is calling me. I try to answer him, "Cal?"

Without any warning I'm back in my body, hearing the silent voice of the Gestalt.

>Node designated navigator's brain has released non-standard neurotransmitter previously observed at moment of non-specialist node deactivation. Control of node designated navigator's body

compromised. Attempts to pacify resistance halted.

"Give me my body back, you bastards!" I slur.

>Attempting direct communication with node designated navigator. Negative. Preserving biological continuity of node designated navigator. Control will not be returned at this time.

My head turns, forcing me to look. The naukara is now less than fifty feet behind me. My head snaps round to look forward before I can examine the threat any further.

There's nothing I can do to take back control of my body, but the way the Gestalt talked makes it sound as if it might return it to me. It is trying to save me from the cyborg-killer. I reach into my mind for the training to help me separate emotion from my decision-making. The only logical thing to do is work with the Gestalt until I can get my body back. I note with pleasure an absence of any reaction to my thoughts. Whatever control it has over me, it doesn't seem able to read that part of my being. I let go and stop trying to take my body back. I swear it feels like my movements become smoother and faster.

>Node designated navigator has ceased active resistance. Target airlock estimated distance is zero-point-six-nine-six kilometers. Remote activation of airlock outer door limited. A glance back over my shoulder. *Hostile approaching within zero-point-zero-eight-seven kilometers.*

I force my lips to move, forming the words as clearly as possible. "There should be a second anchorline. Use it."

>Node designated navigator statement correct. Deploying anchorline.

I start trying to tell it to jump off the hull before firing but it's already acting, kicking off the surface and lining my left arm up with a distant hump on the ship's hull. My best guess is it's the command compartment's airlock, close to the bridge. Will a horde of revenants be waiting for me? It doesn't matter anymore.

The anchorline fires, hits its target. My head turns so I'm looking back and down. The naukara's beneath me, but I'm out of reach. Its electronic eye focuses on me, but it keeps moving forwards. What's more worrying is how far from the hull the jump has sent me. It can't be a long way from the edge of the magnetic cowl and no doubt a lethal dose of radiation. Then the winch engages and the anchorline reels me in, pulling me at high speed towards the airlock and way ahead of the naukara.

I watch with horror as my hands disengage the anchorline, leaving me hurtling towards the airlock with nothing to stop me. Ahead, the airlock outer hatch opens with the slightest puff of escaping atmo—standard security procedure.

As I sail past it, focusing with all my might on getting one of my hands to grab at it, my body twists round, kicks one foot down and against the inner wall of the airlock. The shock is intense—probably enough it'd have dislocated my shoulder if I'd made the grab unassisted—but the servos in my voidsuit compensate for enough of the force of the impact that I'm only a little winded. Maglock engages. The other foot comes stamping down to join the first and I walk inside.

The airlock cycles rapidly and about the time my HUD displays breathable atmo, the first ringing blow sounds against the outside. The damn naukara is trying to tear and batter its way in after me. The thing's clawed fist seems to be almost as effective as bulkhead shears. Shit. Still, part of me wishes it can—after I've gotten out of the way—so the ship depressurizes again, clearing out the control compartment, at the very least.

But that's stupid. It'd leave me locked in with the killing machine. What is the Gestalt's plan? Throw a few thousand revenants at the thing trying to break its way in? The single-minded violence means it has be under the control of the Complex, which removes any doubt that my unwanted guests are the Gestalt.

Given the Complex seems to be trying to kill me and the Gestalt is trying to save me, I begin to see the wisdom of Hiroki's decision to try communication. If it really is rational, it can be reasoned with.

Node designated navigator remains under threat. Extreme measures authorized.

"Wait a minute…" I croak. "What extreme measures?"

The inner airlock opens and I step through, my body turning so I can see the dent the naukara is pounding in the outer airlock.

>Accessing override codes.

My hands work at the airlock's control panel but I can't see what they're doing. The warning light for airlock depressurization goes on and the outer door opens. The hulking beetle-like form of the cyborg soldier swings in and sets its feet down on the airlock deckplate.

"What the fuck are you doing?" I scream.

>Remote degaussing of ship's airlocks activated.

The naukara floats free of the deckplate. My right index finger stiffens, inputting the last of the sequence of numbers it had keyed in. The inner airlock opens. Which shouldn't be possible with the external airlock open. The buffeting of air blasting past me is so great I think I'll be torn free of the deck but the magboots display only amber warning lights in my HUD. The naukara, floating free in the degaussed cube of the airlock is blown out of the airlock by the escaping atmo. Its clawed hand whips out catching a single claw in the pressure seal of the outer airlock.

What the hell can I do? But the Gestalt controlling me doesn't hesitate. It makes my body stomp forward with the rushing gale blasting past me. Every step causes the magboots to flash a red warning in front of my eyes—they don't have enough time to make a secure maglock before they're being dragged forward again. Any moment, I might be blown out into the void.

It's a blur—I close on the naukara and slam my fist into the solitary claw digging into the airlock. The first blow is driven by the voidsuit's servos dialed up with the safety turned off and my muscles firing with more force than I could have ever made them deliver. Pain shoots through my shoulder, arm, back and hip with the extremity of my body's misuse. The worst comes a split second later as the impact with the clawed finger sends a screaming message through my nerves. My hand breaks sending me a level of exquisite sensory detail you wouldn't believe possible. But the Gestalt isn't done. It strikes again and again until I'm trying to flee into unconsciousness to escape the pain of what it's making me do.

The claw deforms and slips free. The naukara blows out, spiraling away.

"Why?" I gasp. "Why didn't you just close the outer hatch?"

The Gestalt doesn't answer but moves me backwards one step at a time. All the while keeping my eyes focused on the receding black shape. Before I lose it against the backdrop of infinite darkness and light, I see the thing which had been coming to kill me has a gun arm quite different from what the other two had held. This is made of the same tines and antennae as the Major's maser had been, but on a larger scale. I can't be sure, but it looks as if the weapon is undamaged. But it must be, otherwise the naukara would shoot me.

The inner airlock closes, cutting off the last of the escaping air. External atmo registers as depleted but returning to breathable.

Returning autonomy to *>node designated* navigator. Disconnecting.

I'm in control of myself again.

"Wait! What the hell?" I shout inside my helmet, bellow it inside my mind but all sense of the presence of the Gestalt is gone.

CHAPTER 25

The command compartment has been stripped bare of all amenities. Everything used in air purification, food synthesis, or water reclamation is gone. Least they left the lights. I search through the crew areas—empty. Armory—my hopes shoot up when I find a single deckgun. Then crash down like a meteor come to extinguish the last of my primal optimism. The stock is cracked and the firing mechanism jammed. Take a damn gunsmith to get the fucking useless piece of plastic shit working again. I take it anyway.

Hunting around leads me to the crew cold sleep compartment—one area that's largely untouched save for the single absent casket. My casket.

I rummage around the storage lockers until I find some painkillers. Jonas Ramirez. Don't immediately remember him but he'd brought on board some heavy-duty narcs hidden in a pack of Peruvian Paradise tabac. Looked like endorphin analogues in a cocktail with dopamine re-up inhibitors. Two-Dee-Pump or something as good as. Narcs on the border of what would've caught serious shit from Dominguez depending on her mood. Someone confident he could get around the Captain...

Of course. *Him!* A picture of a young man begins forming in my mind. Clicks into place. Blond and blue-eyed like a northern Eurussian but otherwise dominated by his southern United American heritage. He'd been a good-looking boy—probably would've gotten round the Captain on the basis of his face and maybe some alternative punishment duty.

He's dead now.

I pop two of the patches on my neck before resealing my helmet. Let the voidsuit sample the air and keep a full reserve but filter every breath. Why the paranoia? Do you have to fucking ask?

I wonder what the Captain would do. Or M'Benga. Or Zed. The self-sacrificing heroic gene I'm so glad must have been edited out of me by my parents, yet another of their gifts to help set me up for a successful life. Bad joke. Anyway, who needs that kind of baggage?

None of that's important now. Only question which matters is—what's the route to survival here? I can't get my head around the absence of revenants—of either flavor—but maybe they're off slaughtering each other.

The agony in my hand, which had been so great I think it's been making me a little bit loco, fades away. And I admit it, I'm a little high. Stoned on duty? Give me a break, I need medication just to deal with the adrenaline come-down let alone the pain.

Surprise, surprise, there's no sign of any medical supply for treatment of my injury. But the nanites inside me are medical, aren't they?

"Hey, Gestalt. Whatever the fuck you call yourself. You're trespassing inside my body so make yourself useful and fix my hand would ya?" I find something about this hilarious and spend a few minutes giggling to myself. I mean, I *am* high.

Eventually, my brain settles down into a balance between the pain being numbed and actually being able to hold two coherent thoughts together. I go to the navicomp. It recognizes me and reports over ten million unauthorized access attempts. So whatever they'd got from me, they couldn't steal the executive authority code lock.

"So that's what you want from me, huh?"

"It's what makes you so valuable, Kara-chan."

I whirl round fast as I can against the confines of the voidsuit. Hiroki stands in the gangway between the crew lounge and the bridge. No voidsuit. A large disc-shaped object in his hands. Behind him, there's a bustle of movement, but whoever—whatever—it is doesn't enter the gangway.

I back up a step but there's nowhere to go. "Who are your

friends, Doc?"

"All in good time, Kara. All in good time. You did well to escape the naukara. I wouldn't even know where to begin to start hacking the airlock. Very impressive." He pauses, quirks an eyebrow at me. "Or did you have help?"

"How the fuck do you know what happened with the airlock?"

His face seems genuinely troubled by the question. Confused even. "You used to be like a younger sister to me, Kara-chan. But always, I found you also had much to teach. I would think by now you of all people would recognize what I have done."

"Maybe I don't have as much data as you think I do. Hard to form a sound hypothesis without data."

"Ah, the attempt to appeal to my rational side. How classic you. Rationality is all I have left. As you taught me, so many times, everything else is a weakness. But let's not stand here debating when we have a job to do. Here..." he holds out the disc—it's about the size of one of the single meal trays we used in the mess. Big enough for a hunk of cornbread and a dollop of synthesized chilli.

I don't take it.

"Come now, Kara-chan. This is no time to be stubborn."

I bring the deckgun up to cradle it across my chest, my broken right hand twinging with the movement but the worst of it still numbed by the drugs.

He mutters something in Japanese but though I hear the words, my weary mind can't decipher any meaning from them. "Slipping back into talking to yourself? Bad sign, Doc. Bad sign."

"I have played nursemaid to you, when *they* would have found a way to break you down and take what they wanted. I found the way to stop them. To keep your mind free of them."

"Bullshit. They can puppet me anytime they want."

"Your body? Yes. Your mind? Never again. I gave you that."

"The cure?"

He nods. "Hai."

"You fucking idiot, Hiroki. Instead of oblivion—at worst, awareness only of the machine code—you've made it so we can become prisoners in our own bodies. Left to scream in vain."

"Don't be foolish. It was a step. A way to share existence with them. In time, perhaps it could have become a partnership. They helped you defeat the naukara, didn't they?"

I glare at him.

"Fascinating. But too late." He moves forward, pressing a panel on the disc he's holding out at arm's length. It vibrates in his hands and emits a soft glow of white light from its center.

The actuators in my voidsuit freeze, the HUD distorts and winks out. Around me the lights flicker but those near Hiroki remain unaffected.

Node designated navigator under electromagnetic assault. Attempting to mitigate… uplink… fail. System reboot. Please input parameters.

"What the fuck are you doing?" I gasp.

"They're in the air. They floated in the dust when there was no atmosphere and coated voidsuits. Even after I removed them they could reinfect you, but the cure could guard your mind. And now, there is a way to reprogram them." He hangs the disc from a strap at his side. The voidsuit HUD reboots, declares a return to factory settings and begins its auto-calibration process.

A cold-water shiver runs through me. Any moment I'm going to start frothing at the mouth like Akima, like Sarah…

Accepting directive. Node controller identity accepted. Command line executed. Standby mode engaged.

"What have you done to me, you sack of shit?" I try to tense my muscles, try to ready a lunge that'll see me drive the butt of the deckgun through his face. I'll wipe that expression of mock concern off. But my body won't respond.

"I'll return control to you once you've heard me out, Kara-chan. Please don't try to fight. You'll only get frustrated."

He comes closer and the shapes moving behind him enter the gangway. Revenants. Mouths full of glowing teeth, but these are shaped and fitted with surgical perfection. The bastard has been upgrading colonists himself.

"Unlike you, these do not have awareness. At least, I don't think so."

"Any minute they're going to turn on you." I want to snap

and snarl at him but that'll get me nowhere. Always before, Hiroki had been… malleable. If I can't get control of my body, then while I can still control my own mind, I'll use every advantage I have.

"No, they won't. Not anymore." He spreads his lips in a wide grimace. His mouth lights blue. There's an instant of blankness in his eyes before they clear. It is Hiroki, but subtly different.

"The Gestalt showed me what I'd been missing. We are one. This is evolution, and as with the origin of any new species, there is pain and an ending to the species it replaces."

He has gone off the fucking deep end.

You can hear me, can't you, Kara-chan?

"Get out of my head!" The sense of violation exceeds even what I'd felt at the distant machine consciousness taking me over.

"As you wish. For now. You'll come to see this is the better way. The only way." He waves at the navicomp. "Now, release control to me and we can be on our way.

"On our way?"

"Yes. Home. Where else?"

"You want to take us back to Earth."

"Evolution is inevitable."

Now, I've been called selfish. Hell, I've been called far worse. What would you do in a situation like this? "What do I get out of this? I do as you say, I end up with a mouthful of glowing teeth doing only what you want, when you want."

"No, Kara-chan. The new human gestalt we form will need a core identity. It's too much for a single ego to sustain. You will be the other half of Us."

"An equal? As what? You telling me you've been lusting after me all this time, Doc?" I try to force a smile, a flirtatious mien but it must look stillborn.

He frowns. "Stop it, please. You were only ever my friend. There will need to be procreation to carry on the evolution of our species, but it doesn't need to be anything as basic as sexual. I have such plans."

He's gone way past plain old space-happy. I let the possibilities rampage through my mind. Part of some new melding of human and machine. Bound to everyone else, and at first, what? An equal partner? When would Hiroki want more members of the privileged few allowed to stamp their identity on a whole species? When would I find myself submerged under another's will? Even if I could wrestle primacy away from him, being mother-goddess to a species of drones holds no appeal. In its way, the possible destiny Hiroki has concocted is worse than the threat the Gestalt poses. Sublimation of the human into the machine or ultimately eradication. Maybe, just maybe, it would one day move beyond that and leave us free again. Sounds like a fucking nightmare either way.

I smile.

"Sounds good, Hiroki. Not sure I'm down with the whole non-sexual reproduction thing, but we can discuss that." I wink and he shifts uncomfortably. "What's the plan for dealing with the Gestalt? Don't want competition when we bring our new destiny back to Earth."

"The ITF military software has given us a tactical edge. A pity to lose the Major but her companions were sufficient. By the time we have turned the ship, I expect we will have eliminated it."

"Didn't you see it as a new form of life?"

"Yes, yes, it is. But it was only a part of the evolutionary process. Something which might be looked back on as a missing link between human and what we are becoming. Nothing more."

"Alright, I think we'll need a gravity assist to make a proper turn at this velocity. I'll need to check the navicomp for the closest object of stellar mass on our current heading."

"Do so." And I am free to move.

"How did you manage all this, Doc? Never realized you knew so much about cyber-intelligence systems."

"I did not. Not before my evolution. Now, what one of us knows, we all know. In time, you will share our knowledge. But it is an adjustment."

I call up the navicomp's data feed. Still showing the same patterns of data as before—manipulated by the Gestalt? Must be, or wouldn't Hiroki have said something?

"Must have taken some programming to get to this next, er,

step of evolution, though."

"Wiping the Gestalt from the nanites was one thing, reprogramming them required assistance, yes. But I had your QI virus. It made it possible."

Steady even breaths. "Had its uses after all then?"

"Yes."

How can I have not seen? "You were always the Complex."

"Not initially, but by the time you woke? Yes. Your choice of name was inspired."

I force my mouth to grin, try to inject a sparkle in my eyes to hide what I'm feeling. Calling it the Complex had secured the idea, the identity of the enemy in my mind. I'd blinded myself.

I pore over the data feed, scowling. There doesn't seem to be a way to send a message to the Gestalt. I hesitate—since when did I decide they're my ally? Desperate times and all…

"A problem?" He walks over to me, in the characteristic twist, release, step, test, repeat rhythm of someone using stikpads.

"The data's still being manipulated by the Gestalt."

"How long have you known this?" His inhuman calm slips.

"We found out when Akima and Joud died. Weren't you tapped into them?"

"An imperfect link. You stayed silent about that." He looks at me with narrowed eyes.

"There might be a way to compensate. Give me a minute."

"They are clever. But we have the edge. It's all about numbers. I'd planned to wipe the navicomp and start afresh when I lost you."

"That would've been one hell of a bad idea…" I call up the core menu, accessing the data feeds from the forward radio dishes and the chronometer.

"Yes, what we were before did not realize. But you were not the only one to understand what it would do."

"Wipe all the data gathered for establishing a positional fix but it couldn't have touched the core—that's shielded. It has to be in case the cowl failed." There it is. Within the streams of data. A false constant introduced to fix the navigational equations. The changes in velocity had caused course correction mode to activate nearly twice a day for the last year. Char*on* 's vector has altered enough so we're no longer heading for Gliese 892 but have entered the binary system Groombridge 34. The primary is close, so close it explains the changing tau that'd got me so worried about going over the redline. So we aren't going to live through the end of the universe in an Anderson scenario after all or go so fast we'll find out first-hand how bad going faster than the weak force propagates would be. Nothing or bye-bye fusion containment… Why does the latter suddenly seem preferable?

"Indeed."

"Who else knew?"

"Oh, one of the ITF agents was trained in the basics. Not as qualified as you, for sure."

"Take a look at this," I say, indicating the display.

He leans forward, "Imagine how it will be when you are comfortable sharing what you see directly to our mind. What are we looking at?"

"Doesn't the ITF agent know? Or doesn't it work like that?"

"He died, sadly. There is only an echo of what he knew. The facts and not his ability to apply them. It is the tragedy of everyone lost to us. Instead of contributing the richness of their experiences, from two hours after death we are left with only data."

Time to weigh up my chances. When he'd leaned over, he'd left himself open. Now, I've never been much of a fighter, but with the boosted strength of the voidsuit actuators behind it, I could deliver a lethal blow…

The time isn't quite right. Who knows how the revenants under his control would react to his death, and wouldn't it be like handing victory to the Gestalt?

"By adjusting for the altered input, the navicomp can function again. We're currently on course to perform a double gravity assist around the binary stars in Groombridge 34. It would send us on a heading to Zeta Cassiopeiae. That's a long way away." I pause, as another problem reveals itself. "It would also bring the Comm Array in line with Earth temporarily between the gravity assists around Groombridge 34 Alpha and Beta."

"Can you alter our course?"

"Yes, simple as ordering the navicomp to change course from our original destination to any other heading. It wouldn't take much to shift our vector off so instead of slingshotting around both, we'll go round Alpha. Still means the Comm Array will be pointing at Earth…"

"Then we will have to send our signal first. Once our identity is established, the Gestalt's will be ignored. And when we return to Earth, every human there will already have been uplifted, ready to play their part in our new species."

Wonder if he knows how fucking crazy he sounds? Probably not. Self-awareness and power-hungry maniacs aren't known to go together.

"This might take a little time. We've got a little under twenty hours subjective before we begin the gravity assist around Groombridge 34 Alpha."

"Then we must redouble our efforts to destroy the Gestalt within that time. For now, we still occupy the Comm Array."

"It'd be a lot easier to maintain control of it if it were depressurized again. We've got most of the proper voidsuits, right?"

"Yes. The Gestalt has not managed to jury-rig more than a few makeshift voidsuits from crew wearalls."

"They didn't patch the hull breaches?"

"No, we did."

"I see. So what about the unpressurised cargo bays? The ones where all the caskets were opened to vacuum?"

"A necessary step to increase the function of our unity. Each of those colonists is a sacrifice on the path of our evolution. Use every resource, that's something we learned from you, Kara-chan. The corollary is to deny the enemy any resource." He was studying my face with a hard, flat stare.

He'd murdered thirty thousand people for a computing advantage over the Gestalt. You can see the logic, maybe but thinking of the actions of Captain Dominguez, of M'Benga, of Zed, and Major Ahmad, I find embracing that rationale impossible. It's too cold. Inhuman. Monstrous. Here's the point where the decision makes itself for me.

"Makes sense," I say. "Glad to see you were paying attention."

He continues to stare at me for an uncomfortable space of several heartbeats. Probably about a hundred of mine, maybe twenty of his, if the lump of withered gristle in his chest still needs to beat. When he turns his gaze back to the terminal, the desire to sigh with relief nearly overwhelms me.

"Change our course. We will depressurize the Comm Array, as you suggest. Then we must find a way to bring you fully into unity." He turned back to me.

Logic. Reason. Keep up your poker face. "Hardware issue or software?"

"You will need more nanites to make the appropriate connections between your cerebellum and cerebrum. It should not be a difficult exercise once we have re-secured the medibay. Then we will truly begin."

"Will it hurt?"

"No, Kara-chan. Unlike the last time, this will be done without pain and without loss of will. We promise. You will grow larger, not smaller."

I nod and force a relieved smile onto my face. "Thank you, Hiroki. Thank you for choosing me."

His smile is as beneficent as any he's ever shown me. Without a backwards glance, he walks away. Two blank-eyed revenants take up position in the hatchway. They're armed, both carrying deckguns. Unlike mine, these must be loaded and functional. Not much of a threat against my voidsuit, but not something to test either.

It doesn't matter if they're Hiroki's eyes, if it's possible to see the being who's stealing the free will of thousands of people as my old friend. He'd saved my life more than once, but who he'd once been is dead. Yes. You have to tell yourself these things. It's as if he'd never returned when he'd been blasted out into the void by the hull breach.

I double-check the navicomp data. This thing I'm contemplating is murder on a scale even beyond his. And the same kind of sacrifice I deride in others. He'd failed to spot the lie. We're less than five hours away from a slingshot around the primary of the dwarf stars in the Groombridge 34 binary system. The ion drive has to engage soon, delivering a full one-g of deceleration followed by a reversal to one-g of acceleration to achieve the course correction the Gestalt wants. It'll take only a small alteration to Char*on*'s vector to do what's got to be done.

My fingers fly over the controls, compensating for the false data being fed to the navicomp, ordering a minute adjustment to the duration of navigational thruster fire, and then hover over the prompt asking me to commit to the course change. This is the single most difficult second in my entire life. Everything I am, wars with the choice. Only my unwanted hitchhikers stay silent. Their quiet promise is what makes me do it.

I commence my final duty as acting Captain of SCCSV *Charon* in this moment.

My next order to the navicomp is to delete all executive access privileges from all users including myself. The navicomp's primitive intelligence queries this and asserts "this is an irregular order." I override its objections, feeling the gaze of my guards pinned on me. Hiroki watching through their eyes.

It accepts my directive but indicates this will only hold until the destination is reached. It's a hard fight to keep the smirk from my face. Machine intelligence. What a joke. It doesn't understand it's receiving false telemetry and can't recognize the ship's new destination.

I stand slowly. We're still in zero-g yet for the first time I can remember I feel truly weightless. A feeling which doesn't last long. Before my final duty is complete, there are a couple of loose ends to cut.

CHAPTER 26

My chaperones let me leave, though they follow a step behind me. I calibrate my voidsuit's internal chronometer to begin three countdowns. The shortest for when deceleration will commence. The next for the start of acceleration following the slingshot around the first star. The longest for a final countdown.

Now for the loose ends. Hiroki is one and the problem of the signal to Earth is the other. Maybe the Gestalt could become an ally but its repeated efforts to send itself on a carrierwave back to Earth means it can't be trusted. If it discovers what I've done, before the ion drive acceleration phase is complete it can simply switch it off. And my plan will fail.

No, there are no allies left for me on Char*on*. Only memories of their sacrifice and the duty owed by an acting Captain.

I approach the nearest of the two revenants. "Hiroki, please have these two lead me to you at the Comm Array. I can be of most assistance there but I don't want to find myself face to face with any of the Gestalt's drones."

The revenant doesn't speak but raises its arm in a gesture I take to mean "follow." I fall in behind, catch sight of the other taking position behind me out of the corner of my eye.

The main corridor is a site of slaughter. Bodies shredded by deckgun, by improvised weaponry, by hand and foot and tooth float amid arcing globules of blood and trailing, uncoiled intestines. The crew had created no less of a massacre but now I know what it feels like to be a revenant, now I have the experience of being awake inside a body I can't control but still feel every sensation from—I flex my right hand and let the pain remind me how it'd felt to break. Now, I have all that, I can't look on the broken bodies. Maybe they had been insensible, all awareness taken over by the machines and maybe they had felt every bite, every punch, every flechette as it tore through their flesh and bone. Maybe they'd screamed both at their own dying and at the horrors they were forced to commit on others. Strangers maybe. But these were colonists and many of them would have come from the same places. The same slums and shanty towns beyond the edge of hope until the offer of a new life had seduced them. Maybe they were friends, or family to those they tore into or maybe it was their loved ones who tore into them. Yet again, we, the human race, have managed to birth an atrocity.

I want to look away. I want to turn my mind to other thoughts and hide from the truth. But now, close to the end, I force myself to look. To see. To know. Their deaths, all of them will be on my hands but at least it will end cleanly. Return to them the dignity of that most human thing of all.

One of the pressure doors opens. Cargo bay Two. A revenant bursts out swinging a length of pipe. My guardians swing up their deckguns in eerie synchronization. The first blasts the charging revenant in the chest, the second destroys its head. Faster than it's possible to see if it's a man or a woman who attacked. Another revenant moves in front of the pressure door, blocking the cargo bay off from the main corridor.

We pass the patched hull breach and I think of the VIPs consigned to an eternal sleep between the stars. I think of M'Benga, drifting out there forever in the death grip of what must have been one of Major Ahmad's ITF agents. Had he given up the false face before he died, or were Zed's features locked in a rictus, grinning for all eternity into Siyanda M'Benga's face?

We reach the end of the corridor and pass through the airlock into the engineering section of the ship. I shuffle around to stand so my feet face towards the bow. The first timer hits zero and I brace myself for the return of gravity. Right on cue the ship begins decelerating. My stomach lurches and my legs ache. Both of my companions sway and one of them vomits. A loss of control of the stomach Hiroki's dominance does nothing to stem. Where you'd react to spilling bile all down your front, the revenant does nothing. Doesn't even wipe its face clean. But in the dilation of its eyes, I see the man trapped inside.

I look away, wanting to engage my suit's helmet and go on internal supplies but I need every minute of air if my plan is to work.

We pass through a hole cut into the space between the inner and outer hull, close to the medibay. The sound of fighting is intense—the bodies of the dying screaming in as much of a reflex as the revenant who vomited. Must not be worth the processing power to suppress.

Can't help but wonder if the Gestalt understands its enemy is no collective entity of near berserk rage but a calculating being serving the perverted wishes of a man I used to call friend.

Maybe it does. Maybe that's why it helped me. Whatever it knows, it's pouring every enslaved life it can into the struggle to take the medibay.

With luck it'll keep enough of Hiroki's forces occupied that I can do what I have to.

They lead me close to the Comm Array but not inside. Instead, I find myself in a compartment squeezed between the hulls. With the return of pressure, it's been opened up and the section of hull Hiroki must have cut to gain access is stowed away, held tight against the wall by temporary suit sealant. Inside is laid out much as the medibay had been—the jury-rigged oxygenator in one corner, lashed to the bulkhead with webbing. Hiroki's battered and scarred voidsuit hangs from webbing, halfway down the wall. Clever—he can reach it from whichever end of the room becomes down.

A lab-bench currently located on the ceiling holds the old-fashioned microscope that'd been in the medibay. Beside it is a clear container filled with shards of crystalline data chips, shaped into teeth. Looks like a set for one person. A shudder runs through me. Who are they meant for? Me.

Hiroki stands in the center of the room with his eyes open and staring. His gaze is fixed on infinity when I enter. Some measure of himself returns to his face as he sees me but it's impossible to shake the impression he's both more and less than the man I'd known. You couldn't imagine this being singing lullabies in a sake stupor any more than you could see him weeping when he realized he'd missed his long dead mother's birthday. And yet, so much of the man remains in this thing. If only there was a way to touch that part of him…

"Is this deceleration in keeping with our new course?"

"Yeah, I had to finagle my way around the Gestalt's false data without giving us away. Unless you've regained control of the ion drive from them?"

"We will shortly. They are giving ground. By current estimate, they will no longer be an effective threat by the time we have completed the slingshot maneuver you have initiated."

If this works, nothing on this ship will be a threat. But I keep my expression loose. This all comes down to poker. Maybe if Zed had been dealt a better hand he'd… well, forget about that. Hiroki can't bluff to save his life and he's never been any good at reading a bluff but one of the lifetimes of experience he's stolen might be. If he's absorbed Zed's memories or the Captain's or even M'Benga's, he'll recognize my tells but maybe there isn't enough time for whatever stolen expertise he has to pick up on whatever subconscious signals I'm giving away.

"We will soon have full control of the medibay. I have prepared a symbol of your new status." He gestures upwards towards the desk.

"Are they really necessary?"

"Of course. If we are to direct the actions of our unity, we must have the strongest connection possible so the extensions of our will are not left without commands. On our return to Earth, we will need to find a superior method, but for now, the crystalline matrix of the casket's circuit boards will have to serve."

I run my tongue along the back of my teeth. He'd better not be planning to start on some dentistry work before I gain access to the Comm Array. Time for a change of tactics, before he gets the idea I need to become a full part of his little insane empire right now.

"Are we safe in here?"

"Yes."

"I don't mean to doubt you, old friend. But two revenants with deckguns aren't going to protect us. And isn't the Comm Array one of the Gestalt's primary targets? Shouldn't we be overseeing its protection?"

"Some of our forces relocated there and have done as you suggested. An easy enough matter to depressurize the surrounding area. The battle for control of the array is mainly within the ship's computer. We are winning."

"Still, I'd feel better knowing it was physically secure."

He turns and the solution to my problem of what to do with him presents itself. The disc he'd used to wipe clean the nanites hiding in my brain and disable my voidsuit is strapped to his hip.

"You still think in the limited terms of one bound to a single body. Oh, when you are set free, Kara-chan. What wonders we will see together."

"I can't wait." *Hold the sarcasm, Kara. Hold it.* "But if you were there yourself, I mean in person, you'd be able to use your EM device to wipe clean any revenant that attacked and then they could join us. Add to us. You know, never be afraid to expend a resource when necessary but don't fail to secure one when possible." A paraphrase of basic Sevran Corp doctrine.

"Yes... yes, you are right. As always. We are finished here for now. Please, wait."

The instinctive urge to attack him then and there is almost overwhelming. Giving up the advantage I have over him while he's out of his suit seems wrong. But this isn't about instinct; it's about cold calculation. I watch in total stillness as he dons the voidsuit and hangs the disc at his left hip.

We're forced to go single file—revenant, Hiroki, me, revenant—as we wend our way between the hulls and out into the engineering compartment where distance contraction is noticeable, giving the unnerving impression the compartment has shortened. It's a thought immediately lost by what I see. The lights are on, and with air and gravity the full horror of the slaughter is plain to see. Among the burned and broken corpses of the revenants Zed had killed, two crowds of human puppets gather. Armed with everything from scavenged deckguns, to broken pieces of machinery, to fist and foot and tooth. Where two armies can only drive themselves so far into savagery, there's no limit for the revenants. They tear at each other even as they died.

One side begins to overwhelm the other but there's no retreat. No surrender. Not even a moment of pause in the tide of flesh as it surges forwards to kill and die. Robbed of any urge for self-preservation, the human drive towards self-annihilation is stripped bare and laid out before me. Hiroki doesn't even glance in the direction of the death-struggle.

The pressure door leading to the Comm Array opens and we enter the gangway where the hole he'd once cut in the bulkhead has been patched. The door seals behind us, cutting me off from the sights and sounds of a primal hell brought to life amid the starry heavens.

With the gravity effect of the deceleration there's no need for the revenants to use stikpads but they still move in the awkward shuffle that goes with it. Try it and you soon find that as tiring as walking in stikpads is in zero-g, it's much worse under gravity. Their legs are probably burning with the effort yet they give no sign of discomfort, faces blank and the faint glow of blue from their mouths. From the way the muscles in their jaws stand out, their teeth must be clenched unbearably tight. I drink in the sight, knowing even at peace there will be no rest in the hive mind Hiroki's vision for human evolution will create. The Gestalt would be no better, lacking even Hiroki's insane grasp on the essence of human existence.

How can it understand us?

My brief moment of communication with it hadn't triggered any direct response beyond bare acknowledgment, it had acted on what I'd said as just another data source.

The ship is experiencing considerable time dilation and distance contraction by now, an hour into the deceleration phase means we're already well within the gravitational grip of the dwarf star, Groombridge 34 Alpha. Navigational thrusters will begin firing on a constant schedule, subtly shifting the angle of approach to keep the ramscoop's magnetic cowl as a barrier between the energies of the star and Char*on*'s hull. Each adjustment will change the angle of apparent gravity ever so slightly. Enough to throw Hiroki off balance if he doesn't engage his magboots. But if I engage mine, he'll realize something was about to happen and do the same. The first thruster burn is my best chance.

The gangway depressurizes, matching the vacuum within the Comm Array. A return to total silence outside the sounds of my body and my suit. I check my air supply—with a careful limit on my exertions and sticking to an oxygen conservation protocol, the voidsuit can recycle breathable air for maybe sixteen hours. Enough? It has to be.

The pressure door silently retracts and my heart jerks in my chest. Three revenants hold position around the array, one armed with a deckgun but the other two carry hand masers—liberated from the dead ITF agents, no doubt. Like the two guarding us, all three wear jury-rigged voidsuits—at a guess they'll have no more than a couple of hours of air each. Past them, the hole Zed and the others had cut remains but now, behind it there's a second cut, a one-meter-by-one-meter opening to the void. Inelegant but simple.

The array itself has been stripped of its external covers, leaving cables exposed and revealing the crystalline sheets of its processors. They flicker with blue light as the optical data exchange takes place, as if they too have been infected like the colonists who've become revenants.

The access terminal shows repeating lines of text. Commands from the Gestalt to rotate and face Earth, I guess. But the mechanism that moves the array is open and blocked by a length of metal. Hiroki must have done it when Zed and the others rescued me.

"You going to do something about freeing the array?" I ask.

>It would be so much easier if we could communicate like this, Kara-chan. The words come in Japanese yet in my mind I understand them as if in my mother tongue. Without effort. And it dawns on me then it's the same as when the Gestalt had spoken in my mind. It hadn't spoken any human language, but the machine code of its essence. Coming in the silent speech of the mind, I'd understood it as if it were English, yet it had been only the meaning transmitted

and not the words. In some way, even separate from the core of my consciousness, being linked in this way alters my mind.

I hate it.

"I'm not ready yet, Hiroki. Not until I am a part of your, I mean our unity. You can understand, can't you?"

"Yes. It will be soon. Very soon. You are right, however, we must prepare the array for our message and purge the presence of the Gestalt from the transmission buffer."

"They're not transmitting now?"

"Yes, directly into the magnetic field of the ramscoop. We must adjust the angle if we wish to send a clear signal."

"Want me to work on the buffer, while you clear the array for repositioning?"

Again the flat appraisal of his inhuman gaze. "Is it not outside your field of expertise?"

"Comms systems are part of fundamental training, Doc. You must have had yours at some point."

"No and yet now we understand it fully."

I mentally cross my fingers, have to keep him close but I also need a chance to confirm my plan can work. The moment we complete our first slingshot maneuver, a signal will be beamed in the direction of Earth. It must not be allowed to carry the Gestalt's message. Anything Hiroki chooses to transmit will be as fatal to humanity's future.

"You may begin wiping the buffer clear of the Gestalt's flawed code. We will upload our gift to the world, it will be simple enough."

He crouches by the blocked mechanism—I want to call it the array's gyro, but engineering details had been Zed's specialty not mine. I focus on the transmission buffer. Right now, the QI virus would come in handy but negotiating the menus of the comm system brings my training back to mind.

The buffer can accept no new data until its contents are transmitted. But the Gestalt hasn't been able to activate the security firewall to prevent access to core commands. It requires an officer's access codes. Hiroki's or mine are the only ones left.

The command options scroll by, everything from bandwidth restrictions to signal compression ratios. First, cut the active signal. Now… Here it is. Purge transmission buffer. Key my voidsuit's comm into the array's systems. Purge the existing contents and slave the buffer to my comm output on channel three. Finally, I engage single user encryption on that channel. Now—so long as my voidsuit comm is transmitting a signal and the array is receiving—it will be the only input the buffer can accept.

I key my comms to record a beacon alert for continuous transmission every few minutes so long as my suit retains power. "This is acting Captain Kara Rozanski of the Sevran Corp Commercial Space Vessel *Charon*. If you are receiving this transmission, it is imperative you find a way to block all incoming radio signals."

"What are you doing, Kara-chan?"

I click over to the channel Hiroki's on. "I think I've cleared the buffer but there's some issue with the input. I think you'd better take a look, it's beyond me."

He stands, holding the length of metal bar and leaving the array's mechanism clear. It adjusts its position, bringing itself into alignment with where Earth will be when we complete the slingshot. For now, the message is transmitting into the dwarf star and this close to it, the signal will be lost in the noise of stellar radiation.

The rotation stops as Hiroki comes to stand beside me. Any moment now the positional thrusters will start firing. If I've got this wrong… I grit my teeth. It should start in ten, nine, eight…

"What have you done?"

Four, three…

He whirls on me, mouth wide and glowing blue—the light reflected from his helmet's visor makes it seem as if blue flames burn in his eyes. Not that it hides the fury in them.

Two, one…

Nothing happens. The revenants in the room face me and begin to advance. Any moment, the order will come that paralyses me and ends this. But he's spluttering in rage at what the piece of shit must see as my betrayal.

"It seems you are not worthy of having a voice in Unity. We would have…"

The deck jerks beneath us, and down is suddenly at a twenty-five-degree angle from the horizontal it had been a second before. Hiroki stumbles and slides across the deck, and I go after him, launching myself to crash into him and take him to the deck. There'd been no goddess in my life, unlike my parents, but now I call to any universal spirit who's listening in a silent cry begging that the EM disc doesn't break in our fall.

Before he can come up, I slam one foot flat on the deck and engage a maglock. It jars my back but the voidsuit actuators lock and spare me any whiplash. Grabbing at the disc as Hiroki tumbles away from me, I snag the strap it hangs from with two fingers. It comes free from him and strikes the deck, denting one edge before I can draw it to me and cradle it against my chest.

Hiroki controls his fall towards the corner of the compartment and we both stand to face each other. Any moment I expect the impact of a deckgun load to strike me or the maser blast that will liquefy me and superheat what's left to vapor. The suit will hold long enough… has to hold. I turn the disc so the emitter side faces Hiroki and his mouth opens wide.

Kara-chan, don't…

There's one touch panel on the disc. I press it. Vibration runs up my arm as something within the disc spins up to speed and the white light glows from its emitter. My HUD flickers at some of the spillover but that's the limit of it.

Hiroki… he's frozen.

The blue glow from his mouth dies and his magboots fail. Locked rigid like a man turned to steel, he slides across the deck to the corner of the room. I follow him, keeping the emitter focused on him. He's saying something, but the disc is doing its job. All electronics are wiped and disabled. His radio too.

I take my eyes off him long enough to see the revenants are standing passively, their weapons down by their sides. The jagged shards of their teeth still glow but otherwise they show no signs of a driving intelligence.

It worked! Just as planned! Damn, am I good at my job or what?

Stomping over to Hiroki, I keep the disc focused on him.

Close enough to see his eyes are clear of their inhuman distance. There's fear in them.

I smile. Move closer still, until the disc is pressed to his chest. I activate my suit's recorder then lean my helmet forward and touch it to his.

"...kill us. Kara, please!"

"Shut up. You brought this on yourself. As senior remaining officer, I am acting Captain of this vessel. In accordance with the articles of the Interstellar Naval Code of Discipline, I charge you with the offence of mutiny. How do you plead?"

"Kara-chan..."

"Your defense of insanity is noted and rejected. My verdict is guilty. Absent a suitable brig, summary judgment is in favor of execution by *foras de nave*. Do you wish to make a final statement?"

"Our revenants, if you do not return control of them to me, they will revert to savage behavior. Please. They will kill us both."

"Your final statement has been recorded. Goodbye, Hiroki. For the sake of the friendship we once had, I'm sorry it has to be this way."

"No, wait..."

I pull my head back. "For the record, sentence will now be carried out."

Hooking the disc's strap around Hiroki's neck, I cinch it tight so it hangs against him. Flexing my sore back and ignoring the sparking agony of my right hand, I grip his legs and drag him up the sloping deck.

He doesn't stop screaming and begging. I can't hear a word, thank fuck. But it doesn't stop him. Keeping an eye on the revenants—still motionless, no wait, they've begun to twitch as if suffering the first stage of a seizure—I drag him to the hole in the inner hull. Through it and out so, he lies on the edge of the outer hull breach. Line him up so his head's in the middle of the hole.

Behind me, the revenants' twitching has become full blown shaking and thrashing about. I don't waste any time.

"Goodbye, old friend."

Disengaging one magboot, I put that foot between his paralyzed legs and kick him from my ship. He falls away, and I turn back—I have no desire to watch him bounce across the hull and spin off into space.

Ten would give you one, he'll fall beyond the protection of the magnetic cowl and be incinerated by the fury of the dwarf star before he asphyxiates. But you wouldn't waste a new-jiao on that bet. Either way, loose end cut.

CHAPTER 27

Of the five revenants, two lie still, twisted awkwardly where their feet remain held to the deck by their stikpads. The other three move in fits and starts. I close on the nearest of the fallen revenants—a young man. His eyes are rolled up in their sockets and his mouth hangs open. The glow from the shards of crystal lattice that have replaced his teeth is faint. Enough to show that in his fitting, he's bitten through his tongue and seemingly choked to death on it.

No time to waste. Tear his deckgun from his limp grip. Swing it up as the other revenants turn to face me. I shred one of the Revs armed with a maser, then try to move round the array to get a clear line on the other two. They move as one. Fast, wrenching their feet from the ground and circling, one to the left; the other to the right. Firing as they come.

Flechettes from one strike my voidsuit causing my HUD to flash amber warnings. I crouch, more from instinct than any real need to avoid the threat. Hadn't M'Benga told me deckguns can only cause minor damage to voidsuits—unless it's close enough to fire point blank into the faceplate or between the armor plates at the joints. It's the one with the maser I have to worry about.

They're predictable these Revs. I line up and blast the one with the deckgun as it comes from the left but the other pops up behind and gets a line on me. Purple light flares… Heat and rad warnings flash across my HUD and I stagger back, expecting the lethal shot. But part of the array blocks the full intensity of the beam.

Instead, the revenant charges and springs on me, trying to jam the maser at the juncture between my helmet and where it connects to its power and air supply. The maser must have a low charge…

There's hope.

I swing at it, but as I'd done to Sarah when I'd been the one without armor, the revenant holds itself to me beyond the voidsuit's range of movement.

Any moment, it'll get the right point and I'll be dead. And then the signal to Earth will turn the nanotech the Superstates have flooded every aspect of their societies with. United America's aerosol nanites will change from a national immune system and become either devices of humanity's enslavement or its scourging. And when one Superstate falls, the others will follow, as their naukara forces tear through their defenses and the nanites in their hospitals turn patients into revenants.

Only one choice, really. I disengage my magboots and stumble back, slamming into the wall. The revenant's behind me and takes the full weight of the voidsuit landing on it, crushing ribs. Its arms and legs spasm and the maser discharges.

My HUD flickers, dies, and I slip into darkness.

I swim back out of the dark to be met by flashing warning displays in my vision, and a chemical smell like burnt conductive cables. The HUD is barely functional, the damage beyond its self-repair system's ability to mitigate. Air reprocessing has been compromised. Power to the suit is limited and the entire right side is getting no power to its actuators.

Marvelous.

I try to turn my head and can barely make out the broken body of the revenant underneath me. The deck no longer slopes away from me. Which can only mean we've reached our final alignment. My suit's chronometer won't display. Without knowing how long I've been unconscious, there's no way to tell how close to the acceleration phase the ship is.

Worse, an interrogatory to the array shows my connection to it has been broken. Most of the voidsuit's on-board systems have failed, and I can't access the recorded message.

Just fucking great.

Using my one functional magboot to anchor me, I stand. The actuators in the suit's left leg whine and strain as they bring me upright. Using every ounce of strength I possess, I manage to drag my right leg level and balance while I disengage the magboot and hobble forward, dragging my paralyzed right leg after me. My right arm hangs imprisoned in the dead weight of the voidsuit. The gauntlet has locked in a fully open position, and the stretch of my broken hand sends shooting spears of hot agony up my arm.

Halfway to the array, the left magboot shorts out but the actuators keep working. I pull myself to the panel.

Two signals are coming from within Char*on*. The Gestalt and whatever Hiroki left behind—an echo of himself, the Complex, or a pure berserk killer. They battle for supremacy. The streams of numbers mean nothing to me, both a dense machine code. I check the buffer and am met with a blue screen filled with white writing. Serious system error, critical damage. Rebooting the array's system gets it into a basic mode. The two signals keep demanding primacy. Both are transmitting, distorting each other. But all it'll take is for one to gain dominance.

I key my comm, begging the universe to have left my radio undamaged. Channel three connects and the array recognizes it as having command priority. Keying the recorded message does nothing but make the fragmented screen of my HUD flash an error message.

Time to acceleration phase? No idea.

Time until I run out of air? No idea.

Time until my suit's power fails or the system breaks down? No fucking idea.

There has to be some way to destroy the array or cut its powerline. Discharging the deckgun or one of the masers into it a few times seems like the first thing to try.

I hobble over to the nearest one. Before I can stoop to pick it up, ceiling becomes the floor and I fall.

Crashing into the deck, ten meters below me with a splitting agony. My HUD goes dead. Consciousness begins to slip from me again, but I fight it back. Gasping in air and willing myself to remain conscious. The tide of darkness rushing into my vision slows and recedes in pulses, one heartbeat at a time.

Focus on your breathing, getting control of yourself.

Then I try to look about. Can't move my head. Maybe I've broken my neck… No, the pain in my right hand and all through my body says that's not the case. I can wiggle my toes in the padding of my magboots but I can't do more than shift the weight of the suit. There's no way I can stand and no way can I drag myself over to one of the fallen guns, even if they haven't broken in the reversal of gravity.

There remains one way to block the signal—a small adjustment to the original plan. Summoning every ounce of strength I have, I twist my body at the hips and lift my left arm up and over so the gauntlet falls against the control panel on my right arm. The left gauntlet has lost power but hasn't completely seized. I strain my arm and fingers until I can key the comm button.

Hoping.

Praying.

There's the reassuring crackle hiss of a connection and a flicker in my HUD showing "transmitting." My suit's actuators may have gone and maybe the power is failing but there's enough for the radio… for a while at least.

I relax and the pressure on the comm button ceases. The connection breaks.

Fucking typical.

I press it again. Start talking.

"This is Lieutenant-Commander Kara Rozanski of the Sevran Corp Commercial Space Vessel *Charon*. This is an emergency. If you are receiving this, you must find a way of jamming this transmission. Repeat, jam this transmission. Your life, dammit, every human life everywhere depends on it."

I repeat the words a dozen times over, in one variation or another. My arm aches from the effort of holding down the comm button. But I have to keep the channel open to stop them sending any message through, until the course correction brings Char*on* to its final destination in the heart of Groombridge 34 Beta.

Start talking. Now you're just rambling. But it doesn't matter.

To my surprise I find myself recounting everything that's happened since Zed woke me. I'm tempted to lie. Make myself seem more deserving of a posthumous promotion to Captaincy. But, you know what, fuck it. I've played that game my whole adult life, earlier even, ever since I'd been assessed as a candidate for the Academy.

Time for a little truth.

There's nothing to hide and no other time to square things with myself and this life. Nothing to lose. No tomorrow to wait on.

"So there we were, thinking it would be easy to get the data sliver…"

"…And let me say right now I hate this. The sacrifice. So fucking noble. So fucking stupid. But at least one thing holds true even now. Even though I've been tearing myself open with words just so I can go on holding this damn button, I've still got my pride. I'm still Captain of this damned ship, on its last mission straight to hot hell. Acting Captain or confirmed, it doesn't matter. I am in command of Char*on* on her sun dive. First human to crash into a star.

"Last of the suit's power's fading… It's held longer than I thought it could. Air's getting thick. Must've been talking for nearly nine hours. They keep trying to send their message, but it's like the Gestalt and that other thing don't know that nothing's getting through. I'm feeling paranoid—like maybe they're waiting me out. Maybe one's been victorious. Maybe it knows how long I have left. Somehow it knows and it's not long enough. Or maybe the little fuckers are in my head, making me see this. Making me hear it. Making me think I've beaten them while I'm walking around with empty eyes and blue lights shining from my mouth. I don't know.

"I'm past caring.

"Before the power fails or I run out of breath, let me say this one more time to you and I hope you never fucking hear it.

"This is Captain Kara Rozanski of SCCSV *Charon*. If you are still listening to this transmission, you're going to die. Jam the fucking transmission. Jam it!

"I'm so tired. So thirsty. My arm went numb so long ago, feels like it's inflated. Doesn't feel like it's part of my body anymore. It's almost comfortable. How long until we kiss a sun? I think I'm going…

"…Not yet…

"…You know, when I was young, my father would sing me to sleep. He did. He really did. For a corporate man, he was soft and gentle. Fucking corporates, you know. But his voice—unlike my mother's tone-deaf drone. Now there was a woman who couldn't sing. What was I saying? Oh. His voice. Yeah, it was sweet. There was this one lullaby, something his own mother had always sung to him and every night I never could sleep without him crooning it to me while I held his little finger in one tight fist.

"I wish…

"I wish I could hear his song now.

"I wish he would sing to me of the summertime and easy living.

"I wish…

"0100010101110011011101000110000101100010011011000110
1001011100110110100000010000001100010011000010111001101100
0101001000000110111001101111011001000110010100111010001000
0000100000010110110001110000001101000011000010000101001000
0010101111000011100000110000101101110011001000001000000011
1010001101111001000000110000101101100011011000010000001
10110001101001011011100110101101100101011001000010000001
110011011110010111001101110100011001010110110101110011001
1101000100000010000100110010101110100011000010000101001
01000001110101011100100110011101100101001000000111001001
100101011100110110100101110011011101000110000101101110…"

ACKNOWLEDGEMENTS

My thanks should include a long list of wonderful people without whom this book wouldn't have happened. These are merely the ones who I can easily remember. That says nothing about those I've forgotten to mention and everything about my scatter-brain. So, in no order of any sort:

Patricia Macomber
Hal Duncan
Phill Pass
David Dodd
Steve Howarth
Charles Phipps
Steve Caldwell
David Wilson

And of course, the long suffering members of my family who've put up with me spending hours muttering and pacing about or else glued to the keyboard. To them I owe a special gratitude.

ABOUT THE AUTHOR

Luke Hindmarsh was born in Oxford before being dragged all over the world by his parents, courtesy of the UK armed forces. Before starting to write full time, he worked as a Criminal Barrister in London for ten years. He now lives in the Scandinavian wilds with his wife and their half-Viking children. When not writing, Luke teaches Shinseido Okinawan Karate and drinks far too much coffee.

CROSSROAD
PRESS